SCORPION INTRUSION

T. Milton Mayer

For my wife Lisa,
whose patience and
understanding allowed me
to pursue my passion.

*From the beginning
men used God
to justify the unjustifiable*

Salman Rushdie
The Satanic Verses

Scorpion Intrusion
By
T. Milton Mayer

This book is a work of fiction. Names, characters, and incidents, except where noted otherwise, are the result of the author's imagination. Any resemblance to actual persons, places, or events is purely coincidental. No part of this publication may be reproduced in any form without the expressed written permission of the author.

PROLOGUE

Steig Bardsonn exited the rental SUV and pulled his coat tightly across his chest. When he was finished, he would have to call the company and report the vehicle as being stolen. Other than a few cars belonging to security personnel, the place was empty. Steig knew from his twenty-five years of working for the company that the research facility would be deserted except for the three guards. They would all be sharing coffee in the break room for another half hour before they resumed their rounds. That gave him ample time to complete his task.

It was the middle of Saturday night in Oslo, Norway and he could feel the ice crunching beneath his feet. The air was cold and burned his nostrils. The wind cut against his face like a thousand razor blades. "This is the last day I'm going to have to put up with this damn cold," he muttered to himself as he zipped up his jacket and walked across the dark parking lot.

He briskly covered the thirty feet from his car to the side door. In spite of the freezing temperature, beads of sweat built up along his upper lip. His hands were shaking uncontrollably, but not from the cold. He was nervous. He was new at this kind of thing. After a few painful seconds, he was able to insert his security badge into the key slot as he entered his personal ID code into the number pad. There was the expected humming sound as the electric lock disengaged and the door opened. He was now committed, and there would be no turning back. There was no reasonable explanation for his presence in this high security research building at three in the morning. Yes, he was taking a chance, but the eight million Norwegian Krona fee made it more than worth the risk. It was the equivalent of over one million U.S. dollars and he had already received a fourth of the amount in advance.

Steig cautiously climbed the metal stairs to the third floor and slowly made his way down the hall toward his laboratory, trying to avoid all of the security cameras as he went. Even if he were recorded, it wouldn't make much difference. By Monday morning they will have already discovered what happened. Their senior research physicist was a thief, but Steig didn't care. By then he would be far away from this godforsaken freezing place. As expected, the lab was deserted but he could feel the anxiety creeping up his spine anyway. After entering his palm print on the scanner, he again entered his personal ID code, and the electronic lock opened with the same audible click that he had heard a thousand times before. When he entered the dark room, he turned on his high intensity flashlight and scanned the space. The small beam of light reflected off dozens of pieces of expensive high-tech equipment. In the far corner sat the four-by-five foot metallic device that he himself had developed several years ago. It was his brainchild, and in exchange for this, he received a paltry annual salary of only seventy thousand dollars. Meanwhile, the company stood to make over a billion dollars from their contracts with NATO, the United States, and Israel. This morning he planned to take his rightful share.

On a workbench, just to the left of the big device, sat the black portable prototype which he had been testing for the past month. It weighed only thirty pounds which was in stark contrast to the one thousand pound weight of the original. The smaller model didn't have the same range but it was still exceedingly effective, and it consistently met all of his expectations. He inserted a fresh battery pack and took a second one for backup. With a little difficulty, he carried the machine into the hall, down the steps, and out the same side door that he had entered just three minutes earlier.

His heart was pounding like a pile driver as he rushed back to his car. "Careful now, don't panic. There's still a lot of time," he reassured himself. The device was stashed next to his suitcase in the SUV's cargo area. After closing the hatch, he got behind the wheel and drove off. Steig repeatedly checked his rear view mirror, expecting to see flashing lights pursuing him, but no-one was there. Still, he had to hurry. Even though the theft probably wouldn't be discovered until Monday morning, he had a lot of ground to cover over the next eight hours. In a few days he would be hiding in a safe place, on a warm beach, thousands of miles away.

After exiting the parking lot, he headed east on a seven hour drive toward the Swedish border. Then he would continue to the Arlanda Airport in Stockholm where a private jet would be waiting. By noon on Sunday, he would be in the air and on his way to a comfortable retirement. That retirement would be short-lived, however. He would never recover the balance of his eight million Krona. He was a liability and his secret employer didn't like liabilities. He'd be dead within the week.

Four thousand miles away in Marietta, Georgia, an employee at the Nordstone-Thorn Corporation was sneaking into one of the company's large assembly warehouses. He was pushing a dolly with three empty five gallon gas cans. They were wheeled toward a one thousand gallon storage tank filled with black iron-ball paint.

Iron ball paint contains tiny spheres of carbonyl iron coated with an insulating layer of quartz. After the paint is applied and is still wet, the surface is treated with a strong external magnetic field which aligns the spheres so that they create their own magnetic orientation. As the paint dries, the spheres become locked in that position. When introduced to high energy waves such as microwaves, the spheres oscillate and convert the energy into heat which is then dissipated into the surrounding air. It was to be another critical aspect of the plan.

Each of the three containers was filled to capacity and wheeled back to the man's truck. He was promised ten thousand dollars for each can of the paint, thirty-thousand dollars in all. It was money that he would never have the opportunity to spend. He also was a liability.

CHAPTER ONE

Nineteen-year-old William Donaldson sat in front of his laptop for what he knew would be the last time. The paragraph was almost complete. It had to be perfect. It was the final summation of his manifesto.

By all appearances he was an average young man: average height, average weight, and average looks. In short, he was essentially invisible just like almost every other student on the Stanford University campus. His mind, on the other hand, was an entirely different matter. It was exceptional to the point of being tragic. He and his two sisters had been raised in a typical lower middle-class home just outside of Bakersfield, California. His father worked two jobs while his mother served lunch in the local high school cafeteria in order to provide a better life for their children. The parents had tried to protect them from the negative influences of the modern outside world by instilling in them a hard work ethic based upon a love of God and love of their country. As the youngest of the three children, William was given the most attention. He had the greatest God-given intellectual gifts, but of him the greatest amount was expected. He walked sooner and learned to talk much earlier than other children. Not surprisingly, he excelled in grade school and high school. Unfortunately, as is often the case in the adolescent culture, that academic success came at the price of social ostracism. He was a loner but not by choice.

William had undertaken an extraordinary metamorphosis over the past year. His parents were excited about his acceptance into Stanford University with a full academic scholarship. Their son was to be the first, after three generations, to graduate from college, and from a prestigious university at that. They were proud and happy but they didn't actually know or fully understand their son. Stanford was their dream, but it wasn't his dream. He was tired of their constant prodding to perform well in school; not that it was at all difficult. He had always been the most accomplished student in any class in which he enrolled. He was accepted into college after only three years of high school. He was, after all, classified as a genius and was driven by the personal expectations of a genius mind.

His parents wanted him to become a doctor, but what was the purpose in that? Money? Surely there was more to life than just accumulating wealth. Yes, he was excelling in a highly respected pre-med program and acceptance into any medical school was a given. Again, that was his parents' dream. It wasn't William's dream. He never aspired to be someone who simply handed out pills for weight loss and high blood pressure to overly indulgent, pampered Americans. He could never envision himself holding the hands of emotionally neglected premenopausal women, reassuring them that everything would be fine, all of the while pumping them full of antidepressants. He was a genius and should be destined for an appropriate level of greatness, not something as mundane as pushing pills. His problem was that he was unable to formulate a plan that would ensure the greatness that he so desperately sought.

He had been adrift for several years and felt he lacked true purpose in his life. He had no actual friends and never really did. He abhorred those around him and could not tolerate their shallow ignorance. Other boys were obsessed with cars, video games, and girls. The girls' intellectual prowess was limited to inane discussions about the most popular reality TV shows or shopping. They were unable to discuss any topic that required anything more than a modicum of original thought. He was essentially alone except for a few loose acquaintances and his family. There was never anyone with whom he could discuss the doubts that constantly plagued him. There was no-one to help answer the questions that the voices inside him posed.

Then finally, the purpose of his life began to unfold for him. It started when he found a place that provided the answers, a website that clarified the ambiguities which had confused him for so long. It was all laid out in a precise way in black and white. His life's destiny was now crystal-clear. Had it not been for the accidental discovery of the site, "Clarity of Life through Modern Islam," he would still be wandering about aimlessly. But now, with the guidance of Allah, his future was mapped out and his legacy would be written. The voices of doubt and accusation would be forever quieted.

Several months after engaging in chat room discussions and posting comments on the website, he was contacted. It occurred on a warm sunny afternoon while he was sitting at a table just outside an off-campus Starbuck's coffee shop. He was studying the Quran when a raven-haired, dark-complected co-ed approached his table. She extended her hand, "Hello William, may I join you? My name is Adara."

How does she know my name, he wondered as he awkwardly accepted her handshake.

"Uh, sure," he replied. She was one of the most beautiful women that William had ever seen. Her eyes were captivating. No girl had ever sought out his company before. In fact no-one at all had ever sought his company before. He had never been in this type of situation and was uncertain as to what he should say next. "Adara... that's an unusual name. Uh, that is, uh, it's a very pretty name," he quickly added.

"Thank you. In my country it means virgin," she giggled.

William's mind started racing at the reference to something so sexual. His brain locked up and he couldn't think of anything clever to say next. The intervening silence was awkward and fortunately, she continued the conversation with some typically flirtatious college small talk. After making sure they weren't attracting undue attention or being monitored, her face turned more serious and she quickly got to the point.

"I couldn't help but notice your reading material, William."

He held up the book. "Oh, the Quran? Yes, I've been reading it now for several months. It's quite enlightening," he said more comfortably now that the conversation had shifted to more familiar waters.

"I would agree. It's a very intriguing book. I've read some of the ideas that you posted on our website about it. I loved the insight reflected in your comments and I shared them with a few of my associates. Everyone is impressed by your grasp of the complex issues that face our people. My friends and I want to know if you would like to explore the world of Islam in more depth."

William, unable to take his eyes off of her replied, "Yes, uh, I would very much like to do that." *Especially if you show me*, he thought.

The young woman reached across the table and held his hand. Her skin was soft and warm. His physical response was predictable. As he lost himself in her dark brown eyes, she said, "I want you to enroll in a special class next semester. It's Professor Jazeer Farouk's *History of Middle Eastern Cultures*." At this point, William would do anything the girl suggested.

She went on to reassure him, "I will become one of your class-mates in order to help guide you on your journey. It will be neces-sary that we spend a great deal of time studying side-by-side," she said as she gently squeezed his hand. She stated that she was look-ing forward to their journey together. The insinuation of some future intimacy hung in the air with the scent of her perfume as the two continued to talk for over an hour.

During the course of the following semester, they spent almost ev-ery evening studying Farouk's lecture notes, the Quran, and the world of Islam. He was infatuated by her level of intelligence and insight into the root causes of the world's problems. Her scent was intoxicating and he drifted into a world of sexual fantasy every time they met. He wanted to take their relationship to a more phys-ical level, but she would always deflect his advances in the name of the Quran. "I would love to, but it's too soon, William. We should wait. We don't want to violate the laws of Allah."

Even after several months of being together almost continu-ously, intimacy never happened. Much to William's disappoint-ment, Adara eventually dropped the class. For hours every day, he would sit at the same Starbucks where they had first met, waiting for her to return. She never did. He searched for her across cam-pus but it was all in vain. Then, on his Islamic Studies mid-term exam, there was a hand-written note in the margin of his test paper. It gave him hope. The message said that he was to meet Dr. Farouk in his office later that afternoon. *Maybe she'll be there,* he wondered…but she wasn't. It was just himself and Professor Farouk.

"You were probably hoping that Adara would be joining us," said Farouk. "She told me to let you know she is sorry about leaving you. Unfortunately, some urgent matters developed that required her immediate attention. But she left instructions that you and I are to work together on your continued instruction."

The two men met several times a week since. It was then that William's true education began. Under the tutelage of the professor, he became deeply enmeshed in the Islamic culture. In time, he stopped attending his regular classes and he discontinued all contact with his family. They were infidels who worshipped the wrong god. He was told how the American culture had been contaminated by the Zionists. There was an unholy alliance between America and the State of Israel, and as a result, all Muslims, especially the Palestinians, were being persecuted. He was shown how American society had become lost in a sea of hedonistic pleasure. The country was so morally bereft that they lacked any sense of spiritual purpose. They were an affront to the word of Allah.

William totally embraced the tenets and traditions of Islam. He was reassured that he was no longer alone but was now part of a worldwide brotherhood. The professor was impressed with his quick mastery of the Quran and his commitment to the Five Pillars of Islam. He was slowly seduced into the world of the jihadist philosophy. When the time was right, he was told that he had been one of only a very few individuals to have been selected for a special holy mission.

"Allah has honored you, William. He has selected you to be the tip of the spear that he will plunge into the heart of America," said Farouk. He further promised, "You will be forever revered as a soldier of Allah and your name will be written in blood in the history books!" Finally, William's quest for greatness would be realized.

The preparations were made and the outline of a plan was revealed to him. He was given detailed instructions on how to proceed over the next two weeks. The first thing he needed to do was take a short trip to Armand's Tailor Shop, located three miles south of the university. William would not be able to see the others who accompanied him. He would be followed and protected by his brothers at all times. They would ensure that he was not being stalked by the spies of the Great Satan. When he arrived at the tailor shop, there were no introductions. Explanations were not necessary. He was simply given a package that contained all of the equipment he would need to complete his mission.

Finally, the time had come. Today would be the day when he would strike back at those who had turned their backs on him and sought to destroy Islam. His would be the opening salvo in the holy Jihad and afterward he would join his brothers in paradise. By then, the entire world would recognize his name and revere him for the level of greatness he had attained.

He finished the last paragraph of his manifesto. After printing his manuscript, he deleted all files from the laptop, and completely destroyed the hard drive. The papers were left neatly centered on top of his desk. He rolled out his prayer mat, faced toward Mecca and prostrated himself as he prayed to Allah, asking for His blessing and guidance. The Adhan was performed three times in a self-mesmerizing chant in Arabic and then in English:

Allahu Akbar, Allahu Akbar
Ash-hadu an la 'ilaha 'ill-Allah,
Ash-hadu anna Muhammadar rasulu-Allah"

Allah is supreme! Allah is supreme!
I bear witness that there is no god but Allah;
I bear witness that Muhammad is the Messenger of Allah."

When finished, he pulled on a pair of khaki cargo shorts, and stepped into his sandals. Then he donned his vest, and secured the triggering device in his pocket. The two hundred ball bearings made it a lot heavier than he had expected but the weight was manageable. Over the vest, he pulled on a red and white Stanford University sweatshirt. Looking in the mirror one last time, he checked himself to be certain that everything was adequately concealed.

After leaving the dorm, he calmly walked across campus to the ten o'clock organic class in the Mudd Chemistry Building. Passing through the front door, he followed the hallway toward the large Braun Auditorium and took a seat in the middle of the three hundred other students attending class. He had been warned by Professor Farouk that there might be some apprehension, but in fact, there was no fear. There was no rapid heartbeat. There was no perspiration on his upper lip. There was just the calm acceptance of fulfillment. Five minutes after the organic chemistry professor began his discussion of ketone metabolism, William stood and yelled out, "Allahu Akbar." He reached into his pocket, pressed the trigger, and then there was oblivion.

Three thousand miles away, on the other side of the country, the hotelier was sitting in his Manhattan office, intently watching the CNN news reports about the horrific attack at Stanford University. "Over a hundred students have been killed and dozens more were injured," the young woman reported. "FBI officials state the attack appears to be the work of a self-radicalized lone-wolf. The suicide bomber was a sophomore in the pre-med program. His name was William..."

A subtle smile grew on the man's face. "So, it begins," he said softly. "You did well Professor Farouk. May your Allah bless you." After several minutes of reveling in similar reports on the other news channels, he checked his schedule and called out to his secretary, "Marie, where is my pilot today?" he asked.

"Your jet was chartered by a private group for a trip to Las Vegas. He's scheduled to fly them back tomorrow," was her reply.

"Contact him and let him know that I want to visit my properties in Seattle, Chicago, Kansas City, and San Antonio early next week. He should have the plane ready to leave early Monday morning. Oh, and you should add Bloomington, Minnesota to the list."

"We have two hotels there, sir. Do you want the one by the Mall of America?"

"Yes, and be sure to notify the managers that I will be coming. Clear my calendar through Thursday."

"Yes sir. Will you be traveling alone?" she asked.

"Yes, and tell the pilot to cancel any further charters. I'll need the plane a great deal for the remainder of the year," was his reply. He picked up an untraceable cell phone and called the leaders of his sleeper-cells in each of the five cities.

CHAPTER TWO

Carver fell asleep on the couch shortly after returning to his home in Park Hills, Kentucky. He had been exhausted after a long weekend of training and he was out as soon as his head hit the pillow. As a former All-American collegiate quarterback, he was in excellent shape, even at forty-three. Nevertheless, the program was still physically and mentally taxing.

He awoke suddenly and bolted straight up in a cold sweat. He had experienced the same dream a thousand times before but it had been over a year since the last one. He knew why it had returned now. It was a disturbing news story that he heard on the radio during his drive home tonight. In his dream, he was again an eleven-year-old boy growing up in the rough coal-mining town of Whitesburg, Kentucky. He and his younger sister, Lisa Marie were playing in the mountains which overlooked the family farm. The two of them heard yelling in the valley below and peeked through the underbrush just in time to witness the brutal murders of their father and older brother. The father had almost been cut in two and the brother's head had been completely blown off by shotgun blasts. It was a bloody and horrifying dream.

But it wasn't just a dream, was it, good buddy, claimed the demon.

No, it wasn't just a dream. Things had happened just that way and Carver had relived the event a thousand times over the past thirty years. The killers were never prosecuted because their family controlled the county. Justice was denied by the system and that left Carver to avenge the murders on his own. It was a ferocious and merciless attack, the source of which was never uncovered. On that day, the demon was spawned, conceived in the dark recesses of Carver's mind. That was the day in which the clawing in his soul had begun. The creature always demanded to be fed and sometimes that demand could not be ignored. Though it gave him an intoxicating sense of power, Carver knew that if he didn't keep it restrained, the demon would totally consume him.

He stood up and went to the kitchen where he made a tall Sapphire and tonic with a lime twist. Then he walked out onto the back deck to get some fresh air. It was a hot August evening, but there was a cool breeze blowing down the river valley.

In the hospital, he was referred to as Dr. Jacob Savich but his close friends called him Carver, a nickname that he had carried since childhood. He took a sip of his drink and leaned against the railing as he gazed out across the Ohio River toward the city of Cincinnati. Like the ancient city of Rome, it was built on seven hills. In fact, the city's name was derived from General Lucius Quinctius Cincinnatus who saved his beloved city of Rome from destruction by marauding invaders. In like manner, Carver saw himself as the protector of the city that he also loved.

The news story that had upset him so much was about a serial child molester from the up-scale Hyde Park neighborhood. The man was given a mere six months in jail for raping a nine year-old boy. The light sentence was handed down purportedly because of alleged abuses that the molester himself suffered as a child. In addition, his attorney argued that he was "mentally slow." It was a ludicrous claim that was made worse when the judge ruled that his release would be contingent upon successful completion of a treatment program. Carver had seen the same process unfold before. Justice was denied because of slick manipulations of the law.

"Bullshit!" yelled Carver in anger at the trees down the hill, twenty feet below the deck. "He'll be back to his normal predatory activities within a month. That's what always happens because you can never cure people like him. It's inevitable. How many more children must be victimized before something is done about him?" At one time, Carver was the one to do that something. He had done so dozens of times before, but not now...not for over a year.

They deserved to die, said the demon. *Just like the others, they prey upon the innocent. You should arrange to meet this fellow from Hyde Park...give him a taste of good old fashioned Savich family justice.*

He considered what he had already done in the name of that justice. He was again plagued by the feelings of doubt and self-recrimination. It had been a long time since he last had the argument with himself. "Am I any better than those whom I have eliminated?" he asked himself. "I am a killer and should I not be treated in the same fashion?" His thoughts drifted to his Sig Sauer automatic. Maybe it's the only thing which can calm the inner conflict, the only thing able to give him peace.

Whoa there cowboy! Just slow down a minute, said the demon.
*Let's not go down that path again. We've already had this discus-
sion. Remember your good friend Sir Edmund Burke? He said "the
only thing necessary for the triumph of evil is for good men to do
nothing." You've never been one to stand by and do nothing, buddy.
You just can't. It's not in your DNA. It's not like you enjoy killing.
You only eliminate the ones who deserve it. It's gotta be done. Who's
going to protect the innocent, if not you? You're the seeker of justice.
You're one of the good guys, buddy. If God didn't want you to do it,
he wouldn't have created you this way. Now let's get that Sig nonsense out of your head!*

Sometimes the demon seemed to make sense, but Carver knew
that it was self-serving. It was only interested in the killing, not
the righteousness. Unfortunately, Carver's prior quests for justice
almost led to the shooting death of his closest friend, a man who
had essentially been a brother. Afterward, he promised the friend
that he would stop the killing; but the clawing inside him could
not be quieted. It became more demanding, and in spite of his
promise, Carver didn't know how much longer he could keep it at
bay. Fortunately, a solution presented itself. He was able to transfer his activities to a more acceptable form. Instead of eliminating
evildoers from his city, he would now eliminate evil threats to his
country. Just over a year ago, he was recruited by a man named
Winston Hamilton III. He was to become a member of a group
that only a handful of people knew about. The group's mandate
was to identify and eliminate all threats to the nation. It was a mandate that Carver and his demon readily embraced.

Ok with me, as long as we get to kill someone, buddy. Let's get on it!

Carver Savich returned to his chair. He was exhausted from his
three day ritual of intense training and tomorrow he had four

hours of surgery scheduled for the morning, followed by a full afternoon of office. He didn't know how much longer he could continue with this. He couldn't train with the Delphi Team and at the same time provide the necessary level of care that his patients deserved. Some changes would have to be made.

As he took another sip of the gin and tonic, he thought about his sister, Lisa. She was under the same stress of trying to balance the rigors of the Delphi Team training program against the need to run her $500 million cosmetic corporation. At the same time, she was trying to maintain her relationship with FBI Special Agent, John Crawford. Adjustments were going to have to be made by everyone.

He felt tired but restless. Pacing the deck for a while, he stopped to again look down the hill toward the river. There had been a drought this year and many of the leaves had already turned brown. It looked like a number of the trees would completely die within the coming months. There would be no imminent relief from the oppressive heat. Below normal rain accumulation and above normal temperatures were forecast for the next several months, but Carver sensed that a storm was brewing out on the horizon. A dark force was gathering. He could feel it and he learned long ago to pay attention to his instincts.

He went inside and picked up the sound system remote. He selected the piano solos channel on Pandora and retrieved his carving tools from one of the cabinets. As the poetic sounds of Chopin's Polonaise wafted across the tree tops, he began the delicate process of sculpting a piece of basswood. He didn't have the usual inspiration of death to guide his hands but he began working on an image anyway.

Perhaps you should carve an image of Mr. Hyde Park. Bet he'd give you some good inspiration alright...some real good inspiration. Maybe we should pay him a friendly little visit next week.

14

After another hour, the effects of the Sapphire and tonic began to take effect. He went back inside, ate a bowl of cereal for dinner, and retired to bed; only to again hear the demon clawing and to again dream the same dream.

CHAPTER THREE

Manny Perez had been working overtime at night to finish up the job at the Allied Marine Company in Ft. Lauderdale. Once he completed the expected work on the 72 foot yacht, he started on the installation of the device. It was a separate, off-the-books project for which he was being reimbursed handsomely, the equivalent of six months' pay. He was told to secure the black box so that it would be hidden in the engine compartment, behind the desalinization unit, and adjacent to the boat's electronic supply terminals. No extra wiring was required because the device had its own shielded set of battery packs. It could function independently of the yacht's power source. He hadn't been told about the purpose of the machine, and he didn't want to know. Because of the insisted-upon secrecy and the huge amount of money he was being paid, Manuel assumed that it could not be for something good. At least he knew that it wasn't a bomb because he had experience with munitions in the Army. He would have recognized any type of explosive device.

"Maybe it has something to do with drug smuggling, like maybe a signaling device," he tried to convince himself. All that he could say for sure about the box was that it was fairly heavy and it had writing on the side that said, "Norwegian Technology Corporation." What he didn't know was that the company had been at the forefront of the development of electromagnetic pulse or EMP generators for NATO. The prototypes had the potential to halt cars, watercraft, and planes by shutting down all electrical power functions within its range. The device had been designed for the purpose of thwarting attacks by suicide car bombers in the middle-east.

He had been having second thoughts about his secret agreement, and was tempted to back out. But his son had been arrested for the third time on charges of crack cocaine possession with the intent to distribute. Manny had been a gang-banger himself when he was young, and he had spent some time in prison. He was well aware of what happened to young men there; they would use his son for sex and he would be corrupted for the rest of his life. Manny couldn't allow that to happen. He needed at least ten thousand dollars to retain the services a good criminal defense attorney and he was to be paid thirty thousand for this small job... and to keep his mouth shut. He had been given five thousand in cash at the time of the initial contact and the rest was to be delivered after he successfully completed the task. He couldn't afford to ignore the financial reward. Besides, he was afraid to say no to the man who had first approached him. There was evil in the man's eyes and he had two fang-like teeth that gave him the appearance of a wild animal, a creature that could easily rip out another man's throat, and enjoy doing it.

Once he completed the installation, Manny took pictures of the device from multiple angles and forwarded them to a pre-specified cell phone number. His employer acknowledged receipt of the pics, and set a time and place for payment of the remaining twenty-five thousand dollars.

Manny arrived at the designated location as instructed at 2:00 am. It was a secluded parking lot behind a Goodwill Store in the Little Havana district of Miami. Having grown up nearby, he was familiar with the area and found it without difficulty. The darkness surrounding the lot seemed to close in around him like the walls of a coffin. He began to feel a sense of panic when he saw the other car already sitting there in the shadows. When the other driver flashed his lights twice, Manny reluctantly responded in kind. He felt uneasy and his instincts told him that he should immediately put his car in gear and speed away, but he still needed the cash for his son.

The man exited the passenger side of the black sedan and approached with a large manila envelope. Manny lowered his car window to receive the payment. He was so nervous that he thought he might throw up. He was looking forward to getting the rest of his money and getting the hell out of there. The man approached his car and smiled. One of Manny's final thoughts was of those two menacing, fanged teeth. Instead of getting an envelope full of cash, he received a single hollow-point .22 caliber bullet to the head. He was another liability.

CHAPTER FOUR

The device weighs over 22 thousand pounds and is the size of several large SUVs. It was developed by Albert L. Weimorts Jr. at the U.S. Air Force Research Laboratory located on Wright-Patterson Air Force Base. The MOAB (Massive Ordnance Air Blast), as it is called, is so large that it cannot be deployed by the typical bomber since standard bomb bay doors are not wide enough to accommodate the massive weapon. It must be delivered by a C-130 Hercules cargo transport plane. The entire rear of the plane opens as a parachute pulls the bomb and its supporting pallet out of the back. The pallet separates as two grid fins open, and the largest non-nuclear bomb ever made is guided to its target by a GPS system. Unfortunately pin-point accuracy is not one of its characteristics. Such a weapon is not meant to deliver a surgical strike. Its purpose is maximal blanket destruction. At a specified altitude, the MOAB deploys a large cloud of a highly volatile mist which is then ignited by the conventional blast. The resulting explosion is widespread, and extensive collateral damage is considered to be an acceptable inevitability. Everything within a half-mile radius is totally obliterated while any living organism within two miles of ground zero is killed instantly. Even at a distance of five miles, there is the potential for severe internal organ damage, concussion, and death.

The man studied the computer screen and read the same information that he had already reviewed a hundred times before over the past twenty years. For generations, his family had lived in a small village nestled in the eastern mountains of Afghanistan. As a young boy, his full name was Abduhl Rahim Wardak but he was simply called Rahim by his family and friends.

On the day that it happened, the temperature was unusually hot, even in the high mountain areas that surround his remote village. He had been assigned the task of tending to the goat herd up in the rocky terrain of the Hindu Kush, three miles away. Rahim was proud of the fact that his grandfather had given him such a responsibility at just twelve years of age. It was an indication that his family now regarded him as an adult. He was given a Pesh-Kabz dagger, a family tradition to symbolize his entry into manhood. Actually, it was the boy's safety more than his maturity that was of paramount concern to his grandfather who was the family patriarch. He simply wanted the boy out of the village for several days. A large army of Taliban had set up a camp less than a mile away from the small mountain community and they were taking all boys over age twelve as conscripts into the mujahedeen to fight in the holy Jihad against the American infidels. The boy's grandfather was desperately trying to hide him without incurring the wrath of the Afghan fighters.

Rahim could remember his grandfather describing the battles against the occupying Russian army just twenty years earlier. At that time, the Americans were the friends of the mujahedeen.

They provided the Stinger missiles that had proven to be the deciding factor that tipped the war in the Afghan's favor. With the help of the US, the occupying Russian army was forced to leave the country. Unfortunately, that left a leadership vacuum and eventually the country fell into the hands of the militant Islamic Taliban. What resulted was the same level of oppression, just different oppressors. Now the Americans were the enemy of the Taliban and the boy didn't understand why. It had something to do with the country harboring a group of terrorists called Al Qaeda and a man named Osama Bin Laden. He was regarded by many as a Muslim hero, but to the Americans he was a Satan.

The boy and his Pashtun village didn't care about the Taliban; they didn't care about Osama Bin Laden; they didn't care about the jihad; and they didn't care about the Americans. They just wanted to be left alone to live their simple lives in peace. So the boy was hidden with the goat herd, in the mountains, several miles away from the Taliban.

Young Rahim was sitting near a mountain ledge, at five thousand feet, under the shade of a hemlock tree. The goats were lazily grazing on the sparse grass growing between the rocks. A gentle breeze made him tired and he began daydreaming about some of the village girls who had recently caught his attention. He had almost fallen asleep for an afternoon nap when suddenly the entire valley below him erupted in an enormous ball of fire that extended from the base of one mountain to the next. It was as though the sun itself had collided with the earth. Several seconds later he heard the massive explosion that left him with a permanent hearing loss. The earth shook and the concussive blast knocked him to the ground. Many of the goats immediately fell over dead, with blood running out of their ears. Others ran over the nearby cliff in a panic.

When the boy recovered a half hour later, the dust cloud had settled. He looked down into the valley and saw nothing but charred earth. Everything was gone. His entire village was gone. It didn't just blow up or burn down. It completely disappeared. Gone were his parents. Gone were his grandparents. Gone were his five brothers and sisters. Gone were his aunts, uncles, and cousins. Everything and everyone important to him was gone. There was only himself and a few surviving goats. On that afternoon, young Abduhl Rahim Wardak died and the Scorpion was born.

CHAPTER FIVE

It had been several years since the vaporization of the tiny Afghan village. Over three hundred miles to the southwest of where that village once stood, a thirteen year-old boy was wandering the streets of Kandahar in search of food. The city boasted a population of a half million people which was large by Afghanistan standards. It was originally designed by Alexander the Great and has been a strategic location for trade and military planning ever since. It had been the capital of the Taliban government until its overthrow by the U.S. during Operation Enduring Freedom. It was now an area under the control of the United States Army and the fragile stability of the region was ensured by frequent patrols.

The boy stood in the shadows, wearing his dirty grey robe and eating an apple. He blended in well with the rest of the poor orphans of the city. He was virtually unnoticeable when a small squad of nine U.S. soldiers pulled into the mouth of the alley. The troops were riding in two vehicles: a tan armored personal carrier and a Humvee. Their .50 caliber machine gun scanned a one hundred eighty degree arc, looking for potential threats in the sector.

The company commander had received an anonymous tip about a hidden cache of Taliban weapons in the neighborhood and the squad had been dispatched on a search and destroy mission. The patrol slowed as it pulled down the alley which was lined on both sides by three-story dusty grey buildings. A few of the locals came to their windows to see what was happening. Seeing the soldiers, they rapidly retreated into the confines of their homes.

After continuing for several hundred feet, the vehicles came to an abrupt stop. The sergeant in charge of the squad didn't like the way that the area looked. There were no good defensive positions out in the street and it smelled of a potential ambush. He had seen it happen before. He heard the copter, looked up, but was unable to see it. The Apache attack helicopter was sent as a protective escort and was patrolling the skies overhead. "Slingshot, Slingshot, this is Bravo-two...over."

"This is Slingshot. I'm just coming up on your six...over."

"How's it look from up there?"

"Just finished checking the perimeter around your position and you're good to go. The rooftops are clear...no bogies. I've got your back, Bravo-two."

"Roger that, Slingshot. Stay close. I've got a bad feeling about this one." The sergeant was uncomfortable so he called for a rapid-response backup team in case things went FUBAR. In the meantime, he wanted to get the mission started so they could finish, pack up their stuff, and get the hell out. He ordered six of his men to proceed with the search while he would remain with the other two members of Bravo-two to stand guard. The six soldiers rapidly exited their armored vehicles and began storming one of the buildings just across from the boy. As the majority of the squad entered the structure and began the search, the sergeant and two of his men scanned the surrounding roof tops and windows for potential threats: two on the ground with M-16 rifles while the third manned the Jeep's .50 caliber.

A group of children, including the boy, surrounded the GIs begging for candy which soldiers often carried with them. It was a distraction. The boy reached under his robe and felt the Pesh-Kabz dagger, the gift from his grandfather. The handle felt firm and solid in his right hand as he gripped it tightly, waiting for the correct moment. While the three soldiers were distracted by the begging children, an explosion ripped through the second floor of the original target building. It had been booby-trapped. Flaming debris and body parts rained down on the street below. At the same time, an RPG was fired from one of the nearby rooftops. It hit the escort helicopter's tail rotor and the Apache lost control. It was no longer able to provide fire support for the remaining ground troops.

The three guards looked up toward the source of the blast. It was for just a brief second, but it would prove to be a fatal mistake. The boy quickly unsheathed his dagger and like a wild cat, leapt onto the Humvee. He was on the machine gunner in an instant. The boy raised his knife in the air and plunged it deep into the distracted man's neck. Quickly drawing the blade back, he severed the soldier's trachea and both carotid arteries. A fountain of crimson gushed out, spraying the vehicle with a shower of blood. The boy pushed the dying man aside and trained the machine gun on the remaining two guards. Before they could respond, both were cut in half by a dozen .50 caliber rounds. A fourth GI, who had survived the initial blast, came running out of the building with his uniform ablaze. He met the same fate as the others. The boy yelled out something that others later translated as "Feel the sting of the Scorpion!" Between the explosion and the boy, all nine US soldiers were either dead or dying. The entire process took less than two minutes. By the time the back-up squad arrived, the boy had already dissolved into the crowd and returned to the back alleys of the city.

The nine deaths added to the Scorpion's record of thirty-one kills and he was now being revered as the "Assassin of Kandahar".

He was drawing the attention of many Taliban leaders and other influential men outside of the country, men who were secretly supporting world-wide Islamic jihad. Without the boy's knowledge, his future destiny was already being secured.

CHAPTER SIX

I t was another spectacular morning in paradise. Graham Maultry looked out over the bow of his new boat at the flat seas lying ahead. He had already checked the ten-day weather forecast and everything looked clear. There was nothing brewing off the west coast of Africa or the mid-Atlantic so he wasn't expecting any threatening storms. He was heading east on a family trip that would take them on a sixty mile cruise from Fort Lauderdale to the Bimini Islands. Although he had made previous trips away from the direct sight of shore, this would be his first open-sea voyage without the guidance of a licensed captain. In spite of his wife's concerns, he felt confident that he could now navigate the waters on his own.

The twin Caterpillar diesel engines were pushing the 72 foot Hatteras Motor Yacht through the water at around 18 knots. Graham adjusted his heading to 119 degrees and set the autopilot on a direct course toward a marina along the northern tip of the island. The depth gauge showed that the boat was in thirty feet of water. He again checked the weather radar screen, the gauges, and the radios. Everything was perfect so he sat back and enjoyed the view.

His wife, Julia had been apprehensive about the trip, but Graham had repeatedly re-assured her that their family would be perfectly safe. He had the mechanics at Allied Marine install all of the most up-to-date sophisticated electronics. There was a GPS integrated navigation system that could be coordinated with the autopilot. Mounted on top was a twenty-five mile radius Raytheon radar unit that could identify any oncoming boats or hazards. A weather monitor relayed a continuous-stream update of weather and sea conditions. There were two ship-to-shore radio systems and a TrakPhone satellite receiver for telephone communications. Finally, he had them install an EPIRB transponder unit similar to the ones used on commercial aircraft to identify the plane's position. In the unlikely event that the yacht started to sink, it would repeatedly ping their position to the Coast Guard. They also had a large capacity dingy with a 150 hp mercury outboard motor as a back-up.

Graham reassured Julia that he had everything under control and had prepared for all contingencies. Even if he did lose his bearings and if all of the navigation equipment failed, all that he had to do was to follow the compass and simply head due west. They would hit the east coast of Florida within several hours. Finally, if there were any non-nautical problems, he had the help of his two best friends, Mr. Smith and Mr. Wesson to help protect them. He also had a twelve gauge shotgun hidden under the bed in the master suite. He was convinced that he had all of the bases covered. However, Graham was oblivious to the unforeseen calamity that was about to befall him and his family that morning.

"Refreshments are being served in first class," said Julia as she climbed up to the bridge with two cups of coffee. "I just brewed it."

She took a seat on the bench, snuggled up next to her husband, and gazed out over the deep sapphire blue water, canopied under cloudless skies. At forty-eight, Julia was still as gorgeous as she was when they married twenty years ago. They had originally met at MIT while he was getting his PhD in aeronautical engineering and she was a freshman in the physics program. They dated off and on for years but school and career demands kept them from pursuing a more permanent relationship. By the time Graham had become VP in charge of research and development at the Nordstone-Thorn Corporation, Julia had finished her doctoral thesis on quantum characteristics of subatomic particles. It was then that they rediscovered each other at a party. She was a stunningly tall blue-eyed blond who was ten years his junior. By his own admission, she was way out of his league, but something worked between the two. They've been happily married ever since.

Graham had been instrumental in developing the initial technology for the Air Force stealth program. In time, he went on to start his own company which provided design and technology support for Nordstone-Thorn and other military aircraft corporations. They were presently pioneering the aeronautical applications of ultra-light-weight carbon and graphene oxide composites in the construction of stealth fighters and bombers. Last year the Maultry Corporation enjoyed an annual profit in excess of six hundred million dollars.

"Oh Graham, it's even more beautiful than I could have ever imagined. I'm so glad we decided to buy the boat."

"What's with the 'we', Julia? As I recall, it was actually my idea and I just about had to get down on my knees to beg you to go along with it," he retorted with a laugh.

She took a sip of her coffee and replied, "Well, that may be true but I gave the final approval." Then, with a coy look on her face, she gazed at him and said, "Besides, I played a key part in the christening ceremony in our stateroom last night."

Graham laughed and said, "I have to admit that it had to be the greatest christening in maritime history. I think we had the boat rocking for over an hour."

"Gosh, I wonder if the kids heard anything," blushed Julia. She and Graham had two obstinate teens on their hands: seventeen-year-old Rodney and the "Princess", fifteen-year-old Tiffany. They had both protested the trip, complaining about how boring it was going to be, stuck on a boat with mom and dad...for days. The only times the two siblings ever agreed on anything was when they opposed their parents, and on this issue they presented a united front. Graham and Julia had hoped for an intimate family voyage that would help heal some of the adolescent fracturing which had occurred in recent years, but they eventually had to arrive at a compromise to make the trip happen. Rodney was allowed to bring his best friend, Tucker Thornton and Tiffany could bring her friend, Jessica Vehr.

Tucker's father had been a decorated hero in the Army. He lost his left leg as the result of a roadside IED in Afghanistan. After a year in a VA rehab facility, Tucker's father had been given a job at the Maultry Corporation. Rodney and Tucker met at a company picnic three years ago. The two boys were polar opposites. Tucker, was personable, confident, and athletic; the kind of boy who would be expected to be class president or prom king. Rodney, on the other hand, was shy, withdrawn, and moody; the kind of boy who everyone would typically forget a year after graduation. In spite of their differences, the two boys became fast friends.

Julia continued, "Well, if they did notice anything, they must have thought that it was a hurricane, you stud," Julia whispered to Graham as she gently jabbed him in the side with her elbow. They both laughed and took another sip of coffee. They sat together and drank in the peaceful tranquility that surrounded them. There was only the soft hum of the engines below and the soothing splash of the water as it was displaced by the boat's hull. It was mesmerizing. They were almost alone. The only other vessel in sight was a deep-sea fishing charter over a mile away.

"Graham, I often forget about just how blessed we have been."

"Yes, blessed by God and a lot of hard work on our part."

Graham looked at his depth gauge and noted that the sea floor was quickly dropping from twenty feet to over a thousand feet. "We've reach the Gulf Stream. The water depth should eventually drop to four thousand feet over the next five nautical miles."

"That seems kind of creepy, Graham. It sounds like a Bermuda Triangle kind of situation." She looked at him and laughed. "But I guess it doesn't matter if you sink in twenty feet of water or four thousand feet of water, the net result is the same."

"You worry too much, Julia. This boat is not going to sink," said Graham with certainty.

"That's what they said about the Titanic and you know how that story ended."

"Always the optimist, Julia." He looked out with his binoculars and said, "I've been watching that fishing charter for over an hour and they still haven't caught anything. Some days can be like that, even in the Gulf Stream."

Graham continued to monitor his instruments and watch the seas as he and Julia resumed the conversation about their difficult teenagers. "By the way, what are the four demons doing?" asked Graham.

"Tiffany and Jessica put on their bikinis and they're laying out on the bow getting a tan."

"Bikinis, I've seen table napkins bigger than what those two girls wear."

"Now, Graham, don't be such an old grouch. Let them have their fun."

"How about the boys? Did they wake up yet?" asked Graham.

"They're on the back deck, hooking up their fishing gear. They wanted me to ask if you could slow down a little so that they can troll for bill fish out the back."

"Sure, we're ahead of schedule. Let me see how things look." Graham leaned over and turned on the SIMRAD fish finder display. Once the screen lit up, he said, "I see schools of bait fish down there so the boys might get lucky and hook a marlin. Call down and tell them to let me know when their poles are set up. As soon as they're ready, I'll ease back on the throttle."

CHAPTER SEVEN

"Do you have them?" asked Ahmad Haq Rasid. He was a former Taliban leader who was responsible for the murder and torture of hundreds of his own people: men, women, and children. Their only crime was a failure to embrace radical Islam. In an ill-advised prisoner exchange program, he had been released from Guantanamo two years ago. There was a thirty percent recidivism rate for those who had been released from the terrorist prison and Ahmad was no exception. He quickly returned to the ranks of the radical Islamists and now he was helping to organize a holy jihad against the U.S. He was sitting in a fighting chair bolted to the rear deck of a 53 foot Viking Sport Fisherman, but he wasn't trolling for large game fish. He didn't even have bait on the end of the lines. No, he was hunting for something bigger and much more valuable; a person who would become a critical part of the decisive battle against the Americans.

"I have them off of our port bow, about two kilometers out," responded his younger partner.

"Slowly take us to within a kilometer and then gradually narrow the distance until we are within the range of the remote control. Do it slowly. I don't want them to become alarmed and run."

"Allah is with us. They will not get away," replied the younger man, Mossaq, as he slowly coaxed the throttle forward. After only thirty minutes they were well within range.

They couldn't risk a direct assault. There was too great a likelihood that Maultry or his wife would be able to send out an SOS distress call on channel 16. No, this had to look like a natural catastrophe so there would be no suspicion of foul play. Ahmad picked up the remote control and sent a test signal. He received a positive response in the form of a flashing green light on his remote control console, indicating that the EMP generator was on and ready for the activation signal. He looked through his binoculars and he could see the man and his wife on the bridge of their yacht drinking coffee. There were two girls on the bow, wearing bikinis and two young men on the stern, apparently fishing.

"Six people, there are six of them!" shouted Ahmad. "There were only supposed to be four. That's going to complicate things. We only have the two of us and the captain who must remain on the boat. We must get control of all of them quickly."

Mossaq responded, "The hand of Allah will guide us. We simply must eliminate the non-family members. That will serve as an inducement to the others that they must follow our orders."

"Yes, Allahu Akbar," responded the smiling Ahmad as he pressed the activation signal. The EMP generator started humming within the engine room of the Maultry yacht.

━╬ ╬━

The two teen boys had been fishing off of the back of the yacht for thirty minutes. They were having about as much luck as the deep sea fishing charter they had spotted earlier. Graham called down on the rear deck speaker, "Hey, are you boys having any...?"

Graham stopped in mid-sentence. Both engines suddenly died. He tried to restart the starboard and then the port diesel engine, but nothing happened, not even the grind of the starters. He looked at his instrument gauges. They were all dead and all of the radar screens were blank. Neither radio was working. The depth gauge and GPS units were out. He had no navigation and his compass was spinning around wildly. He tried the diesel generator, thinking that he had lost battery power, but it too was dead. All of the lights in the cabin were out. He frantically flipped on one switch after another but there was no response to his efforts.

Julia looked at Graham with alarm and yelled, "Graham, what's happening?"

"I don't know. Everything just died. I can't restart the engines and we've lost all of our electronics."

"Now that's really creepy, Graham. I was just kidding about that whole Bermuda Triangle thing earlier, but maybe there's something to it, like some unusual electromagnetic field." Little did Julia realize, that is exactly what had happened. The electromagnetic pulse generator in the engine room had shut down all electrical and mechanical processes on their boat.

Graham ran down the aft stairs to the back deck where the two boys were checking their rods, oblivious to what was going on. Their only concern was that their fishing lines had gone slack. Graham lifted the access door to the engine room and climbed down the six-step ladder. There was no fire and there was no obvious influx of seawater so at least their situation wasn't critical. He climbed back up to the helm and told Julia, "Everything looks OK, no fires and we're not taking on water so we're safe for right now. I just can't figure out what might have happened."

"What're we going to do out here, Graham," asked his wife. "We're at least thirty miles from shore."

"As I see it, we have two options: one is to get the dingy down and try to make the thirty mile trip back to shore, or maybe we can flag down that other charter fishing boat to see if they can help us. Maritime law dictates that they are required to give us a tow or at least notify the Coast Guard for us."

Julia replied, "I don't like trying to cruise the open ocean in a small dingy with six people, Graham. We may not even be able to get it down from the top deck without power to the davit."

Graham checked the switch on the davit and, as Julia suspected, it too was dead. "I guess the six of us could try to lower it into the water by hand but it'll be difficult."

"Before we attempt that, try starting the dingy motor first," suggested his wife.

Graham removed the canvas cover and climbed in. He turned the key and there was no response from the Mercury outboard engine. "I guess that narrows our options down to trying to hail down that other boat. Thank God, someone else is out here with us. I have a signal flare gun in the cabin. Whatever's going on, it shouldn't affect that." He climbed back down the stairs to the inside helm, retrieved the flare gun from a drawer and walked out to the bow. The two teenage girls were still sunning themselves, their ear buds in, listening to their music, and unaware of the situation. Turning the gun upward, Graham pulled the trigger. The bright flare immediately shot three hundred feet up in the air where a small parachute opened and held it aloft. Graham silently prayed the other boat saw his signal and that help would be coming soon.

⋙ ⋘

Mossaq yelled out, "Praise Allah, it worked! They have stopped dead in the water!"

Ahmad looked around in all directions to be sure that there were no other boats in the vicinity. All was clear. He responded to his partner, "Are you picking up any radio transmissions from their vessel?"

"No, nothing at all."

"Good, that means they can't call anyone for help and, as planned, we are their only option for assistance. Give them a few minutes before we respond. We don't want to appear too anxious to help. We want them to keep their guard down."

After about fifteen minutes, Mossaq saw the light. "There's a signal flare! May we proceed?"

"Yes, sound our horn letting them know that we have seen their signal, but approach them slowly. Go on top and make sure the captain has his rifle loaded and ready. You do the same, Mossaq. We have to deal with two more individuals than we expected and we must assume that they have some small arms on board. Shoot if you must, but do not harm the man or his family. He is the whole reason why we are here. The other two are expendable. And remember, this must look like everyone was lost in a boating accident. I want no bodies found floating about. We can't have any evidence of a kidnapping or any other foul play. That might raise concerns in their CIA and our entire plan could become exposed."

When they got within a hundred feet of the disabled craft, Ahmad again pushed the remote button and turned off the electromagnetic jamming device. He didn't want to shut down his own vessel.

CHAPTER EIGHT

Julia heard the horn and was the first to notice the fishing boat had changed course. It was headed toward them. With concern in her voice, she said to Graham, "We don't really know who these people are and we're sitting out here in the middle of the ocean with no-one else around. I don't want to alarm the children, but do you think that you should get your gun?"

"Relax Julia, you worry too much. These guys are just a small group out on a day charter, doing some deep sea fishing. It's not like they're terrorists or anything. We're lucky they happened to be out here and can help us. How's it going to look if I'm standing there with a .45 caliber automatic in my hand?"

"Just the same, a little caution might be prudent."

"OK, I'll tuck a gun under the back of my belt and pull out my shirt to cover it. I hid a loaded shotgun under the bed in the master suite. You can keep it close by, just in case."

"I'm not sure that's a good idea Graham. I know nothing about guns and Rodney isn't much better. Tucker's had a lot of experience shooting and he has a cooler head."

"OK, have him get it, but let's not get carried away with this thing. We have absolutely no reason to believe these guys are anything more than Good Samaritans. It's not like they've been stalking us and remember, we're the ones who sent up a signal flare requesting help."

"You're probably right, but I'm just saying that it doesn't hurt to be a little cautious."

The Viking Sport Fisherman slowed its engines and pulled alongside the Maultry yacht. A young man jumped out, dropped a few bumpers over the side and secured several ropes between the two boats. The captain of the vessel said nothing but stared at Julia like he was keeping an eye on her. It gave her the uneasy feeling that just maybe she had been correct in her concerns. A third person stood on the back deck of the boat and as he spoke to the others he had a distinct Middle-Eastern accent. Cold chills ran down Julia's spine.

As her level of apprehension increased, she turned to Tucker and whispered in his ear, "Neither Rodney nor I have ever shot a gun in our lives, and I know you used to hunt a lot with your dad. I don't like the way these three men are acting. It just doesn't feel right. I'm probably being overly paranoid, but just in case there's trouble, Graham has a loaded shotgun under the bed in the master sweet. Go find it and keep it handy."

Several minutes later, Tucker disappeared below and returned with the shotgun. He hid the weapon behind a curtain just inside the main cabin's aft door.

The oldest of the three men in the other boat appeared to be around forty. He smiled and exposed two broken front teeth that gave the appearance of fangs. It made Julia shudder. He spoke first, "We saw your signal. What seems to be the problem?"

Graham responded, "I'm sorry to interrupt your day of fishing, but we're having some major mechanical problems. Both engines suddenly died and we lost all of our electronics."

"That's OK, we haven't had a single strike today anyway. The problem sounds like something is wrong with the power supply in the engine compartment. That is the only thing that would explain your situation. I own a small marine repair company in Lauderdale. If you'd like, I can take a look to see if it's something simple that I can fix here. Or, if you prefer, we could call the Coast Guard to come get you, and tow your boat back to the marina. However, my experience with them is that in non-emergency situations, they might be a couple of hours."

Much to Julia's dissatisfaction, Graham responded, "If it's not too much trouble, it'd be great if you could take a quick look."

The stranger climbed over the gunwale and onto the Maultry vessel. The younger man followed while the boat captain remained on the flying bridge behind the helm, still staring at Julia. Graham reached down to the deck and lifted open the floor door leading to the engine compartment. Then he and the stranger descended the ladder one at a time, Graham in the lead. The stranger pretended to search around the room and after several minutes he said, "I think I've found your problem. Do you know what this device is?" He stepped back and let Graham bend over to examine the large black box. It had the name Norwegian Technology Corporation stenciled on the side. It was wedged behind the port engine and the desalination unit. Graham struggled to get a closer look.

"I have no idea what that is. It doesn't look like anything that I asked Allied Marine to install," replied Graham as he continued to inspect it. "It looks like it was manufactured in Norway and it has flashing lights on either side. How can it be lighting up while the rest of the boat's electronics are dead?"

Abdul responded, "Because it has its own shielded power source. The red light means that the remote control for the device has been accessed and the green light means that the EMP generator was activated. We had the device installed shortly after you purchased your boat, Dr. Maultry."

Graham suddenly developed a knot in his stomach. He realized that this was no mechanical malfunction. Julia was right! He and his family were now in serious trouble. In his present position, he was unable to reach the gun at the back of his belt. He slowly turned toward the stranger, and found himself looking down the barrel of a large-bore automatic pistol.

"What's this all about? What's that black box for?" demanded Graham.

"It was actually manufactured by a Norwegian company for NATO. It sends out an electromagnetic pulse that freezes the electronics of any vehicle nearby. As an aeronautical engineer, I'm sure that you understand the principal. This particular one was designed to stop car bombings in my homeland but today we used it to stop your boat."

The stranger patted down his captive and found the Smith and Wesson. The man tucked it into his own belt, and with the tip of his gun, motioned for Graham to head toward the ladder. He was instructed to slowly climb out of the engine room. The captor was right behind him with the automatic aimed at the back of Graham's head. When the two men climbed back up to the deck, Julia saw the gun in the stranger's hand. Her heart nearly stopped. She looked at Tucker and almost imperceptibly nodded her head toward the cabin. He nodded back in understanding.

The fang-toothed man looked at his younger partner and said, "Mossaq, head toward the bow and retrieve the two girls." The partner went forward with an automatic rifle and after firing a few warning rounds into the air, forced the two teens to join the rest of the family on the back deck. Graham and Julia were terrified but tried to remain calm for the sake of the children. The two girls were sobbing and Rodney was on the verge of joining them. Tucker however, just glared into the eyes of Ahmad. All the boy could think about was that these were the same people who had crippled his father. His defiant demeanor did not go unnoticed by Ahmad. He looked up at the boat captain in a manner that said to him, "Watch this boy closely."

Mossaq started to secure Graham and Julia while the boat captain stood guard on the flying bridge, keeping his rifle trained on the four teens. Graham said, "Whatever you want, just take it. If the boat isn't enough for you, I'm a very rich man and I can make each of you wealthy beyond your imagination. Just please don't harm my children or their friends."

Ahmad snarled, showing his fangs, "You Americans all think alike. For you, it's only about wealth and material objects. It's not your money that we want Dr. Maultry---it's your mind."

While the captors were distracted in their conversation with Graham, Tucker reached behind the cabin door curtain and cautiously withdrew the shotgun. It's easy to talk about killing another man. It's just a pull of the trigger, a few pounds of pressure by the index finger and boom...easy as pie. A split second later a life is ended. But for the young and innocent of heart, it's the emotional equivalent of scaling Everest. There's the paralyzing sense of unfairness and unrighteousness. So, even though Tucker had been a hunter, he hesitated. He was not his father. He was not a veteran soldier who had already witnessed senseless death. He was simply a teenage kid. His innate sense of fair play dictated that a warning must be issued, a chance to choose life over death. It would prove to be a fatal mistake.

Tucker stepped forward and aimed the shotgun at Ahmad's head. He yelled, "Drop your guns or I'll blow his head off." Tucker was too young and too inexperienced to just pull the trigger, which is what he should have done. The Viking captain raised his AK-47 rifle, and in less than two seconds fired at least five rounds into young Tucker's chest. A cloud of red mist covered the other three teens and the entire back deck. The scene looked like a macabre crimson replica of a Jackson Pollock painting. Tucker died instantly.

"Noooo," cried out Julia as she fell to her knees realizing that she had made the costly decision that resulted in the death of the young boy. Rodney was catatonic, frozen in shock and disbelief. The two girls, covered in hundreds of blood droplets, started screaming uncontrollably. Mossaq calmly walked over to them and turned to young Jessica Vehr, "Quiet you infidel whore!" With that, he hit the teen in the left cheek with the butt of his rifle, breaking her jaw. She fell to the deck, unconscious, bleeding heavily from her mouth. Mossaq turned to Tiffany and said, "Now be quiet or the same thing is going to happen to you."

Graham screamed out, "Leave her alone you bastard," which earned him a vicious punch to the head by Ahmad. After that, all of the hostages remained quiet. They were securely tied, gagged, and placed inside the fishing boat without further trouble. It had only been ten minutes since the terrorists had first boarded the Maultry yacht.

⋙ ⋘

Ahmad climbed back down the ladder into the engine room, walked over to the EMP generator, and removed the bolts that had secured it in place. He had been instructed to remove it and take it with him. Smuggling the machine out of the Norwegian Technology Corporation had been very costly and it was too valuable a weapon to leave behind. After he transferred the device to his own boat, he returned to the yacht where he and Mossaq threw Tucker's body and the still-dazed Jessica down through the deck

43

hatch. There, the two teens were tied to the ladder with nautical ropes so their bodies would not float out to the surface later. Ahmad called out to his own captain and asked, "Depth?" The captain checked his gauges and replied, "Were right over the trench. It's over four thousand feet." Ahmad then grabbed an AK-47 and returned to the engine room where he unloaded an entire magazine into both ten-inch intake hoses of the engines. The resulting gush of sea water immediately started flooding the compartment. After climbing back out, he watched the rapid influx of water and listened to Jessica's final cries for help before she drowned.

He turned to Mossaq, "It should completely sink within twenty minutes. With the Gulf Stream current, it'll drift miles north of here before it hits the sea floor. The boat will never be found and all will believe that the Maultry family members were the victims of a horribly unfortunate yachting accident. No-one will suspect that the brilliant Dr. Graham Maultry has been kidnapped. The American press will love the whole Bermuda Triangle explanation."

After the sinking boat disappeared below the surface of the water, the three terrorists and their captives began the return trip to the east coast of Florida. What Ahmad had failed to take into consideration was the battery-powered transponder device that Graham had Allied Marine install in his new boat months ago. It started pinging the yacht's position as soon as the pulse generator was turned off.

CHAPTER NINE

R ichard Conway stood at the podium and addressed the crowd of over three thousand participants at the Greater Columbus Convention Center. The event was a fund raiser for his party's candidate for the next presidential election. Taking the State of Ohio was essential if they were to win. Richard was the Ohio State political party chairman and he was pulling out all of the stops on this three city campaign tour. He had been one of the first to endorse the man who already had a commanding lead in the polls and who was the presumptive winner of the upcoming presidential race. He was the perfect candidate: intelligent, handsome, charismatic, and a decorated war hero.

The man was a former Air Force captain who had been awarded the Congressional Medal of Honor for valor during Operation Desert Storm. The Black Hawk helicopter, which he was piloting, was carrying a squad of nine soldiers when it was shot down over enemy territory. He single-handedly protected his fellow soldiers from a relentless enemy assault by manning one of the downed helicopter's machine guns. He continued firing his weapon even after sustaining a gunshot wound to his own left arm. The bullet tore through nerves and continued to send several fragments into his chest where a piece is still lodged in the wall of his heart. Six of the nine soldiers survived thanks to his efforts.

After several minutes of enthusiastic applause, Party Chairman Conway adjusted the microphone and said, "Ladies and gentlemen of this great state of Ohio, I have a question for you. Is our country a better place now than it was seven years ago?"

The expected response was not disappointing. In unison, all three thousand responded with a resounding, "Nooo."

"And why is that?"

Again, in unison came the familiar campaign theme, "Lies, scandals, and debt." The chant was repeated over and over, led by local county chairmen.

After a minute, Richard asked, "And what's the solution to the problem?"

"Wagner, Wagner, Wagner, Wagner..."

"Ladies and gentlemen, I present to you a man of his word, a man who says what he thinks, a man who does what he says; no lies, no doubletalk, just truth. I present to you my good friend and the next president of the United States, the Governor of this great State of Ohio, Jack Wagner."

The crowd stood and applauded wildly as their candidate approached the dais. Jack Wagner had ridden the crest of a wave of anti-Washington sentiment that had flooded the country from coast to coast over the past several years. He was politically savvy, and he knew how to work a crowd. Over the past four years he had been one of the most successful governors in Ohio's history. He wasn't afraid to fight hard for what he believed in, regardless of the political consequences. He improved employment in his state by lowering taxes and increasing business investment. With budget tightening measures and elimination of wasteful programs, he pulled Ohio back from the edge of economic collapse. The state was now on solid financial ground and boasted a balanced budget for the first time in years.

He was wearing a button down blue shirt, no tie, and a blue blazer with an American flag pin affixed to the lapel. He looked out over the crowd as though he knew each and every one of his supporters personally, waving at them with his good right hand.

"Thank you, my friends...thank you. The measure of a presidency is the condition in which he and his party leave the country when they leave office. Well, I'm here to tell you what you already know. This president and his party have left our country in a shambles. America is sitting in the middle of a wasteland of incompetence and malfeasance in office.

"There has been an unprecedented abuse of executive power. For the past seven years, we have essentially had an autocracy with little or no adherence to the principals of our constitution. The system of checks and balances established by our founding fathers has been trampled. This president has refused to enforce the laws passed by Congress, while he simply creates his own executive-order laws in order to promote his party's liberal political agenda. Even the Supreme Court has unanimously found his use of power to be excessive and unconstitutional. But, has the result of such abuse been beneficial for our great land?"

"Noooo," responded the crowd.

"No, of course not. By all historic measures, his presidency has been a pathetic failure. We now face a crisis on our borders because the president's attorney general refuses to enforce our laws regarding immigration. They have now caused such an immigration disaster that it will take generations to resolve the problem. We have already seen rioting in California, Arizona, and Texas as those states try to cope with overburdened budgets. The states' economies have already been strained to the max without incurring the additional costs of feeding and housing millions of illegal aliens.

"A porous border is much like a leaking roof on a house. First you must fix the leak in the roof before spending huge amounts of money for repairs inside. That is exactly what we must do. First of all, we must fix our leaking border and then we can go about the task of dealing with the damage. We can implement a fair plan to deal with those who have already established a productive life here. But how does the present Commander-in-Chief respond to the border crises? He halts the deportation process and enacts policies that make further illegal entry into our country even easier. He encourages the establishment of sanctuary cities which refuse to enforce our present immigration statutes. Meanwhile, he promises full amnesty to those who break those laws. This isn't border control. It's not immigration reform. It's a calculated effort to change the voter demographics in our great nation.

"This all comes at the expense of our own national security. Right now our borders are so porous that known terrorists have been able to travel back and forth across them with impunity. Security measures at airports are almost meaningless. The terrorists don't have to fly here anymore. They can simply walk across the border with the other masses that cross every day. There are thousands of them hiding in our cities right now, plotting the destruction of this great nation. I promise you that if I am elected, I will immediately secure our borders and protect our citizens."

After a five minute standing applause, Wagner continued, "This president and his party have absolutely no appreciation of global economic realities. Our national economy is threatened by excessive spending on things which we can't afford, such as: free cell phones for welfare recipients, a Woodstock concert museum, bridges that go nowhere, and subsidies for failing 'green' corporations that are no more than political payoffs. Then there are the tens of billions of dollars that we spend each year on the global warming scam while we ignore the real threat to modern civilization, global terrorism.

"I could go on for hours about the waste. This president and his spendthrift party have brought countless major cities and the country itself to the door of bankruptcy. Our national debt is so high that soon we will be unable to cover the interest, much less pay off the debt itself. Meanwhile, things that are important are ignored. Our border patrol is woefully underfunded. Our police departments are understaffed. Our infrastructure is beginning to crumble. Our VA system is a disgrace. Soldiers who have sacrificed life and limb for their country are dying due to this administration's failure to guarantee timely treatment for their problems. Our boys deserve better and if I am elected, my administration is going to give them just that."

Wagner continued, "Our international policies have been an abject failure because this administration, due to its own inexperience, has no cohesive international policy. They simply react to each individual crisis while jumping from one world disaster to the next, trying to put out brushfires that should have been foreseen and prevented in the first place. We haven't anticipated problems and therefore, we have no policy that formulates a plan of contingencies to address the problems when they arise.

"They have not protected our embassies and the tragedy in Benghazi was a result. There has been a resurgence of the Taliban and Al Qaeda in the Middle East after the president proudly stated that we had already effectively destroyed them. Well Mr. President, I have some surprising news for you…they're still here and they are growing rapidly. For purely political reasons, we abandoned those countries in which thousands of our young men shed blood. The present White House and its party were in such a hurry to publicize our exit from those terrorist havens that they failed to ensure an adequate long-term transition. Our president has been more interested in his social legacy than the welfare of the country that he supposedly serves. He has essentially given Iraq, Syria, and Afghanistan back to the terrorists and now we are more vulnerable than we were before 9/11. ISIS, The Islamic State of Iraq and Syria, is establishing a huge caliphate that will serve as another home for terrorist groups, a place from which more 9/11 catastrophes can be launched in the future. And now, our young men will again have to sacrifice their lives to correct the mistakes of this president and his party.

"Over the past several years, the United States and our allies around the world have been increasingly plagued by radical Islamic terrorists. Mind you, I'm not referring to the vast majority of peace-loving patriotic American Muslims. I'm talking about the savages who kill innocent women and children in the name of their perverse interpretation of Islam. I'm talking about the same savages that this president and his party refuse to acknowledge by name.

"Before one can correct a problem, one must accept the fact that the problem exists. Then you must identify the source and the location of the problem so that it can be eradicated. I can tell you this, the problem is not our allies in Israel. The problem is not our allies in Europe. Certainly the problem is not in the US. The problem is militant Islamists and the countries that allow them to freely operate. The president and his liberal party have kept their heads in the sand too long. What is the president's response to the resurgence of Islamic terrorism? Its malignant apathy…and you all know what must be done with a malignancy. It must be removed and that is exactly what we are going to do in November. We are going to cut them out!"

There ensued five minutes of a standing ovation.

"Seven years ago, the present occupant of the White House promised the country that he would have the most honest and transparent administration in history. Well Mr. President, even the liberal press has admitted that it has been just the opposite. My friends, what do we call that in Ohio?"

"A LIE"

"And what else has he said that wasn't true? If you like your present health care plan and doctor, you can keep it, period."

"LIE"

"I will work with all parties and my administration will heal that which divides us in this country."

"LIE"

"The VA is an excellent role model for a national health care system."

"LIE"

"The Middle East is now secure."

"LIE"

"Al-Qaeda is on the run. We will negotiate a responsible nuclear treaty with Iran. Our borders are more secure now than ever. Benghazi was just the result of a video. The IRS scandal is overblown. Our relations with Russia are excellent."

"ALL LIES," chanted the crowd over and over.

"Yes, lies, lies, and more lies. This president and his party have lied to us so much, that they no longer recognize the truth when they see it. They have lied to us for the past seven years because, as they say in private, they think that the average American is too stupid to understand the complexities that face this country. Well, my fellow citizens, we are not stupid and we are going to make them realize that fact after the next election."

There was another round of enthusiastic applause followed by the chant, "Throw them out! Throw them out! Throw them out!"

"No-one in the world trusts or respects us anymore because the word of this country is now meaningless. The Russians invaded and then annexed the Ukraine and all our administration could do was to draw a line in the sand. What did the president do when that line was crossed? He simply redrew the line farther back. My fellow Americans, this is not leadership, this is nothing more than cowardly capitulation. At the same time, we have abandoned Israel, one of our closest allies. When they are attacked by terrorists, we blame the state of Israel. Is this how we treat our friends while we make excuses for our enemies? How can we expect any other country to trust us as an ally?

"The present occupant of the White House has been the country's worst president since Jimmy Carter. We needed Ronald Reagan to clean up the mess left behind after four disastrous years of his policies and now we again have a mess that needs to be cleaned up. This president and his political party have taken our country to the edge of social, economic, and international collapse. I can't say with certainty whether it's due to naiveté, incompetence, or intent. But what I can say with absolute certainty is that we need a change and we're going to get just that. With the grace of God and with your help, I will begin that change. I will pull this country back from the edge of the abyss that we are now facing. Starting on January 20th of next year, I guarantee you that I will lead this country back to the fiscal stability, trust, and the stature that we once enjoyed. I will put the American citizen first. I will put the welfare of our fine young fighting men and veterans first. I will not tolerate any kind of terrorism or international bullying. I will chase down any organization which attacks our citizens, and I will chase them all of the way to the gates of hell. I will draw a line in the sand and I guarantee you that, by God, I will not allow that line to be crossed. That is my promise to you, Ohio. That is my promise to you America. That is what I say and that is exactly what I will do. Thank you and may God bless America."

CHAPTER TEN

The Muslim captain guided the Viking craft back into Port Everglades in Fort Lauderdale. The boat followed the Intracoastal Waterway north for another ten miles until it reached the dock of an isolated private home. It was a spacious, Tuscany-style, two-story, fifteen thousand square foot mansion constructed with cream-colored stucco walls and a terra cotta tile roof. Multiple tall arched windows looked over the waterway while a large turret dominated the Southeast corner. An expansive veranda with marble balusters extended out the back toward the dock, partially covering a stone lanai and fire pit area beneath.

The four acre property was dotted with a scattering of tall Mediterranean cypress trees, royal palms and colorful flower gardens. In the center of the well-manicured lawn sat a huge fountain made of hand carved Italian marble. The estate was surrounded by an eight foot wrought-iron fence and a thick privacy hedge of bougainvillea. In addition, it was protected with an extensive security system including: camera surveillance coverage of the entire property, motion detectors, a half dozen armed guards, and a pack of Rottweiler dogs that roamed the grounds at will.

The interior of the house was decorated with the most expensive appointments imported from Europe. It contained seven bedrooms and twelve bathrooms. The living room was as large as most houses and had a two story window in the back that afforded a panoramic view of the canal, the dock, and a mangrove marsh on the far side. The mansion had been rented by an off-shore shell corporation several years ago.

The most important aspect of the home was that it contained a large second-floor, self-contained three-bedroom apartment that had been paid for by the new tenant and built to his specifications. It was confined within the interior walls of the mansion and there was only one means of ingress or egress, through a double-locked thick metal door. There were no windows, making the apartment completely isolated from the outside world. Inside, the apartment was as elegantly decorated as the rest of the home. Every room, including the bathrooms, was monitored twenty-four hours a day with video cameras and audio surveillance.

Under the cover of darkness, the Maultry family was blindfolded and led from the boat at gunpoint, across the expansive lawn, around the large fountain, under the veranda, and through a set of glass doors. Once inside the home, they were stopped and their blindfolds were removed. From there, they were led down a hall, up a flight of ornately carpeted stairs, and down a maze of several more hallways whose walls were decorated with original oil paintings of Tuscany and Venetian landscapes. The group was brought to a stop in front of a large grey metal door with a heavy bolt lock on the outside. It was obviously not designed to keep people out but rather to keep them imprisoned within. Mossaq, who Tiffany tearfully recognized as the man who broke her friend's jaw, withdrew a set of keys from his pocket and opened the lock. He pushed the family inside the secure apartment prison and glared at them.

"If you try to escape, you will all die...slowly," he said while grinning at Julia. After the man exited the apartment, Graham could hear him relock the door, followed by the engagement of a second, electronic lock.

We're sealed in tightly, like a tomb. I hope that's not prophetic, thought Graham as he stared at the closed door. He regained his composure, turned toward his family and hugged each of them reassuringly. "Is everyone OK?" Tiffany was weeping while Rodney was speechless, both of the two teens still in shock.

Julia responded, "We're all shaken up but we'll be fine. What's this all about Graham? Are they holding us hostage for ransom?"

"I'm not sure."

"Why did they have to kill Tucker and Jessica?"

"I don't know. I think that they were considered to be expendable. They aren't a necessary part of the plan."

"Well, what in God's name could be their plan?" asked his wife.

"I just don't know for sure exactly what's going on or why. We'll just have to wait until they let us know. I don't think we're in any immediate danger because if they wanted to do something, they would have already done it. For right now, we'll have to try to settle in until we have more information. Then I'll be able to figure something out. I'm going to get all of us out of here, I promise."

The family was allowed to rest and eat, undisturbed, for the next forty-eight hours. To their surprise, each had their own bedroom and each had a wardrobe closet filled with clothes that were of the appropriate size and style. Whoever kidnapped them had the resources to do a great deal of research on them. The captors were apparently interested in keeping the family as comfortable as possible during their stay. All meals were prepared by a full-time, on-site chef per their requests. There was a satellite TV in every room and there were multiple computers available, although all internet access was blocked. For the teens, there were both X-Box and PlayStation systems, including a collection of the most popular games. They were allowed to walk the grounds outside and even had access to the large pool but each was guarded at all times by men armed with silenced Kalashnikov automatic rifles.

⋙ ⋘

On the third day of their imprisonment, Graham was summoned to a meeting in the main part of the house. A young guard by the name of Yassin Aziz escorted him down a stairway and through a network of hallways until they reached an enormous office. Graham found the young man to be surprisingly courteous, at least as much as could be expected from someone who was pointing an automatic rifle against his back.

As Yassin stood guard at the door, Graham entered the lavishly-decorated room. It was furnished with an oversized hand-carved mahogany desk and two opposing large leather couches. The entire back wall of the room was comprised of floor-to-ceiling arched glass bay windows that overlooked a lagoon-shaped swimming pool. An Italian marble fireplace occupied one corner of the room while a mahogany bar sat in the opposite corner. A tall bespectacled man wearing a black suit and tie stood behind the bar. He looked like he might have been a funeral director in another life. Graham again thought of the word, *prophetic.*

Sitting behind the desk and facing the room sat a dark complected man who looked to be in his mid-forties. *Italian maybe, or Arab?* Graham thought. The man was remarkably handsome with black hair and piercing dark-brown eyes. Graham was surprised to discover that the man spoke perfect English.

"Would you like something to drink Dr. Maultry: coffee, soft drink, beer, or a cocktail? We have the finest Kentucky Bourbon."

56

"No thank you," replied Graham curtly.

"Thank you, Mustafa. That will be all for now," said the man.

"As you wish sir," the funeral director replied as he bowed his head slightly and left the room.

The man behind the desk stood and extended his hand as he said, "It's a pleasure to meet you Dr. Maultry. I trust that your accommodations are satisfactory."

Graham noticed that the man looked to be just over six feet tall and wore small hearing aids in each ear. Graham refused to receive the handshake. "They're fine considering the fact that my family and I have been kidnapped and are being held against our will in some unknown location. In addition, two innocent teens were murdered in cold blood."

"Ah yes, that was very unfortunate and I must apologize for the inappropriate actions of my employees," he replied non-contritely. "Sometimes they can be overly enthusiastic."

"You'll have to excuse me if I doubt the sincerity of your apology. The word 'inappropriate' seems pathetically inadequate in describing the atrocities that your people committed. Exactly why have you brought us here and what are your plans for us? Do you intend to kill us also?"

Graham could see a hint of anger in the man's eyes but that look quickly dissipated.

"I think that you and I can agree that the word 'atrocity' can be a relative term, doctor. It depends upon the nature of the victim. What is an atrocity to some might be considered unavoidable collateral damage by others. But, that being said, eliminating you or your family is certainly not our intent. If I had wanted to have you killed, I would have already ordered it. You and your family will be released, unharmed, if you and I can reach a mutual understanding."

"And that is?"

"I have taken the liberty of researching your professional career, and I must say that your credentials are impressive. You are undoubtedly one of the most brilliant aeronautical engineers in the country."

"And?"

"We would like to employ your talents to design a small aircraft."

Graham was astounded. "Are you crazy? I'll do no such thing! What makes you think that I'd ever help you build such thing? Why would I cooperate with a group of savages who obviously have no respect for human life?" asked Graham.

Again, the angry look returned, but quickly disappeared. "Usually, in matters such as this, we provide a substantial cash incentive. However, I am well aware that you are already a very wealthy man, Dr. Maultry. There is no financial agreement that could motivate you; so, I offer you something much more valuable than money. I offer you the health and welfare of your family."

The Scorpion's artificial smile transformed into a satanic grin and Graham could now see the malevolence previously hidden behind those piercing brown eyes. "I would hate to turn your family over to some of my associates who can be even more brutal than those whom you have already met. So, let's not get into futile sparring over what you will or will not do, doctor. The fact of the matter is that you will do exactly as you are told. By the way Dr. Maultry, we are not stupid people. I will have some of my own engineers review your plans to be sure that you have not integrated some device to sabotage our efforts. If you do, someone will pay the price beginning with that beautiful teenage daughter of yours."

Graham was speechless.

"I'll take your silence as a sign that you have wisely resigned yourself to the fact that you have no other choice but to help us."

Graham lowered his head. The man was right. He had no options here. "Exactly what kind of an aircraft and for what purpose? How can you possibly build an aircraft so sophisticated that it would require my design abilities?"

"The type would be a smaller version of a plane based upon the most modern stealth technology available, similar to the stealth bombers that you yourself once helped to design while at Nordstone-Thorn Industries. It must be constructed with a graphene core and covered by a graphene skin so as to minimize weight and maximize structural integrity. Based upon the research that your own company has been doing on this ultra-light, ultra-strong material, you should have no problems with the designs. As you are already aware, graphene sheeting is one of the strongest and lightest materials known to man. A single thin layer is stronger than steel. It makes the plane light in weight while making it virtually indestructible."

"How do you know about my company's research into the aeronautical uses of graphene? That information is a closely guarded secret."

"You would be amazed at our abilities, Doctor Maultry. We have contacts almost anywhere that we need them, and if we don't, we simply pay for them. Most Americans are fairly easy to buy off. It's just a matter of negotiating the right price and it doesn't always have to be money."

"Blackmail," offered Graham.

"Exactly or a guarantee of safety for loved ones."

"What are your design requirements?" inquired Graham.

The man gave detailed specifications.

"I don't think that can be accomplished with the dimensions which you require," claimed Graham.

"That's why you are here doctor. If it were an easy engineering design, I could have had my own people do it. Remember, the lives of your family members are at stake, so don't fail me."

Graham again lowered his head in submission and said nothing.

Now, I will have Yassin show you to your laboratory. It contains the most sophisticated computers and design software available.

In addition, we have all of the equipment necessary to build scale models. I must insist that your final designs be submitted two months from now. Meanwhile, your progress will be monitored weekly by my associate, Mr. Ahmad Haq Rasid. You already met him several days ago when he boarded your yacht. Once our mission is complete, I will have no further need of you or your family. You have my word that you will all be released unharmed, as long as you follow the rules that I already outlined for you."

Unharmed, I'm sure. I'll tell that to Jessica and Tucker when I see them, thought Graham as he already started planning how he and his family would complete their escape. On his way out of the office, he saw the black box with the Norwegian lettering sitting next to one of the couches. He preceded Yassin to the design laboratory, a Kalashnikov automatic rifle again pointed at the middle of his back.

CHAPTER ELEVEN

Dearborn is a city of around 100,000, situated in the southeast corner of the State of Michigan. It was the home of Henry Ford and it contains the world headquarters of the Ford Motor Company. It boasts the Henry Ford Community College and a peripheral campus of the University of Michigan. In addition, Dearborn boasts the Islamic Center of America. The city contains the largest contingent of Muslims in the U. S. While most of them are hard-working patriotic Americans who love their country, a small minority of those 35,000 Muslims embrace the idea that the United States should enact a framework of Islamic law that advocates a change in our freedoms and way of life. Even some of the so-called "moderate" Muslims are painfully quiet when asked to comment on atrocities such as 9/11 or the horrific treatment of women and children by ISIS.

It is in this environment that mullah Muqtoda al-Sadir has prospered. At his Al-Fateh mosque, he has been openly critical of the United States and has been a proponent of replacing its constitution with one based upon Sharia law. In quiet, he has taken things much further. He has been the militant leader of a clandestine terrorist cell that has been working toward the economic and social destruction of America. His activities have allowed al-Sadir to amass a small fortune for himself so as to support a secret, self-indulgent western lifestyle. Paradoxically, he has enjoyed many of the luxuries that American wealth can provide, all of the while preaching a plan to undermine the same source of those benefits.

He was a noticeably obese man who usually dressed in a black robe and white turban. On this particular morning, he was stroking his long salt and pepper beard as he sat in his office, expectantly waiting for a call from a man whom he had never met face-to-face, and hoped that he never would. He had no desire to be confronted by the legendary "Assassin of Kandahar" in person. He was a dangerous man who was best avoided, if at all possible.

After an hour, the phone finally rang and the mullah almost fell out of his chair answering it.

"Mullah al-Sadir, do you recognize my voice?"

"Yes. As salamu alaikum wa rahmatullah wa barakatuhu," replied the mullah.

"And may the peace, mercy, and blessings of Allah also be upon you." Generally the Scorpion did not concern himself with the formalities of Muslim social greetings but there were times when he tolerated them for the sake of his ultimate goal. The Scorpion didn't care about the holy jihad and he couldn't care less about Islam. The focus of all of his thoughts since childhood has been the extraction of the ultimate and final revenge for the hell that America had brought down upon his family and village. But, at times he had to play the Islamic game with fools like this mullah and wealthy Saudi Wahhabis in order to reach that goal.

"Have you been in contact with the Canadian group?" he asked al-Sadir.

"Yes, praise Allah, everything is proceeding according to plan. One of our two contacts has taken a photograph of the containers and the creation of the duplicate is almost complete. We have been given the transfer date and we are on schedule."

"What was the price of the contract?"

"Five hundred thousand dollars for each man."

"A million US dollars total!" exclaimed the Scorpion skeptically. He realized that this was probably an inflated number and the cleric was surely skimming half of that amount into his own bank account. He was all too aware that it was not the principals of Allah that the mullah worshipped most, but rather the US dollar which sustained the man's western lifestyle of travel, expensive cars, and beautiful women. But the Scorpion didn't care how corrupt the man was or the depth of his hypocrisies. This was not a religious quest and he didn't really care if the mullah enriched himself in the process, as long as the mission was successful.

"That's a lot of money. Unfortunately, we will be unable to safely wire any more funds into your accounts. There are too many security concerns. The Department of Homeland Security has broadened their level of cash transfer monitoring, even those coming out of Europe. You're going to have to increase your own activities in order to have enough assets to complete all of the necessary transactions. Get the funds, mullah. Don't disappoint me. You never want to make the mistake of disappointing me. We don't want there to be any complications. I detest complications. Dealing with them can be very messy and too much is at stake."

The mullah understood the implications of the word "messy." He replied nervously, "I will see to it that the necessary funds are in place. With Allah's guidance all should go well."

"It's not the grace of Allah that I worry about," was the short reply as the Scorpion terminated the conversation.

CHAPTER TWELVE

Special Agent John Crawford grew up as the only child of the only black parents in impoverished Letcher Count, Kentucky. After his father died in Vietnam, he and his young mother were taken in by the parents of Jacob and Lisa Marie Savich. In time, he and his mother were considered as part of their family.

He had spent the past twelve months recovering from a near-fatal gunshot wound to the chest. It was the result of being ambushed in a dark Chicago alley while chasing down a pair of serial vigilante killers who had been working the Greater Cincinnati area. He was able to terminate one of them with shots to the head and chest; but the other man limped away after having been wounded in the leg. Two weeks later, the man's dead body was found along the banks of the Ohio River just downstream from Cincinnati. The autopsy revealed the expected healing gunshot wound of the left thigh. In addition there was a fresh high powered rifle shot through the right eye. It had blown out the entire back of the man's skull. Investigators postulated that he was eliminated by other members of his vigilante group. Apparently, the near murder of an FBI Special Agent in Chicago made the man a liability.

In a private awards ceremony at the FBI offices in Washington, John Crawford was recognized for his bravery and heroism in solving what was now being referred to as the "Cincinnati Vigilante Killings". He couldn't help but think that he didn't deserve the award, but he was stuck with the story as it had been told. That acknowledgement, piggybacked upon his recent dramatic success in solving the Cincinnati Rapist crimes, drew the attention of Mr. Lewis Stevenson who was the acting director of the Bureau. Crawford was subsequently promoted to the position of FBI Assistant Director of the Midwest Region of the US, just one of five such regions in the country.

He accepted the promotion with ambivalent feelings. It would require a move to the Chicago Bureau offices. He was as ambitious as the next man, probably even more so, and this new position would make him the only black regional director in the entire Bureau. But it was a double-edged sword. He would have to leave his two daughters behind and his ex-wife was not going to make it easy for him to see the girls, even though she was the one who had left him. Ever since she discovered that he had moved on and started dating someone else, she became furiously jealous. He would never understand that woman. Now, he had someone who was the polar opposite of his ex. He had been in love with her since they were teens in Letcher County. If he transferred to Chicago, he would have to be separated from the woman who he hoped to marry one day, Lisa Marie Savich. It would be impossible for her to follow him to Chicago because she had to remain here to run her own pharmaceutical company, just south of Cincinnati.

He wasn't sure if the two could survive the demands of a long distance relationship. Lisa had already been somewhat preoccupied for the past nine months. She had been away, traveling for three to four days every week and for a while, Crawford was concerned that she might be interested in someone else. But that notion was quickly dismissed. He had known Lisa well enough to realize that if she had wanted to see another man, she would have simply told him up front. No, he concluded, she was not seeing someone else. She was probably just too involved with the recent move of her business to their new national corporate headquarters in Wilder, Kentucky. Managing a half-billion-dollar company was time consuming and he had to remind himself that, prior to the shooting, he had also been extremely busy.

In actuality, Lisa had encouraged him to accept the promotion because she wasn't worried so much about the stress of a long distance relationship. The fact of the matter was that she wasn't sure if their relationship could survive his failure to do so. There would be too much potential for resentment if he didn't accept it, and she didn't want the responsibility of being the basis for a decision which might stagnate his career.

He was in the process of packing up his office when his secretary rang, "I'm sorry to bother you sir, but you have an important call on line three. It's the Director." He stopped what he was doing and picked up the phone. "This is Agent Crawford."

"Well John, it's not going to be just agent for much longer. It'll be Assistant Director soon."

"Thank you, sir. I certainly appreciated the confidence that you've placed in me."

"You've earned it more than anyone I know, John. Listen, I realize you're in the process of getting ready for the transfer to Chicago soon, but I want you to hold off on your preparations for now. Something's come up."

"I don't understand sir. Is there a problem with the new position?" he asked with obvious concern and disappointment in his voice.

"No, no, it's nothing like that, John. You're still our first pick as the man for the job, but something has developed that is going to require your urgent and undivided attention. Your new position is associated with a fair amount of administrative responsibilities that will take you out of the field. For right now, I need my best investigative man working on this new situation full time, and you're my best man. I'm going to need you as the lead investigator in the trenches on this one."

"Thank you, sir. What is it that you need?"

"As you are aware, after 9/11, we've been able to cut off a lot of the cash flow from the Middle East to hidden terrorist organizations in this country. As a result, the enemy has been looking into other options to replenish their funds. For a long time, we've been aware that some amount of the drug trade money has been used to help finance terror cells here and abroad. That may account for the huge increase in heroin traffic in your area of Northern Kentucky and Cincinnati. Now, we suspect that certain other criminal activities are being used for the same purpose. Have you seen the reports about the recent spike in the incidence of armed robberies in the mid-western states?"

"Yes, I reviewed several of them a couple of months ago while I was still recuperating from my gunshot injuries. As I recall, most of the activities involved banks and high-end jewelry stores," replied Crawford.

"That's correct. There's been an 83% uptick in bank robberies and a 47% increase in jewelry store heists in just under two years. The problem appears to be centered in the states of Michigan, Indiana, and Ohio. Based upon this spike in activity, we believe that someone needs to raise a lot of cash quickly. It's too many robberies within a relatively small area to be simply due to chance. Whoever they are, they're well-organized and senior analysts at the Bureau think the robberies might be the work of one or more terror cells."

The director continued, "In addition, my contacts at the NSA say that there's been a dramatic increase in chatter on the internet.

That usually precedes some type of major attack like 9/11. The name 'Chicago' has come up a few times, but right now we don't know what it means; could be a code name, could refer to the city, or it might not be anything. Finally, there have been a number of supposed 'lone wolf' terrorist attacks like the one at Stanford several months ago. A few weeks later there was the suspicious machete attack on a dozen people at the Alamo in San Antonio. If you piggyback these on the attacks at the Chattanooga military recruiting centers and the Boston Marathon, it all points to an organized plan."

"Does the Bureau believe that all of the attacks are coordinated?" inquired Crawford.

"That's becoming the consensus of opinion by many of our analysts and at the Department of Homeland Security. We believe the jihadists are working up to something, maybe an attack of unprecedented magnitude, John. Something big is being planned and we need to find out more information. Right now, the only tangible lead we have might be related to the recent bank and jewelry store hold ups. We need to trace these robberies back to the leadership source ASAP before whatever-it-is happens!

"John, I want you to be the agent in charge of investigating this matter. You'll have the full support of my office. You'll be coordinating all activities. Anything you need, just call me.

CHAPTER THIRTEEN

Mullah al-Sadir picked up his phone and dialed his highest ranking lieutenant, Muhammad Rabbani. He, along with four others, had been smuggled across the Mexican border after the American government softened its stance on illegal aliens.

Muhammad answered the call, "As-salamu alaykum."

"And peace upon you, my friend. I have received a call from our sponsor. All plans are in motion but we are going to need an influx of more money. I would say another two hundred thousand at least."

"I thought we had ample funds. How soon do you need the money?" asked Muhammad.

"Within the month. Our Canadian contacts are demanding more cash," lied the mullah.

"That means at least two big jobs a week! That's going to be very risky. It's becoming more and more difficult and we don't have adequate preparation right now. I've recently discovered that their Federal Bureau of Investigation is diverting a number of assets to investigate the robberies. If we continue, it will be just a matter of time before we are discovered and the mission is compromised."

Al-Sadir responded, "We must do what Allah deems necessary. His will shall guide you and guarantee your success. See that it is done and keep me informed about your progress."

Muhammad Rabbani finished the call and stroked his heavy black mustache as he considered the implications of the conversation. He questioned whether the Canadians actually asked for more. He knew the materialistic side of the mullah all too well. However, he just might be telling the truth and Muhammad couldn't take the chance of a potential cash shortfall.

He decided to meet with his two team leaders the following morning. He had justifiable concerns. He and his Muslim brothers were not worried about dying in the holy war. To die in a jihad for Allah would ensure their place in Paradise. However, he was worried about the additional team members they had to recruit in order to get enough manpower for the jobs. He doubted the commitment of the new American converts to Islam as much as he doubted the commitment of the mullah to the mission. The problem was he had no choice but to utilize their talents. They spoke the language and knew more about how to commit robberies than his Islamic brothers. "Allah's will be done," he said to himself. He decided to put Curtis Johnson on the next jewelry store job and Reggie Patterson would remain on his own team.

⊶+ +⊷

Curtis Johnson had worked at the General Motors assembly plant in Detroit for thirteen years. He was married and had three children. After purchasing his own home, he was becoming uncomfortably deep in debt. However, with his wife also working, they were getting by--that is, until the Detroit financial crisis in 2007 when the auto industry collapsed. The next year, the government bought a majority share of the G.M. Corporation and insisted upon stringent financial controls. Layoffs were the inevitable result and Curtis was on the list to be let go. In spite of the company's promise to find another job for him, there were none available in the Michigan auto industry. Two years later, he gave up and stopped looking for work. By then he had already lost his home, his wife, and his children. He blamed the government. Like many others in his situation, he first turned to alcohol and then crack cocaine to numb the pain. After being arrested at a crack house, he was imprisoned for six months. It was there that he was exposed to the teachings of Islam.

Muhammad Rabbani noticed Curtis hanging around the mosque and eventually recruited him into their organization. Curtis embraced the doctrines of the Quran and spent hours studying it. He learned from Mullah al-Sadir that most of his problems could be traced back to the greedy white Christian Capitalists who ran the country. They were the ones who had destroyed his life. He learned about how the government had intentionally infected the black race with AIDS in an effort to exterminate them. He learned that the Holocaust was a lie fabricated by the Jews of the world in order to justify the stealing of land from the Palestinians. He also learned about how to keep his body and soul pure for Allah, which meant no more alcohol or drugs. It was a welcome change in direction. In time, Curtis Johnson rejected his American heritage. He was now a part of Allah's army in the battle to defeat the people who had destroyed his life. He carried no weapons although he would have loved to shoot some Jews. His job was to act as a lookout, do the talking, and drive the getaway car. He was devoted to his job, he was devoted to Mullah al-Sadir, he was devoted to Muhammad, and he was devoted to Allah.

CHAPTER FOURTEEN

The Ft. Lauderdale based Atlantic Salvage Company had been contacted last month about a recovery mission. Normally, they would only get involved in large commercial operations, not the recovery of pleasure boats, not even seventy-two-foot Hatteras luxury yachts. However, after the Maultry Corporation offered a three million dollar contract for boat recovery and body retrieval, Atlantic Salvage changed its philosophy. They quickly dispatched the red and white painted Jean-Marie, a large ship that was outfitted with a one-hundred-ton capacity crane.

Captain Jerry Kernan rechecked the co-ordinates that the coast guard had given to him and entered them into the ship's GPS navigation system. An intensive ocean rescue search had been initiated soon after the Maultry family yacht had failed to arrive at their scheduled destination in North Bimini. The boat could not be hailed on any of the emergency radio frequencies. One of the vice-presidents of his company remembered that the boss had installed a transponder that would transmit the boat's location in case of an emergency. Graham's secretary had the transponder frequency on file and relayed the information to the Coast Guard. A rescue helicopter picked up the signal well north of the original search area but the actual boat could not be seen. The conclusion was that it had sunk and had apparently drifted north in the Gulf Stream current for fifteen nautical miles before it had stopped moving. The helicopter pinpointed the location and relayed the co-ordinates to the Coast Guard.

Once Captain Kernan reached the site, he put his boat into idle and turned on the underwater sonar. After an hour of methodical grid searching, he pointed to the screen and said to the first mate, "That must be it, right there. Hold this position and send down a few scout divers to see what we're up against."

The divers returned within thirty minutes and reported that it was the missing yacht. The senior diver said, "It's the boat all right. The name Julia Ann is painted on the rear transom. It's precariously perched on a shelf around 150 feet below the surface. It won't take much to knock it over the ledge, boss. After that it's a four-thousand-foot drop straight to the bottom where the signal would have been lost. It's a small miracle that it got caught on that shelf in the first place. If the seas had been rough, the boat would have never stayed where it is. We'd have never found it."

"Could you see any bodies?" asked the captain.

"No, but we didn't really feel safe looking around just yet. First, I think we need to stabilize her. Any wrong move and one of us could be crushed."

"OK. The weather looks clear so we have time. Give yourselves an hour and then put together a team of four. Are you going to need a helium mix in your tanks?"

"I don't think so. It's only 150 feet deep so I'm not too worried about nitrogen narcosis. But it's going to be a little complicated on that ledge and we're going to be down there for a while. We'll need to set up for a decompression stop."

One of the crew dropped the decompression bar over the side and lowered it to a depth of twenty feet. It was secured to two cleats: amidships and aft. Four extra air tanks were suspended from it. The salvage team donned their wetsuits, tanks, and masks and jumped into the water from the back platform. Each used a Sea-Scooter to propel themselves and their gear down to the wreck as quickly as possible. As they descended deeper, they turned on their mask lights, because at this level, much of the sunlight was filtered out giving everything a dark blue-grey color. They approached the sunken ship cautiously.

After they secured their scooters and gear, they began the process of attaching a floatation collar around the hull of the boat in order to stabilize it and prevent it from falling into the trench. Using a compressor hose brought down from the surface, they slowly inflated the collar segments sequentially, until the hull was lifted just several feet off of the ledge. They had to be careful. Over-inflation of the device would have resulted in an explosive surfacing which could destroy the boat and any evidence that might explain why it sank. Once the yacht was stabilized, lift straps were guided under the hull and attached to a four-pronged crane cable.

Using a combination of the crane and the flotation collar, the yacht was slowly raised to the surface next to the salvage barge. Pumps were used to remove water from the bilge and engine rooms. Once the boat was fully surfaced and secured into position, Captain Kernan climbed aboard. No bodies could be seen in the cabin or staterooms. Then he climbed down into the engine room and saw that the intakes of both diesel engines had been destroyed. When he turned to leave he noticed the partially decomposed bodies of the two teens, tied behind the access ladder. It was obvious what had happened. He yelled up to his first mate, "Call the cops! This was no accident. These people were murdered!"

CHAPTER FIFTEEN

The Scorpion stood at the window of his MPC Manhattan offices and looked out over the East River. For the past fourteen years, he has worked as CEO of the Masterson Properties Corporation. The company had prior holdings worth 7.8 billion dollars in the U.S. alone. Their portfolio included over eighty hotels, office buildings, and shopping centers in North America. He had been in the process of selling off many of the properties over the past two years, including a total of twenty-seven luxury hotels under the name of a subsidiary corporation. Thus far the sales have generated over three billion dollars after retirement of debt. He had been gradually transferring that money into various numbered accounts in Switzerland, Croatia, and the Cayman Islands. From there, the funds were converted to gold bullion securities.

He completed an email to the only other owner of the Masterson Properties Corporation, his multi-billionaire adopted father, Prince Alsalud bin Rashid Kabeer of Saudi Arabia. The prince needed to be updated regarding the progress of their plans.

Within the next year, the Scorpion will have taken most of the assets off of the company's books. Today, he would be closing on two more deals. The first was scheduled to happen this morning. It involved the sale of his two major Las Vegas casinos and seven related resort hotels for another two and a half billion dollars. The second was to occur in the afternoon, when he would be selling off another thirty-one properties for a total of two billion. All remaining properties had already been refinanced at one hundred and ten percent of their actual market value. By the end of the day, MPC will have essentially liquidated their entire portfolio of properties. Everything was handled through so many off-shore umbrella corporations that it will take months to sort it out. By then it will have been too late. It'll all be over.

CHAPTER SIXTEEN

The lights were on at historic Wrigley Field in Chicago. Tonight would be game two of the National League Championship series between two unlikely contenders: the Cubs and the Cincinnati Reds. The atmosphere was electric and everyone in Chicago was optimistically excited since the Cubbies took the first game by beating the Reds' pitching ace.

The roads feeding the intersection of Clark and Addison were blocked off as the party atmosphere spilled out of the local bars and onto the streets. Thousands of fans were congregating outside the stadium under the large iconic red Wrigley Field sign. They milled about buying peanuts, beer, and souvenirs. In the midst of them, stood Lazlo Chenko. He already knew he wasn't going to get inside. Security was too tight, a fact he had already anticipated. That was alright. He didn't actually have to enter the stadium. He didn't have any money for a ticket anyway. For that matter, he didn't even have a wallet, or any other form of identification. All he had were the clothes on his back and the heavy necklace that he wore down over his chest. It was all concealed by a thick navy-blue pea coat.

Just over a month ago, Lazlo was still in his native Serbia. His entire Muslim family had been exterminated and buried in a mass grave a mile outside of his village. The Christian government had not spared anyone: not his wife, not his five children, not his parents, no-one. Now, even after fifteen years, he still fostered a deep hatred for all Christians, Jews, and anyone else who supported their anti-Muslim genocidal agendas.

Then he found a way to quiet that hatred. He made contact with a group that would help him extract some revenge. Two weeks ago, he had flown into the Toronto Pearson International Airport where he was met by two members of a Canadian al-Qaeda cell. They gave him all of the equipment and cash he would need for the next several weeks. He completed a drive to the tiny "Walleye Marina" in Leamington, Canada along the north coast of Lake Erie. The next day, he and four others boarded a twenty-five-foot fishing charter that had sailed out of the U.S. earlier in the morning. The boat headed south, back across the lake toward its home marina in Port Clinton, Ohio.

After another five hours of riding in a van, Lazlo arrived at a small Chicago apartment. The other four men from his group proceeded in different cars to their own destinations in Indianapolis, St. Paul, Columbus, and Nashville. For the next two weeks Lazlo studied the local Chicago community, its customs, and the layout of the streets.

Now he was almost ready to complete his mission. He felt under his coat and grasped two of the round metallic objects. As he pulled each, the pins were dislodged and he threw them as far as he could into the crowd, one north and one south. Within a second, he had pulled two more and threw the objects, one to his right and one to his left. In the next second, he pulled one more and held it to his neck. Just as he yelled "Allahu Akbar," his head exploded off of his shoulders and broke up into a misty red cloud with a thousand pieces of bone and brain showering those who had not already been killed by the blast.

Sixty feet away, a five-year-old boy excitedly picked up what he thought was a souvenir baseball. "Mommy, a ball!" he said as he was proudly showing his parents. It exploded in the boy's hand, killing him and everyone around him. In all, over fifty innocent men, women, and children, had been indiscriminately slaughtered. Hundreds more were seriously injured.

The morning after the Chicago attack, the influx of more terrorists continued. Air France flight 3628 completed its journey from Paris to JFK International Airport in New York. Five Muslim men with legitimate French citizen passports exited the plane, separated and proceeded to various landmarks and state capitals. Two took taxis to their destinations in Manhattan. One boarded a connecting flight to Albany while the other flew to Harrisburg, Pennsylvania. The fifth drove to Annapolis, Maryland. Three hours later, Delta Airlines flight 15 from Frankfort Germany landed in Atlanta Georgia. Three German nationals disembarked the 767 aircraft. Two of them made individual arrangements to fly to Tallahassee, Florida and Richmond, Virginia. The third man boarded a flight for Topeka, Kansas. None of the Muslim men was concerned about receiving extra scrutiny at immigration. None of them was listed on any "No Fly" lists and none had any recorded history of affiliation with radical Islamic groups. Each was eventually able to meet up with their respective sleeper-cells without difficulty. The men represented just a handful of those who had already arrived or were about to arrive at other destinations around the country.

CHAPTER SEVENTEEN

They were on the 12th floor of the Great American Tower building in downtown Cincinnati. The room had a huge picture window all along its south side, offering a spectacular view of the Bengal's Paul Brown Stadium and the Ohio River valley beyond. The buyer gazed out the window and studied the bedroom communities along the river's southern shore in Northern Kentucky. The landscape was dotted with thousands of people attending riverside restaurants and walking along rows of old riverboat-captain mansions. A number of pleasure boats were lazily cruising up and down the waterway. *They have no clue,* he thought as he turned around to face the room and take a seat.

At one end of the room was a large credenza upon which sat the obligatory coffee urn and silver tray with Danish pastries that no-one would taste today. Above the credenza hung an original oil painting by Robert Fabe depicting the Cincinnati skyline as it was fifty years ago. In the middle of the room, Rosalyn Rosen sat at a large mahogany table. It was in the main conference room at the law offices of Gerner, Schiff, and Bernstein.

Rosalyn was flanked on either side by her long-term friend Sly Gerner and a junior partner, Richard Weissel. Across from them sat a handsome fortyish man with black hair and piercing brown eyes. He was of average height and wore an immaculately tailored Bottega Veneta suit. He had tiny clear plastic hearing aid stems in each ear canal. Rosalyn wouldn't have even noticed them except for the fact that her husband, Sam wore identical devices before he died. As the man sitting across from her smiled, it was not the cordial smile of someone about to close a business deal, but more like that of a predator. It sent a cold chill down Rosalyn's spine and she understood why Sam distrusted him.

Rosalyn's late husband had mentioned his dislike of the man when Sam was first approached with an offer to buy his company, Microavionics Technologies Corporation, almost a year ago. Basically, the company focused on the production of expensive toys for wealthy adult hobbyists. Sam had started the company, alone in his garage, building remote controlled planes for himself and some of his close friends. Demand grew and he eventually turned his former hobby into a lucrative nationwide business. The sophistication and quality of his products dramatically improved as he expanded into international markets. Eventually, he outgrew the confines of the home garage, and moved his production facility into a fifteen thousand square foot warehouse north of Cincinnati, where it has been housed ever since. It was now recognized as the premier manufacturer of customized remote controlled planes for hobbyists in the US and abroad.

The purchase offer was certainly generous enough and Sam was getting older, but he wasn't ready to give up the company that he had poured so much of his life into. In addition, he didn't trust the potential buyer, so he politely declined the offer. The buyer increased the bid to ten times net earnings and made it a cash offer with no financing contingencies. Again Sam declined.

Three months later, sixty-four-year-old Sam Rosen died in a horrific accident while flying his Cessna Skyhawk to the family summer home in Hilton Head. Afterward, Rosalyn was devastated and the grieving widow didn't know what to do. She knew nothing about how to run the company. Sam had always handled it. Their only child had no interest. After consulting with her attorneys, she was advised to again look into the generous purchase offer that had been made earlier. Phone calls were exchanged and the offer was again extended with the same terms and conditions as previously stipulated. They were in the law offices today to consummate the deal.

She looked at the man sitting across from her and inquired, "I'm curious. Sly told me that your company is primarily involved in the hotel and real estate business. Why are you interested in purchasing a relatively small remote control toy business, Mr...?"

"Darpoli, Martin Darpoli," responded the man. "My associates and I believe that remote control technology is an industry of the future and Microavionics Technologies Corporation is very much at the forefront of that industry. Remote control machinery like robotics, drones, and vehicles is a promising field and we would like to take the company further in that direction. Even though we have paid over twice what the company is worth, we believe that the upside potential for future revenues is unlimited."

"I certainly hope you are correct Mr. Darpoli," she said as she studied the agreement and the final purchase price of twenty-seven million dollars. It would make Rosalyn Rosen a wealthy widow.

Mr. Darpoli opened his cell phone and dialed a number. After several minutes of hushed conversation, he said, "The monies have been transferred to the specified account, Mrs. Rosen. As soon as your attorneys have confirmed this, we can sign the documents." Mr. Gerner looked at his junior partner inquisitively and after a few minutes, there was an affirmative nod. The transfer confirmation code was recorded and over the next hour, all of the necessary papers were signed and witnessed. Handshakes were exchanged and Microavionics Technology Corporation was now under the sole control of the Scorpion.

CHAPTER EIGHTEEN

The black limousine approached the main security gate in Langley, Virginia, just as it did every day, seven days a week, fifty-two weeks a year. The guard reviewed the required identification papers carefully. It seemed to be an unnecessary formality since the he had known both occupants of the vehicle for almost two decades; but at this facility, strict security protocols were followed at all times. After a minute, the driver and his occupant were waved through. The car stopped in front of the main entrance where the passenger exited, and stretched his diminutive five-foot-six inch frame. Cold, black eyes, and a continuous, horizontal smile gave him the appearance of a reptile. Turning back to his chauffeur, he said, "I should be here all day. I'll call you later when I need to be picked up."

"Yes sir, Mr. Hamilton," was the reply.

He entered the building and walked across the large grey and white Central Intelligence Agency logo which adorned the floor of the main lobby. As he did every morning, he paused in front of the Memorial Wall. He reflected upon the number of agents who he had sent to their deaths and hoped that there would be no more; but he realized that more deaths would be a certainty. In this business, loss of life was unavoidable. The men and women represented on the wall were assets, like chess pieces to be moved around where needed and sacrificed only when necessary.

After taking the elevator to the third floor, he walked to room 319. The sign on the door read: *Supplemental Section of the Office of Research and Reports: Winston Hamilton III, Director.* His department appeared to be just another insignificant small piece of the CIA bureaucracy. The interior of the office was anything but. It was as big as a large apartment and furnished like a New York condominium penthouse. There were handmade Victorian walnut bookcases along one wall and a matching desk in the middle of the room. On top of the desk sat a bank of secure phones and an assortment of computer screens. Matching tan leather couches were situated on either side of an antique coffee table. The walls were adorned with pictures of himself posing with a multitude of influential business and political figures, including two past presidents. Being incredibly rich had its advantages.

Winston was raised in a wealthy family from Connecticut and was the sole heir to the fourteen billion dollar family estate. He didn't have to work for a living but he had a passion for what he did. As a teen, he had achieved the level of a grand chess master and was ranked by the World Chess Federation as one of the most promising contenders for the world championship. By the time he graduated from college, Winston became bored with the game in which the stakes were meaningless except for the fleeting satisfaction derived from a victory. For him, it was all just too easy.

He always yearned for a more challenging real-life game in which the stakes were higher; one in which a win might save lives while a loss could be catastrophic. Therefore, after seven successful years in the U. S. State Department, he used his family's extensive political connections to secure a position in the Central

Intelligence Agency. He had an eidetic memory, which allowed him to recall and correlate details of every report he read. He was able to identify significant patterns in seemingly unrelated pieces of data and make insightful recommendations. As a result, he flourished as an analyst and rapidly negotiated his way through the political minefields of the organization until he was promoted to his present position.

He entered his group of offices, said hello to his secretary, Jeanine, and hung up his charcoal grey suit coat. After sitting down, he took a sip of coffee which she had already prepared per his specific instructions: black, strong, no sugar, and at just the right temperature. Winston Hamilton's Research and Reports department dealt in the most valuable commodity in the world: not gold, and not oil, but information. Information was king, especially in Washington. It made him one of the most powerful men in the Agency. It was a fact that few people realized. Yes, information was king and over the past two decades, Winston Hamilton III had accumulated a wealth of information about almost every powerful political figure in the nation's capital. He knew their vices and their indiscretions. In order to get what he wanted, he was able to manipulate them around just like pieces on a worldwide chess board. The type of information he gathered could be a strong motivator in the hands of one who knew how to use it.

After only several years in the Agency, Winston realized that in order to successfully protect the country from those who would do it harm, he could not be subject to the mercurial whims of whatever political administration might be in power. He knew that with the existing systems, the country was unable to adequately defend itself against internal threats. The FBI couldn't do it. They were strangled by the limitations of their own due-process investigative protocols. Meanwhile, the Department of Homeland Security was so large that it was bogged down in a quagmire of administrative bureaucracy. It was very efficient at accumulating data and intelligence, but not very adept at formulating plans of action in response to that information.

The CIA was prevented by law from working within the borders of the US. However, Winston believed that particular law had to be ignored. It was imperative that his agency must in some way be involved in fighting domestic terrorism. The country needed a small nimble team with the moral flexibility to do whatever was necessary to protect its citizens. It was for this reason, he established the Delphi Program; named after the mythological goddess who helped to protect ancient Greece from its enemies. His team was an autonomous group not found on any official rolls of CIA employees. It was an organization that was buried deeply beneath multiple layers of bureaucratic budgeting and accounting. The funding was so convoluted and folded into so many various other budgets that even the shrewdest of forensic accountants couldn't figure it out. What funding his budget didn't provide, Winston covered personally.

No-one in the Agency, including the director, knew of his new organization's existence. Winston answered only to the deputy undersecretary, although even he was unaware of the full scope of Winston's anticipated missions. This provided several layers to shield the higher ups from his activities--activities that even some veteran members of the clandestine services wouldn't be able to stomach. These buffer layers gave his superiors what is referred to as "plausible deniability" if any of his actions became public.

The mission of his clandestine Delphi Team would be to confront terrorists on their own level. The team was to be charged with the task of extracting information from the enemy by any means necessary and then acting upon that information with extreme prejudice. Obviously, this meant they functioned outside the mandates of the constitution. They could not allow themselves to be hampered by the investigative protocols and due process restrictions that hamstrung the nation's law enforcement agencies.

Too much was at stake. They did not deal with criminals; they dealt with soulless terrorists bent upon the murder of innocents and the destruction of this land. Therefore, it was essential that his team use its own set of rules and it took a special breed to do whatever had to be done to protect the country.

Initially, the search for ideal members for the team was rough going. The use of Special Forces veterans would appear to have been an ideal choice, and they would have, if the group's primary responsibility was military black ops missions. For the Delphi program, the use of combat veterans didn't work out. They were too locked into the military chain-of-command mentality and too limited by the uniform code of military conduct restrictions. Winston had tried to recruit sociopaths, who were a lot more flexible in their approach to missions, but they could not be controlled. Indiscriminate collateral killing was the result. The situation became nearly catastrophic and each of them had to be dispatched into an "early retirement."

Finally, after years of searching, he discovered a most unlikely candidate to lead his Delphi Team. He was both intelligent and cunning with an almost uncanny ability to read the thoughts of his opponents. He could rapidly analyze changing situations, anticipate the response of his adversaries, and formulate an effectively lethal response. If Winston had to come up with a phrase to define Dr. Jacob Savich it would be *ferociously clever.* As a former All-American collegiate quarterback, he obviously possessed the necessary physical abilities. The fact that he was a highly respected plastic surgeon in Cincinnati gave him the perfect cover. However, what made him most qualified for Winston's team was a moral flexibility that allowed him to take another's life. He was a serial vigilante killer, motivated by a sense of righteous protection of the innocent. For Winston, it was a matter of redirecting the doctor's activities in another direction.

Doctor Savich possessed instincts which had enabled him to elude detection by the police and the FBI for over a decade. The only way in which Winston was able to identify him was through extensive NSA surveillance data programs and computerized profiling provided by Homeland Security. The new leader and his nascent team had been in training at a secret location for almost a year and Winston was awaiting a verbal report regarding the group's progress. He was going to need to activate them in the near future. Serious problems were looming on the horizon.

He called out to his secretary Jeanine again, "Would you contact Derek Hacker and tell him that I'm still waiting for his report."

"Yes sir, Mr. Hamilton. I spoke to him early this morning and he said the team had a five mile run to do. I'll let you know as soon as he returns your call."

"And Jeanine, would you bring me another cup of coffee?"

"Yes, sir."

As he waited for his coffee, Winston began to page through the stack of reports sitting on his desk. There was a brief internal CIA memo which had been forwarded to Winston by one of the senior analysts. At the top was a hand-written note, "What do you think of this?" The memo stated that a prototype tactical EMP generator had been stolen from the research laboratories at the Norwegian Technology Corporation in Oslo.

Now that could be a formidable weapon in the wrong hands. With enough power, it could bring down a commercial passenger jet...maybe even Air Force One, thought Winston. He was aware that the Reliant Corporation in Canada was developing a high-power variation of a similar electromagnetic pulse generator. They were working in conjunction with the U.S. Air Force to investigate its potential use as a major weapons system. Latest reports have stated that it was fully operational and ready for field testing. He wrote a reply memo to his boss, "This could pose a serious threat and it must be further investigated. I would contact the Canadian PM and recommend increased security at Reliant."

An article in the Wall Street Journal caught his eye. The price of gold had been creeping higher on the international commodities markets over the past six months. It was up over twenty percent and that increase had left some financial experts scratching their heads as to why. For Winston the reason was obvious. It was just a matter of supply and demand. The supply has been constant so prices must be increasing due to a significant increase in demand. Someone or some groups were apparently buying up gold as a hedge against a future global economic downturn. The question was, who. "Why does anyone suspect an impending major economic problem? Except for the situation in Greece and the European Union, the overall world economic numbers looked pretty good," he muttered to himself. In the margin of the report, he wrote, *Pre-attack liquidation of assets?* A similar pattern had developed just prior to 9/11.

Winston returned to the inter-agency reports that he had been reading. He glanced at the executive summary of a recent memo from the FBI about a dramatic increase in bank and jewelry store robberies in the Midwest over the past two years. The Bureau analysts believed that Islamic terrorists were using the robberies and other illegal activities to fund future terrorist attacks.

That's nothing new; we've suspected that for a long time, he thought. *The FBI will have difficulty getting to the source of these robberies in a timely fashion but my new Delphi team could be very useful here. It might be a good inaugural mission for them.* He noticed that Dr. Savich's good friend, Special Agent John Crawford was investigating the robberies for the FBI. *He's a bright man and one of the few in the Bureau who might get to the bottom of the crimes. Then again, the agent could probably use some help and he might be a useful asset,* thought Hamilton. He made a note in the margin of the report.

Winston then went on to read some of the news on the Drudge Report. One item caught his eye immediately. Multimillionaire businessman Doctor Graham Maultry had been missing for several months after sailing out from Fort Lauderdale with his family on a trip to Bimini. Their boat had disappeared in deep water about thirty miles offshore and it was assumed to have been the result of a tragic accident. Last week it was recovered. The report stated, "The vessel had been sunk intentionally. Two bodies have been identified: a fifteen-year-old girl by the name of Jessica Vehr, a friend of Tiffany Maultry; and seventeen-year-old Tucker Thornton who was a friend of Rodney Maultry. They had been murdered. The Maultry family itself is still missing and is presumed kidnapped. No ransom demands have been made and no reason for the kidnapping has yet been established."

"This doesn't make sense," said Winston to himself. "Why would someone kidnap a very wealthy family and make no ransom demands? Why go to all of the trouble to make it look as though the entire family had perished in a boating accident? Why murder two innocent teenagers and leave the Maultry family as witnesses? What would be the benefit?" Then Winston switched his attention to another computer and proceeded to do an internet search on Dr. Graham Maultry. The answer came to him on the screen. Dr. Maultry was one of the key aeronautical engineers involved in the early development of the Air Force's stealth program. His company was currently investigating the use of ultra-light materials in aeronautical construction processes.

"This could be a problem," Winston muttered to himself. "It looks like someone wants to build a high-tech plane and it's not for something good." He assumed the FBI would be involved in the case but they were going to be hampered due to the fact that the Bureau was already stretched thin by all of the investigations at Stanford, the Alamo, and now Chicago. *Besides,* he thought, *they won't really be able to do that which must be done; but my Delphi team can.*

He then scanned another FBI report related to the domestic terror problem. It was about the suicide bombing at Stanford University and he came across the name of a Professor Jazeer Farouk in the Islamic Studies Department. "Now there's a name that rings a bell," he muttered to himself. The report continued to say the bomber, a seemingly normal kid from a normal middle class home, blew up himself and over a hundred fellow students. He had enrolled in one of the professor's classes several months prior to the suicide attack.

Winston did a search on his secure agency computer. He was able to access a sizable CIA file which suggested that Jazeer Farouk had some prior loose affiliation with Hamas and the "Feed the Children" program, which was no more than a radical Islam-friendly front organization. The good professor had been in the FBI's sights for some time, but they were never able to get enough substantial evidence on him for an arrest. The Bureau pushed to have him fired from Stanford but he had tenure and was virtually untouchable. "Quite a coincidence," said Winston to himself. "A normal middle-class boy attends Farouk's class and then becomes a suicide bomber." But Winston didn't believe in coincidences. He began to formulate a plan. He would need to talk to Dr. Savich about having a private discussion with this Professor Jazeer Farouk very soon. His instincts told him that time was of essence and now the Delphi team must definitely get involved.

CHAPTER NINETEEN

After working on his designs for several months, Graham Maultry constructed the final model of his proposed stealth aircraft. It didn't take an aeronautical genius to realize that his captors wanted the aircraft to deliver some type of weapon's system. They planned to kill a lot of people and Graham decided he couldn't let that happen.

He had been meeting in the lab with Ahmad Haq Rasid every Friday to discuss his progress. Last week, he had submitted his final designs. He didn't like dealing with this man who had kidnapped his family and murdered the two teens. He had hateful eyes and when he grinned, he had those evil-looking, fang-like teeth. Graham knew he would have to be exceptionally careful when dealing with him.

He was facing a life and death dilemma. Graham couldn't allow the attack to be successful, but at the same time he couldn't let his family be tortured and killed. His solution was to give them most of what they wanted, but he would omit some critical elements. He decided to leave the external design of the plane almost identical to that which he would use on a standard stealth fighter craft. But he would make some slight but hopefully effective changes.

One of the key aspects in eluding radar identification is the type of paint used on the plane's surface. Graham designs called for the usual black "iron ball paint" that is used in normal stealth construction. While the paint is still wet, the iron particles are subjected to a strong external magnetic field. Their polarity becomes locked in position and oriented in such a way that when exposed to radar waves, they oscillate rapidly. The radar energy is converted into heat, which is then dissipated into the surrounding air. Therefore the waves aren't reflected back to their source and the plane becomes virtually undetectable on radar screens. In his designs, Graham omitted the external magnetic field treatment, effectively causing the craft to become more readily identifiable. He hoped that missile defense systems would then be able to lock onto the plane and shoot it down.

As a backup assurance that the plane would fail, he designed the wing surface area to be smaller than that necessary to provide the required amount of lift for a forty-five pound cargo. If they try to fly the plane with that specified weight, it should crash.

He was expecting that his captors wouldn't be sophisticated enough to recognize the various differences in his designs. He was sadly wrong.

On the first Tuesday after the submission of his plans, Graham was escorted to his lab, as usual, by his personal guard, Yassin Aziz. The guard and prisoner had developed a mutual tolerance of each other over the past several months. He was always armed, but was now more relaxed, and his rifle was no longer pressed against the middle of Graham's back. He seemed to be as personable as one could expect from any guard under these circumstances.

Graham had been studying Yassin's habits carefully. He would strike up conversations regarding the Muslim philosophy. They would often share a pot of coffee over discussions about the Quran. After several months of observing the man's routine, he knew that after Yassin left him at the lab, the guard would wait in the hall for several minutes, unroll his small rug and kneel down to pray. He always looked out a window that Graham assumed faced east toward Mecca.

Today's schedule was a change from the ordinary. After only several hours in the lab, Yassin's cell phone rang and there was a brief hushed conversation. He said to Graham, "You are to come with me."

"Where are we going?" asked Graham.

"Ahmad wants to see you in his office," replied Yassin while avoiding direct eye contact.

"But this is only Tuesday and we always meet on Friday. Besides, we always meet in the lab, not his office. What's this about?" asked Graham with concern. Changes in routine are not a good sign.

"I don't know," lied Yassin. "You are to come with me," he repeated. With the automatic rifle again pressed firmly against his back, Graham was escorted through the house and to the large office where Ahmad Haq Rasid now sat behind the oversized mahogany desk. In front of him, Graham's plane designs were unrolled and sitting on top.

Graham had an uncomfortable feeling when he entered the room. Ahmad stood, turned away, and stared out the large picture window that overlooked the pool. He waited for a minute, leaving Graham squirming. Without turning around, he said, "Sit down Dr. Maultry."

Graham followed the command and felt beads of perspiration forming on his upper lip. His pulse quickened. After another minute of silence, the man calmly said, "Do you take us for fools, doctor?"

"I don't understand."

Ahmad slowly turned around and faced Graham. He sneered, exposing his fangs, and looked like he might suddenly leap across the desk to rip out Graham's throat. He slammed his fist down and yelled, "But I think you do understand, doctor...you understand very well. You were warned that if you tried to sabotage our project, there would be severe consequences for your family."

Graham's mind raced as he began to panic. "Wait. It must be a mistake. Don't do anything."

Ahmad grinned. Again there were the vampire teeth. "I'm not going to do anything doctor. You have already done it yourself. Did you not think that we would recognize your little scheme with the paint? Did you think that our own engineers were not intelligent enough to recognize that you omitted this very important aspect of the designs?" With that, Ahmad nodded to Yassin Aziz who had been standing in the doorway, his eyes looking down at the floor. Yassin reluctantly reached into the hallway and pulled Julia into the room.

She stood just five feet from her husband, head down and sobbing, "I'm so sorry Graham." Her nose was broken and a heavy flow of blood was rushing down over her mouth. Her left lower lip was split open, and her left eye was blackened. Her blouse had been torn, exposing a bloodstained bra. She was supported from behind by Mossaq, the man who had beaten Jessica unconscious on the boat. The knuckles on his right hand were bloodied and he was smiling.

"What have you done, you bastard?" yelled Graham.

With that, Mossaq punched Julia in her right kidney. She doubled over as she screamed out in pain. "You're going to pee blood for a week," he said with a wide grin.

"Stop it!" yelled Graham.

Mossaq drew back his fist and was about to hit Julia again when Ahmad intervened and said, "That's enough Mossaq. I think he got the message." He then turned to Graham and said, "This is all your own doing doctor. When you initially met with the Scorpion, he warned you of the consequences of any attempts to betray us. I am actually being lenient this time. You have failed to provide us with satisfactory plans and that is why your wife was punished. It is you who hurt your wife, not us. If you fail to give us what we need within the week, I will be forced to execute one of your children, and I will make you decide which one."

Julia paid a heavy price for his faulty plans. It was then that Graham realized that no matter what he did, he and his family were going to be killed. *There's no way these savages are going to allow my family to live, especially after mentioning that Scorpion guy, he thought.* No, they were slated to be eliminated even if he did submit corrected design plans. Then, thousands or even tens of thousands of innocent civilians would be slaughtered somewhere. He couldn't win. "I'll submit revised plans within the week," he offered contritely.

Mossaq pulled the whimpering Julia back to the apartment while Yassin gently took Graham's arm to lead him back to the lab. He almost seemed apologetic about what had happened to Julia. As he turned to leave, Graham again noticed the Norwegian black box still sitting next the couch. It gave him an idea.

CHAPTER TWENTY

The four men patiently waited outside the building in the early morning sun. They were eighty miles south of Detroit, just off of I-75, in the small city of Bowling Green, Ohio. The town was home to the Fighting Falcons of Bowling Green State University and it was the home of the First Federal Bank. The men anxiously checked in all directions and everything was clear. Their normal pattern had been to do at least a week of surveillance before they did a job. However, Muhammad said they needed cash quickly and had to get this one done now. It proved to be a critical mistake because they were not aware of the location of all of the surveillance cameras. They were not aware of any extra security measures the bank might have instituted. The business of robbing banks was not one in which it was a good idea to just "wing it."

Reggie Patterson turned to the others, "I don't know about this one. It doesn't feel right to me; too much rushing and not enough planning."

"Just do what you're paid to do, and stop complaining," replied Muhammad.

"Fucking Arabs, I'm not getting paid shit," muttered Reggie, but he had no other choice but to obey orders. There was no place else for him to go. After pulling down their masks, the four men drew their guns and stormed into the small bank lobby. Reggie was the last one in.

Reggie was not a devoted follower of Islam. He had been a local basketball point-guard standout at Detroit's George Romney Central High School and had been awarded an athletic basketball scholarship to a small community college in northern Michigan. But Reggie was prone to getting into trouble. He had a short temper and a violent streak--a bad combination. Within three months of entering college, he was accused of beating and raping a petite white freshman co-ed. That ended Reggie's basketball career and any opportunity for a normal life. No other colleges would consider giving him a second chance. "That rich bitch wanted it as much as I did," he said. "I didn't really hit her. It was just a small slap. I could tell she liked it a little rough anyway. That black eye thing was a setup...probably did it herself. My mothafuckin coach wouldn't help me at all. He coulda pulled some strings just like they always do for the white players, but not for black Reggie. "

He went to prison and like many inmates, Reggie was introduced to drugs. After his release, he got involved in petty robberies to support his habit. That's when Muhammad found him living on the streets of Detroit. He taught Reggie about how he could turn his life around by turning to the word of Allah. Reggie subsequently met with Mullah al-Sadir who interviewed him for over an hour. He was placed in a drug-rehab program and afterward, Reggie was given the opportunity to work at the mosque doing janitorial work. He was fed and was allowed to share a small apartment in the basement with another former addict who had taken the Muslim name of Curtis Johnson. Both men agreed to be instructed in the ways of Islam. They were told about how the white Christians had become rich on the backs of the other races, especially the blacks.

They were taught about the "injustices and atrocities" that the Jews had inflicted on the Arab race. They discussed the Quran nightly. Reggie didn't believe most of what he read or was told, but he didn't want to lose his free room and board, so he played the game. Failure to do so could result in bad consequences and he had already heard about what the Muslims did to infidels. Reggie didn't want to be an infidel.

Then Muhammad approached him one morning and praised him, saying that he had progressed well. "Allah has chosen you for a holy mission, Reggie." As it turned out, the "holy mission" was to rob banks. He had come full circle; he had been a thief, found religion, and now he was a thief again. But now it was OK because it was being done in the name of Allah.

He had been assigned to do all of the talking during the bank robberies. Another of Reggie's primary jobs was to control the employees and any customers that might be present. At six-foot-three, he was good at intimidating others and that's what he was doing this particular morning while his partners grabbed the branch manager and dragged him toward the large vault. He pulled out his Glock and yelled, "All you mothafuckers get on the floor, face down, right now! Don't look at me or I'm gunna shoot you in your fuckin' head!"

Everyone immediately dropped to the ground. That is, everybody except an off-duty cop who had been in the corner, unseen by Reggie and his team when they entered. He had been hired as a plainclothes guard in response to the recent rash of bank robberies. While the others were preoccupied getting the manager to open the vault, the cop came up from behind on Reggie's blind side. He grabbed his gun with one hand while he pulled off the mask with the other. It was a heroic but futile maneuver. Reggie was too young, too strong, and too fast. He turned and fired two quick rounds into the cop's face, killing him instantly. Reggie did lose his mask, however, and when he turned to find it, he looked directly into one of the surveillance cameras. He covered his face with both hands and yelled, "Fuck me!" In a panic, he quickly ran through the bank doors, and disappeared down the street.

The employees and customers screamed as the bank manager tried to run. Meanwhile the rest of the robbers also panicked. They opened fire and shot three more people, one of whom was the fleeing branch manager, the only one who could actually open the safe. All the robbers could do was to clean out the cash drawers and escape before the cops arrived. They ran out to the getaway car with less than four thousand dollars in cash. As he ran, Muhammad knew this was going to be a huge problem and prayed that the news didn't make it back to the Scorpion before he had a chance to explain.

CHAPTER TWENTY-ONE

Jeanine called back to her boss on the intercom and said, "Mr. Hamilton, Mr. Hacker is returning your call on line two."

"Thank you Jeanine. Tell him to hold on a minute." Winston was finishing a Wall Street Journal article regarding presidential hopeful, Governor Jack Wagner. He had a pacemaker placed years ago because a bullet fragment had become lodged in the wall of his heart during Operation Desert Storm. It had resulted in a life-threatening cardiac arrhythmia which has been stable ever since the pacemaker insertion. The opposing party was questioning whether or not Wagner was medically fit for office. However, Wagner jogged several miles every morning and his cardiologist gave him a clean bill of health.

The opposition is getting desperate, Winston thought.

He picked up the phone. He had recruited Derek Hacker out of an Army Special Forces unit two years previously. He was an expert in black ops and munitions. He could follow orders and carry out specific details of a mission, but he was strictly a by-the-book soldier. He lacked the ability to imaginatively plan and co-ordinate complex independent covert operations. At present, he was the eyes and ears of Winston Hamilton, monitoring the progress of the Delphi Team's training.

"Sorry for the delay today sir. We had a five mile run this morning, followed by tactical weapons training.

"OK, Derek, just give me a full report."

"Yes sir. Dr. Savich is doing very well. He's not like any other doctor I've ever met. It looks like you're right about him. He's turned out to be a tactical genius. It's uncanny, and I don't know how he does it. As far as I can tell, he's had no official military training, but he has an instinctive ability to analyze situations and respond quickly, almost as though he could read other people's minds. I think he might be as good a black ops tactician as myself."

Winston smiled and thought, *He's actually far superior to you, Hacker.*

Hacker continued, "He thinks fast and makes adjustments just as quickly.

Moves and countermoves, but faster, just like blitz chess. You have to be quick but you also have to be right. If you're not, you're dead, thought Winston.

"He knows exactly what others are going to say or do next, maybe even before they know themselves. He's athletic, determined, and always figures out a way to win. The other people of the team respect him and I have no doubt that they'll follow him into battle when necessary." Hacker paused for a second and added, "There is just one negative, sir."

"What's that?" asked Winston, although he suspected he already knew the answer.

"There's a dark side to the doctor, something smoldering beneath the surface. I can't put my finger on it but I know it's there, and it could present a problem under certain circumstances like combat. I would worry that he could lose control of a situation."

Winston understood fully and had similar concerns. "That's something we'll need to keep an eye on. What about Doctor Foster?" he asked.

"Initially, I had my doubts about the 'Gas Man.' He's older but the guy's definitely a valuable asset. I think he must be in his mid-fifties or so but he's tougher than most men half his age. He's obviously had some military training, probably in a Special Forces unit. He's one of the best snipers beyond five-hundred yards that I've ever seen. I don't know how he even sees those damn small targets from that distance, but he obviously sees them very well. He has the eyesight of an eagle and nerves of steel. I understand that as a younger man, he was accurate at over three times that distance but now he's still as good a shot as any civilian in the country and he never gets rattled. In addition, he's in great shape. On the morning runs, he's a veritable machine."

Winston Hamilton had already done his homework on Dan Foster. He was a close friend of Dr. Savich who had insisted that the man be included on the team. He was a physician anesthesiologist who had been a Special Forces medic before attending medical school. He had the third most confirmed sniper kills in Iraq, not because he wasn't as good a shot as the others. He simply had fewer opportunities, being the unit's medic.

Hacker continued with his report. "When we run our routes through the hills, the 'Gas Man' and Doctor Savich always tie for second with the rest of us bringing up the rear."

"Second? Well, who usually wins?" asked Winston.

"The woman. She's also the second best shooter after Foster".

Winston was well aware of Lisa Savich's abilities with a rifle and had seen firsthand what she was capable of. If pressed for a description of her it would be that she is beautifully tenacious and just as dangerous as her older brother, Carver.

Hacker continued, "But I don't know about her. She's gorgeous and it's a little distracting. She talks a lot about her company. What's the name?"

"Angel Fire Industries," offered Winston Hamilton.

"Yeah, that's it. What kind of a name is that for a corporation?"

"Well, Derek, it's a half-billion dollar kind of pharmaceutical corporation that she and her brother started from scratch five years ago. That's no small feat."

"Well, she may be successful in business but that's not combat, sir. The trainers here nicknamed her 'Barbie', if that tells you anything about how the rest of the team sees her."

"Don't underestimate her, Mr. Hacker. She's exceptionally bright and has a doctorate in clinical pharmacology.

"She may be smart sir, but I don't want to have to worry about taking care of her if things go FUBAR. I'm not sure I can count on a woman to cover my back."

"She and her brother grew up in the mountains of south-eastern Kentucky."

"Like Hatfield and McCoy country?"

"Exactly, and like I already said, it would be a mistake to underestimate her. Those coal-mine country people tend to be tough and resourceful in spite of external appearances." What Winston didn't tell Hacker was that Lisa Savich had taken out one of his best men over a year ago. She shot the man through the right eye from a distance of over two-hundred yards.

Hacker countered, "Just the same sir, she's a woman and when you're in a fight, you want a partner who you know is going to have your six. You can't rely on a woman to do that. She may have grown up in a tough environment, but she's never faced someone in battle. When we do hand-to-hand combat training, she's always teamed up with an instructor who treats her with kid gloves."

"It sounds like she can take care of herself but maybe we do need to test her a bit. Arrange to pair up with her on the mat and see what she can do."

That'll be a pleasure, thought Hacker.

"Don't hurt her or Carver might just try to kill you," warned Winston. "Again, don't underestimate her just because she's beautiful. She's almost as deadly as her older brother."

Hacker laughed at what he misread as a joke. Winston didn't, because it was far from being a joke. He was dead serious. Carver and Lisa Savich can be a dangerous pair.

That reminded him. He was going to have to make a call to Dr. Savich soon. He had already decided to send him on his first mission and it would have to be without the backup of the full Delphi Team.

CHAPTER TWENTY-TWO

"They have him on camera? That's a problem Muhammad! That's a huge problem! How could that idiot let himself be seen on camera? I knew we couldn't trust those local recruits. They're drug addicts. They're just like all Americans; they lack commitment to any cause. All they want is immediate gratification: sex, money, and drugs. Now you're going to have to clean up this mess before it can be traced back to us."

Muhammad had been somewhat reluctant to give Mullah al-Sadir the bad news. He tended to panic. Muhammad knew the mullah's reaction would be excessive. However, he had to tell the man now and try to control his response. Although officially, Mullah al-Sadir was the head of the Dearborn cell, it was Muhammad who was actually given the responsibility to monitor the mullah and to supervise the Scorpion's overall mission. It was Muhammad who was the mission's actual second in command and who reported directly to the Scorpion. He was one of only a few individuals to know the man's true identity and to comprehend the entire scope of his Great Attack.

Al-Sadir was no more than a figurehead who was being utilized only because he had a better understanding of the nuances of American society. He was just as lazy and unreliable as the local recruits: Curtis Johnson and Reggie Patterson. His father had been a Muslim cleric in Saudi Arabia, but it was in the United States where the mullah actually grew up and was educated. As a result, he had been corrupted by the western culture. He was a self-indulgent coward. If it were up to Muhammad, he would kill the fool. It would be so easy to just snap his fat little neck and be done with him. The problem was they still needed him to procure the Canadian package and the sudden disappearance of such a high profile mullah in Dearborn would raise too many red flags. An investigation would ensue and the mission would become compromised. He would have to postpone dealing with al-Sadir and focus on the present problem. It was, in fact, a huge problem and he knew that it was going to be placed directly at his own feet.

"What would you have me do Mullah?" inquired Muhammad, although he already knew the answer.

"You must eliminate Reggie, before the police get ahold of him. You must do it quickly and carefully. We don't want a lot of nosey reporters snooping around and tracing the guy back to the mosque. We can't have any bodies showing up so you must dispose of him well. Do you know where he is now?"

"No, mullah. He has disappeared but with Allah's guidance, we will find him. What about the other one, Curtis?"

"Get rid of him also, as soon as possible. Neither of those two men is to be trusted. If they're arrested, they will talk. We have to eliminate any potential ties between ourselves and the robberies. We have to get this whole situation under control before the Scorpion finds out. I don't have to tell you what that could mean. We don't want to become a liability. He doesn't like liabilities!"

"I'll get right on it. Curtis will be easy. He's still living here and he trusts me. Maybe I can use him to flush out Reggie before he's terminated."

"Once that's been taken care of, I want you to go into Canada to finalize arrangements for the shipment. Our contact tells me that the material is scheduled to be moved this Sunday at two o'clock in the morning. There should be little traffic at that hour, so that'll make it easier for us. I want you to drive the route several times beforehand so you can select the best location for the transfer. You'll want to the mark the appropriate highway kilometer marker so that the driver can see it easily at night. Locate a good truck in Canada and steal it. The container is going to be heavy so make sure that you have some kind of a lift machine to unload it."

"Don't worry, everything has already been arranged, mullah. I have the cell phone number of our contact person and I plan to call him in several days. Our men have been given the necessary counterfeit identification papers and passports. We already have the truck hidden in a garage in London, Ontario…and it has a fork lift. Once I dispatch of Curtis and Reggie, I'll assemble the group and head into Canada to finalize the plans."

CHAPTER TWENTY-THREE

Several evenings later, Muhammad carried a tray of warm tea down the back stairs of the mosque to Curtis Johnson's basement apartment. After knocking on the door, he entered and found the man involved in his evening prayers. He politely waited until Curtis finished and then entered the room.

"As-salaamu 'alicum, my friend. I had one of the women brew some fresh mint tea. Would you like to share some?"

"And peace be upon you, Muhammad. Thank you, tea would be nice." The two men sat crossed-legged on worn floor-pillows. After several minutes of talk about the fatal shooting at the bank, Muhammad inquired about his roommate.

"Have you been in contact with Reggie?"

"No, he hasn't been to our room in over a week. I know he hasn't called the mosque."

"Has he tried to call you on your cell phone?"

"No, but he never has before so I wouldn't expect him to call me now. Even though we shared this apartment and saw each other every day, we were not close. Reggie would seldom speak to me.

I don't think he believes in the same things that we do. He doubts the teachings of the Prophet Muhammad, praise his name."

"If you were to try to call him, do you think he would listen to you."

"I don't really know for sure. Like I said, we weren't very close. I think he's probably afraid."

"After what he did at the bank, I'm sure he is. He killed a cop. But he can't be wandering around on the streets. Eventually, someone is going to recognize his face and call the police. They'll probably shoot him on sight. The mullah and I are worried about him. I need you to make contact and talk him into coming back so we can provide protection." With that, Muhammad stood and walked over to a table where a cell phone was charging. He picked it up and handed it to Curtis.

"What do you plan to do with Reggie, kill him?"

"Of course not. We simply need to hide him here or at a safe house for a while until this thing blows over."

Curtis wasn't convinced, but he dialed Reggie's cell phone anyway. The man answered on the second ring. He sounded panicky and incoherent. "Reggie, where are you. I've been worried. You need to come home," said Curtis.

"I can't go back there. They gunna kill me for sure."

"That's not true, Reggie. Mullah al-Sadir would never do that. He's a teacher of the Holy Prophet Muhammad, praise his name, and he would never harm another Muslim. He simply wants to protect you from the police."

"I don't know Curtis. I'm scared. Is Muhammad there?"

"Yes, we just shared some tea. He talked about hiding you in a safe house. He's worried about you also. If the police find you, they'll arrest you for murder. Maybe they'll just shoot you."

"I know, I know! I'm fucked no matter what I do! I'm in a real jam here. I don't trust Muhammad but I guess the only thing I can do is to come back…as long as you're sure they ain't gunna hurt me."

"I promise. They have no intention of harming you, Reggie."

"OK, I'll be there tomorrow morning."

"That's good to hear, Reggie. I'll see you then." When he ended the call to his former roommate, Curtis turned and plugged his phone back into the charger cradle. He was still facing the wall when a garrote was suddenly brought over his head and tightened around his neck. Muhammad pulled tightly on the wire until it cut deeply into his victim's neck. Blood began to ooze from the wound and run down his shirt. He tried to get his fingers under the garrote but it was too tight. He struggled in vain as he tried to speak, "No, no, don't do this. You lied to me! You both lied to me! You're Jihad is a lie!" As he was becoming shrouded in a fog of blackness, his final thought was, *forgive me Lord Jesus.*

CHAPTER TWENTY-FOUR

Kathleen Maley and her twenty-four year-old co-worker, Stephanie were sitting at a booth in the Capitol Grill, just a few blocks from the Senate Office Building where they both worked. It was something they did every Tuesday for lunch. Stephanie was an energetic, petite young woman who never experienced a shortage of male attention. Meanwhile, Kathleen was the quintessential frump whose only love in life was her job. The two women worked for Cranston Barnes, the senior senator from the state of South Carolina. Tuesdays were the women's weekly splurge for a lunch which was served at a table rather than the usual sidewalk kiosk fare of hotdogs or mystery meat sandwiches.

After taking a bite of her croissant chicken salad sandwich, Stephanie turned and said, "Kathleen, I've decided. You and I are going to do a girls' afternoon together this weekend. We're going to start out with a make-over at Salon Jean-Paul and then go to Chevy Chase for a day of shopping. We're going to buy some trendy clothes for you."

"What's wrong with what I'm wearing?" asked Kathleen.

"Nothing, if it were two decades ago and you were seventy-years-old, but Kathleen, you're only thirty-nine and times have changed since you last shopped. Somewhere hidden under those baggy old clothes of yours is a beautiful, sexy woman. This weekend, you and I are going to find her."

"I don't know Stephanie. It all sounds very expensive," protested Kathleen, ever the frugal pragmatist.

"Oh, my god, Kathleen. What're you saving your money for? There's more to life than just working in Barnes' office six days a week and watching television. You need to start living a little. That includes feeling pretty and meeting members of the opposite sex. When was the last time that you went on an actual date, and I don't mean just dinner with people from the office?"

Kathleen blushed. "It's been a while."

"I bet it has…like maybe years. Well, we're going to change that very soon."

As the two women discussed their plans for the weekend, they didn't notice the gentleman two tables over. He was staring at them, and had been doing so for some time. Eventually Stephanie noticed and said to Kathleen, "Don't look now, but there's a man to your left who keeps looking at us. Do you know him?"

After casually looking around the room, Kathleen replied, "No, I don't think so. He's probably been looking at you."

"No, I'm fairly positive that he's actually been looking at you, Kathleen. I think he's checking you out," whispered Stephanie.

"No way…Oh my god!" blushed Kathleen. "This kind of thing never happens to me. What should I do?"

"Just look in his direction and give him a subtle flirtatious smile. Maybe flip your hair back. See if he takes the bait."

"I don't know how to do a flirtatious smile!" Kathleen exclaimed using finger quotations. "And my hair is pulled back in a bun."

"Well then, just follow my lead and do what I do."

The result would have been comical if it weren't so pathetic. Kathleen did her best but her smile looked more like a painful grimace, like maybe she had abdominal cramps. *That was an unmitigated disaster,* thought Stephanie, but much to her astonishment, the man stood and approached their table. "Do you mind if I join you two ladies?" Kathleen froze and said absolutely nothing. She simply looked down and poked at her salad with a fork.

Stephanie filled in the awkward silence, "Of course not. Pull up a chair. I'm Stephanie and this is my friend Kathleen." He gently shook Stephanie's extended hand. He turned to Kathleen and waited a second. She finally got the clue and also extended her hand. Before he sat down, the man introduced himself.

"Do you work for the government?" inquired Stephanie.

"No, I'm in the hotel business."

"Really…as in manage or own?" asked Stephanie while flashing a big smile.

"Both."

Stephanie's heart skipped a beat. The man had the most piercing brown eyes she had ever seen. He was about six feet tall and gorgeous! He was wearing an expensive Italian suit and he owned a hotel! She could tell from his demeanor and clothing that the man was wealthy—probably very wealthy. Stephanie developed an immediate interest in the stranger and thought, *he's charming, incredibly handsome, rich, and doesn't have a wedding ring. He may have been looking at Kathleen but he belongs to me now. I'll find someone else for her later.* She began flirting, and put on her best act, but it was all to no avail. Kathleen had his undivided attention. Whenever she faltered, the stranger filled in the conversation with questions about Kathleen and her job. By the time the two women had to excuse themselves to return to work, the man had made a dinner date with frumpy Kathleen for the coming weekend.

CHAPTER TWENTY-FIVE

Carver Savich waited in a black van down the street from Jazeer Farouk's apartment in College Terrace, a quiet neighborhood on the outskirts of the Stanford University campus. Delphi Team partner, Hank, "The Tank" Chmeilewski waited in the shadows behind a cluster of bushes, well away from the glare of the overhead street lights. The professor was scheduled to return from a faculty meeting by 10:00 pm. It was to be a simple snatch and grab kidnapping, after which the professor would be taken to a CIA safe house just outside of Silicon Valley. However, Carver would soon learn that things were seldom simple when it came to kidnapping. Farouk was almost never alone. He usually travelled with an armed body guard, or a pretty young co-ed whom he often brought home for an evening of wine and "private tutoring".

Just get him and slice the bastard's throat. Make him bleed, demanded the demon.

Carver could feel the clawing of the monster. It wanted to be released. It needed to be fed. However, he had to concentrate on the mission at hand and keep the demon contained. Any distractions could be a problem so he pushed it into the back of his mind.

As was his habit, Carver continuously scanned his surroundings for potential problems. He attached a silencer to his Sig Sauer and instinctively chambered a 9mm round. He didn't expect the need for firepower, but he always felt that it was best to be prepared. He was constantly analyzing and re-analyzing his situation, asking himself the question, "What if?" For every postulated complication, he always had a contingency back-up plan. It's one characteristic that made Carver such an effective strategist and leader. The other was his uncanny ability to anticipate his opponent's moves and immediately initiate counter-measures. Just like in Winston Hamilton's game of chess, it was all about looking ahead; moves and counter-moves. Winston pretty much gave Carver free reign in planning and implementing the mission. His only absolute instruction was, "Don't get caught. If you do, you're on your own."

Carver was born as Jacob Emmanuel Savich over forty years ago. He grew up in the mountainous poverty-stricken coal country of south-eastern Kentucky. His father had been a decorated Vietnam War hero who had taught his sons all that he knew about self-defense and military tactics. They were skills needed to survive in their home of corrupt Letcher County. When he witnessed the merciless slaughter of his father and brother at the hands of the county sheriff, young Jacob had to take matters into his own hands if justice was to be realized. Though he was just a boy of twelve, his ultimate response was ferociously cunning and brutal. The bodies were never found. Unfortunately, the event did not quench the boy's thirst for revenge. Rather, it spawned the clawing monster deep within his soul, a monster whose appetite for blood could never be satisfied.

Ever since that time, Carver has been an enigmatic contradiction. After college, he attended medical school and eventually became a plastic surgeon. His selfless compassion and remarkable surgical skill resulted in the rapid growth of his practice. He became well known in the Greater Cincinnati area almost to point of celebratory status. In an effort to give something back to the community which had supported his career so much, he devoted over fifty percent of his practice to free care for the indigent poor and military veterans. He volunteered his time to staff the Congenital Facial Deformities Clinic at the Children's Hospital. He and his sister, Lisa Marie served on the Board of Directors of the Cincinnati Zoo. In addition to being a prominent supporter of his church, he was a tireless fundraiser for the Wounded Warrior Project.

Then, there was that conflicting darker side deeply within Carver's soul. The only way to deal with the relentless monster was to feed it and that entailed the taking of a life. Initially, the battle between the two opposing personas took a heavy toll on him. Carver was constantly plagued by episodes of remorse and guilt to the point of being near suicidal. Eventually, he was able to resolve the dilemma by wrapping his killings in the banner of what he believed to be righteous vigilante justice. It was a natural extension of what he had already done as a young boy. He would eliminate only those who deserved it, those who had destroyed the lives of others and avoided accountability for their actions through slick manipulations of the justice system: killers, rapists, and especially child molesters. In his eyes, the termination of the perpetrators of evil was not only justifiable but also morally mandated by God.

The kidnapping of Jazeer Farouk turned out to be a little complicated. Carver could see the target turning his grey BMW 350i down the street. He adjusted his earpiece and spoke into his throat mike, "Target is approaching, a hundred yards out."

"Roger that, I see him," replied Hank.

Fortunately, the professor didn't have a date with him so the two men wouldn't have to deal with the distractions of a hysterical girlfriend. He did, however, have a passenger.

"We have two packages; repeat, two packages," Carver said into his mike.

Farouk pulled into his designated parking spot, across the street from his apartment building. After raising the convertible top, he exited the BMW and put on his blue blazer. At the same time, the bodyguard climbed out of the passenger side and immediately scanned his surroundings for potential threats. Carver noticed the telltale bulge under the man's leather jacket. Before locking the car, Farouk reached into the back seat to retrieve his briefcase, something which never seemed to leave his side.

Carver again spoke into his mike, "I'll take package one, you take package two. Careful, he's a pro and he's packing."

"So am I," responded Hank.

Carver slowly eased the van forward as Farouk and his partner walked toward the entrance of the condo building. The pair came within ten feet of Hank's position. Like a giant cat stalking its prey, Hank quietly came up behind the bodyguard. The man turned and pulled an automatic, but before he could fire a round, Hank overpowered him and snapped his neck like a pretzel. Farouk took off like a jack rabbit toward the front door.

"We've got a runner," Hank yelled into his mike.

"I have him." Carver had anticipated the problem and was already out of the van, racing across the lawn toward the front of the building. Farouk was running clumsily, not wanting to drop the briefcase. He was too slow and Carver tackled him on the sidewalk. Farouk landed face first, twenty feet away from the front door. When he tried to yell for help, Carver repeatedly smashed the man's head against the concrete, knocking him out and lacerating his forehead.

Smash his head again! Knock his damn brains out! Kill the son-of-a-bitch, demanded the demon.

But Carver stopped. He needed the man alive. Looking up, he checked the front of the apartment building to see if they had attracted any attention. It was just for a fleeting moment but he saw it. "Hank, I saw some movement behind the curtains of one of the second floor apartment windows. I think it was Farouk's place. Get ready; we might have some company soon."

Several seconds later, a third man, sporting a full beard, came running out of the front door, revolver in hand. Carver dropped him in his tracks with double-tap shots to the head.

Carver threw the still-unconscious Farouk over his shoulder and carried him to the rear of the van. Hank lifted the bodies of the other two men like a couple bags of groceries, one under each arm. He threw them into the van, next to Farouk. Carver looked around to recheck the surroundings. There were many lights on in the various units of the complex but no-one was looking outside; no curious eyes to see what was happening and call 911.

The two Delphi Team members jumped back into the van. The entire abduction took less than a minute. Hank looked at the Taser which still hung from his belt. "Didn't need this after all."

"It's a good thing; would've been a waste of good battery power," responded Carver. It was only a ten minute drive to the isolated safe house.

When the professor came to, he was looking straight into a bright light, making everything else in the room non-discernible. By the musty smell, he could tell that wherever he was, it was underground, probably in the basement of an old building. His legs and arms were tightly secured to a metal chair with duct tape, and he could barely move. He had a bad headache and could see blood all over the front of his shirt. He felt along the front of his mouth with his tongue. He was missing several front teeth. He was both furious and terrified.

Standing behind the bright light he could barely make out the silhouette of one man and he could sense another, standing directly behind him. In an angry tone, he yelled to his captors, "Who are you?"

"Who we are isn't important right now. What you should be wondering is why you are here," the silhouette replied.

"OK then, why the hell am I here?" he yelled, not trying to hide an arrogant sarcasm.

The man in front nodded to the man behind. There was an unexpected hard slap. Farouk's head snapped back and a little stream of blood trickled from his nose.

"That was to keep you focused. The reason why you are here, Professor Farouk is that we need to have a discussion regarding one of your former students, William Donaldson."

The look of recognition on his face was fleeting but long enough for Carver to see it.

"I've never heard of him," the professor lied. "I have hundreds of students every semester. How am I to remember just one?"

"Because you spent a great deal of time personally counseling him on how to detonate the bomb that killed over a hundred Stanford students."

Enough with the pussyfooting around, Carver! Just stab the little fucker in the heart! Kill him just like he killed all of those kids, yelled the demon.

"That's preposterous! I did no such thing. I'm the chair of the Islamic Studies Department at Stanford! You FBI agents can't do this! I'm an American citizen! I have my rights! I'll have your jobs for this, you fools!"

"But we're not FBI, professor, and down here you have no rights. You forfeited them when you killed those students," replied the man in the light.

There was another nod from the silhouette and Farouk's outrage was greeted with a harder slap to the side of his head. His smug attitude quickly melted away. When he started screaming for help, he was rewarded with a fist to his left cheek. The chair and the professor were knocked over onto the cement floor. This time, he was momentarily disoriented and fresh blood oozed from the laceration on his forehead. Hank lifted the chair and its occupant upright again.

Often, in interrogations such as this, time would be spent softening up the individual with a little slapping around, followed by a prolonged period of trying to gain their trust. Food and drink would be offered as a reward in exchange for information. Given enough time, a skilled interrogator can turn the most recalcitrant of criminals into a fountain of intelligence. However, Carver and Hank weren't dealing with just a criminal. They were dealing with a religious zealot bent upon the destruction of the country. They didn't have the time for the psychological massaging of the good cop, bad cop routine. Jazeer Farouk was a terror cell leader who probably had information regarding an impending attack on the United States. Many American lives were at stake. They needed information and they needed it immediately. They intended to get it by any means necessary.

Although the professor was a dedicated disciple of radical Islam, he was not a very good custodian of its secrets. After only one hour of interrogation, including just fifteen seconds of waterboarding, the professor started talking as fast as a TV infomercial host... and he didn't stop until he was told to. He actually seemed anxious to brag about what he and his organization had already done and what they were about to do. He proudly admitted that he was a regional leader of a network of al-Qaeda affiliated sleeper-cells that had been organized along the entire west coast of the U. S. over a decade ago. Yes, he had counseled and radicalized the student bomber, William Donaldson. His was just the first of many attacks to come. With some more coaxing from Hank, he also gave up the identity of a dozen other members of his cell, including: the tailor who had provided Donaldson's suicide vest, five matriculated students at Stanford and Berkley Universities, and a number of others who had been illegally smuggled across the southern border. He denied knowledge of the names of other cell leaders in California, Oregon, and Washington. Carver doubted the veracity of that claim but he let it go for the time being. He believed much of that information would probably be fabricated anyway and Carver didn't have the time to ferret out all of the truth.

Farouk also confirmed that the recent, "self-radicalized lone wolf" attacks were actually part of a coordinate nationwide plan to destabilize the country and influence the next presidential election. He claimed that cells of his national organization were responsible for the events at the Alamo in San Antonio, the Wrigley Field attack in Chicago, the Chattanooga shootings, and others. He mentioned a mullah and a man named Muhammad in Michigan but didn't know their actual full names. The most important piece of information, however, he did not provide. That was the identity of the man who gave the professor and the other cell leaders around the country their instructions, the man who was orchestrating everything.

"Who is the one who gives the orders?" asked Carver.

"I don't understand what you mean?" replied Jazeer.

"Of course you do professor. You alone aren't smart enough or wealthy enough to put all of this together. I want the name of the leader of your organization, the one who provides the financing for your attacks. I want his name or do we have to do the water treatment again."

The professor frantically turned his head, trying to see what the man behind him might do. "No, no, you don't have to do that. I don't know his real name; just that he's called the Scorpion."

"That's his name?" asked Hank.

"Yes, yes, that's the only one that was ever used."

"What did he look like, any tattoos or scars?" asked Carver.

"I don't remember any. I only met him one time at a Starbucks near campus. He was about your height, six feet tall with an athletic build. He had dark hair and was dressed in expensive clothes. I couldn't see his eyes because he wore large sunglasses. There is one thing. He had hearing aids in both ears."

"Hearing aids?" asked Hank.

"Yes, the very small ones that are almost invisible," replied Farouk.

"How often did you meet?" asked Carver.

"Like I said before, I only met with him that one time. After that, all contact was made by cell phone through the mullah in Detroit." Then he rambled on about the fact that the Assassin of Kandahar was going to kill him for talking.

After they had obtained all the information they could, the bright light was turned off and the overhead fluorescents were turned on. Hank stepped in front of Farouk's field of vision while Carver took the man's picture with a cell phone camera. After his eyes adjusted to the new lighting, Farouk could make out the details of his two captors. The shorter one was around six feet tall with jet black hair and crystal blue eyes. He wore a black t-shirt pulled down tightly over a well-cut physique. The other man was a giant, at least six-foot-six inches of solid muscle. His arms were bigger than Farouk's waist and at the end of the arms were hands that looked like they could easily snap a man in two; and a look in his eyes that said he had already done so...on many occasions. He wore a black Harley Davidson t-shirt that was stretched across an impossibly wide chest. On his shoulders sat a basketball-sized head without the benefit of an intervening neck. He was an intimidating figure, but the most frightening part of the giant was his calm wide smile. He enjoyed his work.

Farouk realized that since he had now seen their faces, they would never allow him to leave the house alive. He tried to salvage his life by offering to serve as an ongoing source of information about the terror organizations in the US. It was a lame attempt. "I can provide you with a lot more. I can be a valuable asset, a double agent if you will," he pleaded.

I'm telling you, Carver. Just kill the little bastard and shut him up. We're going to miss our chance!

The following silence destroyed any illusions that Jazeer might have had regarding a reprieve. He realized that escaping his present situation would be impossible. In a final act of defiance he yelled out, "You will never stop us, you American fools! You have no idea who you are dealing with. We have infiltrated almost every corporation and university in America. We have over a hundred cells around this country and we will deliver a decisive blow that will destroy you! You'll never see us coming. Allahu... He never finished his statement. Hank raised his Glock and put a bullet through Professor Jazeer Farouk's right eye. The back of his head exploded as most of what had comprised Farouk's mind splattered over the concrete wall behind him.

He looked at an angry Carver and said, "What? I got sick of listening to him yelling." He looked back at Farouk's body and fired another round into the dead man's chest and said calmly, "And that's for the hundred innocent college students you killed."

*Now you blew it! I told you to kill him earlier. This doesn't do any-
thing for me!*

"You feel better now?" asked an irritated Carver.

Hank thought for a second, fired yet another shot into Farouk's chest, and replied, "Yeah, better...much better."

Well good for you Hank! I don't!

Carver was frustrated. He would have preferred to eliminate the professor himself. Hank had unintentionally given Farouk a gift he didn't deserve, the gift of a quick and painless death. To make matters worse, now there was a much bigger mess to clean up, blood and brains all over.

Carver took another picture of the dead man's face as his body sat, still restrained in the chair, blood coagulating around the right eye socket. He bent over the body and searched the pockets. He found an Apple iPhone 6. He handed it to Hank who turned it on and checked the contact list. There was nothing of note except for the fact that there were over three dozen co-eds listed and each had a picture. Everyone looked very young and very cute. Hank said, "Wow, our professor was a busy man. I guess he didn't want to wait for his seventy-two virgins in Paradise. I wonder what he's gunna get now. I don't think he was exactly following the spirit of the Quran."

Carver continued with his search of the body and found a computer flash drive hanging from a thin chain around the dead man's neck. "This must be very important to be wearing it around his neck." He placed it and the iPhone in the man's briefcase and they left.

When they returned to their van, Carver placed a call to Winston Hamilton's office. "We're going to need a cleanup crew. Things are a little messy here. We have two extra packages."

"I'll take care of it," was the reply.

Three hours later, the cleaners wrapped Farouk's body in a sheet and placed it next to the other bodies in the back of the van. The three were unceremoniously disposed of in the hills of the Purisima Creek Redwood Preserve on the western slopes of the Santa Cruz Mountains. They would never be found and Jazeer Farouk would never enter Paradise.

While Farouk's body was being disposed of, Carver and Hank were at thirty-five thousand feet somewhere over Oklahoma, aboard Winston Hamilton's private jet. They were returning to the remote Farmto training facility in Owen County, Kentucky. Hank turned to Carver and said, "We need to get that list of terror cell members to Mr. Hamilton. Somehow he's going to have to turn over the information to the FBI. Maybe it'll lead to something and prevent another attack."

Carver opened Farouk's briefcase and said, "This must be very important for him to try to run while carrying it." He discovered a laptop computer. In addition, there were five throw-away cell phones labeled with the letters D, F, U, Y, and N on the back. In a side pocket, he found two flash drives identical to the one hanging around Farouk's neck. He laid everything on a table in front of him.

He said to Hank, "The iPhone was probably for the professor's personal use. I suspect the others were for communication with his organization. Maybe, if we check out the call logs, we can find a number that might lead us back to the top man."

"What do those letters mean?" asked Hank.

"I don't know for sure; maybe some kind of code as to which one is to be used. I'll see if Norman can figure it out." Carver turned on the computer but was unable to get past the password prompt.

"A lot of this is probably encrypted. I'm afraid to try too much on my own because sometimes these things have self-destruct programs if the proper sequence isn't followed to open it. Then we'd lose everything. We have to get these things to Norman Deets to see if he can get anything out of them. I bet there's a treasure trove of information here!"

"If anyone can do it, the Geek can. The boy's a genius," responded Hank.

Carver used the plane's secure phone to call Winston Hamilton's office. He gave his boss a verbal report about the west coast cells. In addition, he told Winston about the Michigan mullah. Winston did a quick search of the CIA database but he wasn't able to provide anything about a specific individual mullah. There were a number of them with suspicious backgrounds. Carver mentioned the name Muhammad but Winston replied, "There must be thousands of men with that name in the U.S. It's a dead end without more information." Carver also mentioned the name "Scorpion" and Winston could find no record of such a person in the Agency data bank.

Carver thought for a few minutes and finally asked if there was a record about a man called "The Assassin of Kandahar." He could hear the clicking of keyboard strokes as Winston entered the name. After a long pause he replied, "I have a hit here. There's no indication of a specific individual and the title may actually refer to a number of different men. Anyway, during the war in Afghanistan, there were repeated ambushes on GIs in the city of Kandahar. Around thirty of our men were killed over a two year period by someone using a dagger. The locals referred to the killer as 'The Assassin of Kandahar'. Then it looks like he disappeared. There's no further mention of him since."

Winston continued to read the file and after several seconds he continued, "Wait a minute…during one of the attacks, a local witness did mention a 'sting of the scorpion'. At the time, no-one thought that the comment was significant. There's no other mention of the phrase, but it's probably the tie-in. If this was the work of just one man, he was very prolific and he was very good. I have to leak all of this information to the FBI tonight but I need to be careful. We can't have them knowing about the Delphi Team. We don't want to wind up in front of a congressional investigative committee."

CHAPTER TWENTY-SIX

At thirty-eight, Patrick McKeown was not where he expected to be at this point in his life. He graduated from Canada's McGill University with a degree in chemical engineering and a promising future. He had been employed by the Ontario Power Generation Corporation for the past twelve years and made good money...but never enough money. Patrick had a problem. He liked to gamble. He'd gamble on football, soccer, baseball, cricket, the horses, or blackjack. He'd gamble on almost anything. He'd bet on who would be the first one in the office to pee in the morning or the color of the first car to pull into the parking lot. Over time, he gambled away his home, his wife, his family, and eventually his job. Now he was just an overqualified truck driver. He still made pretty good money... but, as always, not enough. He was into a Canadian loan shark for over sixty thousand dollars and time was running out. He had been threatened, but tonight he was going to fix that problem. He would pay off his debt and still walk away with over two-hundred thousand dollars in his pocket. Then he would stop gambling...unless he had a sure thing.

All he had to do was keep his eyes open for the 84 kilometer highway marker. They said it would be bent over so he couldn't miss it. Tonight he was driving last in a convoy of five trucks. They were heading south on highway 401 and were instructed to take the 163 kilometer exit onto Route 6 toward Nanticoke. However, Patrick had his own instructions given to him by the "Arab" as he called the man with the large bushy black mustache. Patrick never knew his real name, just the fact that he offered to pay a great deal of money for Patrick's services tonight.

Another twenty miles and he should see the marker. It was now 3:30 am and Patrick was having trouble concentrating on the road. He turned up the radio to keep himself awake, poured another cup of coffee from his thermos, and thought about what he was going to do with all of his new wealth. "I'll show that ex-wife. She made a huge mistake when she left me. I'm going to be rich and I'll let her know it. I'll buy a new red Porsche and get a pretty young girlfriend. Then, the two of us will drive by her house every day. That'll show the bitch," he said to himself.

Thirty minutes later, he was about a kilometer away from the location. He checked his seatbelt to be sure it was securely fastened and he gradually slowed down until the lead trucks were a hundred meters ahead. When the highway turned left around a bend, he lost sight of the tail lights of the trucks in front of him, and they lost sight of him. It'd take them at least ten minutes before they realized he was no longer behind them. As soon as he saw the bent 84 kilometer highway marker, he cut the wheel of his truck hard to the right, ran across the marker, and through the guard rail. The truck careened down a seventy-foot embankment, crashing through trees and bushes until it finally landed on its side on a service road at the bottom. The back of the truck split open, exposing the cargo.

According to the Arab, the drop was only supposed to be about ten feet. In fact, it was a lot steeper and longer than he was told.

At the bottom, he felt excruciating pain in his left leg and the warm sticky sensation of blood soaking through his jeans. *Broken leg--small price to pay for three hundred thousand dollars,* he thought. He looked up through the shattered rear view mirror and saw the headlights of a smaller truck pull onto the gravel access road behind him. It quickly approached his destroyed vehicle.

Three men exited the other truck and walked toward Patrick. They pried open the cargo area door all the way. A fork lift was used to transfer one of Patrick's containers into the Arab's truck and replace it with a counterfeit container. Two of the men returned to their vehicle to clean up the area, brush over tire tracks, and remove any traces of their having been there. Meanwhile the third man approached Patrick who was still trapped in his seat with a broken leg. The man's bushy mustache curled up at the side of his mouth as he smiled. Patrick assumed that he was going to give him instructions about the final cash payment but instead, Muhammad put his arm around Patrick's neck and with a quick turn, snapped it.

"You were supposed to die in the crash, Mr. McKeown," Muhammad said as he poured a pint of whiskey onto the dead man's lap. Patrick's leg pain was gone. He'd no longer have to worry about having enough cash. He'd no longer have to worry about his gambling debts or impressing his ex-wife. It would look as though he died of a broken neck sustained in an alcohol-related accident.

Muhammad walked away, muttering to himself, "That's another liability taken care of, but there are still several other loose ends to tie up. I still have to find Reggie Patterson." The three men slowly drove off into the darkness with the hijacked container safely stowed in the back. After ten miles, they transferred their cargo to a fresh vehicle with a "Detroit Sanitation" label on the side. Within the hour, the three had safely crossed the Ambassador Bridge back into Detroit.

CHAPTER TWENTY-SEVEN

The official name of the place is 'The Farm II' but the people training here shortened it to Farmto. It's not to be confused with the legendary Farm typically associated with the Central Intelligence Agency. This was not part of any official CIA program. It was a secret joint venture training area. The property was originally a drug cartel manufacturing and distribution center located in the center of rural Owen County, Kentucky. It was confiscated by the FBI after a drug raid and sold at auction to Doctors Jacob and Lisa Marie Savich.

After Jacob Savich had been recruited by Winston Hamilton to be the leader of his clandestine Delphi Team, their personal farm retreat became the team's training facility. The original five-hundred-acre property was too small to ensure adequate security, so Hamilton arranged to personally purchase another three thousand surrounding acres. It provided a total of thirty-five hundred acres of secluded, wooded rolling hills which were protected by a ten-foot chain-link security fence. Motion detectors and surveillance cameras monitored the central one hundred acres while armed guards in camouflage uniforms discretely patrolled the perimeter. The land already had a large house where the team and trainers lived. There were two barns. Under the first sat a subterranean vault protected by a steel door. At one time it had been an upscale meth lab and storage facility. It was repurposed as an interrogation center. The first floor of the barn contained what everyone called "The Mat" where hand-to-hand combat techniques were taught. The second barn is where classrooms, munitions, and other equipment were housed. Just west of this barn was located the firing range which was used every day for weapons training. In addition, the property possessed a runway large enough to accommodate medium sized turbo-prop planes and small jets. The drug cartels once used their planes to ship product into and around the country.

The group had been meeting at Farmto for three-day weekends every week for the past year. They were involved in an intensive training program, transforming them into a cohesive covert fighting team that could carry out pre-emptive attacks against terror cells in this country and abroad. Here they learned about: various weapons systems; munitions utilization; interrogation methods; black ops strategies; self-defense techniques; and Middle-Eastern language skills. After classroom activities, they participated in a grueling personal fitness program and hand-to hand combat training. Two of the newly-formed covert operations team were selected personally by Carver: his sister Lisa, and his good friend, Dan Foster. The remaining three members, Hank the "Tank" Chmeilewski, Norman the "Geek" Deets, and Derek the "Dick" Hacker were selected by Mr. Hamilton.

Why Lisa Marie Savich was here, no-one else except Winston knew for sure. Carver simply insisted that she be on the team. In college, she was a nationally ranked endurance runner and she was one of the best shooters on the team. The fact that she was stunningly beautiful made some trainers question her mettle and whether or not she should actually be here. As of yet, she was still untested. What they didn't know was that Lisa had been her brother's partner in his darker activities. She was no stranger to killing.

Dan Foster, the "Gas Man", was a fifty-two-year-old former Special Forces sniper who had the experience of several tours of combat duty in the Middle East. Although he was older, he was a tough, ferocious fighter. He was the best long-range shooter in the group and he was one of only a handful of men to twice win the U.S. Wimbledon Cup championship for long-range shooting. He was a close friend of Doctor Savich who had insisted that Dan also be included on the team. Lisa and Dan were the only team members who Carver would absolutely trust with his life.

The other three were personally employed by Winston, himself. Hank "The Tank" had been a Navy Seal. After discharge, he went on to earn a PhD in physics. He was recruited by Winston because he was the perfect match of strength and intelligence. No-one would ever guess that this man, who looked like a member of an outlaw motorcycle gang, could in fact have a post doctorate degree. He simply preferred the tangible challenges of military operations to the unanswerable mysteries of subatomic particles. Hacker had also been recruited after he was drummed out of the Special Forces for "inappropriate aggressive tendencies". Finally, Norman "the Geek" Deets had been discovered just after having been sentenced to a five year prison term for illegally accessing various secure computer systems. Nobody in the CIA was aware of their association with the Delphi Team.

"Come on you guys! What's taking so long? You're not going to let a girl beat you again, are you?" chided Lisa. After five miles of running through the woods and hills, she was well over a hundred yards ahead of the rest of the group. At a slender five-foot-seven, anything she lacked in muscle strength, she compensated for with lighting fast reflexes and determination. Her stunning looks and blond hair resulted in her being given the moniker "Barbie," but her disarming appearance concealed the heart of a relentless fighter. Her brother, Carver was running second while his friend Dan matched him stride for stride. Dan had the disadvantage of running in combat boots which was a habit he developed while in the Special Forces. "Builds up the leg muscles," he would reply whenever asked about it. Far behind them were Derek "the Dick" Hacker, and Hank.

Hank yelled out, "Dan, why the hell do you run with those damn combat boots on? It's like trying to run a marathon with a cinder block strapped to each foot."

Dan looked back and replied, "Was that you talking Hank? You're so far back there that I can hardly hear you."

"Yeah, yeah, yeah," laughed the big man.

Dan continued, "I run with these because when it counts, I can run farther and faster than anyone else. The way you're wheezing back there, I'll probably have to carry you in the process, with or without boots." Both men laughed hard as they tried in vain to catch up to Lisa.

Norman Deets didn't participate in the runs or the combat training. He wore crutches as a result of childhood muscular dystrophy. His lack of physical ability was more than offset by a genius mentality. He was the son of a German father and a Jewish mother which technically made him Jewish and eligible for citizenship in Israel. After Deets' grandmother had survived the ghettos of Poland and a year at Auschwitz, she lived with Norman's family until she died. Winston recruited him after the boy and some of his friends had been arrested for hacking into computer systems at several major department store chains and banks. They erased thousands of overdue credit card balances. His biggest infraction was related to several successful incursions into the United States,

State Department database. After his cyber-misadventures were discovered, he was arrested and sentenced to spend five years in prison. He also lost his scholarship and was expelled from MIT. When Winston Hamilton heard about Deets, he decided that the boy had an exceptional talent that was much too valuable to waste in jail. Winston arranged for his release and he has been in Winston's personal employ ever since.

While the rest of the Delphi Team was involved with their daily run, Deets worked on extracting information from the laptop computer which Carver and Hank obtained from the late Jazeer Farouk. First, he removed the two flash drives from the man's briefcase. Deets had a quarantine computer which he used to protect his main computers from corruption or other contamination by outside systems. Occasionally, unfamiliar flash drives contain suicide programs that erase the content of the drive and crash any interfaced computer that attempts unauthorized access. He found no such programs or viruses on either of the professor's flash drives. The first one contained useless information about class lecture schedules. The second contained an outline and three completed chapters of a book that Farouk was writing about the history of Islam and its impact on modern civilization. The third drive, taken from around Farouk's neck, was different. It was encrypted, but Norman was able to decode it within ten minutes. The drive contained detailed information about seven other al-Qaeda connected sleeper-cells in California, Oregon, and Washington. It included names and addresses.

Using his own password-cracker software, Deets was able to access Farouk's laptop. As feared, the computer did contain a suicide program. He was able to bypass the self-destruct feature without difficulty and he scanned the files. There were multiple references to more planned "lone wolf" attacks at various state capitol buildings in the west, the Hearst Castle, Fisherman's Warf in San Francisco, and a cruise ship sailing out of Seattle, Washington.

Others seemed to be in the planning stages but there were no specific details about them. They were all to await some signaling "Great Attack" before launching their plans but there was no indication as to what, when, or where the actual seminal event was to occur. Norman suspected it was the large attack which everyone had been speculating about recently.

There was no clarification as to the identity of the Scorpion or the name of the mullah in Michigan. The name Muhammad appeared frequently but there was nothing that indicated his actual identity. Deets submitted a report about what he discovered to Mr. Hamilton who carefully leaked the information to John Crawford at the FBI. He also forwarded a copy to Carver.

"Little Dick, you're running so far back there, I thought you might be walking. I can hardly see you." Lisa loved to taunt Hacker. He was an arrogant misogynist and she took every opportunity to tease him. "Must have been those cigarettes you smoked when you were younger. Didn't your mother warn you that they'd stunt your growth? That must explain everything."

"Just wait bitch. You're gunna get it in about an hour when we get onto the mat," he growled to himself.

"What?" said big Hank who was running right behind Hacker.

"Nothing."

After the run, they all had classes in Farsi and Arabic. Then, there was an hour of classroom time on munitions use and military strategy. Following a thirty minute break for a snack of protein bars and Gatorade, it was time for personal combat training. They underwent instruction in standard combat techniques and variations of Brazilian jiu-jitsu. After the demonstration and practice of several moves, the agent in charge would usually match two people who would spar for fifteen minutes. The only rule was that excessive force was prohibited.

The instructor first matched up Carver with Hank. At six-foot six-inches, he was an imposing figure to say the least. Carver had been paired with Hank once before but it was a draw. He knew from experience that the guy was too strong to defeat if they got into a wrestling situation. Boxing maneuvers were futile because Hank had a six inch reach advantage and fists as big as anvils. But Hank's large size made him slow and that made him vulnerable. Carver planned to attack quickly and catch the big man off guard. After the instructor said, "Fight," the two circled each other and Hank reached down to grab Carver's left leg in a take-down wrestling maneuver. Carver anticipated this and as the man's weight shifted forward, Carver quickly pulled on Hank's right wrist and pivoted on his own left foot. He swung a vicious round house kick to the back of the Hank's left knee but not with enough force to tear ligaments. The big man fell to the mat like a giant oak tree. In an instant, Carver was on him driving his right heel onto Hank's neck. Hank ceded the bout. The whole contest was over almost before it started.

After he got up, Hank said, "Not too bad for a second string quarterback."

"That was actually a second team All American. By the way, I don't ever remember seeing any All American defensive linemen from Georgia by the name of Hank Chmeilewski."

Hank threw up his hands in surrender, "Ok Carver, I give up. That was a good lesson for me but I'll remember this the next time and I'll be ready."

The instructor did a quick critique of the fight and how they might improve their techniques. Much to the surprise of everyone, he then read out the names of Lisa and Hacker, just as Winston had ordered. Up until this point, the only one to fight Lisa had been the instructor, and he obviously made it more of a training session than an actual fight. Lisa was hoping for an opportunity to prove herself to the group and finally it was here.

It couldn't have been more perfect than if I'd done it myself, she thought. *I'm not going to lose to this idiot.* She pulled her long blond hair into a ponytail as Hacker impatiently paced the mat, like a hungry cat. The instructor yelled out, "Fight."

The two approached the center of the mat and cautiously circled each other. Hacker landed a jab to her jaw, snapping Lisa's head back. She had never been hit that hard and she was momentarily stunned. But she had grown up with several brothers in the rough coal country of southeastern Kentucky, and a simple punch like that wasn't going to stop her. She shook it off and said, "Is that all you've got, little Dick?" She tried to land a right-handed punch of her own. Hacker blocked it easily with his left arm and delivered a hard right-hand blow to her left kidney followed by a left cross to the jaw. She fell over backwards onto the mat and thought she might actually pass out. Carver jumped up and yelled, "Hacker, what the hell was that about?"

"She has to learn to defend herself. Besides, I tried to pull the punch. I guess I just don't know my own strength," he replied with a smile on his face.

"Maybe you should try that kind of crap on me!" yelled Carver.

"Any time you're ready, Doc!" responded Hacker as he motioned for Carver to step onto the mat.

Kill him! Kill him now! Beat his face to a bloody pulp. That'll shut the little fucker up.

Carver could feel it building, the monster awakening. It was always there, impatiently clawing, demanding to be released…demanding it now! Lisa recognized the look in her brother's eyes and knew the monster was about to escape. If not stopped, her brother would kill Hacker in an instant. Like water exploding from a ruptured dam, once started, there could be no stopping the flood of rage. She couldn't let that happen.

Lisa could even feel the monster arousing within herself but hers wasn't as strong. She had learned to quiet the beast and focus it where needed. Just as Carver had told her many times before, she took a deep breath. She got up off the mat, looked at her brother, slowly shook her head, and said, "My grandmother hits harder than this cupcake." She spit out a mouthful of blood and returned to the center of the ring.

Hacker stood there with a smirk on his face and said, "Bring it on if you can, Barbie." The clawing grew louder, but again, she pushed it aside as she approached Hacker cautiously. She subtly shifted her weight to the balls of her feet and inconspicuously moved her center of gravity over her left leg. In almost slow motion, she feigned another punch to Hacker's head with her left hand. When he spread his own legs to balance himself, block her attempt, and throw another counter-punch to her kidney, she placed all of her weight on the left leg. In a flash, she brought her right knee up and slammed it into his groin. As Hacker doubled over in pain, she brought her left knee up and drove it into his face. There was a sickening crunch as Hacker fell to the mat with a broken nose. He was shocked and dazed as he saw his own blood gush down onto the mat in front of him.

"You fucking bitch," he screamed through his bloodied mouth.

"Bad language, little Dick!" she responded and kicked him hard in the ribs, breaking two of them. Fight over. She stood over him and said, "He who wishes to fight must first count the cost... Dick."

Hank turned to Dan and asked, "What was that?"

Dan replied, "Sun Tzu, *The Art of War*. Good book, you should read it sometime. I'm surprised a Seal like you hasn't already."

Lisa turned to the instructor and said with a smile on her face, "Sorry about that. I tried to hold back but I guess I just don't know my own strength." The instructor returned the smile and motioned for several men to get a stretcher.

"There are two lessons to be learned here. Lisa, you can't expect special treatment just because you're a woman. In real life, your opponent will be out to kill you in any way possible. The second lesson is to never, and I mean never underestimate your opponent. It could cost you more than a broken nose and a few ribs," he said to the group. Hacker's career was going to be on hold for a while. Meanwhile, Lisa became accepted as an equal member of the Delphi team.

Afterward, Dan pulled Carver aside. "Carver that was quick thinking back there but that little trick you pulled with Hank isn't always going to be an option. You won't be able to get away with that in a real fight. If you face a dangerous opponent, you'll need backup, like this." With that, Dan withdrew a combat knife with a nine inch blade. It was the same kind of knife that Carver's father had taught him to use when he was just a boy. Dan sheathed the knife and handed it to Carver. "I've found that it's best to have it strapped to your leg. That way it'll always be there just in case."

"Thanks Dan. It's just like the one my father had. I'll see if I can put it to good use someday."

"Just be sure the other guy doesn't have a sidearm. A knife's useless in a gunfight."

"At least it never jams or runs out of ammo," replied Carver.

"Roger that," replied Dan as the two men laughed and headed over to the house for dinner.

CHAPTER TWENTY-EIGHT

After dinner, the group had drinks and discussed the events of the day. They reviewed the information obtained from Farouk's computer and flash drives. Norman Deets pulled out the five cell phones from the briefcase and laid them on the dining room table. He had checked each of them and found that only one had been used. The log on the phone showed repeated calls to and from each of Farouk's cell leaders as referenced in his computer files. There were two other numbers that had been accessed on multiple occasions. They did not belong to any of the west coast cell members. Deets tried to call the numbers but the phones were now dead.

"I bet those calls were made to the top guys calling the shots," said Dan. "Maybe if we give the dates and numbers to Mr. Hamilton, he can have the NSA pinpoint the cell towers used. Then we might get an area of the country where we should be looking."

"Actually, I already did that, Dan," replied the Geek. "The pings are scattered around towers in the city of Dearborn, Michigan. The calls are probably to Farouk's mullah. There's a large Muslim population there, the vast majority of whom are patriotic Americans. Apparently, a few aren't such good citizens."

"They're the ones who find the need to use untraceable burner phones," offered Dan.

The Geek then set all of Farouk's cell phones on the table. "I'm still not sure what these five labels on the phones mean," he continued. While the rest of the team discussed possible complex codes related to the letters D, F, U, Y, and N, Lisa started to arrange them in a row on the top of the table. She asked the Geek if she could use his computer. After a minute, she said, "Maybe we're making this too complicated. I think the letters simply refer to the words Uktubar, Nufambir, Disambir, Yanayir, and Fibrayir.

"What the hell does that mean?" asked Hank.

"You haven't been paying attention in middle eastern language class, Hank. They're Arabic for the words October, November, December, January, and February. Probably those are the months in which each of the phones is to be used. They throw away the last month's phone after destroying the SIM card. That way, even though the NSA and Homeland Security might be able to eavesdrop on their conversations, they can never identify the actual callers."

Norman then said, "That makes sense because the only one that has activity on it is the one labeled 'U' for October. Today is November first and the rest of the months are yet to be used."

Lisa continued, "If the last one is labeled 'F' for February, and there are none for the following months…"

Carver finished her thought, "They don't need any more phones after that because their so-called Great Attack is probably planned for an event in February!"

Lisa asked, "But what big event happens in February? Surely it's not Valentine's Day."

The rest of the team looked at each other with concern and in unison replied, "The Super Bowl!"

CHAPTER TWENTY-NINE

Roger Logan is the divorced father of two girls, ages nine and twelve. They're both in braces and they both attend an expensive private school. The two girls are at an age where designer clothing styles are becoming a more critically important factor in their lives. The oldest is taking gymnastics while the youngest is enrolled in dance classes. Roger still pays the mortgage on the house in which his wife and daughters live. In short, Roger has a lot of financial obligations which he can barely meet. He desperately needs to continue in his present job as plant manager for the Microavionics Technologies Corporation. He had been with the company almost since its inception over twenty years ago. Sam Rosen had been a generous man, and he treated Roger as family. Now he sat in the company's main offices, across the table from a stranger, the new owner.

The man appeared to be nice enough on the surface, but there was something about him that made Roger uncomfortable. He suspected Mr. Rosen felt the same way. His smile seemed fake, like that of a life insurance salesman. He didn't trust the guy but he needed this job.

"It's a pleasure to finally meet you Mr. Logan. May I call you Roger?" Without waiting for a reply, the man continued, "I've been reviewing the company's production numbers since you started managing the facility and I must say that I am very impressed. You've done an excellent job with the people and limited resources that you've had available to you."

"Thank you Mr. Darpoli. Those are kind words."

"However, now it's time for us to look forward. I want you to continue with the company's present business plan but in addition, my partners and I want to take Microavionics in a new direction. As you are aware, remote control technology is one of the fastest growing fields in manufacturing. Unmanned aerial vehicles are the wave of the future. Modern corporations are looking for the option of using fleets of remote control drones for delivery services, security monitoring, and even non-combat military operations. My partners and I wish to expand development of this aspect of the industry because we feel that future potential markets will be unlimited.

"This should have minimal impact on the company's normal manufacturing processes and I don't want to disrupt your present production schedules. You should continue to fulfill your standing order obligations, but you're going to have to devote most of your time to our new endeavors."

The man poured himself a cup of coffee and continued, "Naturally, you'll need more staff and I plan to make the necessary arrangements to hire the right people with the necessary expertise for the job. Since we're going to try to penetrate this new market, I must insist upon absolute secrecy regarding our new projects. I don't want competitors to discover our design plans. Also, in this business, time is of essence. If we act too slowly, another company will seize the opportunity and we'll be left in the lurch. Of course, your compensation package will be adjusted to reflect these new responsibilities."

"Thank you Mr. Darpoli. That's very generous of you. Just let me know whatever you need. We do have a plane already in production that is ideal for various merchandise delivery systems. It consists of a square craft with vertical engine mounts at each corner. It provides excellent maneuverability and the ability to carry a payload of up to ten pounds. It can accurately land in very tight areas. "

"That's good Roger, but it sounds similar to every other delivery drone already on the market. Everyone has seen those on TV and in the movies. I need something that promises better performance ability. If we produce what's already on the market, we'll simply be a me-too company. We can't make any money that way. I want us to separate ourselves from the other drone manufacturers, to take the technology to the next level. Therefore, we'll require high speed capability while being maneuverable enough to fly around buildings and trees. I need you to make sure that the plane can accomplish all of that with an electric motor. We don't want customers or citizens complaining about all of the noise and carbon pollution associated with the gas powered planes. Finally, the electric motor must be powerful enough to handle a forty-five pound cargo."

"Forty-five pounds! That's a lot of cargo capacity. With the motor, battery, and navigation system, that'll make the whole thing almost sixty pounds. I've not seen those requirements outside of military applications. What're you planning to deliver?"

"Don't know yet," he lied, "but if we're going to succeed in this business, we have to stay ahead of the curve. We must provide drones that far exceed what anyone else is building."

After a few seconds of thought, Logan replied, "That shouldn't pose a problem Mr. Darpoli. We already have a large selection of motors in stock. I'll find one that works for you. I can probably juice up the power without adding too much weight. A lot of cargo capacity will depend upon wing surface area. I'll begin work on some preliminary designs tomorrow morning. "

"That won't be necessary Roger. I already have my own engineers working on that. You're primary responsibility will be the actual drone construction and the remote control aspect of the process. The planes must be RPV capable so they're able to accommodate a wide angle camera system with a video feed back to the remote control station."

"That's not a problem, sir. A majority of the planes that we already manufacture contain remote person view or RPV capability. I should be able to accomplish what you need with the equipment we already have in stock. However, the remote still has a direct line-of-sight limitation. That is, the remote cannot be used safely if the plane is separated from the controller by walls or tall buildings. That might pose a problem with delivery situations in the city. The only way to circumvent that problem is to interface the system with satellite GPS technology."

Darpoli replied, "Let's not get involved with satellites just yet. We'll take things a step at a time. There is one other important matter. What's the present range of your remote control systems?"

"Right now, our typical range is about five thousand feet."

"We are going to have to increase that to at least five miles."

"Well, I can ramp up the remote control power by installing a Dragon Link booster. It can extend the control range and it has the potential to allow the navigator to fly between buildings and towers; so it might be able to bypasses the usual direct line-of-sight requirement."

"Might be? Is it one hundred percent reliable? I wouldn't want any of our planes to crash into cars or pedestrians in the city."

"Well sir, the further the distance, the less reliable the control. However, that limitation can be overcome somewhat by stationing the controller at an elevated position. It would allow the navigator to maintain the direct line-of-sight principle, so I can safely accomplish your five mile requirements while maintaining one hundred percent control of the craft."

"That sounds good, Roger. I'll deliver specific design plans to you shortly. I want to have at least six of the craft ready for market testing within three months."

"I'll have to make some adjustments in our schedules, but I'll make it happen."

"That's what I want to hear from you Roger, a 'can do' attitude. That's why I wanted you for this project. If you get these prototypes produced on time, there'll be a twenty thousand dollar bonus waiting for you when you're finished."

"Thank you again Mr. Darpoli. I'll get right on it." Even though a lot of what the man wanted didn't make much sense, money talks. He couldn't argue with the promotion, the raise, or the extra $20,000 bonus. He was starting to like Mr. Darpoli more and more.

CHAPTER THIRTY

"Shit! I'm royally fucked man," screamed Reggie as he paced the floor of his cousin, Michael's one bedroom apartment. Reggie had been hiding there for the past week, and he's been high ever since the bank shooting. He was going to crash soon.

"Maybe it's not as bad as you think Reggie," said Michael, trying to calm him down. Michael's ex-boyfriend had been a tweaker and he was well-aware of how aggressive users of crystal meth could get. He had already seen Reggie like this before and knew that his cousin would become violent if he didn't settle down soon. Violence had always been Reggie's biggest problem.

"Yeah and maybe getting AIDS from your boyfriend isn't as bad as you think," Reggie replied sarcastically to his gay cousin. "They saw my face man! They got a picture of my fucking face! I already got a record so they know who I am. They gunna find me for sure. That damn guard couldn't do like I told him to. Everything woulda been just fine if he'd a done what he was told. But nooo, he had to be some kinda hero. He had to go for my gun and pull off my mask. Why'd he have to go and do that? It was stupid, man. I had to shoot the mothafucker. It was his own damn fault. He did it to himself. Then I see the fucking camera. Can you believe it, a stupid camera that we missed cuz we wasn't ready for the job; too much rushing and no planning. Now I'm gunna fry. Ain't no doubt about that. They gunna fry Reggie's black ass for sure.

Reggie continued pacing the floor, back and forth like a caged animal. "If the Feds don't get me, then the fucking Arabs will. Curtis called me and told me to come back to the mosque. He says he spoke to Muhammad and Mullah al-Sadir and everything was gunna be just fine. They had everything under control, no problems. They gunna protect me and all. Did he think I was gunna believe all that shit? I'm not stupid man. That Muhammad is a mean-ass mutha fucker. I never trusted him. So I says, sure Curtis, I'll come by tomorrow. Then when I try to call him back a half hour later, there's no answer. I call a dozen times on his cell phone. Still no answer. Curtis always answers his damn phone, man. It's always at his side. You know what that means---he's dead. He's real dead and probably lying in some hole somewhere with a bullet in his head. He was a liability man, a loose end, and those Arabs don't like no loose ends.

"I'm next cuz I'm a bigger liability than Curtis, man. The feds got my picture! I know what those crazy fuckin' Arabs do to people they don't like. They cut their fuckin' heads off, that's what they like to do. Do it all the time. Well, I don't want my fuckin' head cut off. I want my head right on my fuckin' shoulders where it belongs. I shoulda never gotten involved with them. I never cared about their fuckin' jihad or their seventy-two virgins. What good are they if I'm in the ground man! Nobody cept crazy people could believe that shit. Besides, once you've used up your virgins, then whatcha gunna do? After that, they're just used merchandise, man. A woman's only a virgin one time. You gunna just wack off for the rest of eternity?"

Reggie kept on ranting, out of control. "But I ain't ready for no paradise yet. Allah can keep his seventy-two virgins. I need to think of sumthin' Michael. I need an idea."

"Maybe you can just turn yourself in and get protection," offered Michael.

"Are you fuckin crazy, Michael? They gunna lock me up and then fry my black ass for killing a stupid cop. You know what they do to the brothers."

"But Reggie, you have a bargaining chip. You think those Arabs are robbing banks just to make money. They need cash because they're up to some of that terrorist shit you see about on TV."

Reggie stopped pacing for a minute and in a rare moment of lucidity, turned toward his cousin. "Damn Michael, you're right! You're one smart mothafucker! They gotta be up to somethin'. That's for damn sure. The feds would love to know about it. I'd have to do some time but I can probably plead down my case and even get some of that witness protection shit. Live the good life on the government's dime. They do that kinda shit all the time for the Mafia. I might even have info that could prevent the next 9/11! Shit man, I could even be a fuckin hero. Maybe I'll even get a reward."

"You just have to figure out how to turn yourself in, Reggie. You need to get a lawyer to contact the Feds for you. You need to get an agreement in writing before you turn yourself in."

"Like I said, you're one smart nigger Michael." Reggie and his cousin talked for another hour discussing a plan. Then, Reggie crashed and slept for two days. When he finally recovered, he and Michael were ready to set their plan into motion.

CHAPTER THIRTY-ONE

It was late in the evening on the first Tuesday in November and the Scorpion was watching the presidential election returns. It was still a little early but both CNN and Fox news had already projected Governor Jack Wagner as the winner. Already, the Secret Service was arranging to increase their protection detail around "The Bulldog" which had been his code name. For the Scorpion, the results were no surprise because the final polls indicated a seven point lead for Wagner the week before, but the extent of the victory was astonishing. Thus far his opponent was projected to win only Massachusetts and New York. Even California fell into the winner's column.

"So the easy days are soon coming to an end for radical Islam. The mood of the American people has definitely changed and they will expect some decisive action by their new leader," the Scorpion said to himself. "Makes no difference. Completion of my revenge against the American Satan will soon happen regardless of the election. They will burn just like my family and village burned three decades ago."

CHAPTER THIRTY-TWO

FBI Special Agent Crawford was sitting at his desk reviewing an anonymous report that had been mailed to his office. "Who in the hell sends a detailed five-page anonymous report that is type-written?" he asked himself. The envelope had no return address or any other indication as to who had mailed it, but the postmark was from Toledo. He forwarded the envelope to the forensics lab for DNA and fingerprint analysis, but he wasn't optimistic about being able to identify the source. Thus far he had no other facts to corroborate the report, but if it was accurate, the information was overwhelming. He was going to have to call the director as soon as he could substantiate it.

The desk phone rang and when Crawford answered, the caller said, "John, it's Tim Hogan."

"Hey, Tim, how are things going in Detroit?"

"Fine...I understand you're going to be my new boss soon. I couldn't have asked for a better one." Crawford had known Tim for over ten years and he respected the man. He had a reputation for being honest and straight-forward.

"Thanks Tim, I'm actually wearing several hats right now and I won't be assuming my official responsibilities until I can get to the bottom of all of these bank robberies."

"That's why I called you John. I had an interesting conversation with one of the higher profile defense lawyers here in Detroit. We've been looking for one of the perpetrators involved in a recent bank heist. His face showed up on a security camera. The guy looked directly at it after he shot and killed an off-duty cop. He had a prior record for rape and he's already in the system, so Detroit PD had no trouble identifying him as a Reginald Patterson. He became an addict and small-time thief after serving three years on the rape charge at the Bellamy Creek Correctional Facility. I guess now he's made it up to the big leagues. Anyway, the local police have had a BOLO out on him, but they havn't been able to find him. It looked like he went to ground."

"Then this lawyer, Sidney Steiner calls the office first thing this morning and says he has a client who wants to meet with us. He says the guy has information regarding some bank robberies and a possible terrorist organization. Want to take a guess at the name of the client?"

"Reginald Patterson," responded Crawford as he moved to the edge of his seat.

"Exactly."

"When can we talk to him?" asked Crawford excitedly.

"I knew you'd want to get on this right away so I scheduled a meeting for this afternoon. I took the liberty of telling your secretary that she should make airline reservations for the next flight from Cincinnati to Detroit."

"That's great, Tim!"

"There's just one problem, John. Before the guy comes in, he wants a signed agreement saying he's not going to be arrested and that we have a deal in place. I told his attorney that I'd have to discuss things with you first."

Crawford replied, "Well, we could agree not to arrest him if he allows us to place him in protective custody. As far as a deal is concerned, were not offering him anything until we see what he has. Tell his attorney that if his information is credible, we could work out a plea deal but he's going to have to do some time. He shot a cop. If he doesn't like those terms, he can stay out on the streets, but the Muslims are going to be looking for him. If they get their hands on him, it won't be pretty, especially if they find out that he tried to talk to us; and I'll make sure that they do."

"I'll inform his attorney and try to have everything set up by the time you get here. It should be around two. One of my agents will pick you up at the airport. See you then John."

By 2:30 pm, Crawford arrived at the Detroit FBI headquarters; an eight story build out of the McNamara Federal Building on Michigan Ave. Agent Tim Hogan met him in the lobby. After shaking hands, Hogan said, "They're both here. I think Reggie preferred protective custody with us rather than taking his chances out on the street. He said the Muslims were going to cut his head off."

"They might have very well done that."

As the two agents rode up the elevator to the sixth floor, Crawford turned to Tim and asked, "What's this attorney, Sidney Steiner like?"

"From what I hear, he's a real weasel. However, in spite of his distorted sense of legal ethics, he does have a good track record as a defense attorney. He's had a lot of experience and he's one of the best in the city. Rumor is that he's good enough to bill seven-hundred an hour for prep time and triple that for court."

"So why's he representing a low-life like Reginald Patterson? There's no way he can afford this guy."

"Because Sidney's a media whore. He could get a half million dollars' worth of free publicity if this case becomes high profile, which it probably will. He has a vested interest in taking this to trial but that's not going to be in the best interest of his client. How do you want to play this, John?"

"I've always found that when dealing with an asshole lawyer, it's best to be a bigger asshole. We're going to have to try to bypass Sidney and negotiate directly with Reggie."

"Here's the sixth floor," said Hogan.

The two men exited the elevator and walked down a hallway to the conference room. They entered and could see a court stenographer sitting at the end of a large table; a tape-recorder in front of her. On one wall hung the familiar blue and yellow circular bronze plaque. Along the perimeter, it was engraved with lettering that spelled out "Department of Justice" along the top and "Federal Bureau of Investigation" along the bottom. At the other side of the room hung a picture of the burning Twin Tower Buildings in New York. The bottom read, "Never Forget."

Sitting on one side of the table was an expensively-dressed fifty-something man who introduced himself as Sidney Steiner. In the chair next to him was a black man dressed in jeans and a Detroit Piston's T-shirt. The man was scratching his arms incessantly. Crawford had seen his type a hundred times before. He had the typical worn-down, hollow-eyed look of a man in the throes of a methamphetamine hangover. He was Reggie Patterson. The two agents took seats on the opposite side of the table.

Crawford began the discussion, "Mr. Steiner, I understand your client has some information which he would like to share with us regarding a string of recent bank robberies."

"Yes Agent Crawford, that is correct. Before we get started however, I want the record to show that Mr. Patterson came to this meeting of his own volition and his presence here should not in any way be construed as an admission to the unfounded charges that he faces. He is here with the understanding that his information is offered in exchange for a favorable disposition of this unfortunate misunderstanding. "

"Unfortunate misunderstanding?" questioned Crawford as he stared at Steiner. "That's quite an understatement, but sure, duly noted."

"Before Mr. Patterson relates his story, we want assurances that he will not be prosecuted for the murder charges. He did not murder anyone. Anything my client might have done at the bank on the morning in question was the result of coercion on the part of those with him. He was afraid for his life. The shooting was an act of self-defense. He was being attacked and the police officer in question failed to identify himself. The charge of bank robbery is open to negotiation."

Crawford again stared for several seconds at the lawyer, and then directed his gaze toward Reggie. The man was nervous as a cat in a roomful of rocking chairs. His right leg was bouncing up and down so hard that the vibrations could be felt in the floor. Reggie was a nut that was ready to be cracked.

"Well counselor, that coercion argument is crap and you know it. Don't waste my time here with that nonsense." He turned and looked directly at Reggie, who was still staring down at the table, "Your client shot an off-duty policeman...twice...in the face. It happened during the commission of a bank robbery. That alone gets him murder one and the death penalty. The guard had not pulled a gun himself so he was defenseless. He was trying to disarm your client here who was threatening to do harm to several innocent bank patrons." Crawford looked at his notes and continued, "In his own words, Reggie told the bank customers, and I quote, 'Stay down or I'm gunna shoot you in your muthafuckin heads'. We have four living eye-witnesses who will testify to that fact. I'm sure you are aware that we have a high resolution video of the altercation and the shooting. We also have documentation that the mask which your client wore was still in the hands of the slain officer when he fell to the ground. We already have a DNA sample on your client from the rape conviction. When we compare it to the DNA retrieved from the mask, it's going to show that the mask was, in fact, Reggie's."

He paused for a second, to let his comments sink in. Still staring at Reggie, he said, "So if there are any courtroom theatrics that your attorney might want to pull regarding the reliability of stressed witnesses, camera quality, or evidence chain-of-custody procedures, that mask DNA alone is going to identify you, Reggie, as the cop killer," he said as he pointed his finger at Steiner's client.

"Please do not address my client personally, Agent Crawford! You should be directing this conversation to me. You're just trying to intimidate him," argued Steiner.

He ignored the attorney and continued to look at Reggie as he said, "Reggie, look at me if you want to make a deal." Reggie looked up for the first time, in spite of protests from his counselor.

"Reggie, I'm sure that you didn't go into that bank planning to kill anyone, but you did just the same. The other three people who were killed are also going to fall on you. As I see it, there are three possible scenarios. Number one, you can walk out of here with your attorney and be on your own out on the street. But you're a cop killer and my guess that you won't last a week before some cops find you. You'll be shot and killed while 'resisting arrest'. The second scenario is that you walk out of here with your attorney but the Islamic militants are going to find out that you spoke to us. I'll make sure of that. They have the resources and they will find you. When they do, you're going to wish that the cops would have killed you first because the radical Islamists are very good at long painful deaths. Or, you can choose to live, by remaining in your chair at this meeting. We'll provide protective custody until you can testify in court against the leaders of your group. But Reggie, you murdered a cop and you're going to have to pay for that. The deal that I'm offering you is life in prison with a chance for parole after thirty years. This offer expires the second you leave the room."

"That's nonsense, Agent Crawford. That's no deal. It's extortion. You just single handedly convicted and sentenced my client. Come on Reginald, we're leaving," protested his attorney as he stood. He glared at the two agents and said, "We'll see you in court."

But Reggie remained seated and continued to look at the FBI agent. He was another black man, like himself, and not like that cracker lawyer, Steiner. Reggie believed the man. His eyes said he was not lying. Reggie knew he wouldn't last a week on the streets and he certainly didn't want the Muslims to get him. He said, "What do you want to know?"

"Start at the beginning," replied Crawford.

Steiner sat back down as Reggie told the FBI agents the whole story. He told them about his history and how a guy with a thick black mustache named Muhammad Rabbani had first approached him. He told them about Mullah al-Sadir and the mosque. He told them about his roommate Curtis Johnson and how he figured they had murdered him. He gave them details of at least three dozen bank and jewelry store robberies over the past two years.

"What was all of the money for Reggie?" asked Crawford.

"I don't know for sure. It was a lot of cash and I damn well didn't get any of it. All I ever got were meals and a place to sleep. I overheard the mullah and Muhammad talking several times about an important shipment coming from Canada. It all had something to do with a guy they called the Scorpion. He sounded like a ba-dass but I don't think they ever met him in person. The way they talked about him, I think he might be their boss and they sure were afraid of him. That's all I know."

"Reggie, I believe your story but I have to warn you that if you've lied to me at all, the deal is off and you'll be facing murder one. Do you understand?"

Yes, Mr. Crawford. I'm telling the truth. I swear."

After the meeting, several agents escorted Reggie down the hall. Arrangements were made to temporarily transfer him to a safe house. Sidney Steiner left the building with no plans to call his much-anticipated press conference. Agent Hogan asked, "What do you think that Canadian shipment is all about, John?"

"I don't know but I have a very bad feeling about it. The information Reggie gave us corroborates some details of a report which I received earlier. We need to monitor all activities of the mullah and this Muhammad fellow."

"You want us to bring them in?"

"No, I'm afraid that if we bring them in, they'll be shut out of the loop and we'll wind up with nothing but bank robbery charges and that's pretty weak. Reggie's testimony would be torn apart by any good defense attorney. Let's start twenty-four hour surveillance on them. In addition, get warrants for taps on all of the mosque's phones. Include computer monitoring also. Let's subpoena the phone records to identify who they may have called in the past six months. Check with border security and tell them to be extra vigilant about anything suspicious coming in from Canada. And let's have Reggie look through the known terrorist files to see if we can get a real identity on this Muhammad guy. He's probably using an alias and I get the feeling he's a major player."

"I'll take him downstairs right now," replied Hogan. "I'll call if he can give us a name."

"Hurry the process Tim. Something very big is in the works and I'm afraid that we're far behind the curve right now. We need to catch up and catch up quickly."

CHAPTER THIRTY-THREE

Two hours after Reggie Patterson told his story, John Crawford placed a call to Director Lewis Stevenson. He presented the facts he had obtained from Reggie and included the information he received regarding Farouk and the west coast terror cells. There was a pause in the conversation. Then, Director Stevenson asked, "Well John, what do you think?"

"Sir, there's a great deal of intelligence suggesting that these multiple so-called "lone wolf" assaults are part of a coordinated nationwide program of attacks to destabilize the country. The cells are well-organized and it's quite possible that their numbers could be well into the hundreds... maybe even more. Up until now, their attacks have been relatively small in scope. We must assume that more and larger attacks are planned for the future. That's their typical pattern. They may be intentionally forcing us to divert substantial investigative resources away from their primary target. I suspect they're presently awaiting instructions from their leadership to launch the major attack. I'm concerned that it's all related to that big delivery from Canada but thus far we have had no reports about thefts of large amounts of weaponry there. We're still looking.

After a few seconds, Crawford continued, "Reggie Patterson identified this Muhammad Rabbani from our known terrorist files. His real name is Muhammad bin Hussein and he's already in our NSA database. He's a former colonel in the Iranian Revolutionary Guard and he's a significant player in the world of international terrorism. He wouldn't be in this country just to organize a few suicide bombings. He's here because something much larger is planned and I'm sure it's related to that Canadian shipment."

Again there was a pause as the director digested Crawford's report. He said, "Good work, as always, John. I'm guessing that you don't want to arrest either Mullah al-Sadir or Muhammad bin Hussein."

"No sir, as tempting as it is to throw them both in jail, I'm afraid that we'd lose the opportunity to find out what's actually going on here. If we arrest them, any other members of their organization will simply disappear and we might wind up with nothing."

"I agree John. I assume that you're going to have twenty-four hour eyes and ears on them. We don't want them slipping through our fingers."

"Already done sir."

Stephenson continued, "Based upon those labeled cell phones from the Farouk fellow, the event should occur sometime before the end of February. These groups like to organize attacks that are symbolic in nature, like the events surrounding that baseball championship game in Chicago. If the Wrigley Field attack gives us any indication of where they're going with this, then I believe they could be leading up to the same type of venue, only on a much larger scale."

"The Super Bowl!" responded Crawford. It was the same conclusion suggested in the anonymous report he had received earlier.

He didn't mention it himself because he wanted the director reach the conclusion on his own.

"Exactly. If everything you have described is true, then I would expect that next February's Super Bowl in Houston could very well be the likely target. What's more of a symbol than seeing a bomb explode on the fifty yard-line during America's big game? There'll be world-wide exposure on live television." Stevenson considered the situation for a few seconds and said, "I'm going to send a hundred agents to Houston in order to start looking around to see if they can come up with anything."

"What do you think, John?" Stevenson asked.

"That's a lot of resources sir, and the Bureau's already stretched a little thin. However, given what we know at this time, it seems reasonable."

"That's it then," added Director Stevenson. "John, continue your surveillance on the two men at the mosque in Dearborn and keep me posted. We still need a lot more information."

"Yes sir," replied Crawford. After the call, he leaned back in his chair and began to worry about the direction this thing was taking. Something was nagging at the back of his mind but he couldn't quite put his finger on it. Muhammad and al-Sadir were the key to all of this. Somehow he had to make something happen... and soon.

CHAPTER THIRTY-FOUR

Senator Cranston Barnes was a four-term senator from the State of South Carolina. It had been ten days since the presidential election and his long-time friend, Jack Wagner had appointed him as chairman of the inauguration committee. President-elect Wagner's only stipulation was that he wanted to keep things simple and wanted to avoid the excessively extravagant affairs that had been characteristic of the event in the past. Therefore the budget for the ceremonies was to be cut by 30%. The Senator was sitting at his desk sketching a proposed schedule for the January event.

After completing his preliminary outline, he called out for his assistant, Kathleen to come into his office to discuss the matter. When he looked up, he was stunned when he saw her walking through the door. Kathleen Maley had always been an unremarkable woman, to say the least. The most generous word to describe her was frumpy. In the fifteen years she had worked for the senator, he had never seen her in anything more stylish than a poorly fitting pants suit and a pair of tennis shoes.

Today however, Kathleen stood in the door wearing an above-the-knee black pencil skirt, a white silk blouse showing a little cleavage, black stockings, and heels. Her hair was highlighted and cascaded down across her shoulders. She looked lovely, sexy even, and for a few seconds, the Senator was at a loss for words. "Uhm, Kathleen, would you please look over this schedule outline and let me know what you think?"

"Yes sir, I'll get back to you in an hour with my suggestions," she replied and turned to leave.

After he was sure she had closed the door to her own office, the senator walked out to his secretary's desk and whispered, "What's with Kathleen. She actually looks very pretty."

"She met a man," was the reply. "She's had a make-over, shopped for a new wardrobe, and has been almost dancing around the office for the past four weeks."

"A man?" he asked incredulously. "I always thought she might be a lesbian."

"Apparently not. He must be very fond of her. He's already sent her flowers twice this week."

"Well who is he?"

"I don't know his name, but I do know that he's wealthy, handsome, and Italian. He's all she's talked about."

CHAPTER THIRTY-FIVE

Before joining the CIA fifteen years ago, Winston Hamilton III worked for the US State Department. He was recognized as an astute analyst regarding international situations. Partially because of an eidetic memory, he was able to coordinate a wide range of seemingly unrelated information and predict future international events. As such, he was sometimes asked to brief the National Security Agency on various pressing matters. On several occasions, he briefed the president directly while accompanied by the Secretary of State. He maintained close contact with several people still within the department and he was on the phone with one of his contacts now.

"That's what I've been thinking Bob. Something very big is in the works, maybe bigger than 9/11. But I haven't been able to get a handle on exactly what it is. There have been all of those individual terror attacks and a lot of chatter on the internet. Besides that uptick in bank robberies, we have no leads." At this time Winston was reluctant to discuss the information Carver Savich extracted from the late Professor Farouk. He couldn't openly say that he knew the lone wolf attacks were part of a coordinated plan. That information had been obtained illegally by the Delphi Team so he had to hold his cards close to his chest.

The State Department contact offered, "One of the FBI offices may have come up with something interesting, Winston. Their reports say one of those bank robbers turned himself in and did a plea deal. In exchange for waiving the death penalty, he offered up names of some people who he claims are heading up a terror cell in Dearborn Michigan. He said they were financing the shipment of something from Canada. With the kind of money they were making, that Canadian thing must be a very expensive shipment."

Winston suggested, "I would have your people check with the Canadian authorities to see if there have been any thefts from chemical companies, munitions factories, or weapons armories. I would also check to see if there have been any irregularities at the Reliant Technology Corporation."

"You mean the ones doing all of the research on EMP generators?"

"That's the one. We know Reliant is transporting a number of their large scale devices to a secure facility in central Ontario for field testing. I'm a little worried that the EMP generators could be the Canadian shipment that the FBI informant was alluding to," cautioned Winston.

"I'll call them right away."

"Before you go, do you have any names that you can share?" asked Winston.

"Yes, two of them: a Mullah Muqtoda al-Sadir and a Muhammad bin Hussein. We ran the names through our database. Al-Sadir has been on our radar for some time. He's in charge of the Al-Fateh mosque in Dearborn, Michigan and he's been pushing for the implementation of Sharia Law in the city. He's been an open critic of Israel and what he calls the unjustified aggression of America in the Middle East. Now he regularly advocates the abandonment of the U.S. constitution and proposes that we become a country governed by laws of Islam. For a long time, we've suspected that he had ties to terror cells, but we've never been able to tie him to anything specifically illegal."

A militant mullah from around the Detroit area? Muqtoda al-Sadir must be the same one who Jazeer Farouk described to Dr. Savich. We must get control of this al-Sadir guy and interrogate him, thought Winston.

"We have a large dossier on the other guy, Muhammad bin Hussein. He's not related to Saddam, but he might as well be. He could pass for Saddam's twin brother. He was a former colonel in the Iranian Revolutionary Guard and was personally responsible for the deaths of thousands of Iranian men, women, and children. One of his favorite techniques of execution was to suspend his victims over a wood chipper and very slowly lower them into it while their family was forced to watch. Then, each one had to take their turn in the grinder."

"Wonderful human being," commented Winston.

"Wonderful like Hitler."

"They were both made from the same mold," added Winston.

Bob continued, "Apparently some of the Ayatollahs thought Muhammad's talents were being wasted in Iran, so he was placed undercover as an international terrorist leader. He was rumored to be the one responsible for that nightclub bombing in London five years ago. After that, he fell off of the grid. It looks like he's now re-emerged in the good old U. S. of A, and I doubt that he's here as part of a cultural exchange program.

"Anyway, the Bureau was in a quandary as to whether or not they should pick these two up. They decided that the best approach was to maintain tight surveillance on them to see if they could get more information about what was being planned. If they are picked up, everyone else might just disappear and then they'll have nothing."

"I agree. Someone has to be the leader, the organizer who calls the shots, and that's the man who we need to identify. I don't think it's either of these two men," offered Winston.

"We still don't have anything on that except for the name, Scorpion; but the Bureau's working it pretty hard."

Winston thanked his friend for the information and ended the call. He made a quick decision. Carver's theory about the Super Bowl being the target of the Great Attack was certainly plausible. It sounded as though the FBI was thinking along the same lines. But he still needed more concrete information and he needed it now. The FBI was good at surveillance but they weren't very good at interrogation techniques when it came to hardened international terrorists. These men weren't the same as the typical criminals the FBI normally faced. They lived by a different set of rules and they had to be dealt with in more effective ways…ways not restricted by due process or Geneva Convention principals. Winston again needed the Delphi Team. This was this kind of a situation for which it was created.

Winston called out to his secretary. "Jeanine, call Tex and tell him to have my plane ready to fly by 4:00 this afternoon. Tell him to file a flight plan for Lunken Airport in Cincinnati." Tex Wallace was a retired Air Force colonel who used to fly F-16 fighter jets. Now he served as the main pilot for the Hamilton family jet, a Cessna Citation CJ4. Winston preferred to fly in his own plane rather than be under the scrutiny of the Agency by flying in one of the CIA planes. The five-hundred-mile trip should take just over an hour. While in the air, he would have Tex redirect the plane to the co-ordinates for the Farmto landing strip.

⊫≓ ⊰⊨

Winston finished his calls and looked at the family photograph sitting on his desk. It was a picture of himself with his wife, two sons, and daughter while on vacation years ago. The photograph had nothing to do with reality. It was only about appearances. There were the obligatory smiles, but there was nothing behind them. Any implied familial bond was nothing more than a façade. The photograph was taken at a time when his wife still somewhat cared about him, but now the best that she could do was to barely tolerate him. That was more than he could say for his boys and his daughter who were now in college. They detested him and hadn't contacted him in over seven years. Winston fully realized that the only reason why he and his wife were still married was his family money and the fact that she seldom had to actually see him. She and the children lived at their home in the Hamptons while he stayed in the family's Georgetown home, on the outskirts of D.C.

In reality, Winston had been married to his job for the past twenty years. Work was his mistress. He'd like to say the reason why he was so devoted to the Agency was to protect his family and country from the forces trying to destroy it. In fact, what motivated him the most was the intoxicating enjoyment he received by totally vanquishing his enemies. To win was not enough. Only total destruction of the opposition was what brought him happiness. Some didn't know why he was wired this way. Psychologists might speculate that it was a mechanism by which he rebelled against the suffocating control of his father and grandfather.

However, for Winston, there was a more practical explanation. It you simply defeat an opponent; he is able to recover and eventually return to do battle again. He has no fear of reprisals. On the other hand, if you completely destroy him, you will always be in his head. He will fear you and never return. This had been Winston's philosophy ever since he had become a chess prodigy.

As a world chess master, he had never been beaten and in the world of covert operations, the same was true; that is, until he crossed paths with Dr. Jacob Savich. It was a near fatal encounter for Winston. He was now on his way to meet the unlikely Delphi Team leader at "Farmto," just fifty miles south of Cincinnati.

Winston's chauffer pulled onto the tarmac by the Executive Jet terminal at Dulles International Airport. The flight attendant welcomed him at the bottom of the stairs and escorted him up to the plane. He entered the Citation jet and said hello to Tex. "How's the weather between here and Cincinnati, Tex?"

"Clear for the entire trip Mr. Hamilton. We should arrive in about an hour. As soon as you get buckled in, we'll be cleared for take-off."

Winston took his usual spot and fastened his seatbelt. The jet taxied to the runway and after just a few minutes, they were aloft. Winston became immersed in thought. He was continuously planning moves and countermoves, just like one did in chess...but this was real life. He reviewed thousands of words a day and his expertise was rooted in his ability to coordinate seemingly unrelated pieces of information. He was able to read between the lines of reports, to see what was not actually there in print. What was omitted often provided more insight than what was on paper. The most glaring omission in this present situation is the how and when; who's pulling the strings, and putting up the cash. That's the key. The robberies provided some money but not nearly enough to finance an attack, the scope of which he was anticipating. Whoever was bankrolling this scheme had access to a great deal of cash and he was spreading it around liberally. In addition, he must hate the U.S. enough to be willing to spend tens of millions for an attack. That places him in a reasonably small group but it's still too large to be manageable. Whoever's in charge is risking a great deal, and not just financially. Look at what happened to Saddam Hussein after he tried to assassinate President Bush. To chance an attack on the U.S., he must feel fairly secure and well-protected. That could only be a foreign president, dictator, or even a member of a royal family. That certainly narrows the field of possibilities further. Hopefully, they can extract some actionable information from the Mullah or Muhammad bin Hussein.

CHAPTER THIRTY-SIX

A week after the beating of Julia, Graham Maultry submitted his revised plans to Ahmad. Time was running short for his family. He wouldn't be able to wait for a follow-up meeting before attempting an escape. He confided to Julia, "Once Ahmad realizes that the revised plans are still faulty, he'll be furious. We're all going to be killed here anyway, so we might as well die trying to get out. At least, we might save some other lives in the process."

Julia had recovered adequately from the beating, so after a careful discussion with his family last night, they decided that today must be the day. Graham discussed his plan with them in as much detail as he could. They'd actually be winging it most of the time. Graham figured that their chances of surviving were maybe ten percent…if they were lucky. If not, hopefully death would be quick and painless. They all knew the risks and the consequences of failure. Surprisingly, his timid son Randy and his self-centered daughter Tiffany didn't hesitate to voice their support.

Their bodyguards had relaxed quite a bit over the past week. Apparently, the captors figured that after the severe beating Julia received, the Maultry family had abandoned any consideration of escape. It was now approaching one o'clock in the afternoon and everyone who didn't have assigned duties stopped to observe one of their five daily prayer sessions.

Graham was counting on them having their guard down. For the past several months, he had tried to establish some rapport with Yassin Aziz, the young man who had been guarding him every day. He had been somewhat successful. The guard seemed to be sympathetic to the family's plight. It was obvious that he was distraught by the way his superiors had treated Julia. Graham had been feigning an interest in the Muslim religion, and was pretending to be more sympathetic of their cause. Yassin became more comfortable around Graham the more he asked about the teachings of the Great Prophet Muhammad. The guard had even given Graham a copy of the Quran which they would discuss together if none of the other guards were nearby.

On this particular morning, just like every other morning, Yassin escorted Graham to the design laboratory at gunpoint. However, the Kalashnikov rifle was now pointing casually at the ground rather than at the middle of Graham's back. Like every other morning, Graham went over to one of the counters where he poured two cups of black coffee and selected two freshly-baked blueberry muffins, which the two men, guard and prisoner, ate together while they again discussed the teachings of Muhammad.

At the specified time of 1:00 p.m., Yassin excused himself, and spread out his small prayer rug. Like every other day, he turned toward the hall window that faced east toward Mecca. Graham seized the opportunity. As usual, his guard carelessly rested his automatic rifle against the lab door frame. After a few minutes, Graham cautiously walked over to the weapon and lifted it by the barrel. He quietly said, "I'm sorry Yassin," just before he hit him in the head. He stood over the unconscious man and noticed blood oozing out of his right ear. He hoped that the man wasn't dead but he didn't have time for regrets. Graham was well aware that he only had a ten minute window until the afternoon prayer time would be over. Fortunately, the flaw in the mansion's elaborate security system is that it was designed to keep intruders out, but not to keep hostages from escaping, once outside of their apartment. The problem would be getting the rest of his family out of their electronically locked door and past the remaining guards. They would not be as easy to dispatch as the unconscious Yassin.

Graham ran down the hall to Ahmad Haq Rasid's large office where Julia had been beaten just a week earlier. Once in the room, he looked around and breathed a sigh of relief. It was empty. Ahmad wasn't there, but the EMP generator was still sitting next to the couch. He grabbed the heavy black box and took off for the family's apartment. He realized that the prayers were halfway over when he heard the repetitive chants of "Allahu Akbar" in the background. He hurried his pace. At the entrance to the apartment he saw another guard who was also kneeling on a prayer rug just outside the metal door. Graham recognized him as Mossaq Hashimi, the man who had severely beaten Julia and broken Jessica Vehr's jaw.

Graham checked his weapon and whispered to himself, "Damn, this rifle doesn't have a sound suppressor. I can't shoot him. I'll have to do this by hand." Graham quietly came up on the kneeling man from behind and hit him in the head with the butt of his rifle. Hashimi fell to the floor and rolled over. He was lying on his back, looking up at Graham, when recognition developed in his eyes. Before he could yell out a warning to the others, Graham smashed the butt of his rifle into the man's mouth, knocking out most of his teeth. "That's for my wife, and this is for Jessica." With that, he pounded the terrorist's head into a mushy red pile of brain and bone on the marble floor.

Graham knelt over the body, working quickly now, searching the dead man's pockets for the keys to the apartment door. He found them, inserted the key, turned the lock, but the door still wouldn't open. "Damn," he again said. "You forgot the pulse generator!" He turned the machine so that it faced toward the metal door and flipped the switch to the on position. There was a quiet hum and after a second he heard the click as the electronic lock released. As planned, his family was already waiting for him. Once inside the door, Graham said nothing but nodded his head as if to say it was time.

"How's it going?" asked Julia with a worried look on her face.

"A few hitches but so far, so good" Graham responded.

"Then let's do this," said Rodney much to the surprise of the others.

"OK, let's do it," replied Graham. He turned the EMP generator around so that it faced outward toward the rest of the house. He checked the lights and televisions. "Good, nothing's working." He didn't know the range of the device but was hoping it would cover the entire mansion, knocking out all surveillance and communications. They had to move quickly. They only had a minute or two at best, before someone noticed the blank security monitors.

He walked out of the apartment and turned back to his family, "Follow me closely but be very quiet. Take a left into the hall and ignore anything you see on the floor. Things got a little messy." He bent over and picked up Hashimi's silenced AK-47 and handed it to Julia. "Just point it at what you want to shoot and pull the trigger. You don't have to worry about aiming."

They headed down a hall and after thirty feet he said, "To the right and down the next hall until we reach the stairway." He led them down the stairs and took a right at the bottom. After another twenty feet, he suddenly raised his right hand, turned, and placed his right index finger against his lips. "Shhh," he whispered. "There's another guard covering the back door. It's the boat captain who gunned down Tucker." Without hesitation, Julia turned the corner, raised her automatic rifle, and fired over a dozen silenced rounds within several seconds. Most of her shots were wild and shattered the glass doors behind her target, but three rounds found their mark, slamming into the man's chest. She smiled and said, "That was for Tucker."

Randy ran over and picked up the dead man's rifle. Graham pulled on the handle and cocked it for his son. "Just like mom's, just point and pull the trigger," he instructed. Julia pulled a Glock out of the dead man's waistband and handed it to Tiffany. Surprisingly, the girl ejected the clip and inspected it. "I have eight rounds left," she said. "How about everyone else?" Then the girl slammed the clip back into the pistol and chambered a round as though she had done it a hundred times before. The others looked at her in astonishment.

"What?" she said, while looking at her family. "I've been watching a lot of CSI reruns on the TV. I've learned a few things. Now, let's get out of here!"

The family took off through the back exit that faced the Intracoastal Waterway. "It's still here!" exclaimed Graham. There, sitting only a hundred feet away, still secured to the dock, was the Viking Sport Fisherman. Graham was praying that the pulse generator's range did not extend that far. They ran at a full sprint across the lawn toward the boat. Halfway, they began to receive fire from guards stationed on the back veranda. There was no cover position here, so they ran behind the large marble fountain. Pieces flew in all directions as they continued to receive fire. Graham was able to take out two of the three shooters. "Spread out and run," he told his family. He then returned suppressive fire at the remaining gunman as the family continued on toward the boat.

He yelled to Julia. "Untie the bow lines and get the kids on board." The final shooter hit Tiffany and she fell to the ground, her pistol flying in front of her. Graham screamed out in horror, "Tiff!" He ran over and scooped up his daughter while Rodney pinned down the final shooter with a spray of automatic fire.

Once they got on the boat, Graham quickly checked his daughter and found that she had sustained a through-and-through wound to her right thigh. "You're going to be fine, Tiff." No major vessels had been hit. He told Rodney, "Put pressure on the wound while I start the engines. Julia, guard the rear of the boat."

Graham ran up the ladder to the flying bridge and started the engines just as two Rottweiler guard dogs came running from the side of the house and charged toward them. Julia took out the lead dog with several remaining rounds in her rifle before it reached the dock but the second one was getting close. Rodney tried to get the dog but missed.

"I'm out of ammo," screamed Julia.

"Me too," responded Rodney.

The dog tried to leap over the back transom of the boat but Randy stopped it in mid-air with a swing of the butt of his rifle, knocking the dog unconscious into the water. They started receiving more fire from the house. There was no time to release all of the lines, so Graham yelled, "Hold on!" as he pushed both throttles full forward. The bow of the boat seemed to jump right out of the water as it snapped the forward deck line in two. The aft line pulled out its cleat and a six foot section of the dock with it.

They got fifty yards down the Intracoastal when Ahmad ran out of the house with an RPG launcher in his hands. As he knelt down to fire, Julia screamed, "Graham, rocket!" Just before Ahmad fired, Graham turned the boat hard to port taking out the corner of another dock across the canal. The rocket passed just over the back deck, so close that as Julia hit the deck, her hair was singed. The rocket exploded in a patch of mangrove trees just beyond them. Graham continued his turn around a bend and disappeared down the waterway out of the line of fire.

He continued to run the boat at its maximum speed of thirty knots through a manatee slow-zone. They were stirring up a five-foot wake while they continued to drag the six foot piece of dock behind them. The speeding boat drew a lot of attention and soon they were approached head-on by a coast guard patrol boat, siren blaring and red lights flashing. As Graham stopped, he yelled down to his family to drop their weapons and raise their hands. The patrol boat pulled alongside the Viking craft, multiple automatic weapons pointed at the family. Graham said in as calm a voice as he could muster, "My name is Graham Maultry. My family and I were kidnapped several months ago. I need an ambulance for my daughter. She's been shot!"

The coast guard captain instructed his men to lower their weapons. He had one of his men tend to Tiffany's leg wound. Then, he turned to Graham and said, "We know who you are Dr. Maultry. We've been looking for you, ever since your yacht was found last month."

"I need to talk to the cops. I have important information about a probable terror attack."

CHAPTER THIRTY-SEVEN

I t was a Saturday night in mid-November. The Delphi Team members were sitting together in the dining room of the main house after a full day of training. Since the departure of Derek "The Dick" Hacker, the atmosphere was more relaxed and the team was bonding well. Lisa was now accepted as a legitimate member of the group after having successfully dispatched of the man. They all had their share of beer as big Hank was regaling them with stories from his days as a Seal. He was as witty as he was intelligent and had the group laughing for an hour.

When things started to die down, one of the instructors entered the room and whispered into Carver's ear. His expression suddenly changed to very serious.

"Let him come in here to meet with me. I want my team to know everything that I know."

The instructor left and returned several minutes later, followed by a man in a dark suit and red tie. It had been a year since Carver had seen the man, but he still had that eerie horizontal smile and soulless black eyes that gave him the look of a reptile. He was small in stature but there was an intimidating aura about him. Carver was always taken aback by the contradiction of the man's cold appearance and his apparent selfless desire to protect the country.

"This is Winston Hamilton," Carver said to the team as he introduced the man to each member of the group.

The diminutive Mr. Hamilton remained standing as he spoke. "It's good to see you again Dr. Savich. I trust that everything is going well with your training program."

"I believe the entire team is ready, Mr. Hamilton," replied Carver.

"Good. From what I hear, you're all performing exceptionally well," he replied as he looked directly at Lisa. The message was obvious. She had taken out one of his men and he was duly impressed. "The reason why I flew down from Washington this evening is because an exceedingly urgent issue has developed. It is the kind of matter for which this group was created. As you're already aware, we have information from a number of reliable sources confirming that there is a legitimate threat of an impending terror attack on our soil.

"The group is headed by a ruthless man whom we will call the Scorpion. For right now, we know nothing specific about the man and I've not been able to uncover any details in either the CIA or NSA databases. He controls dozens of sleeper cells which have been well financed through criminal activities and probably also by wealthy supporters in the Middle East. We suspect that his organization is building up to a large scale attack and it has something to do with a mysterious shipment that will be, or has already been smuggled in from Canada. Unfortunately, we still don't know the exact nature of that shipment.

"As your group has already suggested, some evidence suggests that the target might be the Houston Super Bowl in February. That theory still needs to be confirmed. We're still in the dark as to the scope and the exact nature of the attack. We do know that there are two prominent players in this. According to an FBI informant, Muqtoda al-Sadir is the name of the Michigan mullah that Farouk mentioned during his interrogation. The second individual is Muhammad Rabbani aka Muhammad bin Hussein."

"Any relation to Saddam Hussein?" asked Deets.

"No, same last name, different family, but just as evil. He was a member of the Iranian Revolutionary Guard, and is responsible for the deaths of thousands of innocent Iranian citizens. I'm certain that he is now in this country helping to organize the attack. I suspect he might actually be the number two in command behind the Scorpion. From what I've been able to ascertain, I don't think Mullah al-Sadir is smart enough to be the man in charge. Regardless, the two of them have been orchestrating the delivery of the mysterious Canadian package which I believe to be some type of weapons system. Some are speculating that it could be a powerful electromagnetic pulse generator stolen from Canada's Reliant Corporation, but its only conjecture at this point. The FBI has been maintaining tight surveillance on the two men, trying to get confirmation of the when, where, and how of the attack. Thus far, they've come up empty handed."

Carver injected, "And I assume that's where we come in."

"Yes. This is an urgent situation and we don't have time for the FBI to act. If you think the Delphi Team is ready, Doctor Savich, I would like you to become involved. We need to get our hands on at least one of these two men, preferably both. We need to see if we can convince them to share any information they might have regarding the Canadian package and the attack."

"Understood," said Carver. He and everyone else in the room knew exactly what was being asked of them when Hamilton euphemistically used the word "convince". He wanted the team to break the law by kidnapping the two men. Then, convincing would involve some illegal enhanced interrogation techniques. Carver and Hank had already done it with Jazeer Farouk and neither of the two felt any sense of remorse. It's nasty business, but necessary if they were going to protect the country and potentially save thousands of lives. As he looked at the rest of the team, he saw each of them nod their heads in affirmation.

"We're all on board," said Carver.

"I'll leave the planning up to you and your team, Dr. Savich. Rest assured that anything that you need will be provided. I can't emphasize enough that secrecy regarding our organization is an utmost priority."

"I know, don't get caught," stated Carver. "By the way, who's the lead FBI Agent in charge of the case?"

"Someone with whom you are already familiar--Special Agent John Crawford. I already anonymously fed him the information that you were able to squeeze out of Professor Farouk."

Carver nodded his head and gave a brief glance toward Lisa. She blushed and tried to mask her concern. *This is going to make things a bit more difficult for me,* she thought.

Just so everyone else understood the situation, Carver asked, "And if things go wrong and we are caught?"

"I'll disavow any knowledge of your existence, but I will try to help you as much as I safely can from behind the scenes." Winston Hamilton added, "There's one other important matter. One of my contacts at the NSA reported that the Coast Guard found Dr. Graham Maultry and his family yesterday. He's one of the top aeronautical engineers in the country. His company was involved in the development of improved stealth technology using new ultra-lightweight graphene materials. His actual work has been a closely guarded secret but apparently, the Scorpion found out about it. Maultry told the FBI that he was forced by a group of Middle Eastern men to design a stealth aircraft to be made from the same material. It was his belief that the plane would be used to deliver a weapon of some type. He doesn't know exactly what type of weapon or the location of the attack, although he did mention that his kidnappers possessed an electro-magnetic pulse generator."

"That's the reason for the concern about the Reliant Corporation and the Canadian package?" questioned Deets.

"Exactly," responded Winston.

"But what good does an EMP generator do them at the Super Bowl?" asked Dan.

"That, I don't know yet, but hopefully, the two men from Dearborn can shed some light on the situation."

Winston continued to discuss in more detail what he knew about the two Dearborn men and the threat that they posed. He had detailed dossiers with photographs on both of them. Carver passed copies of the reports around the table. After an hour of discussion, Winston returned to his plane for the trip back to Washington while the Delphi team began to formulate their plan. They didn't have the luxury of time on their side. February was less than three months away.

CHAPTER THIRTY-EIGHT

"Muhammad, I agree that Allah will protect us but we're asking for trouble." Muhammad bin Hussein held his index finger to his lips and pointed to the windows, indicating to the mullah that he needed to be more careful. There was a good chance that the mosque was under surveillance and the mullah tended to be careless. He was out of control and if it were up to Muhammad, he'd dispose of the hedonistic fat man. He was tired of his constant worrying and complaining. But killing him now would raise too much attention and their plan might be at risk of exposure. Fortunately, the mullah was only aware of his small part regarding Canada. He didn't know the specific details of the "Great Attack".

He said to al-Sadir, "Let's take a walk," as he forcefully grabbed the mullah by the arm. They both put on jackets and went out into the cold late-November afternoon. They had to be cautious. Muhammad hadn't heard from Jazeer Farouk in over a week and he was getting worried that maybe the professor had been arrested. If he had been careless and if there had been a breach in their security systems, the Feds might have uncovered some information which could possibly lead the FBI back to the mullah and himself. Muhammad had to assume that the mosque was being monitored.

As soon as the two men exited the building, al-Sadir began frantically waving his arms around as he continued to complain, "That truck has been parked in the garage for over a week now and it's going to be a problem! You still haven't taken care of Reggie yet! You shouldn't have killed Curtis until we had Reggie under control! If the police get hold of him and he talks, they'll have probable cause for a search warrant. They'll find records about that garage even if it is leased through a phantom company. The FBI has ways and they'll find it, believe me. Then they'll be able to trace it back to us. If we're sitting on that container, I don't have to tell you what will happen to us when they find it."

"Perhaps we should notify the Scorpion about your concerns," replied Muhammad.

"No, no, there's no need to bother him right now," responded al-Sadir nervously. "I just think that it would be wise to move the package farther away from the Canadian border and away from us. They're going to need it soon in Cincinnati anyway."

Muhammad paused for a minute. *As annoying as he is, al-Sadir has a point,* he thought. *It would only take four hours to move the canister to Microavionics and then we'd have it there when it was needed. I have to be there to supervise the final construction phase anyway.* Muhammad decided to make the trip that afternoon.

He reassured the mullah, "I'll take care of everything. The truck will be moved later today but I'm going to need some help."

"Use Tarriz. You're going to need him eventually anyway."

"I want him to remain here for a while longer," responded Muhammad. He needed someone to keep an eye on the Mullah once he left. He made a mental note to ask the Scorpion for permission to dispatch of the hypocritical cleric before he left for Cincinnati. He's rattled and he's a liability who is no longer needed now that they had the package. The Scorpion didn't like liabilities even if they did happen to be friends of his father.

Muhammad knew that it wouldn't be just a matter of leaving with the container. If the FBI did have the mosque under surveillance, they'd pick him up before he had driven five miles out of town. Then he'd be sitting there with the package in the back of his truck and a lot of impossible explaining to do. He arranged for Tarriz Muhktar, to stop by the mosque in a furnace repair truck that afternoon. They had enough sympathizers in the community that borrowing one wouldn't be a problem. He could pose as one of the HVAC men and ride to the off-site garage in their van. Then, as long as the coast was clear, he would drive the container directly to Cincinnati.

Muhammad had been unable to reach the Scorpion, so unfortunately the fat mullah was still alive for now. It would have given him great pleasure to have disposed of the man the day he left.

It took three hours for Muhammad to reach I-275 along the northern outskirts of Cincinnati. Fifteen minutes later, he pulled the truck into the back parking lot of Microavionics Technologies Corporation. It was now six o'clock in the evening and most of the employees had already left for the day. Muhammad had been counting on this, but as always, there was a complication. An older gentleman, dressed in jeans and a Microavionics sweatshirt, was exiting the rear steel door. The man was the last one to leave work for the day when he noticed Muhammad's truck pull into the lot. Almost every business had a guy like this: a lower-level employee who believed that he was the one truly in charge of everything. If it wasn't for him, the place would surely fall apart. Nothing happened that he didn't know about.

"I don't think we're scheduled for a delivery today," said the man authoritatively before Muhammad could fully exit the truck.

"I have some parts that Mr. Logan ordered. He said that he needed them right away," responded Muhammad.

"Roger didn't say anything to me about it and he definitely would have told me something. I'm in charge of checking all deliveries. Let's see what you have in there."

Before Muhammad could get out of the truck and stop him, the old man opened the rear of the truck and caught a glimpse of the large container sitting on a cradle. "What the hell is this?" Before the man could say another word, his thought processes were disrupted by a hollow-point 9mm bullet to the back of his head. Brain and most of the front of his skull exploded into the interior of the vehicle. Muhammad pushed the body completely into the cargo area and closed the door.

This was an unexpected problem which he was going to have to clean up. He pulled out his burner phone and called Tarriz Muhktar, "There's a change of plans. I want you to hurry down to Cincinnati right away." Muhammad explained the situation. Tarriz, who was their explosives expert, would drive the truck and container to the hiding place where it would be safer. He hated to leave al-Sadir unsupervised but he had no other choice. The police were certain to discover the package if they came snooping around to investigate the missing man whom he had just shot.

Muhammad called his local team and informed them that he would need a car and a place to stay for several weeks. He then called the project manager, Roger Logan. He introduced himself as Mr. Darpoli's assistant and requested a meeting in the morning to discuss the progress on the drone construction. He needed to be certain that everything was still on schedule. It was several months away from the attack but they still had to complete the final construction phase. Then, he had to deliver the drones to the weapon assembly site where they planned to do some practice runs in preparation for the "Great Attack". He didn't need any more surprises. The Scorpion disliked surprises as much as he hated liabilities.

CHAPTER THIRTY-NINE

Several days after his last discussion with the director, John Crawford was talking on the phone with Agent Tim Hogan. Their surveillance team was housed in a second story apartment, above a bakery, just across the street from the Al-Fateh mosque. They had been watching it for over two weeks. Unfortunately, nothing much had turned up yet. Crawford had just asked Hogan about how extensive their surveillance was.

"We have laser microphones trained on the windows in his office and personal residence apartment. Any conversation will set up a vibratory pattern of voices on the glass that will be transmitted to our monitors. We have taps on all phone lines and have accessed his computers. Anything he does online, we can see in real time. The NSA has expedited coverage of their cell phones although any burner phones will be off the grid. I also have a man outside from time to time but we have to be careful. I don't want to arouse suspicion by having someone prowling around out there too often.

"So what have you found?" asked Crawford.

"There was a very brief comment about Canada but nothing specific regarding a shipment. Bottom line is, we don't have a whole lot so far, John," said a frustrated Hogan. "Other than a furnace problem earlier this afternoon, not much else has happened."

"What was that about?"

Hogan checked his notes. "There was a van from the 'Tamish Heating and Air-conditioning Company'. It arrived earlier this afternoon. Three guys were at the mosque for a several hours. When the van left, I kept a tail on it for a while to be sure they were legit. They made a couple of stops at area businesses but nothing suspicious. It all looked ok."

"Anything else?" asked Crawford.

"Just the usual coming and going of employees. There have been no deliveries or anything else that would look like a truck smuggling a package from Canada."

"The package might already be there," offered Crawford.

"There's no way to know for sure without going in with a warrant. I can arrange for one if you like, John," said Hogan.

"Not just yet. What else do you have?"

"I've reviewed all of the phone logs and nothing suspicious has come in or out. The computers have been silent except for access to some online porno sites."

"Porno sites!"

"Yeah, it seems the good mullah likes the ladies. The window laser microphones have picked up some of his conversations. He frequently calls porno lines and chats for a while. He's actually a pretty sick cookie. You'd be amazed at some of the shit he says. Anyway, he likes to take a dip into the pool of professional female companionship from time to time."

"When was the last time?"

"He actually went out to meet one last week."

"Did you keep a tail on him?" asked Crawford, wondering if it was a cover allowing the mullah to meet up with a potential contact from Canada."

"Yes, but it looked to be a legitimate hook-up. We checked to be sure he didn't sneak out a back door but he stayed there for several hours. The woman who exited with him was the same one we saw on the Internet porno site. We checked her out. She's definitely a pro and she's been in business for over two years."

"How often does he do that? Maybe he's actually meeting up with the Scorpion."

"Maybe once a week. I don't think he's meeting anyone from the organization. He'd take guards if he were. Besides, unless the Scorpion is a hot looking blond with an escort web site, I think it was just for sex."

"Anything else?" asked Crawford.

"One thing was a little unusual."

"What was that?" asked Crawford expectantly as he sat up straight in his chair.

"Mullah al-Sadir and Muhammad went out for a walk this morning. I've never seen them go outside together like that. Al-Sadir never walks anywhere. He's too fat. We couldn't get any audio coverage of their conversation but it was very animated. They seemed to be arguing about something. Then, after only about five minutes, they both went back inside. The whole thing made me wonder. Did they go outside because they suspected that the mosque is being monitored?"

"That's certainly possible," offered Crawford. "This Muhammad fellow isn't stupid and we've been doing a lot of surveillance around those west coast cells. They may have gotten wind of it."

"Maybe it's time to pick them up for questioning after all. We really haven't been getting anywhere with what we're doing now. With Reggie Patterson's testimony, we at least have probable cause for a search warrant and have more than enough to hold them for a while. We might even be able to pressure one of them into talking. From what you've told me about al-Sadir, he might be easy to crack. If we wait any longer and they suspect we're watching them, I'm afraid they might split and go to ground," offered Hogan.

"Sounds like a reasonable idea, Tim. I was hoping to continue surveillance for a while, but you're right. If they're on to us, they might split; so I guess we'd better bring them in," responded Crawford.

"I'll get on it right away. It'll take the rest of the day to get the arrest and search warrants. I'll pick them up first thing in the morning, and I'll call you when they're in custody."

"Just don't let them slip through your fingers, Tim."

"Don't worry John. We have a tight net around them."

CHAPTER FORTY

While Tim Hogan and the FBI were watching the mosque, the Delphi Team was staying in a three-bedroom safe house a half-mile away. Carver and Lisa had completed several days of reconnaissance of the surrounding area while driving a grey aluminum siding company van. They were sitting on a couch and waiting for the rest of the team to return. Hank and Dan had been separately canvassing a several block perimeter around the mosque on foot.

His crutches were leaning against the chair as Norman, "The Geek" Deets sat at the dining room table. In front of him were arranged so many computers, monitors, and cables that the room looked like a NASA command center. After a half-hour of watching him frantically type back and forth between several keyboards, Carver finished his beer and walked over.

"What do you have for me so far, Norman?"

"Well it's interesting boss. There are three things that I've been able to dig up. First of all, the guy's rich, very rich for a cleric. From what I can tell, he must be worth over eleven million dollars!"

"Eleven million! How'd he acquire so much money?" asked Lisa.

"Probably the same way Jimmy Baker and many of the other televangelists do," replied Carver. "He milked the system. He skimmed cash out of the mosque's treasury. I wouldn't be surprised if he also embezzled money from his terror organization. That's a piece of information that we might be able to use later, if we get a chance to interrogate him."

Dan entered through the apartment door, grabbed a bottle of water, and sat down on the couch next to Lisa. He'd been out surveilling the area for the past three hours. Hank followed him inside a few minutes later.

Carver looked up and turned his attention away from the computers. "Did you come up with anything, Dan?"

"I've been all around the place and I caught a glimpse of al-Sadir and Muhammad walking outside. They were fighting about something. I could hear al-Sadir yelling but I couldn't make out what he was saying.

"In addition, I'm pretty sure our friends from the FBI are here. I found two potential sites for surveillance. One's a white Michigan Bell Telephone Company truck with darkly tinted windows. It hasn't moved in the past three hours. It might be legit but we have to consider the possibility that it's a Bureau vehicle. The other site is a second floor apartment across the street from the mosque. It sits right above a bakery. The shades are pulled except for a three inch opening that might allow placement of a video camera. The whole thing screams out 'FBI inside'. "

"How about you Hank?" asked Carver.

"I've spotted about a half-dozen employees coming and going around the mosque. I think we can safely assume that there are a half-dozen more that I haven't seen. So we have at least a dozen people that we must address. Only a handful of the ones that I've seen appear to be guards so that makes the numbers a little better, but just a little. Taking our guys from the mosque would be easy enough from a physical standpoint, but all of the employees are going to present a logistical problem. We wouldn't be able to secure all of them quickly enough and one of them is bound to trigger an alarm. That's complicated by the fact that we want to take two men: al-Sadir and Muhammad. Even if we could grab them together, and that's a big if, the FBI would be certain to notice something. They'll come storming in with guns pulled at the first sign of trouble. I think our best bet is going to be to lure one or both of them offsite. Then we can take them together. It's possible that one might just have to be eliminated."

"I'd prefer to get Muhammad if we have to make a choice. I'm certain he has more information although al-Sadir would be easier to break," said Carver.

"How do we get them out of the house?" asked Lisa.

Dan replied half-jokingly, "We could start a fire. That's sure to force them out."

"And then the FBI agents will really come in with guns-a-blazing," replied Lisa, looking down at the floor. "I have to think about this for a while."

Carver continued, "OK, thanks guys. We're going to have to figure out something pretty soon." He looked at Deets and said, "Norman's been able to hack into the mullah's computer system and was giving us a report. Go ahead Norman."

"Like I said, the guy's rich and he's probably been ripping off his congregation and his terror organization for years. Of greater interest is the fact that while I was hacking into al-Sadir's computer, I discovered that someone else is already looking over the mullah's shoulder. It's the FBI."

"That goes along with what Dan was telling us about potential FBI surveillance locations," offered Hank.

"Is your intrusion going to pose a problem for us Norman?" asked Carver.

"Me seeing them on al-Sadir's system? No, it actually makes things much easier and will give us access to a lot more information. I've been able to backtrack and infiltrate the Bureaus computers with 'Looking Glass'. Now we don't have to wait for Mr. Hamilton to obtain information for us from his contacts in Washington. We'll be able to get a lot of stuff in real time.

"What's 'Looking Glass'?" asked Lisa.

"It's a malware program that some friends and I developed several years ago. We got tired of playing the same old video games over and over. So, we made up our own games to see who could hack into the most secure computer systems."

"Trying to one-up each other," said Dan.

"I guess. Anyway, as part of our game, we came up with 'Looking Glass'." It allowed us to access some exceptionally secure systems. With it, I can look over the shoulder of any computer user without their knowing I'm there. I can monitor al-Sadir's computers and piggyback into the Bureau's system at the same time. It's pretty cool. Now I'm tied into both. I can even backtrack into the Bureau's main computers in Washington if you like."

"Are you sure they won't be able to tell that you're there?" asked Lisa.

"Are you kidding me? I'm insulted that you'd even ask that question, Lisa. I've successfully hacked into over a half-dozen major banks with some of the most sophisticated security systems in the country. They never knew I was there until I wanted them to."

"But you did go to jail Norman," countered Carver.

"That's because I got a little too cocky and hacked into the State Department, but it still took them two months to find me. This thing here is child's play for me. The Bureau's good at eavesdropping on others but they never expect to have an outsider looking at them. Now that I'm tied in, I can go almost anywhere in the Bureau's system. If you want, I can find out more about the Bureau than even the director knows."

"Don't get carried away, Norman. Remember, you did go to jail by overextending your reach. Just focus on the task at hand," replied Carver. "And the final thing?"

"Final thing?" Norman replied.

"Yes, you said earlier that there were three things of interest and you only gave me two."

"Oh yeah. It appears as though the good Mullah likes the ladies...a lot. Judging by his website activity, he's prone to seeking the comfort of women with, ah, shall we say, professional experience," said Deets.

"Like prostitutes!" exclaimed Lisa! "A holy man?"

"Not so holy, I guess," replied Deets. "He's just like some of those television evangelists that Carver mentioned earlier. It's the old do-as-I-say-but-not-as-I-do game. It looks like he surfs porno sites until he finds someone to his liking. Then he makes arrangements to rendezvous somewhere discrete."

"How often?"

Deets again looked at his computer screen, "I'd say once a week, sometimes more often."

"Horny little devil," commented Dan.

"When was his last hook-up?" asked Lisa.

"Just over a week, so he's overdue."

"Lisa, I know where you're going with this and the answer is no," said Carver emphatically.

"It'll be fine Carver. I know what I'm doing. Like Dan said, we need a plan to lure at least one of them away from the mosque. Maybe Muhammad will follow but if not we can at least get the mullah." Lisa turned to Norman and asked, "What type of woman does he prefer?" A plan was already beginning to take shape in her mind.

"Tall blonds," Norman replied and Lisa smiled as she thought, *won't need a wig, just the right dress and some sexy heels.* "Can you establish a web site that can be seen only on his computer?"

Norman looked at one of his screens with concern, "Sure, like I said earlier, it's child's play…but if you're going to do something, you'd better hurry. It looks to me like the Bureau is about to make a move on your two guys…maybe even tomorrow."

CHAPTER FORTY-ONE

After Muhammad left with the container, the mullah was again feeling relaxed and he began to return to his normal pattern of behavior. He decided that he deserved a reward after putting up with Muhammad and his bullying for the past week. He needed to relieve some stress and he knew exactly how to do it. He sat down in front of his computer and started surfing for a date. Almost immediately, an image popped up on the screen. It was a particularly enticing web site that he had never encountered before. There it was, right in front of his eyes, as though it was meant to be there. He lingered for a while to study the image. Unlike the other escort sites, this one appeared to be entirely devoted to just one woman, and a gorgeous creature she was. She was tall and slender with long blond hair that cascaded over her white shoulders. Her warm blue-green eyes seemed to look directly into his soul, inviting him to contact her. He could tell at a glance that this woman was in a class far above any he had encountered before. The cost was high, but she looked to be well-worth it. He had to have her, and he had to have her tonight. After all, he had earned this. He made the call.

⟩⟨

"There's the phone! It must be him," said Lisa with a smile.

"That was quick. It's like chumming water when fishing for sharks," said Dan.

"I'm not sure I like being compared to chum," Lisa said with a fake frown on her face. She answered the phone and spoke to the Mullah in the most seductive breathy voice she could muster. It was hard not to laugh. She could tell that al-Sadir was ready and anxious to get together. She tried to entice him into meeting her at the safe house. It would have been the easiest way, but the man was too cautious for that. She went to plan B.

⟩⟨

The Dearborn Inn on Oakwood Boulevard was an upscale Marriott Hotel located across the road from the Ford Development Center. It was far enough away from the Al-Fateh mosque that al-Sadir was comfortably satisfied that he wouldn't be recognized.

Unbeknownst to him, this was his second excursion into the night with an FBI escort. Two agents, riding in a black Explorer, followed about a half-mile behind him. He was unaware of their presence as he parked his car in the shadows on the east parking lot, well away from the front entrance of the hotel. A minute later, the two surveilling agents pulled in three aisles behind the mullah. Carver had anticipated their presence and made plans to circumvent their involvement. He called in to report that everyone had arrived and were parked in the east lot. "The show is about to start and we have an audience," he told the team.

"Roger that," replied Hank. "How many uninvited guests?"

"Two."

Al-Sadir exited his vehicle. He had exchanged his white robe for a black silk shirt, khaki slacks, expensive black Italian loafers, and a dark leather jacket that he could barely close over his protruding belly. He walked through the front door and, avoiding the front desk, he continued across the lobby until he saw the signs on the wall indicating the direction of room 127. After walking the short distance, he momentarily stood outside the room door. He knocked three times in eager anticipation. Lisa responded from inside, "Just a minute, handsome," and the door slowly opened. When he entered the room, he could smell the subtly enticing scent of her perfume, but she was nowhere to be seen. Then he screamed out as the Taser delivered a burst of fifty-thousand volts to his neck.

⇒⇐

After securing al-Sadir, Lisa gave him a small injection of Midazolam. It left the mullah sedate but able to use his feet. Hank reported to Carver, "The package is wrapped and ready for delivery."

"Roger that. Hold on for a minute. I get the feeling that those two guests are going to start checking all exits in a few minutes. They have to be sure our boy doesn't sneak out the back door to meet someone."

As expected, a few minutes later, Carver saw the FBI agents' car slowly pull around the back of the hotel. They paused for a short while and then continued around the building. After watching the car pull away, Carver said into his mike, "Ok, all clear. I'm just outside the west exit door, but you'd better hurry. I don't know when these guys are going to come around again.

"Be there in two minutes," replied Hank.

Lisa peeked out the room's door to make sure the halls were clear. Then Hank and Dan each supported a side of al-Sadir and half-carried him out of the room. They quickly headed down the hall, much like friends helping a drunken buddy to his car. Dan said, "I'm glad we were on the first floor. I'd hate to have to carry his fat ass down a flight of stairs."

Once out of the hotel, they unceremoniously threw the mullah into the back of their grey van. They then proceeded south on I-75 on a twenty-two mile drive to the small Grosse Ile Municipal Airport, a community airfield situated on an island in the middle of the Detroit River. It provided the necessary privacy for the Delphi Team; no TSA inspections and no Homeland Security issues. Winston Hamilton's private Citation jet was waiting and took off immediately after the team loaded its cargo.

CHAPTER FORTY-TWO

A black Lincoln Town Car pulled up to the curb in front of the large grey concrete structure at 935 Pennsylvania Ave. It was less than a mile away from the White House. As Graham Maultry exited the vehicle, he told his driver, "This'll take about an hour. I'll have your boss call you when I'm ready to return to the airport."

He entered through the glass doors of the main entrance at the J. Edgar Hoover FBI Building and was immediately met in the lobby by Director Stephenson's assistant. After a ride up the elevator to the seventh floor, he was escorted to a conference room that overlooked the traffic on 10th Street. He stood next to one of four tan leather chairs which were arranged neatly around a circular coffee table. On top of the table were several bottles of Evian water and copies of the Wall Street Journal. An imposing FBI plaque dominated one wall and was flanked on the right by an American Flag and on the left by the official banner of the Bureau.

A minute later, the director entered the room. He extended his hand and said, "Dr. Maultry, I'm Lewis Stevenson. It's a pleasure to finally meet you in person. Please, take a seat."

Each man took a chair on opposite sides of the table. "I certainly appreciate your taking the time to fly to Washington to brief me on what's happened. I know you and your family have been through a harrowing experience over the past several months. How're they doing?"

"Thank you for asking. They're all doing quite well, all things considered. My daughter is finishing rehab for the gunshot wound to her leg and Julia is recovering well from the surgery to repair her facial injuries. The family turned out to be much more resilient than I thought. However, we're all still dealing with the emotional trauma of the brutal murder of their two friends, Tucker and Jessica. I'm afraid those wounds will never completely heal."

"That was a tragic and unnecessary loss of life," responded Stevenson. "The men who kidnapped you and your family were ruthless savages. You and your family demonstrated a remarkable amount of courage during your escape. I can't begin to imagine what it must have been like, but you've provided a heroic service to the country. We now have a valuable lead regarding a major terror attack on our soil. I've read the reports submitted by our agents in Ft. Lauderdale but I wanted to hear your story in person."

Graham Maultry spent the next forty-five minutes relating the details of his family's capture and imprisonment. He told them about the drone designs, the existence of the EMP generator, and the captors.

Director Stevenson said, "I understand you were able to identify several of the kidnappers from our computer files of known terrorists."

"That's true. Two of them are dead. We killed them during our escape. Mossaq Hashimi is the one who assaulted Jessica Vehr and my wife. The other one was the boat captain who shot down Tucker Thornton. There are several others who I couldn't identify from your files. To the best of my knowledge, one of the ringleaders, Ahmad Haq Rasid, is still alive."

"We didn't find his body at the mansion, so you're probably right. You and your family are fortunate. We already have a large file on him. He's a very dangerous and sadistic man. He's been identified as the leader of a group that massacred thirty-seven young girls at the Christian Academy School in Lebanon ten years ago. A dozen of the older girls were repeatedly raped before being beheaded."

"That's horrible. I wish we could have shot him also." After a few seconds, Graham asked, "Did you check into the ownership of the mansion?"

"Yes, we have, Dr. Maultry. It was actually under a three year lease to a company which has a chain of so many European subsidiaries that it's going to take months to untangle it, but we will eventually. Interestingly enough, the lease expires at the end of February. That's just several months from now, which tells us that whatever is planned, it's going to happen soon."

"Unfortunately, they never gave me an indication of when or where an attack might occur."

"What're your conclusions about this drone they wanted you to design, doctor?"

"Well, they're obviously planning some attack by air but I have no idea where the target might be located. The group's organization is sophisticated and has certainly done its homework. They were aware of highly confidential work that my company has been conducting using new ultra-light components for stealth aircraft construction. Obtaining that information had to be very expensive; which tells me that they're well-funded and highly connected. The fact that they insisted on the use of graphene materials for construction means that they want to maximize the payload capacity and enhance the stealth characteristics of the plane. They planned upon a forty-five pound cargo capacity, which is a pretty substantial load. However, I designed the drone so that it would carry no more than thirty-five with the expectation that it will crash if they try to fly it. I'm hoping their weapons system has a fixed weight and that they'll be unable to make necessary adjustments. I could be wrong because I couldn't determine the exact nature of the weapon to be used."

Maultry continued, "It's important to note that the design specifications also called for collapsible wings with a maximum wing span of eight feet and fuselage length less than forty-eight inches. I assume the feature was needed for the purpose of concealing the craft inside a box or duffle bag. That suggests that they plan to transport the drone close to the attack site. They're going to have to use remote controlled navigation which would have some inherent range limitations and a line-of-sight navigation restriction. They can't rely on GPS guidance systems because it would make their activities traceable by Homeland Security."

"What about the actual construction of the plane?" asked Stevenson.

"That would take some degree of sophistication. They couldn't just build one in a garage somewhere. A manufacturing facility would be necessary. They'd also need a supply of graphene although they seemed to have no shortage of it at the mansion. You might want to check on recent purchases of the material. There are only a dozen or so suppliers worldwide."

"What about that electromagnetic pulse generator you described? We couldn't find it at the mansion so I must assume they took the device with them. Could that be used as a potential weapon?" asked Stevenson.

"In theory, yes it could. It essentially has the ability to neutralize any device which depends upon electrical current including: computers, radios, televisions, and vehicles. It can paralyze anything within its range, potentially shutting down an entire city if powerful enough."

"What about someone who relies on a pacemaker?"

"It would stop working, and the individual's heart might stop. Obviously, the effects would be catastrophic for that person; but from my experience, this particular machine only has a range of about one hundred-fifty feet."

"So it would have to be delivered close to the target to work," opined the director.

"Exactly," responded Graham.

"What if you can deliver it close to someone by using a drone?"

"Anyone specific?" asked Maultry.

"President-elect Wagner has had one for over twenty years," replied Stevenson. "He's needed it ever since a bullet fragment lodged in the wall of his heart."

"Was that when he won the Medal of Honor?" asked Maultry.

"That's it," responded Stevenson nervously.

Maultry replied, "I'm not a medical doctor but I guess it could be fatal in that circumstance. However, I'm not so sure the terrorists are planning to use the EMP generator as their major weapon. Even after my design adjustments, the drone could probably handle the weight of the one that I used in the mansion. However, the device would actually shut down the plane's electric motor and navigation controls. So I don't think it's their primary weapon; but like I said earlier, I could be wrong. From my discussions with their ringleader, I got the impression that the drone would be used to carry some type of explosive device.

Stevenson then asked, "Could this drone be used to fly explosives over and down into a large stadium?"

"Absolutely it could. It still has the capacity to carry around thirty-five pounds of cargo which is a lot of explosive material. Are you thinking about a large sporting event like…the Super Bowl?"

"That's exactly I'm worried about. Not only that, the word around Washington is that President-elect Wagner is planning on attending," replied Director Stevenson.

"Of course!" exclaimed Graham. "That might very well be it. You couldn't get explosives past the tight security that'll surround NRG Stadium...but you could fly a drone over the top...right into Wagner's lap. The controller could be a mile or more away if he's in the right location. Fortunately, the radar issue might not be a problem. I was able to alter the design of the plane enough so that some of its stealth properties have been eliminated. It almost cost my wife her life."

Director Stevenson interjected, "We certainly appreciate that effort, doctor, but unfortunately, even if it does show up on radar, it'll probably be too late to do anything. We simply must find them before they can launch an attack."

The Director thought for a second and asked, "Is there anything else that might be helpful, doctor?"

"One more thing. The ringleader, the man who captured my boat..."

Stevenson paged through the report, "Ahmad Haq Rasid, the one who got away?" asked the director.

"Correct, he's the one who killed my children's friends and ordered the beating of my wife. My family used to call him the vampire man."

"Vampire man?"

"Yes, because he had two chipped front teeth that made it look like he had fangs. Anyway, during my last conversation with him, he mentioned the name of the man that I initially met when taken to the mansion...the man who I believe is ultimately in charge. I figured Ahmad knew they were going to kill us anyway, so he let the name slip. It was Scorpion."

"I'm familiar with that name. It's come up before," responded Stevenson.

"Who is he?" asked Maultry.

"That, we don't know yet, but we will. Stevenson looked at his watch. "It's getting late and I know that you'd like to fly back home to see your family soon, Dr. Maultry. You've been an incredible help. If you happen to think of anything else, please call the number listed on my card. It's a direct line to my office."

After Graham Maultry left, the Director sat in front of his computer to again access their database. He wanted to double check. As he typed, he said to himself, "There must be something in our files on this Scorpion character. He's got to be one of the world's major terror organization leaders." After an hour of searching, he found nothing there...absolutely nothing.

He called out to one of his assistants, "I need to divert more manpower to the Houston area. Make the calls."

CHAPTER FORTY-THREE

With his warrants in hand, Agent Tim Hogan arrived at the Dearborn Al-Fateh mosque. A frightened housekeeper answered the door, and after a several seconds of discussion, Hogan's face turned bright red. He yelled out to his men to fan out and thoroughly search the premises. He immediately called his two agents who had been tailing al-Sadir last night.

"Where is he?" Hogan asked.

"He's still here. He never left the hotel. She must have been a good one. I bet he won't be able to walk for a week after a night like that," the agent laughed.

Hogan saw no humor in the comment. "That's just hilarious. Go get him, right now! Arrest him and call me as soon as he's in custody!"

He renewed his conversation with the housekeeper and she cried, "Honest, I haven't seen Mr. Rabbani since yesterday morning. Is he in some sort of trouble?"

"Have you ever heard the name, Muhammad bin Hussein?" asked Hogan.

"No, I've never heard that name. Who is he?" Hogan explained and after a second, the seriousness of her situation began to sink in. "Am I in trouble?"

"That all depends upon whether or not you're being honest with me. What about Curtis Johnson?"

"The small black man? I haven't seen him in over a month. They told me he packed up his belongings and left. Is he in trouble? He's such a nice person."

Hogan's cell phone rang. It was the agent at the Dearborn Inn. "Tell me you have him in cuffs."

"Uh, actually sir, we haven't been able to find him."

"What!" yelled Hogan.

"I checked with the manager and he could find no indication that al-Sadir ever registered. I checked the registry myself and no woman had rented a room, certainly not a call girl. The manager was indignant at the implication that he would allow prostitutes to use his establishment; said he manages a high-end respectable hotel that doesn't cater to that type of activity."

"I don't care what the guy thinks, shut the place down, and I mean now! Al-Sadir went there for something last night and it sure wasn't to meet a hooker. I want to know what it was. He might have been tipped off and could be on the run."

"We kept an eye on all the exits, sir. I don't see how he could have left. His car is still here, and…"

"You're not hearing me agent. I don't care if his car is there or not! I don't need to arrest the damn car. I want him! Check the hotel registry again and track down everyone who was there last night. Talk to every patron and employee to find out if they saw anything suspicious. Review any surveillance camera footage to see if a car picked him up. Now turn that damn hotel upside down if you need to! Tell the manager that you're from Homeland Security and that you suspect a terror organization has been using his place as a base of operations. That should scare him enough to co-operate. Get back to me within the hour and you'd better have some good news for me or your next assignment is going to be in Fargo, North Dakota; that's if you're lucky enough to still have a job!'"

Hogan had his agents round up everyone in the mosque, but after several hours of intensive questioning, none of them appeared to be aware of anything untoward going on. It looked like a half-dozen men who might have been guards already took off when the mullah failed to return last night.

After searching al-Sadir's office, Hogan found two computers. He spoke to one of his agents and said, "Get the tech guys down here in a hurry. I want them to go over both of these computers and I want them to find something good for me!" He walked downstairs and found the apartment that Curtis and Reggie had shared. It was just as Reggie had described, but it had been cleared of all personal belongings. Hogan concluded that Curtis Johnson was probably dead; too much of a liability.

An hour later, Hogan's phone again rang. It was the agent from the hotel. "You'd better have some good news for me!"

"Sorry sir, we can't find him anywhere. There was someone checked into room one twenty-seven, but it was a middle-aged man and he appears to have left during the night without checking out. The registration was a fake name. They made a copy of the man's driver's license and that also was a fake. I spoke to a man in room 125 next door and he said that he heard a brief scream at around ten."

"What about surveillance cameras?" asked Hogan.

"We're checking those but there's a problem. The one covering the west exit was damaged so we can't get anything from it."

"That's just terrific. What you're telling me is that you two idiots lost him. Someone kidnapped the mullah from right under your nose and maybe they even killed him. Well, cordon off the room and get a forensics team over there to dust for prints and check for trace evidence. Maybe the kidnappers left something behind. Do the same to his car, which you so adroitly noticed, was still sitting in the parking lot.

⊷ ⊶

Hogan ended the call and then dialed up John Crawford's number in Cincinnati. "John, I have some bad news. We can't find either Muhammad or al-Sadir."

"What! What in the hell happened, Tim? I thought your guys had tight surveillance on them!"

"The housekeeper said that Muhammad has been gone since yesterday and she hasn't seen the mullah since last night. It looked like he was slipping out again to see a hooker at a local hotel. I had two agents on him but they lost contact. I think he was either kidnapped or he just skipped town. That doesn't make sense though because our tech boys tell me that he was logged onto his computer this morning."

"Someone else must have been using it with his password, just to provide cover while he ran," said Crawford. "We just missed them both and now we have no clue as to where either one went. Someone at the mosque must know something. One of them had to be on his computer earlier. Put the squeeze on them. Also, call Detroit PD and the Michigan State Police. Tell them to put out an APB on the mullah's car."

"Al-Sadir's car is still in the hotel parking lot, John. We checked with the hotel manager to see if they have any video surveillance coverage. They do but one of their cameras was intentionally disabled. We're checking to see if a transfer vehicle can be identified on any of the other parking lot cameras. Maybe we can get a plate. By the way, one of the hotel guests heard a scream last night and that's why I think al-Sadir might have been kidnapped."

"Why would someone want to kidnap him? It doesn't make sense. I think someone was helping him escape. Either way, ask the mosque's housekeeper if she knows about any other vehicles that might be registered to al-Sadir. If there are, you can get license plates from the registrations. Homeland Security has plate recognition cameras in every major city in the country. Maybe we can track him down that way. Also, see what you can find out about that HVAC van that was there yesterday. Maybe Muhammad snuck out in it. If I had to guess, he's driving out there somewhere with that Canadian package in the back of a truck, and we have no idea where he went. We're all screwed here and it's going to take a miracle to fix this mess and save our careers."

Hogan offered, "On the positive side, we've retrieved a lot of documents from al-Sadir's office and we're going through those now. We also have two computers and I have our tech guys looking to see if we can find something useful."

"Like I said, we're going to need a miracle and I don't think it's going to come from his computers. However, keep at it and see what you can dig up. Meanwhile, I have the unpleasant task of reporting this fiasco to the director."

CHAPTER FORTY-FOUR

He was known by his brethren as "The Bomb Maker." At the age of 37, he already had an extensive CIA dossier under his full name, Tarriz bin Muhktar. He was born in the Republic of Yemen where he received his degree in chemical engineering at the Yemeni University of Science & Technology. During his senior year, he was recruited by al-Qaeda and was sent to study with their foremost explosive experts. His roadside bombs have been responsible for the death or maiming of several hundred US servicemen. He's credited with being the mastermind behind the Moroccan nightclub bombing and the attacks on two trains in Madrid. After his apprehension in Iraq, he was incarcerated at the Guantanamo Bay facility, but was released in 2013 as part of a prisoner exchange program. Now, he's returned to the work that he does best. Allah has chosen him to design and build his most dangerous weapons system yet: the weapon for the Great Attack.

After completing the overnight seven-hour drive from Cincinnati, he was getting close to his destination. Even though he used the Google Maps feature on his cell phone, it still took him another hour. Eventually he found the gravel drive. It was marked with a tilted rusty mailbox that was standing guard at the far corner. On its top sat a name plaque that read "Yolder".

Finally, no-one will ever think of looking for us here, thought Tarriz. He pulled into the long drive which wound its way up a gentle slope and through a large grove of pine trees. After several hundred yards, the property opened up into a one thousand acre farm surrounded on all sides by thick woods and rolling hills. The Scorpion had purchased the property a year ago from the estate of an elderly farmer whose name was Jeremiah Yolder.

In the middle of the land sat a two story farm house with wooden plank siding, scarred by years of neglect. To the north, east, and west were hundreds of acres of farmland, now overgrown with weeds. A huge three-story barn sat a hundred feet to the right of the house and it was undeniably the most respectable structure on the property.

Tarriz exited his truck and stretched. He was a small man, less than five-feet-five inches tall and maybe one hundred thirty pounds on a good day. He looked in all directions. The surrounding land provided plenty of privacy and open space for practice. As instructed, he looked under a metal milk-can vase on the front porch, and found the house key. He opened the front door and was hit by a strong musty smell resulting from years of the house being closed up. It was sparsely furnished, but by Yemeni standards it was a mansion and would be more than adequate for their purposes. Searching through the house, he found a set of stairs and climbed up two flights until he reached the attic. Tucked away in one corner, sat a suitcase that had been hidden several weeks earlier by a member of the local cell. It was already covered in dust and cobwebs. After cleaning it off, Tarriz carried the case down to the kitchen and placed it atop a wooden dining table.

He opened the lid and, as promised, inside was a manila envelope which he emptied onto the table. Out fell a large wad of fifty dollar bills, five thousand dollars in all, for equipment and living expenses. Next to the cash was a set of pickup truck keys which he put in his jeans pocket.

Tarriz walked outside into the cool December afternoon and proceeded toward the barn. Its large double doors were secured with a long piece of chain and a padlock. He fished into his pocket and withdrew the truck keys which he had found minutes earlier. On the key ring was a small key for the lock. He opened it and pulled the doors apart. The entire back wall of the barn was occupied by a long work bench where the final assembly would occur. After rummaging through the drawers, he found a few of the tools he'd require, but he'd still have to get some things from the local hardware store.

In front of the bench was parked a red Chevy pick-up truck. He inserted the key into the ignition and turned it. The engine immediately came to life. "Praise Allah, it works!" he said to himself and he backed the truck out of the barn onto the gravel drive. When finished, he pulled his own truck containing the Canadian package inside.

His first priority would be to get rid of the body of the old man whom Muhammad shot at Microavionics. He opened the rear cargo door and gazed at the large Canadian container, still covered with dried blood, brain, and pieces of skull. The old man's body was disposed of in a shallow grave a hundred feet behind the barn. When finished, the doors were again locked shut. Tarriz checked his surroundings to be sure that no-one had seen him thus far. All was quiet. He got behind the wheel of the red pickup truck and headed out to the nearest grocery store, which was seven miles away. One month's provisions for three men were purchased. On the way back, a stop was made at a Home Depot store to pick up some overhead fluorescent lights, a drill, a scale, and some other tools he would need.

Tarriz returned to the farm and climbed into one of the beds. He hadn't slept in over thirty-six hours. There wasn't much to do but wait for the arrival of Ahmad Haq Rasid from Florida and Muhammad bin Hussein from the Microavionics warehouse in Cincinnati. Then the final preparations would be made.

CHAPTER FORTY-FIVE

When he first came to about twenty-four hours ago, Mullah al-Sadir found himself strapped to a chair in the middle of a stainless steel-lined room. It looked like a laboratory of some type. He couldn't be sure of the amount of time that had elapsed since his kidnapping because there were no windows and the lights were kept on continuously. A huge man, wearing a hood, would bring in a bottle of water or food from time to time, but he never spoke. Twice, his restraints were released and he was allowed to use a toilet in the corner. The last time the hooded man entered, he didn't leave. He remained standing right behind the mullah. He was so close that al-Sadir could feel the man's breath on the back of his neck. As the mullah searched the room, he noticed a camera mounted on opposite corners of the ceiling. *They're watching me* he thought but there was nothing he could do; so he sat and waited… and waited. He couldn't imagine who had taken him and he was frightened beyond comprehension.

⇒⊹ ⊹⇐

The members of the Delphi Team were seated around several television monitors displaying the image of Mullah Muqtoda al-Sadir locked in the underground vault.

"He looks very nervous," observed Lisa.

"He should be," replied Norman. "I would be too if a giant like Hank were standing behind me breathing like a dragon." The group chuckled.

"I think he's just about ready to talk. He just needs another several hours to worry about his predicament," said Carver. "Let's take a break and get something to eat. Tell Hank that he can leave the room for a while. After we get back, you'll be on Norman. Are you ready?"

"Yeah, I've been practicing my grandmother's accent all day and I'm good to go," replied the Geek.

After what seemed like an eternity, but was only a few hours, the enormous hooded man again entered the room and stood directly behind al-Sadir. This time he wasn't carrying water or a food tray. The mullah could hear the man breathing heavily, almost growling. Then, without any warning, he smacked al-Sadir along the right side of his head, nearly knocking him out of the metal chair. Afterwards, he again just stood there, arms crossed and breathing. The mullah was terrified. Within another minute, he was hit again. Al-Sadir screamed out, "Why are you doing this? Who are you?"

"Are you ready to speak to us?" a calm voice asked over the overhead speaker.

"Who are you and what's this about?" the cleric demanded, which resulted in another blow to the head.

"We will ask the questions and you will answer truthfully. Do you understand?" Al-Sadir noticed that the man asking the questions spoke English but had a distinct accent... *Israeli perhaps?*

"Yes…yes I'll talk! Just stop hitting me!" answered al-Sadir.

Norman Deets began with questions to which they already knew the answers. This was a technique used to get the subject into a rhythm of answering truthfully. It established a flow of conversation.

"What is your name?"

"Mullah Muqtoda al-Sadir."

"And you are a mullah at which mosque?"

"Al-Fateh in Dearborn, Michigan. Where am I now?"

He was hit again and this time he fell over sideways onto the concrete floor, still strapped to the chair. The large man picked him back up.

"We will ask the questions. You are to answer the questions. Do you understand? I won't say it again."

"Yes."

"Where were you born?"

"Medina, Saudi Arabia."

"How long have you been in the United States?"

"About thirty years. My father was a Saudi but my mother is an American. She brought me here to visit her family when I was ten. We never returned."

"Are you a U.S. citizen?"

"I have dual citizenship: U.S. and Saudi."

"How long have you been stealing money from your mosque?"

"I haven't…" He stopped himself and winced, expecting another punishing blow to the head. "For about seven years."

"Good. We're making some progress here."

"Are you familiar with a man named Reginald Patterson?"

The mullah shuddered in fear for he knew where this would be going. "I don't know anyone named Patterson," he lied. Immediately he was hit so hard that the blow almost knocked him out. Blood trickled from his nose.

"It will be best for you if you stop lying to us. We already know the correct answers to most of our questions, so we will know if you are not being truthful. If you try to deceive us, there will be a heavy price to pay. Now, just so you are aware of what might be in store for you if you fail to cooperate, I'm going to show you what happens to those who try to lie to us."

With that, the large hooded man dragged a metal table across the floor to the front of al-Sadir. The scraping noise achieved its purpose. It was unnerving, like nails scraping across a black board. The man then threw several pictures onto the table top. The mullah became nauseated and thought his heart might stop. There, in front of him were pictures of Professor Jazeer Farouk. Just like himself, Jazeer was restrained in a metal chair, but he had a bullet hole through his right eye and blood over his cheek. That was all it took to loosen the mullah's tongue. He freely talked about his knowledge of activities surrounding Professor Farouk and the cells he headed along the west coast; but he claimed that he didn't know the identity of any other leaders across the country. There were many sleeper-cells, probably hundreds but he didn't know any specifics about all of the members. He confessed that he had been pressured into arranging over three dozen bank and jewelry store robberies over the past several years. The money was used to finance some of the cells' activities.

"And you put over half of that money into your own personal accounts, didn't you?" asked the voice.

Al-Sadir lowered his head and said "Yes." He claimed that a man named Muhammad Rabbani was the actual mastermind of the activities, but he didn't know the man's whereabouts at this time. When asked about Curtis Johnson, the team was told that Muhammad had killed the man and disposed of his body, but the mullah didn't know where. The team suspected he was lying about the extent of his own involvement in the robberies and the killing of Curtis, but they didn't care about that. They had more important matters to pursue. His information thus far simply confirmed much of what they already knew. The next sets of questions were the important ones.

The voice then asked, "Who is the Scorpion?" The color drained from al-Sadir's face and he again lowered his head. His mind raced, *How do they know about him? I can't deny my association with the man or I'll get a bullet in the eye, just like Farouk. If I talk, the Scorpion will slit my throat. I can't win.* "I know of him. He has a reputation as being a ruthless man, one to whom you never say no. I've never met him in person. If I ever do, he'll probably kill me."

"Is he the one who gives the orders and provides financing?"

"Yes."

"Where did he first contact you?"

"He called the mosque several years ago and asked to speak to me. When he gave me his name, I recognized it immediately. He's well known within certain groups in the Middle East."

"Terror organizations like Hamas and ISIS?"

"Yes, and the Muslim Brotherhood, Hezbollah, al-Qaeda, all of them; but his true identity is known by only a few people. He's highly respected and feared. When he called, he told me what he wanted me to do and promised that there would be a handsome reward if I complied. I knew that if I refused, he would have had me killed. He's the one who put me in contact with Muhammad Rabbani."

"Hussein," said the voice with the Israeli accent.

"I don't understand."

"Rabbani was an alias. His true name is Colonel Muhammad bin Hussein and he's from Iran. He's probably responsible for over a thousand brutal killings in his own country alone. We believe he's within the Scorpion's inner circle and probably reports directly to him. We suspect that one of his responsibilities was to keep an eye on you. You alone aren't intelligent enough to put all of this together. If you worked closely with Muhammad, you're lucky to still be alive."

Al-Sadir shuddered.

"Was all communication through you or Muhammad?"

"Me...that is, I thought it was me; from what you say, it might have been Muhammad. After that first call, all of our communication was by cell phones which we changed every month." That information confirmed what Lisa had already figured out about the letter codes on each of Farouk's cell phones.

Carver reached over and turned off the microphone. "I want to think about my next set of questions."

⊷⊶

Deets asked, "How was my accent, Carver? It was the best that I could do from what I remember of my conversations with my grandmother."

Carver stared at the television monitors again. After thinking for a minute, he turned to his tech expert, "Your accent was great Norman. I don't think this guy could tell the difference between a real Israeli accent and a fake one anyway. Do you think that you could use some Hebrew and mix in the word 'Mossad' a few times? I want you to do it in such a way that he believes that it's an accident. Maybe leave the microphone on and pretend you're having a discussion with associates."

"Mossad?"

"Yes, it's the national intelligence agency for Israel, like our CIA."

"Aren't they the guys who assassinated the terrorists who kidnapped and slaughtered members of the Israeli Olympic team?"

"Yes. It was in Munich in 1972. It took years, but they pursued every one of the killers and assassinated them. They're incredibly efficient and lethal. Anyway, I want al-Sadir to believe that he's been kidnapped by the Mossad. I have an idea. Turn the mike back on."

⊷⊶

"What about the package delivery from Canada?" the voice asked. The question caught al-Sadir off guard. Again the color drained

226

from his face, and he started to tremble. He knew that any answer to this question could very well get him killed but he had no good options. *Lie and I'll get a bullet like Farouk. Tell the truth and I'll probably get a bullet anyway.*

"The Scorpion is planning what he calls the Great Attack on your country. The package is related to that. My job was to arrange for the hijacking of the contents of a truck carrying its cargo through central Canada. Muhammad did so and is now delivering it somewhere, but I have no idea where."

"The Great Attack?"

"Yes, that's what the Scorpion calls it. It is to be just the opening salvo, but it will be so devastating that the entire world will take notice. Then, within days, there will be hundreds of smaller regional attacks that will cripple the country."

"Where and when is this attack to occur?"

"I don't know. I was never told much about it. Like I said, my only responsibility was to get the package."

"And what was the Canadian cargo?" the voice asked impatiently.

"Spent fuel rods from the Darlington Nuclear Power plant. They were being transferred to a dry storage facility in Ontario. We were able to substitute an identical replacement canister so the Canadians never realized what had happened."

Now it was the entire team's turn to be shocked. They stood silent for a minute digesting the ramifications of what al-Sadir just said. They didn't anticipate this.

"Are you telling me that you arranged to have a large amount of nuclear material smuggled into this country and now you have no idea where it is?"

"Yes...I'm sorry," cried the mullah.

"Do you know how it is to be used or where the ultimate target of this so-called Great Attack is?"

"Like I said, I was never told anything about any of that. My only job was to procure the nuclear fuel rods and that was it."

"I want the names of your contacts inside the Darlington Nuclear Power facility."

"There were two men. One gave us the information about the date and logistics of the transfer operation. He provided specifications and photographs of the storage casks so that we could make a dummy replacement. I don't know his name. He was recruited by the other man who was the actual driver of one of the trucks transporting the material. The driver's name was Patrick McKeown and I'm afraid that he is dead. He was killed by Muhammad on the night of the hijacking. Unfortunately, he was the only one who knew the identity of the inside man."

"What do you know about the incidents at Stanford, Chicago, and the Alamo?"

Al-Sadir almost laughed and said, "You mean the ones that your press still calls "The Lone Wolf" attacks. The Scorpion has a supposed lone wolf ready to strike targets in every major city in the US. You have no idea what you're up against. We have a hundred different sleeper-cells with a thousand men across the country. His organization has infiltrated most major corporations and recreational areas in the U. S. He even has affiliates in command positions in the military. They're all simply waiting for the triggering event."

"Which is the so-called Great Attack?"

"Yes."

Carver again reached over to turn off the microphone.

―――

Dan spoke first. "Hank, you're the nuclear physics man. What do you think of this? What are those fuel rods all about?

Hank thought for a second and replied, "Canada is heavily invested in nuclear power. From what I've read, they have over a dozen nuclear reactors, most of which are located in the Ontario

Provence just north of the U.S. border. They use Candu 6 reactors which utilize Uranium 235 as their nuclear fuel. The controlled nuclear reaction generates heat which is converted to steam that turns the electric turbines. After about eighteen months, the uranium loses enough of its radioactivity that it can no longer produce energy efficiently. The U-235 pellets in the fuel rods are referred to as "spent" but that's a misnomer. They're anything but fully spent. The uranium is still dangerously radioactive and short-term exposure within a distance of only one yard can result in incapacitation or death within days. Therefore, safe storage of the material is mandatory.

It looks like the Canadians were in the process of transferring a number of fuel rods to an off-site facility for long term storage. I've read that they're facing a huge problem in trying to store all of it safely. Reports show that there are over forty-thousand metric tons of the stuff and the only way to deal with that amount is to secure it in underground bunkers. They must have had a caravan of trucks transporting the rods when they were hijacked. Muhammad was smart though. By making a dummy cask, the Canadians never realized that they were missing an entire container of nuclear material."

"Can they make a nuclear bomb out of it?" asked Lisa.

"No. They wouldn't be able to sustain a fissionable reaction. However, when combined with standard explosives, it can still be an extremely lethal weapon."

"A dirty bomb," said Carver.

"Precisely. It's something the feds have worried about for a long time," replied Hank.

"We need to get this uranium info to Winston Hamilton right away," said Dan. "He needs to feed it to the FBI!"

Carver stared at al-Sadir on the television monitors for several seconds. "You're right Hank, but I have an idea about how to release him."

No way, Carver! Get in there right now and slit this guy's throat, ear to ear. He deserves it, yelled the demon.

"Release him? I thought that you were planning on killing the son-of-a-bitch," said Dan. "I volunteer for the job."

"Sorry Dan, I would actually enjoy doing just that myself. But Winston Hamilton is going to need a way to leak all of this information to the FBI without them knowing who we are. Using al-Sadir in that capacity might take care of the problem. Besides, I owe a favor to a friend. We probably damaged his career when we kidnapped al-Sadir, and I need to try to salvage it for him," he replied as he looked at Lisa.

"There's just one more thing I want to do before we drug him and send him north."

Carver explained to the team what he wanted to do. The Israeli voice returned over the loudspeaker, "At this point, we are finished with our questions. Where we go from here depends upon you." The giant behind him grabbed the mullah and pulled his head back. Another hooded man entered the room and withdrew a military knife as he approached al-Sadir.

Now you're talking, buddy. Like I said before, make the fat bastard pay!

After the screams stopped, the restraints were cut and the two hooded men left the room.

CHAPTER FORTY-SIX

John Crawford hung up his office phone. He had just received another anonymous tip, and this time, it was an electronically disguised voice. "Who are these people?" he asked himself. "Whoever they are, they're pros," he added. He called a junior agent into his office and told him to trace the source of the call. He wasn't optimistic though.

He contacted Captain Joseph Watters of the Cincinnati Police Department. The two men had worked together previously on several high-profile cases.

"Hello John, it's good to hear from you. We haven't talked since you solved that serial rapist case several years ago. What can I do for you?" asked Captain Waters.

"Well, I need your help on something urgent, Joe."

"Sure thing John, what're you up to this time?"

"I'm going to need some backup right away. Could you send a couple of squad cars to 4013 Eastern Drive? I need to block the street in both directions. Tell them it's a code 3."

"Eastern Drive? I know that area well. We've busted up a couple of crack houses down there. It's a rough neighborhood. I'm not sure what's going on, but you always seem to get into some real badass shit, John; just like when you were shot in that Chicago alley last year. Knowing you, I think I'd better send an entire SWAT team. Do we need to break down some doors?"

"No, just the backup. It would help if you could send your bomb squad too. I'm a little concerned that this could be a set-up and the place might be booby-trapped."

"Bomb squad? OK John, exactly what's going on? I need to let my men know what they're going to be up against." Crawford gave him a brief summary about a terror cell working the area.

"Damn, John! That really is some bad-ass shit."

"I'm afraid something deadly is being planned somewhere and I need to find out exactly what's going on."

"I'm on it, John. I'll have everyone there within the hour and I'll emphasize the code 3 status, no lights or sirens."

"And Joe, I'm sure that I don't have to tell you that absolute confidentiality on this issue is mandatory."

"You just did. Don't worry, I'll keep a tight lid on this thing."

Crawford parked on the street, a hundred feet south of the old two-story home. As he waited for his backup, he checked the surroundings and saw no activity around the place. It was eerily quiet. No-one entered or left the building. Once the SWAT team arrived, they placed blockades along both ends of the street and a third group was sent to cover the alley behind the house. After he received the sign that everyone was in position, he cautiously walked up the porch steps and approached the front door with a member of the bomb squad on either side of him. They checked all around the door and front window frames. The leader said, "No trip wires.

Let me have the drill." He drilled a small hole through the front door and inserted a fiber optic telescope. "I don't see any detonation devices. Get the sniffer." They used the nitrate detection meter to sample the air and could find no residual traces of explosive materials.

"All clear, Agent Crawford. It should be safe to enter but stay behind us."

The SWAT team knocked down the front door and everyone stood aside for several seconds. When nothing happened, they entered cautiously in a low crouch behind mobile anti-blast shields. Crawford was right behind them.

When he stood up, he gasped. There, in the middle of the living room, was the elusive Mullah Muqtoda al-Sadir. He was naked, blindfolded, and his mouth was gagged. He was secured to a rusty old metal kitchen chair with layer upon layer of duct tape. What caught Crawford's attention the most was the Star of David that had been carved into the man's forehead.

He was so shocked by the scene that he initially didn't notice the audio tape that had been secured to the man's chest with the same duct tape. He waited for the SWAT team to clear the rest of the house and for the bomb squad to tell him that al-Sadir himself was not booby-trapped. After he was given a thumbs-up, Crawford removed the gag from al-Sadir's mouth. Frantically, the man said over and over, "Need to talk to Special Agent John Crawford."

He wrapped a blanket around his prisoner and took him into custody. After providing some clothes, he placed the cleric in an interrogation room. He had one of the junior agents start with some preliminary questions while Crawford listened to the tape. At the conclusion, his only words were, "Holy shit!"

He immediately placed a call to Agent Tim Hogan in Detroit. "Tim, do you remember when I said we'd need a miracle to save our jobs?"

"How could I forget? I figured it was the last day of my career. Why, what's up?"

"I think our miracle just landed in my lap. I found al-Sadir!" He proceeded to relate a summary of what he had heard on the audio tape.

"Holy shit," responded Hogan.

"That's exactly what I said when I listened to it. I need you to get a team back to the Al-Fateh mosque and that off-site garage they were using to hide the package. Check for the presence of any residual radiation levels. Be sure you do it discretely. We don't want to incite a wave of panic around the country. We need to keep this information under wraps until we know more about exactly what's going on. If what the mullah said is true, the rods are sealed in radiation proof cylinders. However, we don't know whether or not that wacko Muhammad bin Hussein has opened the cask and removed any of the rods."

"If he did, he won't be alive for very long. Even though those rods are considered to be spent nuclear fuel, they're still very lethal. I'll make sure we do the radiation checks quietly. I'll get a truck from DTE energy and tell anyone who asks that we're checking on a gas leak."

"Good idea, Tim. I'm going to question the mullah further to see if I can confirm what's on the tape."

"By the way, John, I have some good news of my own. The tech boys finished going over al-Sadir's two computers. There was nothing on them relating to the ultimate site of the attack. However, we did find some recurrent correspondence with someone from the Middle East. We don't have a specific name on him yet because the emails were run through a series of encrypted servers from around Europe and the Middle East. From the content of the letters, the guy sounds very wealthy and very connected. I think he might be the one who is ultimately bankrolling this entire thing."

"Thanks Tim. I'll ask al-Sadir about it and see if I can get a name. Maybe we can send your information to Quantico and ask them if they can backtrack to the source of the emails."

⟝⟞

After several hours of questioning, al-Sadir pretty much confirmed what he had already confessed to on the tape. When asked about the encrypted emails on his computer, he claimed they were to an old childhood friend from Saudi Arabia. He wasn't afraid to lie to the FBI. He knew they couldn't repeat the same things which he had been subjected to at the hands of the Mossad. He was a U.S, citizen and he had rights. All they could do was to put him in prison and that was going to happen anyway. He didn't talk about the prince, although he did give up a name. It was fake.

Finally Crawford asked, "You say that you were kidnapped?"

"Yes, in Dearborn."

"Where were you taken?"

"I don't know. I was unconscious. When I came to, I was strapped to a chair in the middle of a metal room."

"You certainly weren't taken by any of our people, so who were they?"

"Probably the Jews."

"What?"

"The Jews. They had Israeli accents and I overheard them talking about reporting to the Mossad." Crawford thought to himself, *Maybe that explains the Star of David carved into his forehead but it doesn't make any sense. Why would Mossad advertise the fact that they are working illegally within our borders. They do anyway, but why send this message? Are they just trying to frighten the jihadists? Why am I getting so many gifts handed to me like the anonymous tips and now al-Sadir with a taped confession? I feel like a puppet; but who's pulling the strings and why?* He'd have to figure that out later. For now, he needed to call Director Stevenson.

CHAPTER FORTY-SEVEN

Roger Logan rolled over in bed and again looked at the clock on his nightstand. It was one in the morning. He had been tossing and turning for over two hours. He just couldn't get some problems out of his head. The whole thing at Microavionics with Mr. Martin Darpoli and the drone program didn't make any sense. It had been gnawing at him ever since he first met the man. Deep down inside, he had known from the beginning that something bad was being set into motion, but he had been blinded by the promise of money. "What good is the extra cash if my two daughters have to live under the threat of some catastrophic disaster?" he said to the dark bedroom. He had ignored all of the signs but could no longer kid himself.

First, old Joe Thompson disappears and then, that Muhammad fellow shows up the next day and takes over the entire drone program. He always wondered why they would need a forty-five pound cargo capacity in a commercial drone. In addition, why the insistence on high-tech, ultra-light graphene in the construction? Yes, it increases load carrying capacity but the added manufacturing costs make its use, cost prohibitive. Finally, he could tell from the design plans that the drone possessed stealth properties. There was absolutely no need for that in a commercial environment. His inescapable conclusion was that the drone was going to be used to carry some type of weapon. "How could I have been so stupid? I should have contacted the FBI as soon as I saw the final designs and now I might be considered an accomplice. Something has to be done, and I'm the only one able to do it. I need to find out exactly what's going on," he said to himself. He made his decision.

Logan rolled out of bed and walked into the closet where he pulled on a pair of jeans and a University of Cincinnati sweatshirt. It only took him fifteen minutes to complete the drive from his condo in Montgomery, Ohio to the Microavionics building. He parked his car and was relieved to see that the employee lot was empty. The only vehicles there were three Microavionics delivery vans. He walked up to the rear door which was bathed in the yellow glow of an overhead security light. As he looked at the surveillance camera mounted above the light, he unlocked the door and walked into the dark warehouse. Feeling to the right, he flipped on some interior lights and turned left into the main offices. After sitting down in front of one of the company's computers, he turned it on and began to scan all files and recent correspondence related to the drone project.

Even after forty-five minutes of searching, he found nothing suspicious. He paused and thought for a few minutes. "There must be something," he said. All of the new employees hired by Mr. Darpoli were obviously from the Middle East. They're probably illegal, and the same goes for Muhammad," Logan said out loud. He turned his attention back to the computer, typed in the name, Muhammad Rabbani, and engaged the search button.

Roger heard the noise behind him before he actually saw the figure standing in the doorway. Logan instinctively logged off and turned around. He recognized the man and forced a smile.

What he didn't recognize was the silenced Luger in the man's right hand. "What are you doing here at this late hour Mr. Logan?" The question was rhetorical and Roger Logan had no opportunity to answer. All of his cognitive processes ceased as a hollow point twenty-two caliber bullet destroyed his brain. A second shot followed, ensuring that Roger would never speak again. "You should have just let it go, Mr. Logan," Muhammad said to the corpse. "I didn't have instructions to eliminate you."

⇒⇔⇐

Muhammad was hoping to simply disappear with the drones tonight but Logan's presence forced him to again alter his plans. He destroyed the camera security disc that had just recorded his arrival. He then proceeded to do what he had actually come to the warehouse for in the first place. He went over to the safe and dialed in the combination. Multiple one-pound bricks of C-4 explosives were withdrawn. Two of them were placed on one of the warehouse work benches. The others were loaded into a cooler which was then carried outside and placed in the back of one of the Microavionics delivery vans. After re-entering the warehouse, Muhammad checked the completed prototype drones sitting on the assembly counters. He collapsed the wing assemblies of each and loaded them into the van, next to the cooler. An identical number of remote control consoles and extra battery packs were also loaded.

Muhammad returned to the warehouse and looked around. He hadn't wanted to attract attention to the building but he was left with no other choice. There was a murder that had to be covered up and he had to destroy any evidence of what was going on here. Blasting caps were inserted into the two blocks of C-4 that he had left sitting on the workbench. To these, he connected a delayed-time detonator device and set it for twenty minutes.

In one of the storage cabinets, he found several cans of flammable glues and solvents used in the manufacturing processes. After removing one of the five-gallon containers, he proceeded to saturate the business office and Logan's body. A trail of the liquid was then poured through the entire perimeter of the warehouse and continued toward the exit. The remaining containers of the flammable liquid were stacked around the blocks of C-4. He surveyed the area one last time before leaving. The two office computers drew his attention for a second, but he decided they contained no information regarding the "Great Attack" or himself. Therefore, he didn't take the extra time to destroy the hard drives. Muhammad exited the door through which Roger Logan had entered just over an hour ago.

He looked around for potential witnesses and seeing none, lit the solvent trail. By four o'clock in the morning, Muhammad was driving in his van ten miles away, heading toward the Yoder farm. He was far enough away that he couldn't hear the explosion that ripped through the Microavionics building.

CHAPTER FORTY-EIGHT

John Crawford paced back and forth across his Cincinnati FBI office after placing a call to Washington. He had just finished his interrogation of Mullah al-Sadir and was too excited to sit. After a few minutes, Director Stevenson came on the line, "Hello John, I hope you have better news than the last time you checked in. That's when you told me you had lost al-Sadir."

Crawford cringed, "I hope so sir. First of all, I have an unusual question for you. Have you heard anything about the Mossad working in this country?"

"Israeli intelligence? I'm sure they're always working in this country just like our CIA is always working in theirs. It's all off the books, however. We have to keep a close eye on what our good friends are up to. Why are you asking about the Mossad?"

"Well sir, it has to do with Mullah Muqtoda al-Sadir. I've tracked him down."

"That's great news John! I knew that somehow you'd turn this thing around. If anybody could do it, you could."

"I've had a chance to interrogate him, and he has quite a story to tell. First of all, Dr. Maultry's analysis was correct. We don't have to worry about Wagner's pacemaker being a target anymore. The EMP generator is definitely not the weapon; at least it's not their primary weapon."

"That's great to hear," responded Stevenson.

"Probably not, sir." He proceeded to relay a detailed report about the information obtained from the mullah.

"My God, John. This is bad news, very bad news."

"Yes sir, I know. I have Tim Hogan checking around the Al-Fateh mosque and surrounding property to see if they can pick up any signs of residual radiation."

"That's good. We need to get a better handle on this thing. I'll keep shaking the bushes to see if any of our agents in Houston have come up with anything. Maybe we can do background radiation scans to localize the site of where they're hiding the stuff."

"There is another thing, sir. Agent Hogan had the tech boys in Detroit analyze the mullah's computers. They found a number of emails that were re-routed through a series of encrypted international servers. Someone was obviously trying to cover their tracks. They tracked it down to Saudi Arabia and it certainly looks like it's someone with a lot of power. Al-Sadir claims that it's just an old friend but I think that the person might just be the one who is bankrolling this whole scheme. He gave me a name which I suspect is bogus. I wanted to send everything to the lab at Quantico to see if they can pinpoint the source of the correspondence. Maybe you can expedite things, sir."

"Absolutely John, send the hard drives and I'll call the lab to give them a heads-up. It'll be top priority."

"Yes sir. I might also suggest that we contact the Canadian Nuclear Safety Commission to see if there are any irregularities in inventories at their dry storage facility. Specifically, they should check any spent-rod canisters delivered on the night of the truck crash when Mr. Patrick McKeown died. Tell them we have reason to believe that one of the canisters is a counterfeit. You might also ask them how lethal the contents of those canisters are…although I think we both know the answer."

Crawford thought for a second and then asked the important question. "Do you think they can use this uranium to make a nuclear bomb?"

"For years we've had meetings in Washington about this same issue, John, and the answer is no…at least not in the conventional sense. They mix boron carbide and gadolinium oxide with the uranium, so that critical mass cannot be achieved in nuclear fuel rods. Fortunately, without critical mass, a sustainable fissionable nuclear detonation won't occur."

"But they could use it to make a dirty bomb," offered Crawford.

"Exactly, and such a weapon could be catastrophic with a massive loss of life. I'll contact the people at the Canadian nuclear facility right now. And John?"

"Yes sir?"

"Good work as always. I'm not going to ask you further about this Mossad story. Right now, I don't care where you got your information. We need all the help that we can get on this."

"Thank you sir."

When Crawford hung up the phone, he thought about a dirty bomb exploding at the Super Bowl. He had an uneasy feeling scratching at the back of his mind, something he couldn't quite reach. He pulled up overhead photos of the Houston Stadium area on his computer. After fifteen minutes of studying the screen, he saw the problem.

CHAPTER FORTY-NINE

The Boeing 747 jet taxied to a stop at gate forty-three of the Charles de Gaulle International Airport in Paris. He arose from his first-class seat and retrieved his briefcase from the overhead bin. After ignoring a flirtatious turn of the head and inviting smile from the flight attendant, he disembarked the plane and proceeded to the baggage claim area. He approached a man wearing a white button-down shirt, black suit, and a matching black tie. He was holding a sign that said "Darpoli". Martin nodded to the driver and said, "I have one bag on the carousel." The man retrieved his client's bag and led him outside to where a black Citroen limousine was waiting at the curb.

Forty minutes later, he could see the top of the Eiffel Tower as the car pulled onto the Avenue des Champs-Elysees. The limo pulled up to the front of the Paris Marriott Hotel and the driver said, "We are here monsieur Darpoli." After getting out of the car, he paid the fare and tipped the driver handsomely. Looking down the avenue, he noticed the Arc de Triomphe standing proudly to the west. He had always admired the structure and would have loved to examine it more closely, but he was not in Paris for sight-seeing. This leg of his trip was to be no more than a diversion.

Darpoli entered the hotel lobby and approached the front desk. He gave the bellman a generous tip and checked in. Once inside his luxury suite, he ordered room service, unpacked his bag, and showered. By the time he finished, his meal arrived. "Merci beaucoup," he said and then gave the waiter one hundred Euros. He wanted to be remembered.

For the next two days, he had several meetings scheduled around Paris, ostensibly regarding the potential purchase of a half dozen hotels in Paris, Marseilles, and St. Tropez. In addition he had a private appointment with the world-renowned art dealer, Marcelle Duboise. He intended to pick up a gift for the next part of his trip. He studied the item carefully and it took him only twenty minutes to finalize the purchase, once the authenticity papers were confirmed.

After completing his business responsibilities in Paris, Darpoli placed a "Do-Not-Disturb" sign on the door of his room and took the elevator down to the lobby. At the front desk he spoke to the hotel manager and left specific instructions. "I am going to be involved in a number of intense confidential meetings for the rest of the week and under no circumstances am I to be disturbed by anyone, even housekeeping." He gave the man one thousand Euros to emphasize the importance of his request. The manager replied, "I understand fully Mr. Darpoli. It will be as you wish."

Martin exited the hotel through the front doors and turned east in the direction of the Louvre Museum. He crossed the avenue and continued to casually stroll down the Champs-Elysees, past a number of sidewalk cafes for which Paris was so famous. After ensuring that he wasn't being followed, he hailed down a cab, and in French instructed the driver to take him to the airport. He would not be returning to the Charles de Gaulle Airport today. This time, his destination would be the smaller Le Bourget airfield just eleven kilometers northeast of Paris. Darpoli wanted the anonymity that only this business airfield could provide. There would be no inconvenient immigration interviews to deal with and no need for a passport record. His trip was never designed to be a Paris business trip. It was merely a cover to disguise his actual destination. He couldn't allow his passport to be stamped by the Kingdom of Saudi Arabia.

Per instructions, the driver proceeded through a side executive gate and directly onto the tarmac where a private Boeing 737 jet was waiting for him. As the driver pulled alongside the plane, a lovely tall brunette met him at the bottom of the air-stairs. She was wearing a tight black pencil skirt, floral black and white blouse and black heels. She approached him, held out her hand, and speaking perfect French said, "Welcome Mr. Darpoli. I'm Sharina, your personal flight attendant. Your father sent one of his smaller jets for your trip home." She escorted him up the steps and inside the plane. The jet had a dozen tan leather luxury seats facing forward. Behind them there was a lounge where two opposing couches sat on either side of the cabin. In the rear of the plane was a stateroom. Satin sheets were turned down on the bed and a pair of pajamas sat on one of the pillows.

Martin selected a seat near the front of the cabin and fastened his seatbelt. As soon as he heard Sharina secure the door shut, he could hear the two Pratt & Whitney jet engines begin to rev up. The plane taxied to the main runway for takeoff. Within five minutes of his arrival at the airport, they were airborne. Once cruising altitude was reached, Sharina served him a breakfast of Eggs Benedict, orange juice and coffee. Afterward, he walked aft to the state room where he undressed, and put on the pajamas. Fifteen minutes later, the tall brunette flight attendant opened the door and said, "Do you need anything else, Mr. Darpoli...anything at all?"

The offer was tempting and she was magnificently beautiful, but he replied, "No, that'll be all. Thank you, Sharina. Please give me a wakeup call forty-five minutes before we land. I would like time to shower and shave before we arrive."

"As you wish, Mr. Darpoli. If you change your mind about needing anything, simply give me a call on the intercom," She closed the door.

Martin sat on the edge of the bed and said to himself, "My father," as he shook his head slowly from side to side. The prince was a devout Muslim, but only when convenient. He never let his beliefs stand in the way of his pursuit of worldly materials or carnal pleasures. He again thought about Sharina's offer and pressed the intercom button.

"Do you need anything, Mr. Darpoli," she asked.

"Yes, Sharina; I've changed my mind."

⊱✦⊰

After landing, the jet taxied into a private hanger. Martin Darpoli exited the plane and was hit in the face by the suffocating air. It had been a long time and he had forgotten about the arid, stifling heat. He wondered how the five million people who lived here tolerated it. Again, the traditional customs and immigration desks were bypassed. A member of the royal family was never subjected to such common treatment. There would be no official record that he had ever left Paris or arrived here.

Darpoli was met inside the hanger by a dozen members of his father's security team. They were wearing reflective sunglasses, dark suits, and ties as they vigilantly stood guard around three armored vehicles. There was a Mercedes limousine flanked on either side by a Chevy Suburban, all with heavily tinted windows. He was escorted toward the cars and ushered into the Mercedes as the security team scanned the surroundings for potential threats. A suited chauffeur spoke over the limo intercom and said, "Welcome home, sir. I have cold refreshments inside. I would suggest that you fasten your seatbelt securely. We will be traveling fairly quickly and the ride can be a bit bumpy." Once he was safely secured inside the limousine, six members of the security detail climbed into the escort vehicles and the caravan took off for the palace.

They passed down a major highway and then exited through a maze of smaller roads, kicking up a plume of sandy dust behind them. The Riyadh police had already cleared a path for them and all side roads had been blockaded. It would not be safe for such a high profile caravan to stop or even slow down. Though Riyadh was a fairly secure city, the potential for danger lurked around every corner and on every rooftop. They continued for almost thirty minutes until they reached a plush area that contained a huge palace standing in the middle of a sprawling estate, an oasis of green surrounded by the white sand. The grounds were protected by a decorative eight-foot concrete wall. Martin remembered from his childhood that the top of the wall was further secured by an electrified barbed wire coil. Anyone who tried to scale the barrier would either be electrocuted or cut down by one of the three-dozen snipers stationed on the palace roof.

The front of the estate was guarded by a large wrought iron gate, upon which hung a solid gold plaque displaying a script letter 'K' for Kabeer. The gate was flanked by a guard house which was staffed by three armed men. After their identities were confirmed, the gate was opened and the caravan was waved through. They proceeded up the quarter-mile drive, past multiple manicured gardens and fountains, toward the front of the palace. When his car stopped, Martin exited the vehicle and was met at the bottom of an expansive marble entrance stairway by an entourage of a dozen people who would care for his every need during his visit; every one of them willing to sacrifice their life for Prince Kabeer.

A silver-haired elderly man who he had known since first arriving at the palace twenty-five years ago, stepped forward, kissed him on both cheeks, and said, "Welcome home, sir. Praise Allah, for your safe return. It has been far too long since we last had the pleasure of seeing you."

"Over ten years I believe," responded Darpoli in Arabic. "How is my father?"

"He is well and very anxious to see you. He's presently waiting for you in his office. Would you like me to take you there?"

"It has been a long time, but I believe I can still find the way."

"As you wish, sir."

Prince Alsalud bin Rashid Kabeer had essentially adopted the boy shortly after learning of his activities in Afghanistan. He had joined the Taliban effort several months after his village and family had been annihilated by the Americans a quarter century ago. He never donned the attire of the Afghan fighters and didn't join in the large battles against the enemy. Waging his own private war, he preferred to wander the back alleys in the city of Kandahar, living under the guise of a homeless orphan. When the opportunity arose, he would deliver a merciless death to any unsuspecting U.S. soldier by plunging his Pesh-Kabz dagger into their neck. He had amassed a record of over thirty kills.

In time, his accomplishments were brought to the attention of Prince Kabeer. As a member of the Saudi royal family, the prince had amassed a fortune in oil investments, a world-wide chain of over two hundred luxury hotels, and dozens of expansive indoor shopping malls in the Middle East and Europe. Forbes Magazine had estimated his net worth to be in excess of fifty-five billion dollars, making him the fourth richest man in the world. Although he gave the outward appearance of being a friend of the West, he actually despised the "imperialistic" attitudes that the American and European governments embraced. This hatred festered in spite of the fact that he made billions providing the trappings of a western lifestyle to others. He considered himself to be a strict Muslim who adhered to the conservative principles advocated by the Wahhabi movement. He secretly funded the construction of hundreds of militant Muslim schools across the Arabian Peninsula. Such institutions were the spawning ground for many of the world's most vicious terrorist organizations such as the Taliban, al-Qaeda, and more recently ISIS. They preached the destruction of the infidels and the establishment of a global state of Islam governed by strict Sharia law.

After hearing the story about what had happened to the boy's family, and after learning of his relentless search for vengeance, the Prince summoned him to his palace in Saudi Arabia. He was well aware that the boy's thirst for revenge could never be quenched by the blood of only several dozen American soldiers. His soul would not be at peace until his enemy was completely vanquished. That desire made the boy a valuable weapon in the holy jihad; one whose steel could be molded and forged into a spearhead for Islam. In time, the prince came to love the boy even more than he did his own sons, and wished that they could be even half as courageous as the young Afghan. But they were mired in the hedonistic trappings his wealth had provided.

The young boy was moved into the Prince's extravagant palace where private tutors were hired to educate him in finance, the arts, and the nuances of western cultures. He became fluent in English, French, German, and Italian. It was then that his official name was changed from his Afghani name of Abduhl Rahim Wardak to the name of Martin Darpoli. A new history for the fictitious Martin Darpoli was created and he was given a full set of papers establishing himself as a natural-born citizen of the United States. He completed his education at Princeton University and Harvard

Business School. His position as CEO of the Masterson Properties Corporation allowed him to freely travel across the U.S. and live a life above suspicion, a life that would hide the true identity of the Scorpion. He prospered amongst the enemy, waiting to strike when the ideal opportunity presented itself. Now, that opportunity was near.

CHAPTER FIFTY

The Scorpion made his way through the labyrinth of elaborate palace halls until he stood in the open door of his father's study. He looked around the same room that he had known so well as a boy. It was still adorned with the same hand-carved furniture imported from around the world. The center of the detailed mosaic tile floor was adorned with a six-foot script "K" outlined in solid gold. Ornate Persian rugs were strategically arranged to protect the intricate floor designs. On the walls hung an extensive collection of original oil paintings by Matisse, Renoir, Monet, and others. There had been a number of additions to the collections since he was last here. The Scorpion knew that in spite of his father's strict anti-western cultural beliefs, the prince loved the works of the French Impressionists. He possessed one of the largest private collections in the world and that didn't even include the illegally obtained works hidden in a vault deep below the palace, many stolen from the Jews during the Holocaust. For Prince Kabeer, that fact alone made the paintings all the more precious.

Behind the ornate desk, reading financial reports, sat his father. The man had aged a great deal since he last saw him over ten years ago. He was wearing a loose white silk shirt, cream-colored dress slacks, and handmade Italian loafers. His grey hair was combed in such a way as to hide the thinning that had taken place. His reading glasses were perched on the end of his generous nose. When he looked up and saw his adopted son, he removed the glasses and hurried across the room. His intense dark brown eyes softened as he greeted Martin.

"As-salamu alaykum," he said as he grabbed his son in a hug.

"And peace be upon you father," replied the Scorpion.

"Allah be praised, it's been too long since I last saw you. You have become a handsome man. Come...come in and sit down. What is that which you hold in your hand?"

"A gift for my father, open it."

Prince Kabeer removed the brown wrapping and to his astonishment saw a painting by Georges Seurat. "What a magnificent piece of work. It looks to be one of the preliminary studies of *A Sunday on La Grande Jette*. I only have a few French neo-impressionist paintings and this will be one of the finest in my collection. I will hang it in a place of honor. Thank you my son."

"Through Allah, you have blessed me father. It is but a small sign of my gratitude."

"And it is one I will always cherish." The prince turned toward a silver tray sitting on the table. Would you care for some tea? I had it prepared for your visit, just the way you like it."

"Yes, thank you. It's been a long time since we have shared tea together."

"May I call you by the name that Allah gave you? Martin Darpoli is not a real person."

"I would like that, father. It's been decades since anyone called me Rahim."

"Abduhl Rahim Wardak it will be as long as you are here. Well then Rahim, tell me, how has your life been in America? I hope that you have not been seduced by all of the temptations of that country."

"Thanks to you and Allah, I have been very prosperous and have lived very comfortably there. It has been necessary for me to embrace the western culture and to live somewhat lavishly, but I must keep up appearances if I am to be accepted as one of their own. I have not forgotten from where I came, however."

"That is good to hear. I wish that I could say the same about my two sons. The only things they care about are fast cars and faster women. They have forgotten the traditions of Islam and the history of their ancestors. It's the influential dark shadow cast by the American movies and music. Their infidel way of life can sneak up on the unwary, so you must always be vigilant to resist their temptations. But that will all soon come to an end, will it not?"

"Yes father, Allah willing," replied the Scorpion.

The old prince looked around the room, gathering his thoughts, and then asked, "How are the plans coming along?"

"All is falling into place. There was an initial problem due to a delay in the purchase of the Microavionics Corporation. I had to be patient because it was the only company available that could manufacture the drones. The owner was an old Jew who simply refused my very generous offer. Eventually, I had to dispose of the man and subsequently his widow was anxious to rid herself of the business. She accepted the terms of the deal and the company is ours.

"I've met with the plant manager and insisted upon an aggressive production schedule. I've been told that the drone design is complete and we have a number of working prototypes available for practice and testing. We will be ready in time. If all goes as planned, we will be able to deal a decisive blow against the enemy.

Their government will be in turmoil and their economy will collapse."

"What about the men you selected for the mission?" asked the Prince.

"All of our men are dedicated to the word of Allah and the Holy Jihad. Unfortunately, Muqtoda al-Sadir is a different matter. I find him to be weak and careless. Like your sons, he has become interested in material possessions and the lifestyle which America provides. He is easily distracted by women and money."

"Does he know the full scope of the plan, Rahim?" asked the Prince.

"Fortunately, he only knows about some of our cells and the procurement of the Uranium 235. However, he does pose some risk. He's not a strong man and if he falls into the hands of the enemy, he'll probably talk. He could lead them back to us and compromise the mission. We might have to eliminate him."

The Prince nodded his head in understanding. "I will be sorry if that becomes necessary. I was a friend of his father for many years before he died. He was a holy mullah and teacher of Islam. It brings sadness to my heart that his son, Muqtoda has become a casualty of the American way of life. If he truly has become a liability, then he must be eliminated."

The Prince took another sip of the warm tea. "What about the follow-up attacks?" he asked.

"Once the Great Attack is successful, the United States will have no leader. Then we will launch the subsequent attacks across their land. There have been sleeper-cells scattered around the US for over fifteen years. Up until now, they have lacked a leader and a unified sense of purpose. Now, you and I have provided that. We have over a thousand men ready to act on my signal. Once it is given, we will hit every state capital, every national landmark, and every major financial institution. Chaos will ensue. In addition,

I have formed an alliance with The Muslim Brotherhood. They already own land in the U.S. where they run over two dozen different jihad training camps. On my command, they will launch guerrilla attacks on the American infrastructure. Our success will be final and the destruction of America will be complete."

"Ah yes, the Jamaat ul-Fuqra organization. I never cease to be amazed at the naiveté of the Americans and their failure to shut the camps down. We have used their own constitution against them."

"I must confess that there has been one possible complication," cautioned Rahim.

"Yes?" replied the Prince with concern in his voice. He set down his cup of tea and leaned forward.

"Doctor Maultry, the engineer who designed our drones, escaped with his family before he could be neutralized. He has been placed in protective custody and we must assume that he has warned the FBI about the attack."

"How much does he know about our mission?"

"Nothing, other than the fact that he was forced to create plans for a stealth drone. He has probably figured out that the plane will be used to carry a weapon of some type but he knows no specifics about our ultimate Great Attack. He has seen me but he does not know who I am and cannot trace any of our activities back to you."

"That is a serious complication because it will place their security agencies on higher alert. However, they don't know when, where, or how the attack will occur. The possibilities are endless. This should not affect our schedule, but we must be very careful. Even though the Americans are fat and complacent, they can be unified into a formidable enemy. Fortunately for us, their greatest failure is their inability to see the world in the context of history. They forgot about the Twin Towers five years after the two buildings fell. We, on the other hand, look at the world in terms of centuries. They are so preoccupied with their immediate future needs that this entire threat will blow over within a few weeks, and they will again let their guard down."

"That should help insure our success, father," the Scorpion replied without true conviction in his heart.

"Yes…we have had a friend in the White House for the past seven years but that will soon come to an end. I'm afraid that the next president will be a much stronger and determined man. He will not be so soft in confronting the jihad. Therefore, we must act soon. In spite of this Maultry complication, the moment must be now. This is our best chance to deliver a decisive blow against the Great Satan and its allies. Previous attempts like 9/11 were symbolically significant but that's all they were. They did nothing to propagate our cause. They only served to galvanize the different American factions into a united front against us. It strengthened their resolve to destroy us and they almost did. As a result, we lost Afghanistan and Iraq. We also lost many great leaders like Osama bin Laden. Had it not been for their Islamic-friendly president, our quest might have been permanently thwarted. But he handed us a gift by pulling out of the Middle East and backing down in Syria. By the will of Allah we have been given a second chance. Our brothers in ISIS have retaken the land that was lost and more. This time, we will not squander the opportunity. This time we must completely paralyze them so severely that they will not be able to mount a response. Anything less than a complete and absolute success would be an unmitigated disaster for us and the world of Islam. But you have formulated an ingenious plan my son and I am proud of you. With Allah at our side, we will be gloriously successful and Islam will be spread across the world. It is Allah's wish."

The two men, father and son, shared their tea in quiet for a few minutes. Then the prince turned to Rahim and asked, "And what about the transfer of our assets into gold. I have noticed a gradual increase in prices on the international markets over the past year. I assume that is due to your efforts."

"Yes. I have had to do so gradually so as not to spark a speculative buying frenzy. Between the nearly eight billion from the liquidation of our assets in the United States and what you have generated on your own, we now have the equivalent of over thirty-eight billion U.S. dollars invested in gold and gold derivatives in secret accounts."

The prince replied, "Well done Rahim. After the Great Attack, the American economic markets will collapse and the price of gold will quadruple. We will become the wealthiest and most powerful men in the entire world. I will have the resources to organize all Arab sects: Sunni, Kurds, Shiite, ISIS, Muslim Brotherhood, and the others into a single unified group to fight against our common enemy. After the United States falls, we'll eliminate the president of Iran and replace him with our own man. Our own government won't be a problem. The Saudi monarchy will collapse with the fall of America and I will assume leadership as a member of the House of Saud. Then the entire Middle East will be ours. The formation and funding of ISIS was just my first step. Once the Great Attack has been successful, we can expand our influence and spread the word of Allah around the world. One way or the other, the culture of America and the western countries will collapse under the weight of Allah's commands. Their time has come to an end and the age of Islam is emerging.

The two men stopped for a minute to reflect upon Prince Kabeer's words. "You have brought me much joy, my son. I was blessed by Allah the day that he delivered you into my life."

"Yes, praise Allah," responded Rahim. The Scorpion loved his adoptive father but did not adhere to his beliefs regarding Allah and Sharia law. For him, the Muslim quest was nothing more than a vehicle by which he could exact his revenge on the country that murdered his family. He spent another two days at the palace with his father, finalizing plans before flying back to Paris to resume his identity as Martin Darpoli.

CHAPTER FIFTY-ONE

John Crawford had just returned from a lunch date with his girl-friend, Lisa Savich when his cell phone rang. It was Captain Joe Watters of Cincinnati PD. "Good afternoon John. I seem to be talking to you a lot recently."

"That's for sure, Joe," responded Crawford. "What do you have for me?"

"I came across some information that I'm sure you want to hear about. I just received a call from the head of the Cincinnati arson squad. Last night, there was a warehouse fire and explosion just north of the city. They found a body buried under some debris. On closer examination, the fire inspector discovered that the guy didn't die from the fire. He had several .22 caliber bullet holes in his skull. We identified the body as that of a Mr. Roger Logan, a long-term employee of the company. That's not all; there was defi-nite evidence that accelerants were used."

"Sounds like a routine murder with the fire used to cover up evidence. What's this have to do with the FBI, Joe?" he asked.

"I'm getting to that. The arson boys also found some remnants of C-4 explosives and other bomb-making materials. After the fire started, someone used the C-4 to blow up the building."

"C-4? I'm getting interested. What else?"

"We pulled the hard drives from two computers found in the company's front office and we were able to retrieve some information. It seems as though at around 3:40 a.m., the victim was doing a search on an individual that you might be interested in. We have no record of him arriving in this country legally."

Now Crawford sat straight up in his chair. "What's the guy's name?"

"Muhammad Rabbani."

"Holy shit!" He seemed to be saying that a lot recently. "That's an alias. His real name is Muhammad bin Hussein and I've been looking for him."

"Like Saddam Hussein?"

"Same last name, same ugly mustache, different bad guy. Is he around anywhere?"

"Not a trace of him. Does this have anything to do with that fellow we helped you apprehend in the crack house last week?"

"Yes, but that's just between you and me. By the way, you said that the fire was at a warehouse?"

"Yes, at around 4:00 a.m."

"What was the name of the company?" he asked with an uncomfortable feeling in coiling up in his gut.

"Let's see," Watters said as he paged through his notes. "It's called Microavionics Technologies Corporation. They manufacture a line of high-end remote control toys for the rich and famous."

"Like planes?"

"That seems to be most of what they sell," responded the police chief.

"Ok Joe, thanks a lot. Let me know if you hear anything else from those computer searches, like where this Muhammad character might be holed up?"

"Will do, John."

"Holy shit!" Crawford again exclaimed to himself.

⥤⥢

He picked up his office phone, called Director Stevenson, and relayed all that he had uncovered.

"This is serious John. It pretty much confirms what Dr. Graham Maultry was thinking. They plan to use a remote controlled drone to deliver a dirty bomb. The story circulating around Washington is that President Wagner is definitely planning to attend the Super Bowl on February fifth. His assassination must be the Great Attack."

Director Stevenson continued, "We still don't have enough specific information yet, but I need to notify Parker Davis. He's the new White House Secret Service agent in charge of the presidential protection detail. He can start making some adjustments in Wagner's plans but I don't think Wagner is going to cancel his appearance. Being a former military hero, he's not one to run away from a fight or the threat of danger."

"If I may, sir," offered Crawford. "We're committing a lot of man power and we're already" stretched thin after the Stanford and Chicago investigations."

"But I don't see how we have any other choice," argued Stevenson.

"Well sir, I've been studying aerial photographs of the NRG Stadium area. While a great deal of the evidence seems to point in the direction of a dirty bomb attack at the Super Bowl, it's probably not going to be the site of the attack."

"Really! That runs contrary to everything we've been thinking up until now." exclaimed the astonished director. "How convinced are you of that opinion John?"

"Eighty-three percent certain, sir."

"Eighty-three percent! That's a pretty strange number, John. How'd you come up with that?"

"Logic sir. As I mentioned, I was studying the stadium aerial photos yesterday. I noticed something very important. The NRG stadium has a retractable roof."

"And?" countered Stevenson, pushing for further elaboration of Crawford's point.

"Historically the roof is open about eighty-three percent of the time, but there is no absolute certainty that it'll be opened or closed for any given event. The final decision isn't made until just several days prior to the game. The stadium officials make it based upon the three day local weather projections at the time. So there's a seventeen percent chance that the roof could be closed, and those are bad odds for the terrorists. I have to believe that these guys are too well-organized to have their plans foiled by something as unpredictable as a last minute unfavorable weather forecast. I just don't see it. There's something else that has been bothering me about the whole Super Bowl theory."

"What's that, John?" asked the director who was becoming more convinced of Crawford's position.

"Terror groups usually like to raise the bar for any attack. Although hitting the Super Bowl would be certainly be devastating, it wouldn't be that much more significant than taking down the twin towers on 9/11. Yes, if Wagner is there, it would be a much more dramatic attack, but the terrorists had no way of knowing for sure that he would be present when their plans were being formulated. In short sir, I don't believe Houston will be the site of the attack but I can't say so with absolute certainty. It's my gut feeling. There is a chance I could be wrong."

"Damn, I thought we were getting this thing narrowed down," said Stevenson. "Now we're back to square one. Do you have any ideas regarding their potential target?"

"Unfortunately no sir, none at all; but I do think that it's a mistake to commit all of those resources to the Houston area. You still have to cover things there because there is a small chance that I'm wrong. However, I think I would hold back as many men in reserve as you comfortably can, ready to deploy them once we get a better handle on things."

"Good idea, I think I'll do just that. Keep up the full court press on your end, John. I'm afraid time is running short and we're still in the dark.

After disconnecting the call, Crawford said to himself, "I'm getting closer but he's still a couple of steps ahead of me. I've got to catch up and soon." He knew he was rapidly running out of time, especially since February the fifth was now probably off the table.

CHAPTER FIFTY-TWO

Thanks to the Geek and his "Looking Glass" program, Winston now had access to all internal memos written in the FBI computer systems, even the highly confidential ones. He reviewed everything the Bureau had accumulated regarding Jazeer Farouk, Reggie Patterson, Mullah al-Sadir, Muhammad bin Hussein, and Graham Maultry. He was concerned. Now they had the information about the Microavionics Company in Cincinnati. It didn't take a genius to realize that the Scorpion and his organization were planning to deliver a dirty bomb by means of a stealth drone. The problem continued to be that they still didn't have a specific target or a specific date, and without that information they were still dead in the water. Wherever this bin Hussein fellow is, would give an indication as to the site of the attack. He is the key but where could he be hiding?

Winston Hamilton had been at this game a long time and he had developed keen instincts. He had looked at the overhead photographs of the Houston Stadium and came to the same conclusion as John Crawford: it could not be the site of the attack. He was concerned that the FBI was diverting too many resources to Houston. They were already spread thin investigating the other events around the country. He believed that the Chicago game sports venue might have been a misdirection play. He was convinced that he was missing something important but he couldn't quite put his finger on it.

Winston got out of his chair and paced the floor of his office. He gazed at the books on the shelves and pulled out a copy of 'The Prince' by Machiavelli, leafing through the pages as though the answer could somehow be found there. "Think Winston, think like a terrorist," he chided himself. Replacing the book, he stopped to look at his bank of computers and lingered on the family photograph sitting on his desk. After a few seconds, his attention was directed toward the wall pictures of himself posing with various political celebrities. Suddenly, he stopped pacing and stared more closely at one of the photographs. He studied the background of the picture and began considering the possibilities. Sitting back down at his desk, he quickly paged through his monthly calendar. "Oh my God!" he almost whispered. He immediately placed a call to Dr. Jacob Savich and told him to assemble the Delphi team. They were told to clear their schedules for the rest of the week and await further instructions. The situation was becoming more critical and now time was even shorter than he had thought.

CHAPTER FIFTY-THREE

Tarriz Muhktar was finishing the process of installing a bank of overhead fluorescent lights so he could work through the night. He was just completing the wiring on the last one when Muhammad bin Hussein pulled into the Yolder farm's long gravel drive with the drones and C-4 stored in the back of the van. Ahmad Haq Rasid had arrived several days earlier and was inside the house studying a detailed map of the target area. He came outside and the three men greeted each other, "As-salamu alaykum."

The van was unloaded and its contents arranged on the workbench along the back wall of the barn. Tarriz took one of the planes and unfolded its wings back to its full span of eight feet. It would have been much easier and cheaper to have simply purchased the drones, but that would have raised a lot of red flags at Homeland Security. It was a mistake which Rezwan Ferdhaus, the unsuccessful terrorist from Massachusetts, had made in 2010. He tried to purchase a remote controlled scale model of an F86 Sabre Jet. He was going to fill it with plastic explosives and fly it into his target. The FBI set up a sting operation that led to him being arrested and incarcerated for seventeen years.

Fortunately, the Scorpion was too smart to make the same mistake. We made our own drones so there's no way to track us down, thought Tarriz proudly. He checked the dimensions of the cargo area under the fuselage and concluded that the size would be more than adequate. Time was running short, so he got right to the business at hand. It was essential that he determine the exact load carrying capacity of the drones. He began a series of several practice runs using various payloads, gradually adding weight to the cargo hold each time. After several hours of trial-and-error efforts, and after essentially destroying two of the drones, he discovered that when he exceeded a cargo weight of thirty-four pounds, he was unable to successfully launch the plane without crashing it. It was substantially less than the forty-five pounds that was initially promised by Dr. Maultry's designs, but he would have to make do. He subtracted two pounds to allow for some variation in the power of the different motors and lift capabilities. That gave him a net thirty-two pounds with which to work. Using four one pound bricks of C-4 would comfortably allow for a twenty-eight-pound payload of Uranium 235 pellets. "It's not the amount which we planned, but it's still a lot of explosive power and radioactive shrapnel," he reassured his partners.

After a night of prayer and studying the target maps, the three men arose the next morning for a full day of practice. They each needed to be able to launch the drone comfortably. It would take time to become familiar with the process of navigating while only looking at a small four-by-six-inch monitor screen on the remote control console.

Each of the three men took a drone and folded its wings back into the storage position. They then reset the wings into the flying position. They repeated this process until they could complete the assembly even if blindfolded. Then the group studied the remote control consoles. Each one was eight by twelve inches. In the center sat the monitor screen which received feeds from the plane's nose camera. On either side were joystick controls, the left for velocity and the right for navigation. In the center, just above the monitor screen, was a button covered with a hinged red cap. It was the remote detonator switch...to be used when the drone was in position.

The men familiarized themselves with the remotes and completed a dozen practice flights until they were comfortable with the navigation process. Each plane was then stowed in a large duffel bag along with its corresponding control unit and an extra fifteen pounds to duplicate the weight of necessary supplies. Tarriz had already labeled the bags: Alpha, Beta, and Gamma; the first three letters of the Greek alphabet. He smiled at the irony of the code names he had selected.

That afternoon, they shouldered their individual duffel bags and climbed a ladder up to the roof of the barn. They needed to simulate the launch of their drones from a high altitude position. The roof of the barn provided a view of over five miles in all directions. The skies were clear with a moderate breeze. It was enough to make it feel cold and made their footing somewhat precarious on the pitched roof.

"This is good," said Tarriz. "We must become comfortable controlling the planes in challenging situations."

Tarriz Muhktar was the first to unpack his drone and secure the plane with his right hand. In spite of the graphene construction, the payload still made the plane fairly heavy, but Tarriz was able to successfully hold it aloft by bracing his right elbow against his side. He turned toward the wind, secured the remote control in his left hand, activated the velocity joystick, and increased the propeller rpms to the maximum. When he could sense the necessary amount of lift, he released the drone and it sailed into the air.

After only ten minutes, he was able to effectively navigate the drone by using the monitor on the remote console. He found that he had to keep it near the treetops in order to maintain his sense of orientation; too high and all he could see were blue sky and clouds. Then, he would have to put the plane into a nose dive to see the ground and get his bearings. A second camera in the belly of the plane would have been optimal but it would have come at the expense of payload capacity. It was too late for any modifications anyway. They would have to make do with what they had. "Allah will guide us," Tarriz reassured his partners.

He flew the plane straight out away from the farm to check the remote control at long distance. When the plane was at what he estimated to be around three miles, he put it through several maneuvers and it performed magnificently! He brought it back and went through the difficult process of landing. The plane wasn't designed for such because on the day of the attack, the drone would be sent out on a one-way trip.

The other two men took turns with their own planes and practiced for the next two hours. When all three were confident in their abilities, they returned to the house, ate, prayed, and retired for the evening.

The following morning, they repeated their practice drills from the previous day. In the afternoon, Tarriz had one more test to complete. He went back down inside the barn, retrieved one of the bricks of C-4, and returned to the roof. He placed the explosive into the drone's cargo area, connected blasting caps to the battery pack, and launched the plane. He flew it straight out over a wooded area, about a mile away. When he pressed the red detonation button on the control console, the plane exploded into a ball of fire.

Tarriz smiled at his two partners and said, "Tonight I will complete the final assembly of the weapons systems. The time for victory is drawing near. "

In unison, all three men said, "Praise Allah for he is great."

⸻◄┼ ┼►⸻

Caleb Miller was taking his thirteen-year-old grandson, Joshua for one of their monthly hunts together on the family farm which was adjacent to the Jeremiah Yolder place. The two walked quietly side by side, wearing their identical dark coats and straw hats. At about the same time that Caleb flushed out a pheasant, both he and Joshua saw something flying overhead, just above the trees.

"What was it Grandpa?" the boy asked his grandfather.

"I don't know for sure what it was, boy. It looked like a small airplane, but I've never seen one quite like it before. Its making no noise and it looks very peculiar. Maybe it's some kind of toy." The plane returned and the two watched the thing make turns to the north and then abruptly to the south. It would climb and then suddenly dive down. Then it disappeared, only to reappear after fifteen minutes. "Very odd, must be the new neighbors," said Caleb as they continued with their hunt.

After another forty-five minutes, both of them heard an explosion overhead and just caught a glimpse of the fireball. Caleb turned to the boy and said, "Something's not right here boy. We better return home and check on Grammy. As soon as he walked through the door, he said to his wife, "Some strange things are going on over at the Yolder place. I don't know what's happening, but something's not right there. You and Joshua can go ahead and eat dinner without me. I need to talk to the sheriff right away. I'll be back in several hours." He went out to the barn where he hitched up one of his horses to the buggy. He then set out on the one hour trip to a nearby grocery where he asked the owner to call the sheriff's office.

Sheriff Walter Lange had been dealing with the Amish community around Lancaster County for over two decades and he was familiar with their non-aggressive but no-nonsense ways. After hanging up the phone, he thought, *If Caleb Miller says he saw something strange flying around the Yolder place, then something strange was actually going on. The man wasn't prone to overstatement and if he saw an explosion, then there was an explosion.* He gazed around his office as though he were looking for an answer. "Something fishy is going on but damned if I know what it could be," he muttered to himself. However, it was dusk and getting too late to check things out tonight. He planned to drive out to the Yolder farm tomorrow.

CHAPTER FIFTY-FOUR

That evening, Tarriz Muhktar stood in front of the workbench, studying the stack of C-4 bricks. Composition 4 is just one of several types of plastic explosive. The plastic is combined with the explosive material so as to make it more stable and safer to handle. It's so safe that it can be lit with a match and it will simply burn without detonating. Even shooting it with a rifle round won't result in an explosion. Only a detonator with a blasting cap will work. Another function of the plastic is that it also makes the compound malleable. It can be molded into different shapes so as to focus the direction of the explosion.

He walked to the truck and opened the back door. The large cylindrical container was still covered in the dried bloody remnants of the old man. He realized that as soon as he opened the canister, the clock would start counting down on his own life. Using a pipe-wrench and hammer, he unscrewed the six large bolts that secured the top, rotated the lid aside and thought, *my fate is now sealed. I'm a walking dead man. It's just a matter of time.* He tried to withdraw one of the five-inch diameter rod clusters, but it was too heavy for just one man, especially one as small as Tarriz. He couldn't recruit the others to help him. They couldn't afford to have all three of them exposed to the radiation this early in the process.

He looked around for a solution, and he retrieved the length of chain that had initially been used to secure the barn door. He wrapped one end around the rod and the other end around the front bumper of the red Chevy pickup truck. He started the engine, put it in reverse, and slowly backed up until he had withdrawn about six feet of one rod. A hacksaw was retrieved from the workbench and was used to cut off the six-foot section, spilling some of the pellet contents onto the barn floor. He wasn't concerned about contamination. It was too late to worry about that.

After carrying the section to the workbench, he weighed out seven pounds of the uranium pellets and placed them in a lead bag. It would contain some of the radiation and delay its effects for a while. He repeated the process until four bags were complete. The tops were sealed and the four bags were placed into the cargo area of his drone, lining each toward the sides and bottom of the compartment. He then sandwiched four bricks of the C-4 between them and molded them in such a way that the blast would be directed laterally outward and down toward the ground.

When detonated, the C-4 and the twenty-eight pounds of Uranium 235 pellets would expand outward at a rate of 26,400 feet per second. Unlike in the American movies where the hero often outruns the explosion, there can be no escaping this five miles-per-second blast. Those who aren't killed instantly from shrapnel will die within a week from radiation sickness. The overall death toll will be well over ten thousand and the city will be uninhabitable for over a century. The Great Satan will finally be brought to its knees.

After loading the cargo area, he went about the task of arranging the detonation fuse that would be triggered by manually depressing the red button on the remote control console. He then affixed an additional detonator. Ideally, the explosion would occur a hundred feet above the target, which would allow for maximum disbursement of the Uranium 235 pellets. Tarriz installed the additional fuse as a backup in case the operator of the plane somehow becomes incapacitated. If he is unable to depress the remote trigger on the console, the plane will still explode. It would not be ideal, but would still be lethally effective. He repeated the process on the remaining drones. Afterward, he joined his two partners in the house. He looked at the two men and nodded his head, "All is ready."

The three men completed their final preparations. After a week of studying the topography of the city, and practicing with the planes, they were now ready for their mission. They spent their final hours together praying to Allah, performing wudu and other rituals of taharah; the purification of themselves for their entrance into paradise. They retired to their rooms but none of the three slept. They were too excited about the destruction they would soon rain down upon the United States.

At dawn, on Tuesday, they climbed into Muhammad's van and began their journey into history. Tarriz was in charge of driving and once they arrived at the outskirts of the city, he dropped Muhammad Hussein at a Hampton Inn just to the south. Ahmad was taken to a Marriott in the north, while Tarriz would keep the van and briefly check into a Holiday Inn. All of the necessary reservations had already been made through the offices of Martin Darpoli. Each of the hotels is owned and operated by his Masterson Properties Corporation. Since all of the arrangements were made in advance through the corporate offices, none of the men actually had to register. All they had to do was pick up a packet at the front desk. It contained their keys and a thousand dollars in cash.

Whatever they needed for their individual missions had already been delivered to their rooms. The three men were instructed to carry no wallets and no forms of identification. Contact between them was forbidden. The only communication would be between themselves and the Scorpion who would co-ordinate their efforts from an undisclosed location.

After dropping off his two partners, Tarriz stopped at the Holiday Inn and proceeded to his room. As promised, his uniform was sitting on the bed. While the other two rested, Tarriz had more immediate matters to attend to, beginning this very evening. He had to make an important visit and by tomorrow at this time he would be in position. Ahmad and Muhammad were to scout out their own locations and on the following Thursday evening, they too would be at their assigned stations. All was falling into place, just as the Scorpion had planned.

CHAPTER FIFTY-FIVE

The following morning, Lancaster County sheriff, Walter Lange stopped at Benny's Café for a breakfast of biscuits, fried ham, and eggs. After he finished his second cup of black coffee, he got into his cruiser and headed east on the forty-five minute drive to check the Yolder farm. When he reached the rusted mailbox, he pulled the cruiser up the long gravel drive, and parked his car in front of the house. He called out, "Hello?" but no-one answered. The place was as quiet as a cemetery at night. He called out again but still there was no answer. He walked up the steps to the front porch and knocked on the door, but again, no answer. He checked all of the windows but was unable to see anything except some plates, coffee cups, and papers in the kitchen. He knew that someone had been here recently because there was still food on the plates.

After returning to his car, he removed his hat and did a three-hundred-sixty degree inspection of the property. The farm appeared to be deserted. The double barn doors were partially open so he walked over, thinking someone might be inside. Something seemed unusually eerie about the place, so Walter instinctively un-holstered his service Glock and chambered a round. Using the tip of the automatic, he called out "Police!" and slowly pushed the barn doors fully open, ready to return fire if necessary. After flip-ping on the overhead lights, he saw the workbench and his heart skipped a beat. Having spent twenty years in the army as an MP, he knew bomb making materials when he saw them. As he was backing away, he noticed the partially opened truck cargo door. He cautiously opened it fully, and was shocked to see dried blood and bone splattered everywhere. When he noticed the radioactive material logo on the side of the opened container, he yelled, "Oh my God!" He immediately ran back to his cruiser and made an urgent call to the FBI.

CHAPTER FIFTY-SIX

T he building was completed in 1899 and looked much like a
large cathedral. It stood as a monument to the stature and
prestige of the United States Postal Service. At the time of its
completion, it was the largest government building in the District
of Columbia and the only one to boast an attached bell tower. It
spite of its magnificence, the architectural style of the building was
roundly criticized.

Within fifteen years, there were repeated efforts to have the
structure torn down. Fortunately, it survived at least seven such
attempts over the next six decades. Eventually tastes changed, and
those in power began to appreciate the beauty of its Richardsonian
Romanesque architectural style. Renovation plans were initiated after a Congressional act authorized the necessary funds.
In 1983, the building was reopened as the home of the National
Endowment for the Arts and various retail businesses. Great
Britain's Ditchley Foundation gave the US Congress a bicentennial
gift of ten large bells which were placed in the building's unique
tower. The bell chimes are rung on the opening and closing of

Congress, on important state occasions, on national holidays, and on Presidential inaugurations. They would be rung in spectacular fashion in just three days by a group of registered bell stewards. The sequence of the chimes is so varied and complex that weekly practice sessions are required every Wednesday to insure proper ringing. This week would be no exception.

In addition to being a magnificent example of period architecture, the Old Post Office Tower also boasts the title of being one of the tallest buildings in D.C. When standing on the tower's 315 foot high observation platform, visitors are rewarded with a panoramic view of Washington and the National Mall. More importantly, it provides a commanding view to the east, down Pennsylvania Avenue toward the western steps of the nation's Capital Building: the site of presidential inaugurations and the site of the Scorpion's "Great Attack" in several days.

CHAPTER FIFTY-SEVEN

He had just returned home after a full day of work. At age 64, Walter Giles was in his final three months of employment in the federal government. After January 20th, he will have served under no less than six different presidents over the forty years of his career. During that time, he had escorted over fifty-thousand tours of various national landmarks around D.C. This March, he would turn in his National Park Service uniform and keys for good. Then he would head out to Everglades City, Florida where he had already purchased a small condo and a Cobia center-console fishing boat. As he looked into the mirror to unbutton his shirt, he gazed upon a picture of Mary, his wife of forty-one years. She had died five years earlier from complications related to her diabetes. The doctors had tried to get her on a diet to lose weight but she just couldn't do it. She eventually gave up and so did her heart. Walter had to fight back the tears, thinking about the fact that the two of them would be unable to share their golden years together. He was alone. He picked up his wife's picture from the dresser and kissed it, saying, "Miss you Mary. I'll always love you, babe." His reverie was interrupted by a knock at the door and a voice which said, "UPS delivery. I need a signature Mr. Giles."

"Now what can that be?" he asked himself. "I haven't ordered anything. Could be papers related to my condo purchase; but I thought the real estate agent had already handled everything."

Walter walked to the door and looked through the peep hole. He could see a small man dressed in the characteristic brown uniform of the delivery service. He was holding a large manila envelope in his hand. Walter unlocked the door and opened it, but he wasn't greeted by a UPS man and he wasn't given the package. The only delivery Walter received that evening was a 9mm bullet into his forehead. He died instantly. There would be no golden years in Florida and no fishing the back waters of the Everglades for snook. There would be nothing.

Tarriz Muhktar holstered the silenced Beretta and pushed the body of Walter Giles back into the living room. He quickly retrieved a towel from the bathroom and wrapped it around the body's head to prevent any more blood from seeping down through the floor into the ceiling of the apartment below. Inspection of the man's park service uniform revealed that, other than a spray of blood over the shirt collar, it was clean. Tarriz went into the closet, pulled out a fresh white shirt, and put it on over his clothes. Then, he removed the green U.S. National Park Service uniform from the body and also put it on over what he had already been wearing. The fit was a still a little large in spite of being worn over his other clothes, but it would be satisfactory. Giles' uniform was then removed and placed in a white garbage bag. After retrieving Walter's Park Service identification badge, he studied it carefully. It would be passable if Tarriz put some grey coloring in his hair and used some glasses. "Allah willing, this should get me in without too much trouble," he said to himself. Tarriz placed Walter's ID badge into the bag with the uniform and set it by the front door.

He dragged the body into the bathroom where it was placed in the tub. There was no concern about the body and he wasn't worried about leaving behind any evidence. He was simply buying time. Walter Giles would not be missed by anyone for at least four days and by the time his body was discovered, it would all be over.

A wave of nausea passed over him, and Tarriz vomited a swirl of bloody liquid into the toilet. It wasn't the thought of the dead body that made him sick. He had seen thousands of dead bodies before. It was the Uranium 235.

After closing the bathroom door to contain the smell, the thermostat was found and the temperature was set as low as possible. He exited through the same door which he had entered thirty minutes earlier, and locked it behind him. Once back at the hotel, Tarriz fine-tuned his disguise and Walter's ID photograph.

CHAPTER FIFTY-EIGHT

The next morning, on Wednesday, January 18th, a National Park Service guide was carrying a heavy black duffel bag over his shoulder as he walked past the statue of the first postmaster general of the United States, Benjamin Franklin. After entering through the heavy double doors, he walked across the large pavilion courtyard toward a sign that read: Nancy Hanks Center: Tower Tour Elevators. Standing guard at the elevator doors, he waited for the bell-ringers to arrive for their weekly Wednesday practice session. Today would be especially important for them because of the events scheduled in forty-eight hours. After checking his watch for the third time, he saw the small group approaching, right on time. When they reached the elevators, Tarriz addressed the leader of the Washington Ringing Society, "Mr. Wilmington, if you will please follow me, I am to accompany you and your group up to the bells this morning. Due to the events scheduled in a few days, extra security precautions are in place." The leader of the group inspected the man's official name tag and responded, "Certainly Mr. Giles. You lead the way."

Mr. Wilmington glanced at the duffel bag with an inquisitive look in his eyes. Tarriz noticed, tapped the bag, and said, "New security cameras for the observation deck."

The group entered the glass elevator and exited at the bell ringing chamber. Multiple heavy ropes descended from openings in the ceiling of the room and the ringers began to position themselves around them. Once they were situated, Tarriz said, "I will allow you to complete your practice session. I have some matters to attend to with the camera installation. It will take me a while and you'll probably finish before me, so you may leave on your own when you are done." With that, Tarriz exited the small room through a back door and climbed the rest of the way up toward the observation platform via a rear set of metal access stairs.

Must move quickly, he thought as another wave of nausea hit him. He exited the service stairway through a maintenance door into a space just above the elevator shaft that housed the motors and cables. Tarriz crawled into a small cubbyhole in the back, behind the large cable coils, where he couldn't be seen from the access door. For the next forty-eight hours he would hide there with the duffle bag containing his equipment, food, and water. He wouldn't exit the space until after the Secret Service completed its final inspection of the tower tomorrow. At that time, the building would be sealed and closed off to the public, because it is well within sniper range of the capitol building.

Once in position, he pulled an untraceable cell phone out of his duffel and whispered, "Alpha in place." There was no verbal response, just a double click that acknowledged reception of the message. Tarriz looked down at the phone and a saw a drop of blood land on the display screen.

The Scorpion sat on a couch in his top floor suite at the JW Marriott Hotel on Pennsylvania Avenue. He was just a half-mile away from the Old Post Office. He double-clicked a radio response to Tarriz. Alpha was in position and would be ready on Friday, as long as he wasn't discovered by the secret service. The Scorpion didn't expect the man to live more than forty-eight hours anyway. He was already showing early signs of radiation poisoning, but he was expendable. That had been part of the Scorpion's original plan. The Old Post Office was to be little more than a diversion.

He turned on the television and switched the station to the Weather Channel. The five-day forecast was for highs in the mid-forties and only a ten-percent chance of rain. The conditions were optimal. More importantly, winds were projected to be from the east at less than five miles-an-hour...perfect flying weather.

"Soon," he said to himself, "Very soon." He called his girlfriend, Kathleen Maley to be sure that they were still on for this Friday at her condo.

CHAPTER FIFTY-NINE

Late on Thursday afternoon, January 19th, the day after Tarriz took his position at the Old Post Office, a priest exited the side door of the Basilica of the National Shrine of the Immaculate Conception at 400 Michigan Avenue. On the southwest corner of the Cathedral sits the carillon. Rising 329 feet into the air, it is ranked as one of the tallest buildings in the District of Columbia, second only to the Washington Monument. It's commonly referred to as the Knight's Tower because its completion was financed by funds donated by the Knights of Columbus.

As the cleric approached the base of the bell tower, he was met with, "Good afternoon father, or should I say good evening." The elderly custodian was in his usual position, sitting at a desk just inside the tower entrance, in the same chair which he had occupied for the past twenty-five years.

"Good afternoon," the priest replied.

The old man looked perplexed as he asked, "How may I help you this beautiful evening?" He looked at his watch. "You know, the tower was closed to tourists as of fifteen minutes ago. I was just on my way up the elevator to make sure the observation platform is empty. I'm afraid that if you want to ride up, it's a little too late." There was the hint of an Irish brogue in his speech and more than a hint of Irish whiskey on the old man's breath.

"I apologize for the lateness of my visit but Archbishop Mahoney is concerned about some problems with the normal ringing sequences of the bells. One of the official ringers reported that one of the bells might need to be serviced. The Archbishop expects a number of VIP visitors in D.C. tomorrow and he asked me to check things to be sure that all would be functioning properly in time for the festivities."

"So late in the afternoon? There's hardly time to fix them if anything's wrong," stated the caretaker.

"I'm sorry if it's an inconvenience but it's the earliest I was able to get here," replied the priest. "Hopefully, it's something that can be fixed with a minor adjustment."

"That's strange, the Ringer's Society was here just three days ago for practice and Mr. Wilmington didn't mention anything about there being a problem. Normally he would tell me about it since I'm the curator of the tower." The old man was becoming skeptical and something didn't quite add up with the priest. He had never actually seen the man before and he knew most of the clergy in the diocese. He looked at the large duffel bag the priest was carrying.

The priest noticed and responded, "I brought a few tools just in case I could adjust the bells myself."

"Still, I don't understand why Mr. Wilmington didn't say anything to me about it when he was here."

"He and his team have been extremely busy practicing at all of the different bell towers around the city. You know how overloaded everyone's schedule is this week. I guess Mr. Wilmington was distracted and simply failed to mention it; but then he called the Archbishop's office this afternoon."

"I guess that must be it, Father...?"

"O'Reilly, Father James O'Reilly."

Another strange thing, thought the old man. *If this guy's Irish then I'm Chinese. Something's very fishy here. And those teeth when he smiles-- they look like fangs.*

"OK father. Let me just check your bag of tools before you get on the elevator," said the curator as he slowly checked his belt to be sure he had his pepper spray. "You know how the Archbishop is about rules and protocols."

"Sure thing, you can never be too careful," said the priest as he lifted the bag onto a small inspection table and unzipped it. The old curator was startled when he saw the contents. Something was seriously wrong.

"What's this? You can't go up in the tower with this stuff!" he exclaimed while trying to pull out his pepper spray canister. He was too slow.

"I'm afraid that's going to pose a bit of a problem," snarled the priest as he withdrew a silenced Glock 37 from under his cassock and put two rounds into the middle of the old man's chest. Ahmad Haq Rasid, the same man who had captured the Maultry yacht and the same man who had killed the two teens, hid the old man's body in a corner. After locking the entrance, he jammed the curator's desk against the handle to further secure the door. He wasn't worried about witnesses because, as the old curator stated earlier, the tower was now closed to the public. He picked up the duffel and walked up three flights of stairs to the tower elevator. Ahmad pushed the button for the observation deck level. Once there, he locked down the elevator, eliminating access to his location.

After checking the platform to be sure he was alone, he crawled over to the outer deck and looked out across the balustered railing. He could see Michigan Avenue as it coursed southwest to intersect with North Capitol Street. He was then able to follow North

Capitol until it terminated near the Capitol dome, just over three miles away. The famous Statue of Freedom was perched on top.

"It's a perfect spot, just like the Scorpion described it. We're going to tear down that infidel monstrosity and fly the flag of Allah in its place," he said to himself. He turned on his phone and said, "Beta in position." Several seconds later was the double-click reply. He pulled out a bottle of water and settled down for what would be a cold but calm night.

CHAPTER SIXTY

At about the same time that Ahmad Haq Rasid was taking his position in the Knight's Tower, a major from the United States Marine Corps was exiting a visitors' center across town. He wandered slowly through the various paths which wound their way through the site, pausing occasionally to admire some of the statues. On his chest, he proudly wore medals that documented his participation in Operation Desert Storm, and Operation Iraqi Freedom. He had two purple hearts, a Silver Star, and a Distinguished Service Cross.

He casually gazed around and as expected, the tourist crowd was gradually dissipating. The facility was closing early tonight because of the big event on the National Mall tomorrow. He gazed up the hill and saw the mansion. The columned Greek revival-style home had been built by the adopted grandson of George and Martha Custis Washington. It now served as a memorial to General Robert E. Lee. The major smiled at the irony of the fact that the mansion was associated with two famous generals in American History: one the father of this country, and the other a general who tried to divide it. But tomorrow, it would serve as another historic milestone for the United States. It will be the launching site for the Gamma phase of the Scorpion's planned attack, and it will mark the end of the United States government.

He veered to the right across a gravel path until he reached the walkway that took him up the hill toward the rear of the historic building. There, he found the small grove of pine trees which would serve as a temporary hiding place. The sun was on the horizon and dusk was settling in. Once it was sufficiently dark, he stood up to check his surroundings. As expected, there was no activity since the building had closed hours ago. Security was minimal. Most assets had been reassigned to the National Mall and Capitol building.

He knelt down in the grass, unzipped his duffel bag, and withdrew a grappling hook with fifty feet of rope. "Allah guide me," he prayed. Quietly approaching the back of the building, he threw the hook onto the roof. As he pulled on the rope, it fell to the ground. It took several more tries but eventually he met resistance and knew that he had acquired a good bite. He crawled back to the cover of the trees and waited to see if the noise had attracted any attention. All was quiet.

Another fifty-foot-length of rope was withdrawn from the bag. One end was tied to his waist while the other was secured to the duffel. A silenced 9 mm Sig Sauer automatic was placed in his waistband. He wasn't planning to shoot anyone, not because of an aversion to taking a life. He had done so hundreds of times in the past and certainly would kill many more tomorrow. He simply didn't have time to deal with a dead body.

After looking around once again, he was satisfied that it was safe, and he carried his duffel to the back of the mansion. Pulling himself up the grappling rope, hand over hand, he made his way up to the roof. The bag and the ropes where then hauled up and stowed against one of the building's two chimneys. Muhammad bin

Hussein removed his fake Marine Corps uniform and exchanged it for a black sweat suit.

The surrounding view provided a perfect vantage point. He gazed toward the National Mall as he slowly stroked his black mustache. The lights of the Capitol Building with its famous western steps could be easily seen, just 3.1 miles away. Tomorrow there would be a hundred thousand civilians, politicians, and government officials gathered there. Everyone would be present: all members of congress, the senate, the Supreme Court, the Speaker of the House, the President pro tem of the Senate, the Vice President and most importantly, the new President of the United States, Jack Wagner. He picked up his phone and said, "Gamma in position." The silence was disrupted by a double click.

CHAPTER SIXTY-ONE

It was late in the evening on January 19th. John Crawford sat at his desk, reviewing all of the reports related to Muhammad bin Hussein, looking in vain for something that might give him an indication of where the man could be hiding, and more importantly, the site of the attack. The solitary silence in the offices was shattered by the ring of his phone. He was the only one left in the building to answer it.

"I need to speak to Agent Crawford please. It's urgent."

"This is John Crawford."

"Hi John, it's Agent Mitchell Scott from the Harrisburg office. We met each other a couple of times at Quantico."

"Sure Mitch, I remember. You beat me twice in racquetball. What has you calling me at this late hour?"

"Well it's complicated John." He went on to relate how he had been contacted by the Lancaster County sheriff's office late on Wednesday. Per the sheriff's request, he sent a pair of his agents out to an old Amish Farm in the area.

"My guys found an open container with a yellow and black nuclear material logo stenciled on the side. They called a HazMat team which checked for radiation in the barn and their instruments lit up like a Christmas tree. We isolated the immediate area and are calling in a nuclear team to better analyze the situation, but I can tell you right now that there's a lot of radioactive material scattered around the place. One of the guys said he was surprised there weren't any dead bodies lying around. I thought you should know."

"Was there anyone there?" asked Crawford anxiously. This is the lead he had been waiting for.

"No, the agents checked inside the house and all around the property but no-one was found. However, someone was there very recently because there was still food on plates and coffee in cups on the kitchen table."

"How many plates?"

"Three. Also, they found a map sitting on top of the table."

When he described the map, John exclaimed, "Holy shit! I've gotta call you back later Mitch. Thanks!"

Crawford called his boss, Director Stevenson who was attending a D.C. cocktail party. "It's John Crawford, sir. Sorry to disturb your evening, but I've come across something important."

"No problem John. I hate these boring things anyway. What's up?"

"We were right sir. Forget about Houston, and forget about February. The attack is going to occur tomorrow afternoon in Washington."

"Are you sure about that?" the director asked incredulously.

"Absolutely sir, no doubt about it. You realize, of course, what's happening in Washington tomorrow?"

"Oh my God, they're going to target the inauguration ceremony of President-elect Wagner. That's less than twenty-four hours from now. Do you realize what this means, John?"

"Yes sir, I do. The entire government of the United States will be there. That includes everyone in the line of succession for the presidency. It'll be a constitutional catastrophe. There'll be no-one left to run the country. The entire government could collapse. Wall Street and the world economies will go into a free fall."

"And according to your reports, it'll be followed by attacks at every state capital. We have to stop this thing, John. I'm sending my jet to Cincinnati. I want you here in Washington ASAP. I'm going to recall as many agents as I can back to D.C. I need to talk to Parker Davis at the White House again. He needs to be aware of the seriousness of this matter.

CHAPTER SIXTY-TWO

On the same evening of Thursday, January 19th, Winston Hamilton met with the Delphi Team at Carver Savich's estate home in Park Hills, Kentucky. Everyone was there, including Derek Hacker who had joined the team several weeks after recovering from the injuries that Lisa had inflicted. When she saw him, she asked coldly, "How're the ribs, Hacker?"

"All healed and ready for action. How's your foot?"

"My foot?"

"Yeah, your foot. You kicked me so damn hard, I figured you had to have broken a toe or two." There was a pause as he searched for the right words. "Look, I'm sorry about hitting you. We needed to test you in a real combat situation and I got carried away. Much to my chagrin, you excelled."

"Apology accepted…but you're still a chauvinist ass, Hacker."

"I know I am, but being an ass is what I do best; don't know any other way."

The two looked at each other for a few seconds, and then, both broke out in laughter. All was forgiven and Hacker had developed a newfound respect for his female teammate. He also earned a new moniker, "Rib Man." The old wounds were healed and the Delphi Team was again fully intact.

The other members of the group poured themselves a drink or opened a beer while selecting seats in the living room. Meanwhile Winston sipped on a glass of Woodford Reserve Kentucky bourbon as he gazed at the contents of two glass display cabinets on either side of Carver's floor-to-ceiling fireplace. Both cases contained an extensive collection of wood sculptures. He admired the artistic intricacy and graceful flow of the lines of each piece. It was difficult to comprehend that these magnificent works could be the creations of a serial killer; yes, one who believed in the righteousness of what he did, but a multiple murderer just the same. Each sculpture represented one of his victims. Like most serial killers who collect trophies, Carver shaped beautifully abstract free-form images of his victims, capturing the essence of their evil.

On the second shelf of the right cabinet, he saw a cherry wood plaque. It was hand-engraved with a quote by Dr. Martin Luther King, "Injustice anywhere is a threat to justice everywhere." It provided some insight into the motivation behind Carver's twisted psyche. Winston had to admit that there was a Quixotesque charm to the man, an undeniable need to "right the unrightable wrong" as the song says. The unlikely combination of his purity-of-purpose juxtaposed against his psychopathic need to kill was an enigma that Winston would never fully comprehend. Perhaps it was that mix of viciousness and sensitivity that made him such an effective leader of the Delphi Team. He guessed that it all stemmed from witnessing the brutal murder of Carver's family when he and Lisa were just children.

While still facing the cabinets, he said, "You may proceed Dr. Savich."

Carver began, "We have a theory as to what is being planned by the Scorpion. Thanks to Norman's efforts, we are privy to all information at the disposal of the FBI. Earlier today, Mr. Hamilton and I discussed in detail what has transpired over the past several months and we have come to a conclusion. We know the when and where of the Great Attack and it's not the Super Bowl." He went into a detailed explanation of what will happen and the reasoning behind his beliefs.

"A dirty bomb like the one which Hank described at Farmto; right in the middle of the National Mall!!" exclaimed Lisa.

Winston was still turned away from the group, studying Carver's sculptures. "A drone can provide the perfect delivery vehicle, especially if detonated several hundred feet over the target. That will create a much wider dispersal range of radioactive material and proportionately more casualties. Of course, the major concern here is the target, which is the president and the entire leadership of our government. We simply can't let that happen. We must identify the location of the terrorists and stop them."

Carver added, "That's our major problem. We can't kill them if we don't know where they are. We need a plan...a good plan, and right now I don't have one."

The rest of the group offered their opinions and argued about potential scenarios. All during the meeting, Norman Deets had his laptop computer open in front of him. His fingers danced across the keys like a concert pianist. "Carver, I think I may have something here. I've done some more research on those remote control drones. In order to ensure one-hundred percent continual control of the planes, the navigator must maintain a direct line-of-sight access." Deets continued to type. "That limitation could be somewhat overcome with the addition of a power booster but control would still be chancy around buildings and trees."

"That's their Achilles heel!" exclaimed Carver. "The bad guys wouldn't risk a loss of drone control at this point. They can't access any of our GPS satellites without raising a dozen red flags at Homeland Security so that leaves them with only line-of-sight navigation."

Lisa added, "That means that the operator will have to either be fairly close to the target or be sitting in an elevated position like a tall building, or maybe a helicopter."

"I doubt that a helicopter would be feasible. The air space around Washington will be locked down tighter than a drum," offered Dan. "I need a topographical map of the area to search for spots I'd use for a long-range shot. Probably any such position would also be an excellent place from which to launch a drone."

Deets again worked furiously on his laptop. After a few seconds, he looked up and said, "I have a list of the ten tallest structures within five miles of the D.C. area. That should cut down the size of the search area."

"Great work Norman. We can focus our efforts on those sites," responded Winston.

"What is of supreme importance in war is to attack the enemy's strategy," added Deets.

"I'm impressed Norman. You actually read Sun Tzu's book," said Dan.

"Not as interesting as my video game magazines, but still worth reading," replied Deets.

"We're going to need a bank of helicopters in place and ready to fly. We can use Norman's list to find the right building," offered Dan.

"Excellent idea," said Winston. "We need to pass our thoughts on to the Secret Service. It would probably be best if we can get Dr. Foster here stationed in one of the helicopters just in case his sniper talents are needed."

"Roger that, Mr. Hamilton. I'd love the opportunity to take this drone out," responded Dan.

"I don't think it's going to be that easy," said Deets with a concerned look on his face as he studied the computer screen. I just intercepted an urgent internal FBI memo between Director Stevenson and many of his field agents. He's recalling them from Houston and redeploying them around Washington. The Bureau just found Muhammad's hiding place. It's a farm in eastern Pennsylvania. A search of the house revealed detailed maps of the Washington area. It confirms Mr. Hamilton's theory about D.C. being the target. The farm's less than a hundred miles away so they may already be in position. It looks like the FBI also found evidence of several drones and at least three team members."

"Multiple points of attack?" asked Dan.

"Possibly," replied Winston who continued to face the cabinets. "It dramatically raises the level of complexity and our chances of failure." He continued to study Carver's sculptures, seemingly lost in thought. After several seconds, he turned to face the team. The look on his face was even more serious than usual. "We have an important problem, above and beyond the obvious dirty bomb threat. I was hoping to run this entire operation by proxy through your FBI friend, John Crawford. I've been able to do so up until now, but I can't anymore. We're running out of time and the stakes are too high. This thing is a potential endgame and if we're dealing with several drones being launched from different sites, we must pull together all of our resources to stop them. We need to openly handle some things ourselves, and that might very well expose us. We are an illegal entity involved in very illegal activities. All of you need to be aware that the entire team, including myself, could be charged with serious crimes including kidnapping and murder. I want each of you to consider the ramifications of our actions before we proceed any further."

Winston looked at each team member in the eye and there was a positive nod from all of them. Carver responded, "We understand the risks Mr. Hamilton, but as I see things, there's no other choice but to attack this thing with everything we have."

"Good, I thought you might say that. Now I have some very urgent phone calls to make. One of those must be to Parker Davis, the man in charge of President-elect Wagner's protection detail. Once I talk to him, our small organization will be exposed and we'll be at the point of no return. In the meantime Carver, I'll let you and your team come up with a plan on how to identify and neutralize all of the terrorists. I'll have my jet ready at Lunken Airport in two hours.

The Delphi Team members began to organize the gear they brought from Farmto. Meanwhile, Carver walked outside onto his deck and gazed across the Ohio River toward the lights of Cincinnati. It was an unusually mild evening for mid-January and he didn't wear a coat. He was too distracted by the group's situation to worry about the cold anyway. The welfare of the entire country was at stake and everything was falling squarely on his shoulders. He lit up a Maker's Mark cigar as his good friend Dan walked up next to him. Dan took a sip from his bottle of Heineken and said, "How do you want to play this thing tomorrow, Carver?"

Carver shook his head. "No matter what we come up with, our chances of success are miniscule. There are so many unknowns and variables. If there are actually three points of attack, they only have to get lucky with one of them. We must be one hundred percent on target with all three. Those are bad odds."

Together, the two men worked as best they could on the outline of a plan, knowing that the first casualty of any battle was usually the plan, itself. It would likely have to be chucked after the first few minutes of combat. Then, they'd be flying by the seat of their pants.

CHAPTER SIXTY-THREE

Forty-seven-year-old Parker Davis had been a member of the Secret Service for the past twenty years. The first five years were spent paying his dues working in the financial crimes division, fighting counterfeit rings. After repeated requests, he was finally transferred to the protection division. The next seven years were spent watching various presidential candidates and ultimately he was promoted to the full-time Vice Presidential detail.

Then, there were the debacles surrounding the White House Secret Service team. Some agents were disciplined after bringing prostitutes into their hotel rooms in Columbia, just prior to a presidential visit. On one occasion the president was allowed to ride on an elevator with an armed convicted felon while visiting the Centers for Disease Control near Atlanta. The straw that broke the camel's back occurred when Omar Gonzalez scaled the White House fence and made it all of the way to the East Room before he could be apprehended. The Secret Service director resigned under accusations of tolerating a culture of incompetence and complacency. That resulted in a big shake-up in the agency bureaucracy and paved the way for Parker's rapid promotion to the position he had always wanted: protection of the President of the United States, or POTUS as he was commonly called. Parker was President-elect Wagner's personal selection to be the head of the elite group based in the White House. The welfare of POTUS and his family was now in the hands of Parker Davis, and he would allow no harm to come to them under his watch. He or any of the men and women serving in his detail would not hesitate to take a bullet for "Bulldog"--Wagner's code name.

It quickly became apparent that protecting this particular president would not be an easy task. The man had been a decorated Air Force captain in Desert Storm before he was forced to retire after sustaining a disabling injury. He only had partial use of his left hand, and a bullet fragment was still lodged in his heart; but he never allowed that fact to slow him down. He was a relentless fighter. He appeared to have no fear of the potential dangers associated with his new position. Parker didn't know whether that lack of fear was attributable to his past military experiences or just due to the dogged stubbornness for which the man was known. Parker only knew that keeping a protective leash on the Bulldog would be the most challenging task of his career.

It was late and Parker Davis was in his office, reviewing plans for tomorrow's inauguration when his secure cell phone rang. Only a select few people had his number and the source of the call was blocked. Almost no-one could do that. He answered, "Hello?"

"Mr. Parker Davis?"

"You must know it's me if you were able to access this number. What's this about?"

"My name is Winston Hamilton and I'm with the CIA. I have some important information that I must discuss with you immediately. Is your phone secure?"

"Of course," replied Davis.

"I have a brief story to relate." As Winston explained the information he had available and his theory as to what was about to occur the following afternoon, Parker's pulse quickened. Hamilton's story co-related with some preliminary reports he had received from the FBI weeks earlier. Now there was corroboration from a second source that a dirty bomb might be used in an assassination attempt on Jack Wagner.

"You must inform Wagner about this situation and get the inauguration moved to a more secure location," warned Winston.

"I'll try but he's a very stubborn man. I'm not sure he's going to go along with it."

"Then it's imperative that my team and I meet with you by six o'clock tomorrow morning. How about in front of the Capitol Building?"

"Sure, I'm going to be there anyway. What do you look like so I can notify my men. "

Almost as soon as he terminated the call, Davis' cell phone again rang. "Hello?"

"Is this Parker Davis?" *Déjà vu all over again* thought Davis. "Yes."

"This is Lewis Stevenson."

"Yes sir, Mr. Stevenson," replied Davis while a headache started to build in the back of his neck. Stevenson had already warned of a possible assassination attempt on Wagner at the Super Bowl. Now, the venue for the suspected attack has been changed to Washington. He relayed almost the exact same story Winston Hamilton had just told him minutes ago. His report contained no new information other than the fact that the terrorists had been holed up just ninety minutes away on a farm in Pennsylvania. They had to assume the terrorists were already in D.C. and had probably been there for several days.

"We need to convince Wagner to change the inauguration venue."

"I'll talk to him right away Mr. Stevenson, but you've met him before. You know how he is."

"I'm sending my agent in charge to meet with you first thing in the morning."

"What's his name and what does he look like?"

Stevenson gave a description of the man. "His name is John Crawford."

Tell him to meet me at the western steps of the Capitol at six. I'm already meeting someone from the CIA there at that time. Hopefully, I can get Wagner to move things out of the D.C. area."

Parker Davis immediately met with President-elect Wagner. "Mr. President, the NSA, CIA, and FBI all have credible evidence of a possible terrorist attack during the inauguration ceremonies tomorrow. They believe a group plans to somehow launch an attack with a dirty bomb. I suggest you move the site and time of the inauguration."

"I understand your concern, Parker, but so far it's only a suspected threat. We had previous warnings about the Super Bowl and now this. We have no concrete evidence that they are actually here or even have the ability to pull this off."

"But Mr. President, as you are aware, the entire government will be congregating in a space the size of only two hundred square yards. That's not to mention the hundred thousand visitors that will be present on The National Mall. As head of your secret service detail, I must strongly encourage you to cancel the present schedule and arrange for a smaller indoor ceremony. The chief justice can swear you and the VP inside the Capitol Building, or even better, in Philadelphia at a more secure location with a small group of witnesses present. Independence Hall would be an excellent option. It's a site where you can be more readily protected. There is an established precedent for such a process, especially if January 20th falls on a Sunday."

"Well January 20th isn't going to be on a Sunday this year, Parker. It's on a Friday. For the past twenty years, there's been an almost continuous threat of some kind of terrorist attack or another. Most of the stories don't pan out. We can't turn tail every time we get nervous about another threat. The enemy's main goal is to psychologically cripple our land. If we change our routine in response to every suspected threat, the terrorists will have already accomplished that goal. The signers of the Declaration of Independence didn't hide, knowing their lives and fortunes would be under attack by King George. Well, I'm not going to run and hide, either. That's not how I do things. I refuse to give the enemy that kind of a victory. As a candidate, I made a vow that I would take a strong stand against terrorism and I will not back away from that stand tomorrow. It's high time the leader of this great country stood his ground. My first act as President will not be to back down from a fight. I will not hide in the shadows. I will proudly stand at that podium on the steps of the Nation's Capital tomorrow and address the citizens of this great country.

Parker persisted, "Sir, I understand your position, and I don't mean to belabor the point, but I would prefer that you change the inauguration venue to a site where my staff and I can provide better protection. If I may, sir, sometimes discretion is the better part of valor."

"Yes Parker, I know. I've read Shakespeare. But what he should have added is that not if discretion portrays an image of cowardice. Falstaff, as you know, was a coward. This country has looked cowardly enough over the past eight years. I promised that I would return this great country to a position of respect around the world, and that's what I'm going to do. I want our friends to know that we are not afraid to stand up to evil and I want our enemies to know that we do not fear them. I can't do that if I'm hiding somewhere behind closed doors at the first hint of danger. The country expects to see their president at that podium tomorrow, proudly delivering an inaugural address, and that's exactly what they're going to get. Like Churchill said, 'It's time to draw the sword of freedom and throw away the scabbard.' We possess the most sophisticated technology and the best trained personnel in the world. Use them Parker. Have the Service, the FBI and the CIA add men to their details and establish a strong perimeter of security within a three mile radius of the Capitol Building. Now get about the business of protecting me."

"Mr. President, I admire your stand, but if I might suggest, perhaps it would be wise to have an early swearing-in ceremony in order to ensure a proper transition of power; just in case something were to happen. We don't want to leave the country in limbo without a recognized leader. It's mandatory that there is an established chain of command just in case some catastrophic event does occur. You and the Vice President may be sworn in by the Chief Justice several hours before the actual ceremonies. That way, I can take measures to ensure that the continuity process of succession will be protected."

"You're right Parker. This isn't just about the position of one man. Just make sure that nothing does happen to me or the Vice President. By the way, I'm not Mr. President just yet. That man is still in the White House until tomorrow."

"Yes sir, Mr. President," replied Parker as he smiled at the new Commander in Chief.

CHAPTER SIXTY-FOUR

Early on the following morning of January 20th, the sun was still below the horizon as Parker Davis looked out over the National Mall. He was planning his response to the information he received last night when his thoughts were interrupted by his cell phone.

"Now what," he said impatiently as he checked the display screen. It was a call from his command center. "This is Davis," he said.

"Sorry to bother you sir, but I just received a message from the telecommunications center at the National Security Agency. They intercepted three separate brief cell phone transmissions sent over the past thirty-six hours. They traced the numbers and all three were assigned to unregistered burner phones. Each call was less than five seconds duration so they were unable to isolate the exact location of the sources. They could only say that, based upon the cell tower pings, the calls definitely originated within a ten mile radius of the Capitol Building. The first was recorded on Wednesday afternoon, January 18th and it only said 'Alpha in place'. It was followed several seconds later by a double click on the receiver. Then late yesterday, there were two more similar messages just thirty minutes apart: 'Beta in place' and 'Gamma in place. Each was also followed by the same double click. The NSA ran all three messages through their voice recognition database but nothing popped up."

"Contact the FBI, CIA, and the armed services to see if any of them are running ops around Washington that might be using those same code names," ordered Parker.

"I already have, sir and it's a negative. It looks as though the double-click signal is an acknowledgment of reception of the messages."

"I agree. Notify everyone on the protection detail that I'm raising the level of alert to stage four." That is just one level below an actual attack on POTUS.

Parker Davis froze in position while he thought about the implications of the radio transmissions. There was definitely going to be some type of attack, but how? Alpha, Beta, and Gamma are the first three letters of the Greek alphabet and are sometimes used in operations to designate different teams. They also refer to the three types of radiation emitted from a radioactive source. He shuddered as he considered the possibility of a dirty bomb detonation. The effects would be devastating. He was also now certain the terrorists were planning to use three separate teams and that made his job infinitely more difficult. The enemy only had to get lucky with one of them, but Parker had to detect and destroy all three. Anything less would be catastrophic. It was a nearly impossible task.

"I can't believe it. My first assignment as protector of POTUS is already turning into a major clusterfuck!" he said to himself as he paced back and forth in front of the Capitol Building. He gazed down at the western steps toward the podium. He walked down and stood behind it, exactly where President Wagner would be standing eight hours from now. He studied the bulletproof glass shields which were designed to withstand multiple .50 caliber rounds. In front of him, the open space of the National Mall was framed on either side by rows of the massive museum buildings that comprised the Smithsonian Institute. He looked farther west toward the Washington Monument, a mile away. The huge obelisk, which stood nearly in the center of the mall, was by far the tallest structure in Washington. Behind that were the World War II memorials, the reflecting pool, and finally over two miles away, at the far end, sat the Lincoln Memorial with Honest Abe sitting in his chair looking back toward Parker. He thought, *It's a majestic sight, fitting for the inauguration of the next leader of the entire free world. But Abe just might be witnessing the end of the country that he had fought so hard to preserve.*

Parker's palms started to sweat from the overwhelming responsibility that faced him. He again stared out across the expanse of the National Mall, looking for any potential points of attack. After hearing the earlier reports about possible assassination attempts, he beefed up security more than usual. Every vulnerable location had been checked and double-checked. All buildings within a one mile radius of where he now stood had been thoroughly searched, closed, and sealed off to the public. Armed military guards were posted at all building entrances. He had assigned six teams of snipers, one spotter and one shooter each, to be stationed on the roof of all Smithsonian Institute buildings, the Senate office buildings, the Congressional office buildings, and the top observation level of Washington Monument. Each team was equipped with shoulder-launched Stinger missiles. Military transport vehicles, armed with .50 caliber machine guns, blocked every major intersection surrounding the mall. On the roof of the Capitol Building were stationed a half-dozen more sniper teams and the four permanently-placed batteries of radar guided surface to air or SAM missiles to guard against any attack from the air. His big problem now was that he couldn't just shoot down the drones with a missile if they contained nuclear material. The resulting radioactive cloud would shut down the city for a hundred years.

He had three hundred men in cars, on horse, and on foot patrolling the entire area around the National Mall from behind the Lincoln Memorial all the way to the east entrance of the Capitol. Explosives sniffing dogs and their handlers would be scattered throughout the crowd looking for bombs. In four hours, the Air Force would also scramble two pairs of F-16 fighter jets to patrol the skies over the District. He ordered the closure of both Reagan International and Dulles International Airports between noon and five. In addition, he ordered the closure of all small community airports within a fifty mile radius of the Capital, beginning two hours before the ceremonies, and lasting until two hours after they were complete. The Potomac River had already been closed to boat traffic forty-eight hours ago and the coast guard was running regular patrols.

Parker had designed what he hoped would be an impenetrable dome of protection around the incoming president and the public. However, he had learned one painful fact during his years with the Secret Service. No plan is perfect and the other side can always find a way to breach any protection if they have the resources and the necessary commitment. The group that he faced today appeared to have both. Now he knew there were at least three assassins who were already in position and ready to attack. They could be hiding within his dome of protection right now. If so, his defenses might very well be worthless. He again scanned the mall, looking for weak points in his plan.

He didn't really know this Winston Hamilton from the CIA, but the man apparently had a lot of clout and he was obviously someone who Parker should listen to. Per the CIA man's request, the Air Force promised to provide four new super-silent Sikorsky Stealth Black Hawk helicopters similar to the ones used in the 2011 successful assassination attack on Osama bin Laden. The newer ones were equipped with noise-cancelling blue-edge rotor blades that made them almost totally quiet, so the crowd and hopefully, the terrorists would be mostly unaware of their presence. They should arrive shortly.

It takes someone with a fair amount of power to obtain them and apparently this Hamilton fellow had the connections.

Parker checked his watch and it was almost six o'clock, just eight hours away from the administration of the presidential oath, a thirty-five word affirmation that will officially make Jack Wagner the President of the United States. The temperature was cool and the skies were clear. It was going to be a beautiful day for a presidential inauguration. In a few hours, the plaza area would be filling with visitors, placing their chairs in the prime spots. Governmental VIPs would then be arriving and mingling about, jockeying for position that would reflect their status in the new governmental hierarchy. Archbishop Mahoney would soon be here to rehearse his convocation address. He would be standing near the semicircular terrace that housed the elevated podium. The sound engineers were already here balancing out the speakers as dozens of huge American flag banners hung down between the tall columns of the Capitol Building. On either side, network employees were standing atop temporary towers which were erected to house the dozens of television cameras covering the event. "That's just great. The entire world will be able to witness the catastrophe," said Parker to himself.

He looked to his right and saw a group approaching: five men and a woman in black uniforms. One of them was being pushed in a wheelchair. Their leader, a man in a blue suit, stepped forward, extended his hand and introduced himself as Winston Hamilton.

After the man showed his credentials, he again described in detail the scenario that he believed would unfold that afternoon.

Parker became more and more concerned as the reality of Winston's report sunk in. All of his defenses were designed to intercept an attack from the air, from the buildings, or from the crowd. He was not prepared for a drone attack from just above the tree tops. If the planes, in fact, contained nuclear material, he couldn't use stingers to shoot them down because the explosion would disseminate a huge radioactive cloud, killing tens of thousands.

After finishing, Winston asked, "Did you talk to President-elect Wagner about changing the venue for the inauguration?"

"I tried last night but Wagner's having none of it," replied Davis. "At least he authorized an early swearing-in ceremony. He and the Vice-president will assume office this morning." Then Davis asked Winston, "Have you been working in tandem with the FBI?"

"Why is that?" replied Winston, already knowing the answer.

"Because in a few minutes, I'm supposed to meet an FBI agent regarding this same matter. Their story is almost exactly the same as yours. He's trying to help organize a group of agents to thwart the attack."

"Would that man's name be Agent John Crawford?"

"Yes, but how did you know?"

Just then a very tall black man began to climb the side steps to the terrace but was intercepted by Secret Service personnel. "He's ok," Parker yelled to his men, "He's with us." As the man approached, Winston extended his hand and said, "Agent Crawford, I'm Winston Hamilton from the CIA. We've actually been working on the same case involving the Scorpion character."

"You must be the one who's been spoon feeding me all of the anonymous information about this case; the one who kidnapped al-Sadir; the one who he thought was the Mossad."

"I'm not sure that I know what you're talking about," replied Winston with a smile. He turned to his right and said, "Agent

Davis, this is Special Agent John Crawford from the FBI. He has a lot of insight into the group that's planning the attack."

The three men shared all of the information that each could provide and all concluded that, in fact, a three-drone attack with dirty bombs would be launched, probably during the presidential address. That meant they only had about six hours left to find and destroy the drones.

Crawford said to Parker Davis, "I have over a hundred FBI agents arriving within the next hour. Where would you like them stationed?"

"For right now, I would deploy them along a two block perimeter surrounding the National Mall. Have them search every suspicious vehicle, just in case the enemy is transporting the drones closer to the target area," replied Davis.

After Crawford finished issuing the orders, Winston turned to him and said, "We find ourselves in a somewhat difficult situation. I believe that you know several of the other members of my team. They've been working on this for several months." With that, Carver, Lisa, three other men and a little guy in a wheel chair approached the stairs. "Carver, Lisa? What in God's name are you two doing here?"

Winston intervened, "No time for explanations. We can discuss the whys and hows later. Right now, we must get moving on this thing together, and Dr. Savich is the team leader."

Crawford looked at Lisa with a confused look on his face. She could only shrug her shoulders.

Carver turned to Parker and said, "The Washington Monument is the tallest structure in the city, correct?"

"Yes"

"And your men have completely cleared all levels to be certain that no snipers could be hiding anywhere?"

"Correct."

"And I assume that you have men stationed at the top of the Monument to watch the crowds and nearby buildings?" asked Carver.

"Yes. Three groups of two: one sniper and one spotter for each of the windows facing north, south, and east toward the western side of the Capitol. Each shooter is equipped with a Barrett M107, fifty caliber rifle. Why?"

"From what my tech guy has found, after the Washington Monument, the closest tall building to the Capital is The Old Post Office building. It has a 315 foot tower that looks directly down Pennsylvania Avenue toward us. It's less than a mile away and it's one of the most likely sites for a drone launch."

"That's correct, but we've already checked that building twice. It's been sealed off and under armed guard for the past forty-eight hours," replied Parker.

"It's still possible that someone might have gained access to the tower and was able to hide away for several days before it was actually sealed. Get one of your Washington Monument spotters on the radio. He should be able to see the Post Office Tower well from his location. Tell him to check the tower's observation platform with his scope. Ask if he can see anyone hiding up there."

Parker spoke into his radio and relayed instructions to the spotter. The response was "I have good visualization sir and it's a negative. I don't see anyone...wait a minute...yes, there's some movement at the northeast corner. Hold on," he said as he refocused his scope..."Yes sir. I have confirmation. There's one man present. I couldn't see him initially because he was bent over behind the railing. He looks to be vomiting. Yes, that's affirmative, sir. He's vomiting heavily, and I believe he's been shot! He has blood all over the front of his shirt. He's holding on to the railing and he's having a hard time standing up."

"Shit!" exclaimed Dan Foster. "He wasn't shot, he's vomiting blood. It's probably radiation poisoning. That means he's already been exposed to a large dose. He must have a lot of radioactive material up there. This is a very serious problem. We can't let him trigger that device."

"Do you have a solid head shot?" Parker asked.

"That's a negative sir, but I can give it a try."

Carver said, "You can't just try. He must to be taken out with one shot. You have to be one-hundred percent certain. If he's only wounded and can still get to the triggering mechanism, he'll detonate that thing on top of the tower. The radioactive cloud will spread for miles. Casualties will be huge."

Carver thought for a second and added, "We need a couple of guys to hit that tower and get in fast for a close head shot," responded Carver.

"I'm on it," said Crawford. "I'll take the big guy and the other guy next to him with me," he said as he looked at the Hank and Hacker. The three men ran down the side steps of the terrace toward Crawford's car which was parked nearby on Pennsylvania Avenue. They got in and raced down the road to the Old Post Office tower.

Parker Davis turned to Carver and said "That's one, but based on our radio intercepts, there are at least two more sites."

Carver replied, "Our research shows that there are nine other tall buildings which could serve as possible launch sites. I'd suggest you get two of your stealth helicopters airborne and have them check the rest of the locations on the list as quickly as they can." Carver looked at his watch. "It's now almost nine and the ceremonies begin at noon. I'd have the president wait inside a secure location for as long as possible. I realize that he's adamant about standing his ground, but maybe you can convince him to stall for a little while. Everything in government runs late anyway."

Parker Davis got on his radio and did as was suggested.

Winston said, "I'd recommend that a member of my team accompany one of the helicopters if possible. He's one of the best long distance combat snipers in the country and he has extensive combat experience. If anyone can take out these guys from the air, it's him."

"Done. I have my own snipers but they're already deployed. I'll take all the help I can get," replied Parker.

CHAPTER SIXTY-FIVE

"Allah, give me the strength to fulfill your wishes," muttered Tarriz Muhktar weakly. He didn't realize how painful it would be. He had spent the past forty-eight hours hidden in the tower elevator shaft in the Old Post Office Building. Initially, he was only having trouble with episodes of nausea and vomiting. Then, the vomiting became more frequent and turned bloody. The entire front of his shirt was now covered in red. On the second day, the diarrhea started and rapidly progressed. He had to remain hidden in the elevator shaft and there was nowhere to go to relieve himself or clean up.

"Look at me. I am not worthy to see Allah today," he moaned. Now on the glorious day of their victory for Allah, he could barely crawl out of his hiding place and up to the observation deck. Once there, he immediately vomited a huge amount of bloody fluid. Repeated episodes of cramping pain in his abdomen dropped him to his knees, causing him to pass out for a short while. After a few minutes, he collected his strength, stood up, and looked down Pennsylvania Avenue. It was quiet except for a single car speeding down the middle of the road in his direction. It had been closed down for the upcoming presidential parade from the Capitol building to the White House. Tarriz prayed that the parade would never happen. Rather, Pennsylvania Avenue would become a river of blood glorifying Allah's battle against these infidels.

He dropped back down to the deck surface and pulled his duffel bag closer. He again vomited, this time all over the bag and its contents. He passed out and when he came to, a few minutes later, he was moving more slowly. He withdrew the plane from the duffel and with great difficulty, he slowly unfolded the wings. The cargo compartment was opened and he inserted the lead bags containing the Uranium pellets. The blocks of C-4 were sandwiched between them. He smiled a grotesque smile of the nearly dead as he thought about the storm of fire that he was about to unleash. He took the remote control device and checked it. All was working well. He connected the remote detonator blasting cap wires to the C-4 blocks and then attached wires to his back-up system. "There is no way that they can stop me now," he said to himself in an almost inaudible whisper. Then he again vomited a large amount of blood, this time onto the drone's remote control console.

Crawford brought his car to a screeching stop in front of the building. He, Hank, and "Rib Man" Hacker got out and raced to the front door. After he showed his identification badge to the two marine guards stationed at the entrance, a sergeant unlocked the door and allowed them in.

"Tower elevators," shouted Crawford over his shoulder as he passed. The guard pointed across the courtyard and said, "To the right." They ran through the pavilion to the elevator banks and pushed the button. There was no response.

"They've been sabotaged. We need to take the stairs," said Crawford.

Hacker looked at Hank and said, "Three hundred fifteen vertical feet, we should've had Lisa for this one."

Hank replied, "Let's go ladies. We have less than two hours."

After thirty minutes of difficult climbing and a lot of heavy breathing, they made it to the access door of the observation platform. Crawford tried to quietly turn the knob, shook his head and whispered to the group, "Locked. We're going to have to break it down. Hank, you take out the door, Hacker go low to the left and I'll go right. Shoot anything that you see and ask questions later. We have no time for Miranda kinds of shit."

Tarriz propped himself against the railing of the deck and he waited. He sensed that the time was drawing near. "Just a couple more hours and I will be in paradise." He only needed to await the final signal from the Scorpion. He had the plane and remote control sitting in front of him, and his rifle lying across his lap. Suddenly, the deck door exploded open and an enormous man pushed through. He was quickly followed by a short white man and a tall black man. Tarriz raised his automatic rifle and unloaded the clip into the closest one. Hacker collapsed with a dozen bullet holes in the chest.

Tarriz reached for the remote control unit and flipped the cover off the red detonator button. He pushed it...nothing happened. The wires had shorted out after he vomited on the console. Instead of detonating the nuclear device, he got two of Crawford's .45 caliber bullets into the center of his chest. The only thing to explode was his heart. Any hopes of entering paradise that afternoon died with him.

Crawford got on the radio and hailed Carver. "Alpha is neutralized and the package is secure. From the looks and smell of him, I think we did him a favor. Put him out of his misery. Rib Man is gone. He took most of an entire clip in the chest. Died instantly but Hank is still running strong."

"Roger that, good work. Sorry about Rib Man." replied a shaken Carver.

"What about the bomb?" asked Parker Davis.

"It's here and it's secure. I've disconnected the wires to several blocks of C-4 so it can't be remotely detonated by one of the other terrorists. I don't want to mess around with things any more until you can get a HazMat team up here. I don't want to wind up like this poor sucker."

"Roger that. I'll send a team and some extra people to secure the area," replied Davis.

"One down but we still have to find Beta and Gamma," said Winston.

Davis responded, "I'll notify the president."

Winston turned to Carver, "Have your helicopter teams identified any other launch sites?"

"Both teams have checked in and six buildings have been negative so far. Dan's on his way to the seventh so, including that one, we have four to go," responded Carver.

"Tell them to hurry it up," responded Winston. "We're running out of time."

CHAPTER SIXTY-SIX

As Archbishop Mahoney was delivering the opening invocation for the ceremonies, Dan Foster was on his way to the next building on the Geek's list, riding in one of the Sikorsky Black Hawk helicopters. He was secured by a harness with the side door open, and his right leg hanging outside. *It's eerie,* he thought. *This coptor's almost completely silent, unlike the missions in Iraq where the noise was deafening.* All he could hear was the wind rushing past him. He knew they were running low on time. The presidential inauguration address was now less than an hour away and he was getting anxious. Seven of the other prospective launch sites had been checked and were found to be empty. There were only three left and two more terrorists to be identified, a sixty-seven percent chance that this one would have a bogie.

They were approaching the Knights Tower on the southeast corner of the National Shrine of the Immaculate Conception. The coptor's co-pilot was using a pair of stabilized binoculars when he yelled out, "I've got one bogie on the tower. He's on the southwest corner of the observation platform, about fifteen feet from the top. He's pretty well hidden but someone is definitely there and he's holding some gear.

"We need to come up from behind so he doesn't see us. Where's the sun? We don't want to cast a shadow." Dan checked the surroundings and then said, "Take a wide arc to the east, but we must move quickly. I just hope this thing stays as quiet as it's supposed to be."

"Don't worry," said the pilot. "He won't know we're there until we're just about on top of him."

"Get me as close as you can. I need to get off a clean head shot so he can't activate that damn detonator!" Dan knew this would have to be the shot of his life. Hitting stationary targets from a mile out was one thing, but sitting in a helicopter with one leg hanging out the side and trying to hit a moving man's head, even from only a hundred yards was something else. There was no room for error. Failure could be catastrophic. As the pilot gradually approached the target, the terrorist turned around and fired in their direction.

"We're taking fire, hold on!" yelled the pilot. He banked the helicopter hard left. If it hadn't been for the harness, Dan would have fallen out the door.

Ahmad Haq Rasid didn't hear the copter as much as he sensed its presence. He looked up and snarled through his two vampire teeth. He picked up his AK 47, pushed the selector switch to full automatic, and opened fire. The AK 47 rifle was designed for the Soviet Union by Mikhail Kalashnikov after World War II. It's a weapon that was made to withstand all of the abuse that combat situations could inflict. It's virtually indestructible and undeniably reliable, but that reliability comes at the expense of accuracy. Any hit at over a hundred yards is likely to be no more than an accident, especially if the target is moving. Not surprisingly, Ahmad's spray of automatic fire didn't even come close.

＝◁┼┼▷＝

"Get me back down there fast!" yelled Dan. "Don't worry, he's already out of ammo." Dan didn't have a clear shot yet. He tried to center his sights on Ahmad but the man was taking cover behind the stone balusters of the observation deck. The distance to the target was closing, but this was no long-range shooting contest where he had the benefit of a bipod and was in a stable prone position. There was no time to control his breathing and no time to slow his heart rate. He was straddling the side door of a rapidly moving, Sikorsky Black Hawk helicopter traveling at almost two hundred miles an hour. It was not a long distance by Dan's standards, but it would be the most difficult shot he had ever tried. Finally, he took it.

＝◁┼┼▷＝

With the setting on fully automatic, Ahmad's thirty-round magazine was expended within ten seconds. He dropped the rifle, and squatted down behind the balusters for protection from what he knew would be coming. Although he didn't stop the helicopter, he hoped that he had slowed down its attack long enough. He had already assembled the plane and the bomb. It was ready for launch. He was supposed to wait until he received the signal from the Scorpion but there was no time for that now. He had to begin his attack right away. He bent down and lifted the plane with one hand, while he secured the remote with the other. He stood up and launched the drone. It soared away beautifully. Using the remote, he accelerated to its maximum speed and guided it down Michigan Ave. He studied the console screen, looking for the left turn that would take him down North Capitol Street and toward the target. He maintained a level just above the trees and power lines. He could see the street several hundred yards ahead.

"Praise Allah, give me just a few more minutes and your glory will be seen by all." Apparently Allah wasn't listening because A second later, Ahmad's head exploded into a misty red cloud of brain and bone. He fell to the deck as a rapidly expanding pool of blood radiated outward from what used to be his head. His hand was still holding the remote, but his hand was no longer attached to any cognitive center. As he fell, the remote navigation control was pushed forward, pitching the drone into a sharp dive to the left. Within three seconds, it plummeted into the Glenwood Cemetery. There was a loud explosion and a rising cloud of dust... radiation-contaminated dust. Fortunately, any breeze had completely stopped.

⸛ ⸛

"My God!" shouted Dan. "How in the hell did that damn thing explode? I know the son of a bitch couldn't push the remote detonator switch. He died instantly. The C-4 wouldn't just explode like that."

"They must have had an impact detonator on the thing," replied the pilot. "I guess they installed one as a backup just in case the navigator was neutralized."

"We're lucky it detonated inside that cemetery. The place is empty; must have been closed down by the Secret Service. Based upon the size of the dust cloud and the lack of a breeze, dispersion of the uranium should be limited to the cemetery and hopefully just a few surrounding streets. Be sure we stay away from the area. We don't want our rotor wash to stir up that cloud," warned Dan.

"I'll climb to five hundred feet and head west toward the next building on your list," responded the pilot.

Dan commented, "I guess Allah was watching over us more than Allah was watching over him."

"Maybe Allah doesn't like insane mass murderers," added the pilot.

"Roger that." Dan immediately hailed Carver on his radio. "Carver, we got Beta, but the drone crashed."

"Yes, we just heard the explosion. Did he push that detonator switch?" asked Carver.

"No, he didn't have a chance. He was dead as soon as I shot him. The drone has a backup impact detonator. If the guys with the guns see the third drone in the air, tell them that they can't shoot it down. I repeat, do not shoot it down. That backup trigger mechanism will detonate on impact when the plane crashes," warned Dan.

"What about the radiation risk there?"

"I think it's mostly limited but you'd better have Parker Davis send a HazMat team over to the Glenwood Cemetery and contain a two block perimeter just to be sure. They should evacuate everyone in the area until it's been cleared. They can tell the neighbors it was a gas explosion," said Dan.

"We still haven't identified the third terrorist and we only have two other buildings left on the Geeks list," said Carver.

"We're on our way to check them now. I'm not optimistic because they're not as tall and they're farther out."

"That's a problem but I have an idea. I'll let you know about it later."

"Carver, we may not have a later. If Gamma is close, and he heard that explosion, he's going to get ready to launch. I don't have to tell you what'll happen if his drone comes down close to the Capitol. You can't let Gamma launch. Once it gets in the air, there's going to be no way to prevent a disaster!"

"I'm working on it."

"How far along are the ceremonies, Carver?" asked Dan, trying to figure out how much time they had left to work with.

"Wagner's been given the oath of office and should start his inauguration address shortly. Let me know as soon as you've checked those final two buildings. Gotta go."

⊨⊹⊰⊱⊹⊨

President Wagner had just finished reciting the oath of office when the explosion could be heard. The crowd began to stir and some started to run. Parker yelled into his wrist mike, "Secure the Bulldog, secure the Bulldog!" Immediately, the president was surrounded by a half-dozen Secret Service agents as they tried to pull him inside and out of harm's way. But he struggled loose and approached the podium.

"Ladies and gentlemen, there's nothing to worry about. Unfortunately, my first duty as the Commander-in-Chief is to let you know that it appears as though one of the presidential battery canons fired prematurely."

There was a collective sigh of relief and nervous chuckles from the crowd. Parker Davis looked incredulously at President Wagner who simply raised his eyebrows.

CHAPTER SIXTY-SEVEN

Dan called Carver five minutes later, "We just finished checking One Franklin Square and the National Cathedral. They're both negative. We could continue working down the next five on the Geek's secondary list, but we're getting pretty far away."

Carver responded, "Forget about the rest of the list. Gamma's closer than that. I just know it. I want you and the other copter to increase your altitude and circle through a three mile radius of my position. Use your scope to see if you can spot anything on the rooftops. You're the sniper. Look for places that you'd use for a good shot. If you find him, kill him, and ask questions later. Let me know."

"Roger that, Carver."

After his conversation with Dan, Carver scanned his surroundings until he found what he was looking for. A hundred feet away, stood an older man who was wearing an olive green uniform and a ranger hat. His face was tanned and severely wrinkled from the many years he had spent outdoors as a guide. He was a senior member of the U.S. National Park Service. Carver pointed at him and told Winston, "I need to talk to that fellow right away!"

The confused man was brought to Carver who looked at his name badge and said, "Hello, Mr. Morgan. I have a question for you. If I asked you to show me the best place around here to get the widest view of the National Mall area and the Capital Building, what would you suggest?"

The old ranger automatically went into one of his tour routines. "Well, the best view would be from the top of the Washington Monument. It's five hundred fifty-five feet high and...

"Yes, yes, I know," interrupted Carver. "What if I asked you the same question but wanted you to exclude all of the tallest and most famous structures in D.C.? Maybe somewhere more obscure."

The man paused, pursed his lips, and stroked his chin for a few seconds. Then his eyes lit up with the idea.

"Tourists, and even most D.C. residents aren't aware of this, but one of the best overviews of the city can be seen from a hill behind the Kennedy Memorial. It's where the historic Custis-Lee mansion sits. It was built on the highest point in the region by George Washington's grandson in 1803. I haven't been up on the roof but I imagine the view is nothing short of spectacular up there."

"You mean in Arlington National Cemetery?"

"Yes, but you can't go there today. It's closed for the inauguration ceremonies."

"How far away is it, would you say, maybe as the crow flies?"

"I guess around three miles."

"That's it!" Carver exclaimed to Winston and Parker Davis. "I need one of those super-quiet helicopters that you put Dan on and I need it thirty minutes ago!"

"We already have one ready on the South side of the building," replied Parker Davis.

"Tell the pilot to get the rotors turning. Lisa, get your rifle and come with me." Carver grabbed hold of the Geek's wheelchair and pushed him along, running as fast as he could. Lisa was right at his side, step for step.

The Geek was shocked and said, "Me? Are you sure you want me along? I've had no combat training! I can't even shoot!"

"You're more than well-trained for what I have in mind," replied Carver. "Let's go!" he yelled to the pilot after he got the Geek and Lisa aboard.

CHAPTER SIXTY-EIGHT

Martin Darpoli turned on Kathleen Maley's television and began surfing between the various news channels until he settled on Fox News. "Nice picture," he said nonchalantly. He went to the kitchen to get a beer and sat down on the cream floral-patterned couch. Kathleen's body was still warm and dressed in her robe, her lifeless eyes staring out toward eternity.

He had arrived at her Georgetown condo three hours ago, ostensibly so the two of them could watch the inauguration ceremonies together on television. They were invited to attend one of the many gatherings honoring President Wagner later that evening. As the assistant to Senator Cranston Barnes, and the one who actually arranged the schedule for today's events, Kathleen was selected to attend the most prestigious party. She had been looking forward to introducing her new boyfriend to the Senator and maybe even to President Wagner himself. But, the Scorpion had always known that it was never going to happen. He simply needed Kathleen for the specific details about the inauguration...details that only she could provide. Now she was a liability, and he didn't like liabilities.

After he arrived at her condo earlier, they had sex...twice. She seemed to have an insatiable appetite for it. Afterward, Kathleen made sandwiches. The two ate lunch in the kitchen and shared a bottle of chardonnay. After a shower, he got dressed while she put on a robe over her naked body. They sat on the couch. She snuggled up next to Martin, pulled her legs up to the side, and laid her head on his left shoulder. She was in love. He reached around with his left hand and began gently rubbing her neck. With his right hand he softly caressed her breasts. She moaned and he thought the two of them might have sex again. However, he looked at his watch and there was not enough time. He slowly raised his right hand from her breast to her chin, and turned her face up toward him as if to give her a kiss...but there would be no more kisses for Kathleen. With a quick counter-rotation motion of both arms, he snapped her neck. She died instantly. It was his final gift to her, a quick and painless death.

He turned his attention back to the TV, increased the volume, and picked up the cell phone he planned to use to signal the initiation of the Great Attack. He looked at the schedule notes which Kathleen had left on the coffee table. Right now, President Wagner was being administered the oath of office by the Chief Justice of the Supreme Court. After that, the Marine Corps Band would begin the playing of ruffles and flourishes followed by "Hail to the Chief". At that time, the twenty-one gun salute was scheduled to be carried out by the Presidential Guns Salute Battery. Once those are heard, the three drone navigators would know that they should get ready for his signal. Then the president was scheduled to approach the podium and deliver a thirty-minute inaugural address. It was during the speech that he would transmit the message to initiate the attack.

The Scorpion held the cell phone in his right hand as he studied the TV screen. The camera scanned the dignitaries sitting behind the podium. There was Mrs. Wagner, standing proudly next to her husband. Seated were the vice president and his wife, the outgoing president and first lady, all nine justices of the Supreme Court, the head of the senate, the leaders of both political parties, members of the new cabinet, and members of the Joint Chiefs of Staff. The entire United States government and its military leaders were gathered there in a space less than the size of a football field.

"How thoughtful of them," the Scorpion snickered to himself. There was some scurrying about and Wagner said something at the podium but the Scorpion missed it. He was distracted by the anticipation of his coming revenge. It was so strong, he could taste it. He stared at the screen again, reveling in the total destruction of the very country that had destroyed his family and village years ago. The firing of the twenty-one gun salute was completed and he again studied each face before transmitting the attack signal. President Wagner approached the podium and gazed out over the tens of thousands of civilian attendees sitting on the National Mall lawn. He adjusted several of the swan-necked microphones. In front and on both sides of him was the bullet-proof glass shield. "That shield will do you no good today, Mr. President. Today, the fires of hell will rain down from above."

One more time, the Scorpion looked at the faces of leadership, following in his mind the normal line of succession to power. His sardonic smile slowly melted into a worried frown. Something was wrong. He stood up and dropped the cell phone onto the floor. "This shouldn't be!" he screamed at the television. Conspicuous by his absence from the ceremonies was the third in line behind the president and vice president, the Speaker of the House.

"Where is he? He's supposed to be there! He must be there! The success of the entire mission depends upon the total elimination of everyone in the chain of succession. Their government will still be crippled but without killing all of them, the government will still continue." The Scorpion had done his research on every major leader. The press had referred to the Speaker as a no-nonsense, self-made man. He had grown up in a tough neighborhood and he brought that toughness with him to Washington. Like President Wagner, he was not afraid of a fight and the public liked him for it.

"He has to be there somewhere. Kathleen told me he would." He looked at her notes again and there it was: Speaker of the House in the front row. He was supposed to be right next to the vice president, but the Speaker wasn't there! What the Scorpion didn't realize was that at the suggestion of Parker Davis, the Speaker was being held at a secure location inside Andrew's Air Force Base fifteen miles away.

The Scorpion continued to stare at the screen, rage welling up inside him and an acidulous knot coiling in his stomach He picked up the remote and repeatedly changed the channel hoping to see something different on another station, but the man definitely wasn't there. He smashed the TV control against the wall. As he stared at the pieces on the floor for several minutes, he regained his composure. "I underestimated the Americans. I will not do so again. It's time to start work on the backup plan. I've been patient this long. I can be patient a while longer," he said to no-one but himself. He initiated a cascade of calls that would inform every sleeper-cell leader in the country to stand down for now. The follow-up attacks must be postponed. He picked up Kathleen's car keys from a dish on the hall table, checked his coat pocket to be sure that he had his ticket, and headed for the door. While looking back at the TV one more time, he said, "I can't completely destroy your country yet, but I can still deliver a devastating blow." Holding up the cell phone, he pushed the send button.

CHAPTER SIXTY-NINE

Muhammad bin Hussein was unaware that their plan had been exposed. He was unaware that Alpha and Beta had been eliminated. He was unaware that he was the Scorpion's last chance for success. Remaining in a crouched position on top of the Custis-Lee mansion, he peaked over the edge of the roof. He scanned the deserted grounds of Arlington National Cemetery and marveled at the thousands of headstones. Multiple monuments had been erected over the years to honor their fallen heroes, famous soldiers like: Audie Murphy, General George Patton, General Omar Bradley, and Admiral William Halsey. The eternal flame, marking the grave of their President Kennedy, could be seen a hundred yards in front of him. To his right sat the Tomb of the Unknown Soldier with its adjacent Memorial Amphitheater. Even though the cemetery was closed today and there were no visitors, a lone Army guard in full military dress uniform continued pacing back and forth on the black mat; twenty-one paces to the north and then twenty-one paces to the south until the hourly ceremonial changing of the guard. It continued twenty-four hours a day, seven days a week, three hundred sixty-five days every year. He couldn't help but be impressed by the way this shallow country of infidels honored their fallen warriors. There would be many more fallen warrior bodies to bury after today. A grin twisted the bushy mustache at the corners of his mouth.

To the north, he could make out the Arlington Memorial Bridge which he would soon follow with the drone, across the waters of the Potomac River. Looking further, he could see the Lincoln Memorial, the Washington Monument and the Capitol dome. *Today, we will launch a glorious attack that will unleash a hundred similar attacks across this country. We will completely erase the vestiges of their decadent society. Their stock market will collapse and the other western economies will soon follow suit.*

He could hear the sounds of the twenty-one gun salute reverberate across the river. "Soon it will be time," he quietly said to himself. He assembled the drone, inserted the Uranium 235 bags, attached the blasting caps into the C-4, and looked at his cell phone screen, waiting for the Scorpion's signal.

CHAPTER SEVENTY

After the three members of the Delphi Team boarded the copter and secured their safety belts, Carver yelled to the pilot, "Head south and work your way around Reagan International. We need to come up on Arlington from behind. I don't want to spook this guy into launching that drone before we get there, but we don't have much time."

"Yes sir. I'll stay low on the trees so he won't see us coming. We'll be there in three minutes."

Carver looked out the open door of the Sikorsky and saw the Potomac pass below them. Within a minute, they crossed the airport's perimeter fence and were heading west toward Arlington. The Pentagon sat just to the north, the scars from 9/11 all but invisible. Carver turned to Lisa and the Geek and told them his plan, which actually wasn't much of a plan. "Lisa, get your rifle ready and Norman, just wait. I'll let you know when you're on. You'll have to act quickly if this is going to work."

Carver's radio squawked. It was Parker. "Carver, how're you doing with that third drone?"

Carver looked through his binoculars. "Hold on a minute. We're almost there. I can see the top of the mansion. He's there! We'll get him in a minute."

"Well hurry up. I'm getting nervous down here."

Lisa prepared her Knight 110 sniper system. She put the selector switch on three-shot bursts and looked through the scope in the direction of the target. They were getting closer now. Her father had taught her how to shoot when she could barely walk and she was more than prepared for this mission. She was no stranger to killing, and she could feel the clawing increasing inside her, the monster wanting to be released. It was the same demon that had plagued her brother since the two were children. She knew from experience that she needed to contain it until the time was right

They crossed the Arlington western perimeter fence and she could feel herself enter into the zone. The coptor was at tree top level and right below her, she could easily see the headstones, all precisely lined up in neat military rows. She again brought the scope to her eye and visualized the target. They were getting close and fortunately, he still seemed to be unaware of their presence. She controlled her breathing and willed her heart rate to slow as she prepared herself mentally.

"I have him...but I don't have a clear head shot!"

"Well get one," yelled Carver. "Shoot something. I don't see the drone. I think he already launched it!"

She fired.

Muhammad felt the vibration of his cell phone and looked at the screen. The message was just one word, "Attack." He stood on the slanted roof and braced himself against the chimney for stability. He held the drone aloft while holding the remote control console in his left hand, just as he had practiced. The plane lifted out of his hand and he watched it fly down over the Arlington Cemetery visitors' center at tree-top level. It continued along the Arlington Memorial Bridge across the Potomac River. His heart was racing in anticipation. He turned to the console screen for further navigation. He could see the Lincoln Memorial straight ahead. Once there, he turned right and began heading across the Reflecting Pool. From there, he would skirt around the Washington Monument, just above the crowd, and continue toward the Capitol Building. In his mind, he could visualize the tens of thousands of Americans who would be killed on worldwide TV. He yelled, "What a glorious day for Allah and ..."

His thoughts of glory stopped. He felt a sudden pain in his arm as two of the three shots that Lisa had fired tore through flesh and bone, severing his left arm at the elbow. A split-second later, the pain became excruciating as blood gushed forth from the stump. The remote control console, with Muhammad's hand still clenching it, fell to the roof and slid down into the gutter, where it became lodged. He instinctively fell for cover behind the mansion's chimney. When he tried to make it back to the console and the detonation trigger, he was pinned down by Lisa's automatic rifle fire.

⫘⫘⫘

"Get me down on that damned roof!" Carver screamed to the pilot. "Lisa, keep that son of a bitch pinned down. Don't let him reach that control panel."

The pilot put the helicopter's nose into a rapid dive, pulling up at the last second, just three feet from the roof. When Carver landed on the pitched surface, he stumbled, dropping his 9 mm Sig Sauer sidearm. The gun slid down the roof and all of the way to the ground. Muhammad jumped up from behind the chimney, running at him like a screaming banshee, a snarl of bloody saliva showing underneath his mustache.

"Shoot him," Carver commanded but Lisa didn't have a clear shot. The two men were too close together. Muhammad was tearing away at him like a one-armed madman. Carver tried to reach his ankle holster for his back-up .380, but Muhammad had him tied up.

The problem for Muhammad was that he no longer had a left arm, leaving Carver's right arm free. He reached down along his right leg and found what he needed. He unsheathed the nine inch combat knife that Dan had given him at Farmto. He quickly brought it up under Muhammad's chin and pushed it upward through the base of the man's tongue. Blood poured out of Muhammad's mouth and he loosened his grip. Carver pulled his left arm free and drove his fist into the heel of the knife handle. He slammed the tip of the blade through the base of Muhammad's skull, slicing the man's brain in half. The clawing quieted while he watched Muhammad's eyes widen in shock and disbelief as his life slipped away into oblivion.

Carver dropped him and immediately slid down the roof toward the control unit. He pulled it out of the gutter and threw Muhammad's still-attached hand to the ground. Running back up to the copter, he jumped in, and said to the Deets, "OK, Norman, you're on. Do some of that geeky computer-game stuff that you do."

To the pilot he yelled, "Stay within two hundred yards of that drone so we don't lose control."

Norman straightened the console in front of him, shaking uncontrollably. "Settle down," he told himself. "It's just like a video game that you've played a thousand times before." He looked at the screen and yelled, "Shit, its heading directly for the Washington Monument." He slowed the drone and banked left to avoid the famous obelisk, missing it by only a few feet. Then he again yelled, "Fuck, fuck...too slow... it's gunna stall." He pushed the velocity joy-stick forward and banked the plane farther to the left.

Lisa looked over his shoulder and screamed, "Norman, you're headed for the White House!"

"Shit! Shit! Every direction I turn this thing, I'm headed for a collision! I'm gunna kill everyone down there."

Carver said, "Easy Norman, get some altitude up over the trees and buildings."

Norman pulled the nose up until all they could see were clear blue skies.

"Now bank left and complete a one-hundred-eighty-degree turn." Norman followed Carver's instructions. "Good, now gently lower your nose so that we can see the ground and figure out exactly where we are."

When the Geek completed the maneuver, they could see that the drone was headed back in the direction of the Reflecting Pool. "That's perfect Norman. Straight ahead, there's the Lincoln Memorial. Do you see it?"

"Yeah, got it," replied the Geek.

"Now, turn a little more. Do you see the Jefferson Memorial?"

"Yeah, just to the left."

"There's a large tidal basin directly in front of it."

"I see it."

"Try to circle around and keep it in view while you slowly descend."

"Carver, if I try to land this thing, that impact detonator is going to trigger a radioactive explosion and there must be a couple thousand people down there! I'll kill all of them!"

"Just do as I say, just like we planned. Go slowly now...slowly lower...circle around and lower...lower." The plane gradually dropped until it was just a few feet above the water. At that point Carver yelled, "Now! Pull the nose up and cut the power!"

Norman pulled the nose up. It was perfect. The tail of the drone hit the water first and then it skimmed along the surface for about fifteen feet. The drone's motor stopped and the nose gently settled into the water...no impact and no detonation.

"You timed that perfectly, Norman!" said Lisa.

"Not really," replied a terrified Geek. "I was so damn nervous that I didn't cut the power. The battery just ran down. I almost screwed it up. I almost killed thousands of people."

"I won't tell anyone if you don't Norman. Sometimes it's better to be lucky than good," said a relieved Lisa.

⊷⊶

Carver placed a call to Parker Davis, "Gamma is down! I repeat, Gamma is down! The package is stable and secure. We need another HazMat team near the tidal basin by the Jefferson Memorial. The drone is floating on the surface.

"You've been busy, Carver. I certainly hope you don't have anything else planned for today. I'm running out of HazMat teams."

"No, I think everything's been taken care of. I'm going to take the afternoon off and maybe have a beer with the rest of the team. By the way, how's the president?"

"He's just finishing up his address and people are already giving him a standing ovation. He and Mrs. Wagner are about to begin the parade down Pennsylvania Avenue to the White House. I gotta go."

EPILOGUE

A week after the attempted attacks, John Crawford was meeting Director Stevenson in his office at the J. Edgar Hoover Building. The two men were sitting in high-backed leather chairs, facing each other. Stevenson took a sip of his coffee and set it down. "That was great work, John. Because of everything you did on this case, our country avoided an unprecedented disaster."

"Me and some very effective people from the CIA," responded Crawford.

"Yes, I'm aware of their involvement but someone with a lot of clout has put a tight lid on whatever they did." After another sip of coffee, the director continued, "John, I wanted you here today so that I could tell you something in person."

"Sir?"

"I've spoken to the president several times in the past week about you and your investigation. He wants you to be promoted to the job of Assistant Director in Charge of Domestic Terrorism. You'll be one of the top three people in the Bureau."

Crawford paused for a while and said, "Thank you sir." This promotion was one of the highest non-political appointments in the FBI. Still, he had the same mixed feelings he had experienced when he was being promoted from Cincinnati to the Chicago office.

Now, just three months later, he would be going to Washington, even farther away from his daughters and away from Lisa.

Stevenson sensed Crawford's hesitation and understood. "I know this will be a big change for you, John, but you'll still be able to commute back and forth to Cincinnati every weekend, using one of the Bureau's planes. President Wagner wants you on this, John."

After another second of hesitation, he replied, "It would be a privilege, sir."

"Good. I'll submit all of the necessary papers. We'll make the promotion effective as of today. Now, we need to get to the bottom of who's responsible for the attacks. Fortunately, we've already come up with a great deal of information. The drones were made at the Microavionics Technology Corporation."

"The site of the warehouse fire. That's where Muhammad bin Hussein had been working."

"Exactly. We've tracked down the ownership of the company. It was purchased just over six months ago by an offshore subsidiary of the Masterson Properties Corporation. The CEO is a man by the name of Martin Darpoli. Two days after the attacks, the D.C. police found the body of a Kathleen Maley on the couch in her Georgetown condominium. She was an assistant to Senator Cranston Barnes and was in charge of creating the inauguration schedule. She was naked and her neck had been snapped. She had recently had sex, presumably with her killer. We have semen samples for DNA analysis and we're awaiting the lab report."

"I think I know where you're going with this. So she pretty much knew the exact schedule for the day's events; who would be where and when," added Crawford.

"Yes. Maley recently started dating a man whom we are now looking for. Would you like to take a guess at his name?"

"Martin Darpoli."

"That's not all. We've discovered that the three terrorists each stayed at a separate hotel on the evening prior to the attacks. All are owned by the Masterson Properties Corporation."

"So Darpoli is probably the Scorpion. What's his connection to jihad?"

"We don't know yet. All we do know is that Kathleen Maley's car was found in a short-term parking lot at the Philadelphia International Airport. We assume Darpoli took it after killing her. The ticket in the car shows that he entered the lot just about three hours after Wagner finished his address. Looks like he skipped out as soon as his plan collapsed. After that, he just disappeared. We couldn't find his name on any passenger manifests. "

"New identity?" inquired Crawford.

"Probably, or maybe he flew out on a private jet. We just don't know yet. That's where you come in, John. I want you to track down this guy. In addition, we need to determine the identity of anyone else who might have helped organize of the attacks. Darpoli's rich and smart but he didn't do this alone. He had to be helped by someone with a great deal of power. See who else was on the Board of Directors at Masterson Properties and what private jets might have flown out of Philadelphia on Inauguration Day. That might lead us in the right direction. The president wants everyone involved in this attack brought to justice. You'll have the full power of my office and that of the CIA."

Assistant Director John Crawford exited Stevenson's office and walked down the hall to his own new offices. He turned to his secretary and said, "Would you please reserve the Bureau plane for me for this Friday evening? I'll be traveling to Cincinnati."

He was going to have to arrange a face-to-face discussion with his old friend Dr. Jacob Savich. There were a lot of matters that needed to be explained. In addition, he had dinner reservations for two at Otto's restaurant in Covington this Saturday evening. He and Lisa also had a great deal to discuss, especially regarding the future of their relationship. He needed some answers to questions that he really didn't want to ask. He didn't know if he actually wanted to hear her answers. How did she get involved with the CIA? Exactly who was this woman who he thought he had known his entire life…but apparently didn't know at all? He thought she had been the love of his life…the woman he planned to marry.

He reached into his suit coat pocket and touched the small velvet box which he had purchased at a jewelry store just four weeks ago. He wondered.

—⊰+⊱—

Winston Hamilton III had a very important meeting scheduled at the White House later in the morning. First though, he had another function that required his presence. He was attending a ceremony commemorating the fallen Derek Hacker. He sat with a group of a hundred other department chiefs. Before them, the CIA director stood at a podium in front of the 'Memorial Wall' which was located in the main lobby of the Langley Headquarters. The left side was flanked by the American Flag while on the right side stood a flag bearing the seal of the Central Intelligence Agency.

The Director began, "Behind me is a wall containing one-hundred-ten stars. Each one commemorates a fallen comrade. Many of us knew some of the heroes represented here. Most of us didn't. At the top of the monument, it reads, 'In honor of those members of the Central Intelligence Agency who gave their lives in the service of their country.' The man who we honor this morning personified those words." The director went on to speak of dedication, bravery, and sacrifice but no actual name was mentioned.

Since Hacker's activities were officially off-the-books, Winston had to lobby hard to have his star etched in the wall. In spite of his cold pragmatic veneer, such loss of life always weighed heavily on

Winston's soul. Hacker's star represented the valor and service he had provided at the expense of his own life. No-one, not even his own family, would appreciate the circumstances or the full extent of his sacrifice. The only record of the honor was the inscription of Derek Hacker's name into the Moroccan leather-bound "Book of Honor". After the ceremony, the book was returned to its locked stainless steel box, and covered by a thick glass protective cover.

Then, it was all over. The atmosphere might have appeared cold and impersonal to the outsider, but the area was filled with an air of respect and appreciation. After the dedication, the attendees returned to their offices, back to the task of protecting the country. Winston spoke to a few colleagues, then exited the front door, and headed toward his limousine.

━◈ ◈━

As Winston was escorted to the Oval Office, he saw Parker Davis leaving the same room. "Hello, Mr. Davis."

"Hello yourself, Mr. Hamilton." The two men shook hands as Davis pulled Winston aside and whispered, "I don't know exactly who you are, but what I do know is that you and your team saved this country. You also saved my ass in the process. I'll never forget that fact and neither will the president."

Parker Davis turned to one of his agents, who muttered something urgent. The two men quickly walked away without further comment. Winston took a seat in a hallway chair just outside the Oval Office door. Ten minutes later, he was told to enter.

President Wagner dismissed his advisors and the Secret Service detail from the room. He stood and walked around his desk to shake the hand of the man who might be one of the country's greatest unspoken heroes. By appearances the short-statured man was an unimpressive person. His wide mouth and cold black eyes gave him an uncanny resemblance to a reptile, but this man, probably more than anyone else, was responsible for saving Wagner's life and saving the country from disaster. "It's an honor to meet you in person, Mr. Hamilton."

"The honor is all mine, Mr. President."

"Have a seat." The two men sat across from each other in leather chairs next to the fireplace. "Shall I have my staff bring in some coffee or tea?"

"Coffee would be nice, Mr. President; black, no sugar."

After the two men were served, Wagner leaned forward in his chair and said, "I want to thank you personally for what you have done for the United States. I must confess that I underestimated the full extent of the threat the terrorists posed. Without the actions of your team, it would have been a disastrous mistake on my part."

"Thank you Mr. President. I'm just happy that my team was able to help. How's the recovery process going?"

"Unfortunately the entire upper floors of the Old Post Office Tower continue to show fairly high levels of radiation. We're lucky that your team got to the man before he could actually detonate the bomb. The tower will be closed for now but hopefully it'll be open again by mid-summer. As far as the Glenwood cemetery is concerned, I'm afraid it'll take years to completely clean it up. A great deal of radioactive material was spread about by the blast and it'll be closed to the public for a long time. At least the surrounding neighborhoods are clear and no civilians were exposed to any significant levels of radiation. Fortunately, whoever landed that third drone in the tidal basin did so in such a way that there was no measurable contamination. It was an ingenious plan. The Park Service is still testing the water and the shoreline, but everything is clear so far. We plan to open up the basin area and the Jefferson Memorial in time for the cherry blossom festival."

"That's good to hear, Mr. President."

"Mr. Hamilton, let's get straight to the point. I've had extensive discussions with Parker Davis about what happened leading up to and including inauguration day. He filled me in on what you and your team have accomplished over the past three months. I think I can connect a lot of the dots from there. I want to reassure you that he's a man who I respect and trust; he knows how to remain quiet about certain sensitive areas. He'll carry any secrets revealed in this room to his grave. I understand that as part of your activities, you may have exceeded legal limits set forth by U.S. statutes and I want you to know that I don't care. Without your help, our country would have experienced one of the greatest tragedies in its history. I've taken all necessary measures to keep a lid on your team's involvement in the recent events. I'm committed to the protection of our citizens at home and abroad, and I'll do whatever it takes to ensure their safety. Our country is at war, and we're going to have to respond to these situations accordingly."

"I agree wholeheartedly, Mr. President." That's what Winston liked about the new president. He didn't tolerate a lot of nonsense or politically correct wishy-washy policies. He's a bottom-line guy who is more interested in results than the show.

"I also understand that you've uncovered some disturbing information. You reported that there are over a hundred organized sleeper-cells and training camps in this country. Some of them are openly training jihadists."

"Unfortunately, that's true, sir. Because of a wave of irrational political correctness in this country, the FBI has been prevented from aggressively pursuing them. The Bureau's been hamstrung in what it can accomplish. In all fairness it was designed to fight crime but we aren't fighting criminals here; we're fighting clandestine groups bent upon our destruction," replied Winston.

He thought for a second to consider the correct words. "I'm afraid that we must become as ruthless as the enemy if we are to defeat them. We must do so without becoming that which we seek to destroy."

"That is a fine line to try to negotiate, Mr. Hamilton; but I'm ready to walk it," replied President Wagner.

"As am I, Mr. President," responded Winston.

"Well, the old approach is coming to an end," added Wagner. "Trying to be the world's best friend hasn't worked and it's time to take the gloves off. The rules of engagement are going to have to be altered. I would like you and your team to uncover those illegal cells and training camps. Deal with them by any measures necessary. I believe the term used in the Agency is 'with extreme prejudice'."

"My team was designed for that very purpose, sir. They're very adept at carrying out just such missions, Mr. President."

"I'd like to meet the team members and thank them personally for their service," said Wagner.

"No offense, Mr. President, but it's imperative that the actual identity of the individual team members be protected. Government leaders and the mood of the public eventually change, and the team members don't want to fall victim to a politically motivated future attack by the opposing party or the liberal press."

"I fully understand. The identities of your team members will be kept confidential. The only persons who will know about your activities will be myself and Parker Davis who will serve as our go-between. As far as you are concerned Mr. Hamilton, I would like to propose your name as a Deputy Director of the CIA. The country needs a man of your abilities in a position with enough power to make a difference."

"Thank you Mr. President. I appreciate your confidence in me, but in all honesty, I believe that I can be more effective right where I am. I have all of the power I need."

"Yes, I've heard that from Mr. Davis. I appreciate your desire for personal anonymity. That being the case, you should continue your work at Langley in the..." Wagner had to look down at his notes as he smiled, "Supplemental Section of the Office of Research and Reports?"

"That's correct, Mr. President."

"To make your work more effective, I am going to rework next year's budget so that more funds and assets are at the disposal of the Department of Research and Reports. You can never have enough research," said Wagner with a wide smile on his face. "It'll be done in such a way that it's well-hidden in the accounting process."

"Again, thank you, sir," replied Winston. He continued, "There is one more important matter which we need to discuss."

"Yes?"

"As a result of talks with several of the forensic accountants at Homeland Security, I believe we have identified the ultimate ring leader of the organization that tried to assassinate you."

Wagner again leaned forward in his chair, "The one to whom that Scorpion fellow reports?"

"Yes. As you are well aware, in the months leading up to 9/11, there were billions of dollars in cash and securities transferred out of the United States. Many individuals from the Middle East knew what was about to happen in New York and took steps to protect their investments. That same pattern of activity repeated itself prior to this recent attempted attack. We've been looking back at major financial transactions in our country and internationally over the past several years. Mr. Martin Darpoli, whom we now know was the Scorpion, sold off over seven billion dollars of properties of the Masterson Properties Corporation in this country alone. He hid his activities well, but we were able to correlate those sales with the subsequent purchase of billions of dollars' worth of gold equivalents. A search of computer hard drives at his company revealed a close association between Darpoli and Prince Alsalud Bin Rashid Kabeer from Saudi Arabia. It appears as though he also converted tens of billions of dollars and Euros into gold. I believe that he was counting on a collapse of the U.S. and European economies."

"Which would have sent the price of gold through the roof! It would have made him the wealthiest man in the world," continued Wagner.

"Exactly. That's why I'm certain that the Prince was the ultimate financier of the failed attack. It appears as though his plans were motivated by greed as much as religious conviction. I think you might want to call Director Stevenson at the FBI to solidify the case against the Prince. Then you might want to have some confidential discussions with the present Saudi King. Prince Kabeer's recent activities would have not only toppled our government but also the Saudi monarchy. Meanwhile, he was poised to fill the resulting leadership vacuum himself. I'm convinced the Saudis will want to take appropriate measures to be sure that such a thing doesn't happen in their country again. They need to send a message and their Ministry of Interior Security is very adept at sending such messages. I expect the prince will soon disappear somewhere in the desert. His body will never be found."

"Seems to be a fitting end." Then President Wagner asked, "What about this Martin Darpoli, aka Scorpion?"

"He's a ghost sir. He disappeared shortly after the failed attempt but he's still out there somewhere. I doubt that we have heard the last from the Scorpion. Darpoli, on the other hand, no longer exists. Actually, he never really did exist until twenty-five years ago. Before then, we have no idea who he was. His identity appears to have been created by Prince Kabeer."

"Then they've been planning this thing for a long time," said Wagner. "I'll make all of the necessary calls today and again, thank your team members whoever they may be."

After his meeting with the president, Winston Hamilton placed a call to Dr. Jacob Savich. At the same time, President Wagner called Director Stevenson at the FBI and then placed a call to the King of Saudi Arabia.

⬧⬧ ⬧⬧

"What type of suture do you want to use, Dr. Savich?" asked the circulating OR nurse.

"Let's use some 6-0 Prolene and mild chromic." Carver was performing revision surgery of a cleft-lip nasal deformity that had been improperly repaired by another surgeon several years ago. She was the daughter of a wounded veteran and of course, there would be no bill.

"Are you ready, Dan?" he asked the anesthesiologist, Dan Foster.

"Just about Carver. She's almost asleep."

"Did you two enjoy your one month sabbatical in Europe?" asked the scrub nurse.

Dan looked over his mask at Carver and replied, "Oh, pretty typical medical stuff."

"Yeah, pretty boring couple of weeks, as a matter of fact," added the surgeon.

Just before he began his scrub, Carver's secure cell phone indicated a text message. It simply said, "Assemble the team for next week and clear your schedule. We still have a lot of work to do."

The clawing began to stir;

Time for a little hunting again, eh buddy.
Gunna get us some more bad guys.

He forwarded Winston's message to Lisa, Dan the "Gas Man," Hank the "Tank", and the Geek.

⬧⬧ ⬧⬧

The eight hour flight from Tehran to Beijing was long but uneventful. He had just finished reading an article regarding the disappearance of Prince Kabeer from Saudi Arabia. He hadn't been seen in public for over a month. *Probably in an interrogation cell in the basement of the Ministry of Interior Security,* he thought. *Or his body might already be somewhere out in the desert.*

After the plane landed, Faizel Sassani closed his laptop, stood up from his first class seat, stretched, and retrieved his carry-on bag from the overhead bin. He followed the crowds through immigration where he presented his passport which was scanned into the computerized recognition system. After he was cleared, he proceeded to the exit where he was met at curbside by an armored black Hongqi limousine with heavily tinted windows. The driver opened the door and Mr. Sassani took a seat in the back next to a colonel in the People's Liberation Army. There was no greeting and there was no conversation as the vehicle proceeded to the campus of the Liuang Computer Corporation's research center.

As his piercing brown eyes gazed out the window, Sassani inserted his hearing aids and smiled. He thought to himself, *the Scorpion always has a plan B. I have waited for over thirty years for my revenge and I can wait a few years longer. The Chinese have already had the components in place for over a decade. I just need to get the access codes to activate their systems. This time I won't make the mistake of underestimating the Americans.*

Made in the USA
Lexington, KY
25 June 2017